"Have you a taste, Lads," called Policrates, "for precious wines and delicate viands?"

"That we have, Captain," called a man.

"Have you a taste for well-tooled leather and fine clothes?"

"Yes, Captain!" called men.

"Have you a taste for more gold and silver, and jewels, than you know what to do with?" called Policrates.

"Yes, Captain!" called dozens of men.

"Have you a taste for luscious slaves, to train with whips to your pleasure?" demanded Policrates.

"Yes, yes, Captain!" called hundreds of men. I heard weapons unsheathed and clashed. "Yes, Captain! Yes, Captain!" shouted hundreds of men.

"Then, Lads," cried Policrates, "take the port of Victoria! She is yours!"

GUARDSMAN
OF GOR

John Norman

DAW BOOKS, INC.
Donald A. Wollheim, Publisher

1633 Broadway, New York, N.Y. 10019

FIRST PRINTING, NOVEMBER 1981

1 2 3 4 5 6 7 8 9

DAW TRADEMARK REGISTERED
U.S. PAT. OFF. MARCA
REGISTRADA. HECHO EN U.S.A.

PRINTED IN U.S.A.

Contents

I

SHIPS OF THE VOSKJARD

Most Gorean ships have a concave bow, which descends gracefully into the water. Such a construction facilitates the placing of the ram-mount and ram.

I watched, fearfully, almost mesmerized, as the first of the gray galleys, emerging from the fog, moving swiftly, like a living thing, looming now, struck the chain.

Battle horns sounded about me. I heard them echoed in the distance, the sounds first taken up by the *Mira* and *Talender*.

There was a great sound, the hitting of the huge chain by the galley, a sound as of the striking of the chain, and then the grating sound, scraping and heavy, of the chain literally being lifted out of the water. I saw it, fascinated, black, dripping water, glistening, slide up the bow, splintering wood and tearing away paint. Then the whole galley, by its momentum, stopped by the chain, swung abeam. I saw oars snapping.

"The chain holds!" cried Callimachus, elatedly.

Another galley then struck the chain, off the port bow.

"It holds!" cried Callimachus. "It holds!"

I was aware of something moving past me. It was swift. I almost did not register it.

"Light the pitch!" called Callimachus. "Set the catapults! Unbind the javelins! Bowmen to your stations!"

I saw, amidships, opposite our galley, on the enemy vessel, two bowmen. They carried the short, stout ship's bow. They were some forty yards away.

I looked upon them, fascinated.

They seemed unreal. But they were the enemy.

"Down!" called Callimachus. "Protect yourself!"

I crouched behind the bulwarks. I heard again, twice, the slippage of air, sliding and divided, marked by what I now recognized was the passage of slender, flighted wood. One arrow struck into the stem castle behind me and to my left. The sound was firm, authoritative. The other arrow with a flash of sparks struck the mooring cleat on the bulwark to my right and glanced away into the water.

I heard the snap of bow strings on my own vessel, returning the fire.

"Hold your fire!" called Callimachus.

Lifting my head I saw the enemy galley back-oaring on the starboard side, and then, straightened, back-oaring from the chain.

Some fifty yards away I heard another galley strike at the chain.

A cheer drifted across the water. Again, it seemed, the chain had held.

Across the chain I heard signal horns.

Callimachus was now on the height of the stem castle. "Extinguish the pitch!" he called.

I tried to see through the fog. No longer did there seem enemy ships at the chain.

Callimachus, twenty feet above me, his hands on the stem-castle railing, peered out into the fog. "Steady!" he called to the two helmsmen, at the rudders. A sudden wind was pulling at the fog. I heard the rudders and rudder-mounts creak. The oar master set the oars outboard, into the water.

"Look!" cried Callimachus. He was pointing to starboard. The wind had torn open a wide rift in the vapors of the fog.

There was a cheer behind me. At the chain, settling back, its concave bow lifted fully from the water, its stern awash, was a pirate galley. Men were in the water. Beyond this ship, too, there was another pirate galley, crippled, listing.

"They will come again!" called Callimachus.

But this time I did not think they would attempt to so brazenly assault the chain.

This time, I speculated, they would attempt to cut it. In such a situation they must be prevented from doing so. They would have to be met at the chain.

"Rations for the men!" called Callimachus. "Eat a good breakfast, Lads," he called, "for there is work to be done this day!"

I resheathed then the sword. The Voskjard had not been able to break the chain.

It seemed to me then that we might keep him west of the chain. I was hungry.

"They are coming, Lads!" called Callimachus from the stem castle.

I went to the bow, to look. The fog now, in the eighth Ahn, had muchly dissipated. Only wisps of it hung still about the water.

"Light the pitch!" called Callimachus. "Be ready with the catapults! Bowmen to your stations!"

In a moment I smelled the smell of burning pitch. It contrasted strongly with the vast, organic smell of the river.

I could see several galleys, some two to three hundred yards away, approaching the chain.

I heard the creak of a catapult, being reset. The bowmen took up their positions behind their wicker blinds.

Here and there, on the deck, there were buckets of sand, and here and there, on ropes, some of water.

I heard the unwrapping and spilling of a sheaf of arrows, to be loose at hand behind one of the blinds. There are fifty arrows in each such sheaf.

A whetstone, somewhere, was moving patiently, repetitively, on the head of an ax.

I saw Callimachus lift his hand. Behind him an officer would relay his signal. On the steps of the stern castle, below the helm deck, the oar master would be watching. The oars were already outboard.

I doubted that any of the enemy galleys would be so foolish as to draw abeam of the chain.

I could not believe my eyes. Was it because the flag of Victoria flew on our stem-castle lines?

I saw the hand of Callimachus fall, almost like a knife. In an instant, the signals relayed, the *Tina* leaped forward.

It took less than an Ehn to reach the chain. The iron-shod

ram slid, grating, over the chain and struck the enemy vessel amidships. The strakes of her hull splintered inward. Men screamed. I had been thrown from my feet in the impact. I heard more wood breaking as we back-oared from the vessel, the ram moving in the wound. I heard water rushing into the other vessel, a rapid, heavy sound. She was stove in. A heavy stone, from some catapult, struck down through the deck near me, fired doubtless from some other galley. A javelin, tarred and flaming, snapped from some springal, thudded into the stem castle. Arrows were exchanged. Then we had backed away, some seventy-five feet from the chain. Some men were clinging to the chain. I heard a man moaning, somewhere behind me. I snapped loose the javelin from the stem castle and threw it, still flaming, overboard.

Here and there, along the chain, we could see other galleys drawing abeam of it, and men, in small boats, with tools, cutting at the great links.

Again, in moments, the hand of Callimachus lifted, and again fell.

Once more the ram struck deep into the strakes of an enemy vessel.

Once more we drew back.

A clay globe, shattering, of burning pitch struck across our deck. Another fell hissing into the water off our starboard side. Our own catapults returned fire, with pitch and stones. We extinguished the fire with sand.

"They will lie to now," said Callimachus to the officer beside him. "We will be unable to reach them with the ram."

I could see, even as he spoke, several of the pirate vessels drawing back, abeam of the chain, but far enough behind it to prevent our ram from reaching them. Off our port bow we saw one of the pirate vessels slip beneath the muddy waters of the Vosk, a kill of the *Mira*.

Small boats again approached the chain.

We edged forward again. A raking of arrows hailed upon our deck, many bristling then, too, in the stem castle.

"Bowmen!" called Callimachus.

We spent a shower of arrows at the nearest longboat. Two men fell from the boat into the water. Other men dove free into the river, swimming back about the bow of the nearest pirate vessel.

"Do not let them near the chain!" called Callimachus to the bowmen.

We swung to port, to threaten another longboat. This one did not wait for us to approach, but withdrew behind the shelter of the nearest galley.

I watched the long, looping trajectory of a bowl of flaming pitch, trailing a streamer of smoke, near us, and then fall with a hissing splash into the water nearby.

"Save your fire. Steady!" called Callimachus. Then, later, he called, "Back oars!"

An occasional stone, or globe of pitch, was lofted towards us, but fell short.

Callimachus, with a glass of the builders, surveyed the chain.

"Look, Lads," called he. "See what small respect they have for you!"

I, and some others, went to the bow. Some five longboats were crossing the chain.

"Places, Lads!" laughed Callimachus.

I had no station, so I remained in the bow. The others, mostly oarsmen, returned to the benches, and the stern.

The men in the longboats carried swords and grapnels. Did they truly think to engage us? Our galley, like most of Gorean construction, was low and shallow drafted, but still its bulwarks would loom above the gunnels of a simple longboat.

The *Tina* knifed toward the chain. We rode over the first longboat, shattering it, its bow and stern snapping upward, its crew screaming and leaping into the water. Another was fouled in the oars of our starboard side and capsized. The other three fled back toward the chain.

I saw then that their action had been diversionary, to occupy us while other longboats, fixed with wicker shields, of the sort used for naval bowmen, lay along the chain. Behind those shields, like shapes and shadows, distinguishable behind the wicker, men tore with saws at the chain.

The diversion, though, had been too brief.

Once again the *Tina* approached the chain, swinging about now, broadside to the chain.

"Fire!" cried Callimachus.

Arrows lanced into the heavy wicker but, though several pierced it by a foot, they did little damage. The shafts were caught in the heavy wicker. Too, now, from the pirates' galleys, protecting their longboats, there sped a fierce counterfire. The wicker shields of our own archers were now bristling with feathers and wood.

A heavy stone broke away the railing of the stern castle of the *Tina*.

"Closer! Closer!" called Callimachus.

I heard the hiss and snap of our catapults, the twisted ropes snapping loose. When the largest one fired I could feel the reaction in the deck boards beneath my feet.

Flaming pitch was flung at close quarters. Arrows traversed the air in swift menace.

An arm suddenly appeared over the bulwark. Then a man, wet, scrambled aboard. I met him with the sword and, grappling, kicking, I forced him back overboard.

Burning pitch spattering and exploding out of a clay vessel skidded across the deck.

I could hear battle horns to port and starboard.

Not more than a dozen feet away I could see a pirate longboat behind the chain, protected by wicker shields.

Stones and pitch, at point-blank range, pounded and exploded between ships.

I could see, clearly, the eyes of pirates, no more than a few feet away, we separated from them by the chain, and a few feet of water.

A man rose from behind the bulwarks of the enemy vessel, bow in hand.

Then he was reeling back, an arrow in his chest.

I heard the chain scraping at the side of the *Tina*, then the shearing blade on our starboard side, swinging to starboard, struck the wood of a longboat. We slid along the chain, then, the oars on our starboard side striking loose the wicker shielding of another longboat, too close to the chain, and spilling men into the water.

I saw pirates, on the galley opposite, shaking their fists at us.

But the *Tina*, the chain cleared, was now swinging about. There was the wreckage of two longboats in the water. Half submerged, a wicker shield floated behind the chain.

I heard men behind me extinguishing the flames on the *Tina*.

"Back oars," called Callimachus. And the *Tina* backed away again from the chain, her bow facing it.

The pirate vessels, too, had withdrawn from the chain. It was near the tenth Ahn, the Gorean noon.

Callimachus descended from the stem castle, leaving his officer at that post. He took some water in his helmet and, using it as a basin, splashed his face with it.

"We have held them at the chain," I said to Callimachus. He wiped his face with a towel, handed to him by a fellow.

"For the time," he said.

"Do you think the Voskjard will now withdraw?" I asked.

"No," he said. He handed back the towel to the fellow who had given it to him.

"What will we do now?" I asked.

"Rest," he said.

"When do you think the Voskjard will try again?" I asked.

"What do you think?" he asked.

"Tonight," I said.

"Of course," he said.

II

NIGHT

Slowly, in the darkness, the *Tina* prowled the chain. The sound of the oars, softly entering the water, drawing and lifting, was almost inaudible.

"They are out there, somewhere," said Callimachus.

"Still?" I asked.

"Of course," he said.

Two ship's lanterns, suspended on poles, thrust over the bow, to port and starboard, cast pools of yellow light on the water. In the light of the starboard lantern, here and there, where the chain was visible above the water, as it was between certain pylons, we could see the dark links; generally, however, it was invisible, concealed by the surface.

"Quiet," said Callimachus. "Hold!" he called, softly, back to the oar master, who stood now behind the stem castle. The oars of the *Tina* lifted and slid partly inboard. The ship, with its momentum, drifted forward, south along the chain. We heard the chain grate then, on the hull, below the starboard shearing blade.

"What did you hear?" I asked.

We looked over the side, at the chain, suspended some six inches here above the water, and at the water, flickering in the lantern's light. "They were here," said Callimachus. "I am sure of it. Do not enter the light."

I drew back.

"It is hopeless," he said, dismally. "They may come and go as they please, withdrawing at our approach."

"There is little we can do about it," I said.

"Extinguish the lanterns," said Callimachus. "Wait! Bucklers and swords! Bucklers and swords, Lads!"

Almost at the instant that he had spoken grappling irons looped over the bulwarks and snapped back, the points anchoring in the wood. We saw tension in the irons as men climbed the ropes secured to them. But they were met, as dark shapes at the bulwarks, screaming and cursing, by fierce defenders, thrusting them back with bucklers, darting steel into their bodies. They were emerging from longboats and must climb up and over the bulwarks; they could not, bulwark to bulwark, leap to our deck; the advantages were fully ours; only one reached the deck, and we threw his lifeless body, thrust through in a dozen places, back into the Vosk, after its retreating fellows.

Callimachus wiped his sword on his cloak. "Additional insult have they done to us," he grinned. "Do they think we are an undefended merchantman, to assail us so boldly, so foolishly?"

"As you slew a man," I said, "you cried out with pleasure."

"Did I?" asked Callimachus.

"Yes," I said.

"When you, too, drove your blade into the body of a man, I thought you, too, cried out with pleasure," said Callimachus.

"I could not have done so," I said.

"You did," grinned Callimachus.

"I do not recall it," I said.

"In the press of battle," said Callimachus, "it is sometimes hard to be aware of all that transpires."

"You seem exhilarated," I said.

"I am," said he, "and so, too, seem you."

"No," I said, uncertainly, "it cannot be."

"But it is," said Callimachus.

"I do not think I know myself," I said.

"You are a man," said Callimachus. "Perhaps it is time that you made your own acquaintance."

"We were as fierce as they," I said, wonderingly, "as swift, as vicious."

"It would seem so," smiled Callimachus.

I was silent.

"Do you fear to look upon the hunter, and the killer, in yourself?" he asked.

I did not speak.

He clapped me on the shoulders. "We have now, I suspect," said he, "taught the men of Ragnar Voskjard some respect for honest men."

"Yes," I said, "let us think of it in such terms."

"Do you not wonder, sometimes," asked he, "why honest men, honest folk, such as ourselves, permit pirates, and such, to exist."

"Why?" I asked.

"That we may have someone to kill," he said.

"Are we so different from them, then?" I asked.

"I do not think so," said Callimachus. "We have much in common with them."

"What?" I asked.

"That we are men," said Callimachus.

"It is not the killing," I said, "for executions would not suffice."

"No," said Callimachus, "it is the sport, and the risk, and the killing."

"One must fight for causes," I said.

"Causes exist," said Callimachus, "that men may fight."

"I am troubled," I said.

"Extinguish the lanterns," said Callimachus to a fellow. "The pirates may still be about."

"Let us put down the longboat," I said to Callimachus. "With muffled oars we may patrol our sector of the chain."

"Why would you do this?" he asked.

"Our vessel, even with the lanterns extinguished, cannot approach the chain as silently as a longboat. The pirate boats, at the chain, need only draw back."

"The longboat," said Callimachus, "should be west of the chain, that it may approach the pirate boats less suspiciously."

"Of course," I said.

"Why will you do this?" he asked.

"Why, to defend the chain," I said.

"True," smiled Callimachus.

"You have tasted blood," said Callimachus. "You want more."

"Such thoughts are too terrible to think," I said.

"The sword must drink until its thirst is satisfied," said Callimachus. It was a Gorean proverb.

"I will not think such thoughts," I said.

"Consult your feelings," said Callimachus. "Do you find yourself desperately committed to this bold venture, that you may imperil your life in order to protect the chain? Are your motivations those of discharging a dangerous and unwelcome duty, one which no man has placed upon you?"

"No," I said.

"What then?" he asked.

"I have met the enemy," I said. "I am eager to meet him again."

"I thought so," said Callimachus. "I will put the longboat down. I shall call for volunteers."

"Who is there?" called a voice, in the darkness.

We rested the oars in the oarlocks.

"Ready," I said to the men with me, softly. We approached the chain from the west. The longboat had been put down across the chain, the *Tina* abeam of it, a quarter of an Ahn ago. We had actually passed within a few yards of pirate vessels, anchored in the river.

"Who is there?" called the voice.

"Now!" I said. Five men, behind the gunnels, suddenly rose up, bows in hand. The arrows were discharged at almost point-blank range into the other boat, as we struck against it. I heard men scream, tools cast down. I, and five others, swords drawn, boarded the other craft, hacking and slashing about us. We did not speak. The cries, the screams, were those of the pirates. More than one saved himself by leaping into the water. I thrust the body of another over a thwart, and then rolled it, sprawling, over the gunnel into the water.

"What is going on out there?" called a voice, from one of the pirate vessels, back from the chain.

We struck down with an oar, driving back a man trying to reach into the boat.

"What is going on out there?" called the voice again, as we slipped away.

"Be off! Be off!" cried a voice, frightened, in the darkness.

"Back oars," I said. Then I said, "Steady."

The longboat rested on the waters, rocking in the darkness, silent.

"We know you are out there!" cried a fellow in the darkness, near the chain. "We are armed! Approach at your own risk! Identify yourselves!"

I smiled, discerning his fear. I gave no orders.

"Identify yourselves!" called the voice.

We were silent.

I saw no point in attacking. The element of surprise was no longer with us. We had taken three longboats in the night. That there was danger at the chain was now well understood by the pirates. They had thought to work with impunity, and had found that we had not chosen to permit it.

We were silent.

"Return to the ship," said the voice in the darkness. "Return to the ship!"

We let the longboat move past us, some yards to starboard, judging by the sound of the oars.

I then had the longboat move to the chain, where I felt the links. In one of the great links I could feel a concave roughness which then gave way, as the tool had bit in, to a sharp, geometrically precise crevice, too small to feel inside. I felt about the link, to the limits, on both sides of the link, of the crevice. It was diagonal, and, at its deepest point, toward the link's center, about an inch in depth.

"What is it?" asked one of the men with me, an oarsman, behind me and to the right.

"They must have been working here about a quarter of an Ahn," I said.

"How bad is it?" he asked.

"The chain has been weakened," I said.

"What shall we do?" he asked.

"We shall continue to patrol the chain," I said.

"Did you hear it?" asked one of the men with me.

"Yes," I said.

"A fish?" asked one of the men.

"Divers, I think," I said.

"What are you doing?" asked one of the men.

"Return for me in five Ehn," I said.

I put aside my weapon, in its sheath, in the bottom of the longboat. I removed my sandals and tunic.

"Give me a knife," I said.

"Here," said one of my fellows. I put the blade between my teeth and, silently, lowered myself over the side of the longboat. I treaded water. The longboat, almost noiselessly, the oars muffled, the wood wrapped with thonged fur at the fulcrum points, the oarlocks similarly served, moved away.

It was cold and dark in the waters of the Vosk.

After a few Ehn the longboat returned, and I was hauled aboard.

"Here is your knife," I told the fellow who had loaned me the weapon.

"Was it a fish?" asked a man.

"No," I said.

"The knife is sticky," said the man to whom I had returned it.

I spit into the Vosk. "Rinse it," I said.

"How many were there?" asked a man.

"Two," I said. "They were not patient. They returned to work too soon."

"What shall we do?" asked one of the men.

"Return to the *Tina*," I said. "We shall need our sleep. There will be war tomorrow."

"Was the chain damaged?" asked a man.

"Yes," I said.

"Seriously?" he asked.

"Yes," I said.

"It could have been done in a hundred places," said a man.

"I think so," I said.

"Then, tomorrow," said a man, hesitantly, "the chain will not hold."

"I do not think so," I said.

"Perhaps we should flee while we can," he said.

I shrugged. "Let the crews and their commanders make decision on the matter," I said.

"The divers," said a man, "did you kill them both?"

"Yes," I said.

"Then the Voskjard will not know that the chain is weak at that point," said a man.

"No," I said, "he will not know that it was weakened at that point."

"But there will be other points," said a man.

"Of course," I said.

"It is impossible to protect the chain," said a man.

"Sooner or later, if not this night, it will be cut," said another man.

"The Voskjard has been delayed," said one of the men. "It is said he is not a patient man."

"We are not naval personnel," said another man. "In a free battle, on the river, we will stand little chance against the swift ships of the Voskjard."

"We have with us the ships of Port Cos," said a man.

"There are too few of them," said another man. "Presumably, if the chain is cut, they will withdraw to protect Port Cos."

"If the Voskjard should join with Policrates," said another man, "and the forces of Port Cos and Ar's Station are divided, no town on the river will be safe."

"Pirates will own the Vosk," said another man.

"We must flee," said another man.

"Decision on that matter can be made in the morning by the commanders and their crews," I said.

"But single men can flee," said another.

"I will kill the first man who deserts his post," I said.

"What manner of man are you?" asked a man.

"I do not know," I told him.

"Command us," said one.

"Put about," I said. "Return to the *Tina*. We shall think further on these matters in the morning."

"Do you think that the urts of the Voskjard will discontinue their nibblings at the chain because we choose to rest?" asked a man.

"No," I said.

"Then we must remain at the chain," he said.

"No," I said.

The longboat then put about and, slowly, made its way northward along the chain. The fate of the river, I had learned, did not lie in the fate of the chain.

We were hailed by men in pirate vessels, as we passed near them, but we did not respond.

"We have encountered no further evidence of work at the chain," said a man, as we neared the location of the *Tina*, east of the chain, a single lantern swinging on one of her stem-castle lines.

"Perhaps the Voskjard has given up," said a man.

"Perhaps no further work has been done," said another man.

"Perhaps," said another, "the work has been completed by now, to his satisfaction."

"The chain must hold," said one of our oarsmen. "It must!"

"What do you think, Jason?" asked a man.

"Let us hope, fervently," I said to him, "that it holds."

"But do you think it will?" asked a man.

"No," I said.

"We must flee," said a man.

"Would you surrender the river to men such as Policrates and Ragnar Voskjard?" I asked.

"No," he said.

"Is that you, Jason?" called Callimachus.

"It is," I responded.

The *Tina* then, in a few Ehn, came abeam of the chain. We threw lines up to her.

III

THE CHAIN HAS BEEN
BROKEN IN THE NORTH

The long galley, some eighty feet Gorean, sped toward the chain. Its bow as lifted, unnaturally, from the water, did not even touch the water.

"Superb!" cried Callimachus, commending the enemy.

"What is it?" I called up to the stem castle.

"They have redistributed the ballast," called Callimachus. "Splendid!"

The vessel continued to approach the chain. I could hear the stroke of the hortator's hammer even on the *Tina*. Such a speed could be continued for only a few moments. I saw more of the hull, and its keel, dripping, lifting out of the water.

"Are they mad?" I called.

"It is their intention to ride over the chain," said Callimachus.

I clutched the rail, in wonder. Every bit of sand in the lower hold must have been thrust to the stern of the vessel. Gear, too, and catapult stones, had been slid to the stern deck. Even the crew, other than oarsmen, their weapons ready, had congregated there.

Then the concave prow of the vessel had cleared the chain. There was a great scraping as the chain tore at the keel. Then the galley, half on the chain and half off, moved eccentrically, teetering, like a ship caught on a bar, stranded and buffeted, assailed by conflicting currents.

"Out oars!" called Callimachus. "Ready!"

We saw another galley from the west, too, its prow high, speeding toward the chain.

The first galley, its oars stroking, slashing at the Vosk, its hull twisting, careened forward and to the side.

"It will clear the chain!" I cried.

"Two points to port!" cried Callimachus. "Stroke!" His officer, by hand signals, conveyed his message to the helmsmen and oar master at the stern.

"It is clearing the chain!" I cried.

Already the *Tina* was speeding toward the intruder. I flung myself to the deck. We took her in the starboard bow, as she slid, grinding and splintering, from the chain.

"Back oars!" called Callimachus.

The impact had slid me back on the deck for a dozen feet.

"Back oars!" called Callimachus.

The *Tina*, shuddering, backing, with a splintering of wood, freed her ram.

I, crouching, peered over the side. The forward deck of the enemy was already awash.

I saw men there, in water to their knees, clinging to rails. The catapult on the enemy's stern castle had broken loose from its large, rotating mount. Its ropage hung down, dangling in the wind. The strands seemed narrow, from the distance from which I viewed them. The largest, however, would be some four inches in diameter. I saw a man leap from the stern castle into the water.

"Look!" cried out a man, in misery. He was pointing to starboard. The second enemy galley had ridden over the chain.

"The first of the Voskjard's ships has crossed the chain!" cried another.

We saw other galleys, too, approaching the chain.

"Another has crossed!" cried a man, pointing to starboard. Beyond that ship we could see another galley, too, but this one was striking at the chain.

The *Mira* was hastening to engage the galley which had ridden over the chain.

The *Mira* made good her strike. There was a cheer from our vessel. The starboard rudder of the enemy galley had been torn away in crossing the chain. The galleys of the Voskjard, like most Gorean ships, were double ruddered.

"Hard to starboard!" cried Callimachus.

As we came about a pirate galley knifed towards us.

"To starboard!" cried Callimachus. Then he cried, "Oars inboard!"

Her ram missed us. Her port shearing blade tore at our strakes.

"Oars outboard!" called Callimachus. "Come about!"

The two ships had slid past one another. As the ships passed I had looked into the eyes of a pirate. He had not been more than five feet from me.

"Two more ships are over the chain!" called the officer with Callimachus, pointing to port.

"Ships of Port Cos are approaching!" cried another man. There was a cheer on our vessel. Ten such ships were at the chain. Twenty others lay to in the waters near the south guard station, which post was held by Callisthenes. These ships, those of Port Cos, were our hope. It was only these, we feared, who might be able to match the forces of the Voskjard in even combat. The ships of Ar's Station could bring numbers to bear in our favor, but we did not regard them, ship for ship, as the match of either a galley of the Voskjard or of Port Cos. The naval tradition of Cos is an ancient one, and many of the officers of Port Cos were native Cosians, mercenaries or veterans of the Cosian navy, on detached duty to the colony, that the interests of the mother island might be defended on the Vosk.

"There is a ship of Ar's Station!" called out the officer on the stem castle.

There was a cheer at this cry.

We had now come about, but already the galley which had nearly torn us open was facing us.

"She has quick lines," said a man.

"Why has she not attacked?" asked a man.

"She is waiting for support," said a man.

"No," said another. "If we move to the chain, she can ram us amidships."

"She is defending her sisters," said a man.

"We can no longer protect the chain," said another.

But then we saw the galley swinging to starboard. Another galley, one flying the pennons of Port Cos, was speeding towards her.

There was another cheer from our men. "Back to the chain!" called Callimachus, elated.

"Another has slipped over!" cried out a man, angrily, pointing over the bow.

It was free of the chain. We could not catch her. She slipped behind us on the waters of the broad, muddy Vosk.

"How many have passed the chain?" asked a man, glumly.

"Who knows?" asked another.

Here and there, at the chain, again and again, pirate galleys were striking at the great links, and then backing away, and then again, patiently, renewing their attack.

"Doubtless they are hammering at points where they know the chain was weakened in the night," said a man near me. He had been with me in the longboat last night.

"Yes," I said. "Look there!"

I pointed to one of the truncated pylons rising out of the river. It had been splashed with yellow paint.

"Catapults!" called Callimachus.

Two stones looped into the air and then, gracefully, began their descent toward one of the pirate ships.

Huge spumes of water rose into the air as the great rocks plunged into the Vosk.

"Bowmen!" called Callimachus.

We neared the first of the galleys and flighted arrows toward her.

She drew back.

"There are others," said a man.

We moved along the chain. We came upon the wreckage of a pirate galley, broken in two, deserted. It had broken, attempting to ride over the chain.

"There is a pirate galley behind us, a pasang back, lying to!" called out a man, aft on the stern castle.

"We remain at the chain," said Callimachus.

"It seems to list," called the man. "I think it is crippled."

"We remain at the chain," said Callimachus.

I smiled. He was a good commander. He would not be lured from his post. A ship can be made to seem to list by repositioning the ballast in its lower hold. If the ship were truly a cripple I did not think it would be lying to. An oared fighting ship is seldom helpless. Too, if the ship were crippled, it posed no immediate threat. And, if it were not crippled, it needed only be kept under observation. Isolated ships can be dealt with on a piecemeal basis. Our duty lay at the chain. He who thoughtlessly abandons his defenses strikes a poor bargain with fortune.

"Look there!" called the officer on the stem castle with Callimachus. He pointed ahead, half a point off the starboard bow.

Callimachus took the glass of the Builders from the officer. "It is the *Sita* of Point Alfred," said Callimachus, "and the *Tais* of Port Cos."

"They fly distress signals on the stem-castle lines," said the officer.

"Bring her about," called Callimachus.

"It can mean but one thing," said the officer.

Callimachus snapped shut the glass of the Builders.

I could now hear the sound of the horns drifting towards us.

"Acknowledge," said Callimachus. Flags were run on the stern-castle lines.

I could not interpret the horns.

"What is it?" I called up to Callimachus.

"It had to happen," he said.

"What?" I asked.

"It happened to the north," he said.

"What?" I asked.

"The chain has been broken," he said. I held the rail, looking astern.

The *Sita* and the *Tais* were now clearly visible.

"Where are the *Talia*, the *Thenta*, the *Midice*, the *Ina*, the *Tia*?" asked the officer.

"I did not see them," said Callimachus. He handed the glass of the Builders back to the officer. "Do you see them?" he asked.

"No," said the man. "No."

"Quarter stroke," said Callimachus.

"Quarter stroke!" called the officer to the oar master.

"Quarter stroke!" he called to his men.

The *Sita* and the *Tais* were now abeam, to port.

We moved southward, along the chain.

Callimachus descended from the stem castle and made his way back, between the benches, to the stern castle. I accompanied him. He carried the glass of the Builders.

"There were seven ships," I said. I stood beside Callimachus on the stern castle.

"Perhaps some survived," he said.

"I see ships," I said, pointing astern. There were specks at the horizon line, marshaled specks.

Callimachus handed me the glass of the Builders. "Ships of the Voskjard," I said.

"Yes," said Callimachus.

"Apparently the Voskjard has more than fifty ships," I said. I had counted at least forty. And there were several others, I knew, here and there at the chain.

"The information of Callisthenes was apparently mistaken," said Callimachus. "That is a sore and unwelcome flaw in our intelligence."

"How many can there be?" I asked.

"I do not know," said Callimachus. "Sixty, a hundred?"

"We can never match such ships in open battle," I said.

"Port Cos must fight as she has never fought before," said Callimachus.

"They are not hurrying," I said to Callimachus. I had been counting the strokes per Ehn.

"They do not wish to tire their oarsmen," said Callimachus. I handed the glass of the Builders back to him.

"Port Cos is the hope of the Vosk," said Callimachus. "We of Ar's Station and of the independent ships must support her in her battle."

"The odds are overwhelming," I said. "Can she win?"

"She must," said Callimachus.

"At least she is commanded by men such as Callisthenes," I said.

"His twenty ships, summoned from the south guard station, will be crucial," said Callimachus.

"We shall need each of them if we are to make a showing," I said.

"Without them," I said, "it would be a slaughter."

"With them, in spite of the odds," said Callimachus, "the tide might be turned in our favor."

"You seem troubled," I said.

"I am only hoping," he said, "that the chain has not been cut south of us."

"We have protected it as well, and as long, as we could," I said.

"Let us hope that the time which we have invested in that work will prove itself to have been well spent," he said.

I shuddered. "I shall hope so," I said. If our fleet did not have time to group, or if our flank were turned, it would be indeed a tragic day for our forces upon the Vosk. The planks of our fleet might litter the river to the wharves of Turmus.

"Have you orders for me?" I asked.

"Sharpen your sword," he said. "And get what rest you can."

"Yes, Captain," I said. I turned away from Callimachus.

"Do you look forward to the fight?" he asked.

"Yes," I said, not turning to regard him.

"That is interesting," said Callimachus.

"Is it significant?" I asked.

"Perhaps," said Callimachus.

"What does it mean?" I asked.

"Do you think you will be able to sleep before the engagement?" he asked.

"Of course," I said. "Why? Are these things significant?"

"What do you think?" he asked.

"I do not know," I said.

"Sharpen your sword," said he, "and get what rest you can."

"Yes, Captain," I said, and then descended the steps of the stern castle. I made my way toward the bow. The rowers were working only at quarter stroke. I sat down near my gear and, for a time, with a stone, whetted the blade on the weapon I carried. When I was finished I set a light coat of oil on the steel, that it might be protected from rust. Then I lay down on the smoothed deck, near the starboard rail, and, near a coil of mooring rope, fell soon asleep.

IV

THE WEDGE;
RAMS AND SHEARING BLADES

"How many are there?" I heard an officer inquire of Callimachus, above and behind me, on the deck of the stem castle.

"Forty-two," said he.

We lay to, twenty-two ships, in a double line. Our oars were inboard.

"The chain held," said a man near me.

"Yes," I said. It had been broken in the north, but here, closer to the southern shore of the Vosk, it had held. This had permitted us to group. Too, the left flank of our position was protected, still, by the mighty links of the Cosian chain, transported to the Vosk, slung between its pylons.

"Where are the ships of Callisthenes?" inquired an officer of Callimachus.

"They will join us shortly," said Callimachus. "We must hold our lines until they arrive."

Even this far south, and from the height of the stem castle, one could not see the southern shore of the Vosk.

"They are forming the wedge," said an officer beside Callimachus.

Our right flank was protected by seven ships of Port Cos, seven of the ten which had been originally abroad on the

river. The *Midice* and *Tia* had been lost. The *Ina,* her starboard oars sheared, had been boarded and taken as a prize.
The *Talia* and *Thenta,* the first of Point Alfred and the second of Jort's Ferry, had been lost in the same action. Both
had been merchant ships, acting in support of the ships of
Port Cos. Of the group the *Sita,* of Jort's Ferry, and the *Tais*
of Port Cos, had escaped. In this first engagement, in the
north, we had lost five of seven ships. The Voskjard, as we
had learned, had lost four.

"Yes," said Callimachus, handing the glass of the Builders
back to one of the officers, "it is the wedge."

From my position at the starboard rail, near the bow, below the stem castle, I could not well see the arrangement of
the Voskjard's formation.

"There are other ships of the Voskjard west of the chain,"
said a man, glumly.

These were the ships which, for better than a full day and
night, beginning with yesterday's dawn, had been essaying the
chain in our sector.

"We can no longer keep them out," said a man.

"True," I admitted.

The chain could now be cut with impunity, behind the
shield of the Voskjard's northern fleet, that now some half
pasang off our bows.

We had not been able to make a determination on the
ships west of the chain in our sector. It was speculated, however, that the southern fleet was larger even than the
northern, which had been successful in its strike against the
chain.

Acting on the information supplied by Callisthenes we had
conjectured that the Voskjard commanded in the neighborhood of fifty ships. This intelligence had now been revealed
as substantially in error, perhaps by a factor of two.

"By now," said a man, "the chain has probably been cut."

I recalled the yellow paint, splashed on the pylon.
Doubtless, too, other points of weakness had been similarly
marked. Even now, behind the shield of the northern fleet, it
was not improbable that the ships of the southern fleet were
proceeding unimpeded between the pylons. The chain had
held long enough, however, to permit us to draw southward
along the chain and group. Too, of course, it held, still, protecting our left flank, in our immediate area.

"We have little hope," said a man.

"They are forming the wedge," said another.

"Where are the ships of Callisthenes?" asked someone.

"They will be here," said another man.

"Captain," said one of the officers to Callimachus.

"Yes," said he.

"Shall I order that the ships be chained together?"

These signals could be conveyed by flags and horns.

"No," said Callimachus.

"How else can we withstand the weight of such a wedge?" inquired the officer.

"We will not impair our mobility," said Callimachus. "We will not render our rams and shearing blades useless."

"We must be a floating fortress of wood," said the officer. "At such a citadel the wedge must pound in vain."

"The ships of our interior line would be prevented from engaging," said Callimachus. "We would be then nothing but a tethered, placid target, one impossible to miss. If our flank were turned, too, we could no longer protect ourselves. Only our undefended strakes could be presented to the rams of the enemy. In an Ahn your floating fortress of wood could be a wreckage, awash, of timbers and chains."

"Then let us withdraw," said the officer.

"It is too late for that," said Callimachus.

The officer, white-faced, looked over the rail of the stem castle. "The fleet is moving," he said.

"Yes," said Callimachus.

"What can we do!" cried the officer.

"We must hold the line until the arrival of Callisthenes," said Callimachus.

"We can never withstand the strike of the wedge," said the officer.

"Here are my orders," said Callimachus.

It was a galley, heavy class, fit for the open sea. It was the point of the wedge. I had never seen a galley move with such speed. There were two men to each oar. Our bow was aligned, as though to take its ram on the ram shield. The strike, should it occur, I feared would snap our keel.

To our port side, gunnels almost touching, lay the *Mira*, our sister ship, from Victoria.

I saw, some hundred yards away, on the stem castle of the

speeding galley, her captain move his arm. Almost instantaneously the galley, responsive at that speed to the slightest rudder pressure, veered a point to her starboard. It was her intention not to be stopped at the *Tina* but to shatter between us and the *Mira*, opening the line. At her stern quarters, like running, heeling sleen, were two other galleys, to exploit the opening the point must make. Fanning out, too, behind the supporting galleys, were others. And, in the wake of the first galley, plowed several others. Our line, it seemed, must be cut. Our communications, it seemed, must be disrupted. Enemies would be among us. Flanks to be defended would be multiplied. We would be divided, handicapped in our attempts to reinforce and support one another. Divided, hunted, we could be herded, and surrounded. We might then make good sport for the pirates. The Voskjard had been held at the chain in the south. I did not think that this would have pleased him. I did not expect that prisoners would be taken.

"Now!" cried Callimachus.

There are three poles which, customarily, with Gorean ships are used in casting off, in thrusting away from the wharves. There were, of course, three such poles on the *Tina* and on the *Mira*. Our oars were inboard.

Suddenly, as the enemy galley veered to knife between us, and the *Mira* men with poles, and, too, with oars, on our ship, and on the *Mira*, thrust the ships apart. There was a shattering and a scraping but the enemy galley, which had thought with force to press us apart, meeting little resistance was, by her momentum, almost immediately astern of us. Almost simultaneously other men, on the *Tina* and *Mira*, with ropes and grappling irons, drew the ships more closely together. The two ships following the first galley had intended to follow her into our line, exploiting the breach. But now there was no breach. The point of the wedge, harmlessly, save for splinters and paint torn from our hull, was behind us. The two supporting ships ground their hulls together. Burning pitch and arrows rained upon their decks. I heard rams clash to port and starboard. Then one of the supporting galleys was struck in the stern by a following ship, unable to check its momentum. The pirate galleys began to back oars, frantically to extricate themselves, but, clumsily, half swung about, they must accept our fire. Two other ships from behind them, unable to slow themselves sufficiently, struck into the milling ships.

I turned about. The first galley, isolated behind our lines, was trying to swing to the southeast, to avoid the chain and find the open water to the east. As she did so the *Tais*, come from our right flank to reinforce the line, circling about her, took her full in the port side. The strike was high, but water poured into her hold. I saw men dive from her decks. She lay then in the water, listing, unmanned. As she lay the rupture in her hull was lifted above the water line. I saw men from the *Tais* board her, moving about on the tilted deck. Then, in a short time, they returned to their ship.

"Run flags on the stem-castle lines," called Callimachus. "Blood for Port Cos!"

There was a cheer from our benches.

I watched the *Tais* draw away from the disabled vessel. Then I saw the stern of the vessel swing eccentrically about.

"She is caught on a bar," said a man near to me.

"Yes," I said. No longer did she move sluggishly, turning, carried by the current, toward the chain.

"It is the *Tuka*," said a man near me.

"Is that a well-known ship of the Voskjard," I asked.

"Yes," he said.

"It is the wedge again!" cried a man.

I looked out, over the railing, northward. The enemy fleet had reformed.

The crew of the *Tuka* had swum west of the chain.

"They are approaching at only half stroke," said a man.

"They will not repeat their first mistake," said another.

This time it was their intention to force our line apart with consistent pressure, not as a shattering bolt, but as a flood, a pressing, an avalanche of wood and steel, regulated, controlled, responsive to the tactical situation instant by instant. Not again would the point of the wedge be lost fruitlessly behind our lines, spending itself in vain against emptiness and spray.

Flags, torn by the wind, snapping, sped to our stem-castle lines. Signal cloths, pennons and squares, in mixed colors and designs, acknowledging these commands, ran fluttering and streaming onto the stem-castle lines of the *Tais*.

"She is at full stroke!" said a man.

The *Tais*, her stern low in the water, her ram half lifted from it, knifed to the northeast.

"The wedge of the Voskjard approaches!" called an officer on our stem castle.

"Let us chain the ships together, while we may!" begged another officer.

"No," said Callimachus.

"Look!" cried a man, miserably, clinging to a projection on our stem castle. "Look!" he cried. He was pointing to the east. "The *Tais* is leaving our lines! The ships of Port Cos attend her!"

"Our flank is unguarded!" cried a man in fear. There seemed consternation on our benches.

"The Voskjard is committed to the wedge!" I said to the man next to me.

"Our flank is in no immediate danger," said he. He set an arrow to the string of a short ship's bow.

"No!" I cried laughing. "No! Look! It is the flank of the Voskjard which is now unguarded!"

The *Tais* and her swift, lean sisters, emerging unexpectedly, circling, from behind our lines, stern quarters low in the water, rams half lifted from the water, wet and glistening in the sun, at full stroke, oars beating, drums pounding, like loosened weapons, sped toward the wedge.

Our oarsmen stood on their benches cheering.

The lead ship of the wedge was trying to come about, swinging to starboard. Her immediate support ship, fifty yards astern, could not check her flight. Her ram took the lead ship in the stern, tearing away wood and breaking loose the starboard rudder. Almost at the same time the seven ships of Port Cos, fanning out, each choosing an undefended hull, exposed, helpless before the hurtling strike of the ram's brutal spike, to the tearing of wood, the rushing of water, the screaming of men, made contact with the enemy. Efficiently did they address themselves to the harsh labors of war.

I did not see how Ar, in her disputes with Cos upon the Vosk, could hope to match such ships and men. The ships of Ar's Station, with the fleet, seemed more round ships than long ships. Some lacked even rams and shearing blades. All were permanently masted. Few of these ships boasted more than twenty oars. All seemed undermanned. Ar, I thought, might be advised to tread lightly in her politics on the Vosk.

The ships of Port Cos, led by the *Tais*, backed from the subsiding, shattered hulks they had smitten. The Voskjard's fleet was in confusion. Ship struck ship. Signal horns sounded frantically. Ships struggled, crowded together, trapped in the wedge, to come about. Again, and again, hunting as single marine predators, the *Tais* and her sisters, prowling the outskirts of that confused, sluggish city of wood, almost at will, almost fastidiously, selected their victims.

How could Ar, I asked myself, compete with such men and ships upon the mighty Vosk?

Laughable were the miserable, squat ships of Ar's Station when compared with the sleek carnivores of Port Cos or, indeed, those of Ragnar Voskjard.

"The *Tais* has made her third kill!" cried a man.

There was cheering upon the *Tina*.

On each of the ships of Ar's Station there were long, heavy sets of planks, fastened together by transverse crosspieces. These heavy constructions were some twenty-five feet in length, and some seven or eight feet in width. They were mounted on high platforms near the masts, one at each mast, and could be run out on rollers from the mast, to which they were fastened by adjustable lengths of chain. At the tops these constructions leaned back toward the masts, to which, at the top, they were secured by ropes. Projecting outwards from the top of each of these constructions there was, like a curved nail, a bent, gigantic, forged spike.

"The fleet is coming about!" cried a man.

To be sure, amidst the wreckage and crowding, and even grinding against the chain, the fleet of the Voskjard had managed to come about.

"Flee!" cried a man near me to the crews of the *Tais* and her sisters, as though they could have heard him over the water. "Flee!"

"They must run or they will be crushed!" cried a man. The rams of the Voskjard's fleet swung toward the *Tais* and her sisters. Between them, drifting apart, listing or awash, lay what must have been the wreckage of some eighteen ships. Several had already gone down.

"Run! Run!" cried more than one man near me. But the *Tais* and her sisters of Port Cos lay to.

"The fleet of the Voskjard has been marshaled," said a man next to me.

"Pity the brave lads of Port Cos," muttered a man.

"Stroke!" called Callimachus.

"Stroke!" called his officer.

"Stroke!" cried the oar master. The ringing of the copper-covered drum struck with the fur-wrapped wooden mallets suddenly rang out behind us.

"Yes, yes!" I cried. "The Voskjard has exposed his flank to us!"

The *Tina* and her line moved forward.

"Withdraw! Reform!" called Callimachus.

That island of wood in the midst of the Vosk, those grating, striking ships, twisted at the chain. Rams now, and concave bows, threatened us.

We backed from the wreckage.

We, the line of our ships, had caught the fleet of the Voskjard in its right flank, as it had turned to confront and punish the *Tais* and her sisters of Port Cos. This audacious act on our part had taken the fleet of the Voskjard by surprise. That ships such as those of Ar's Station and of the independent towns, mostly refitted merchantmen, would dare to leave the security of their lines to launch their own attack, not bolstered by the ships of Port Cos, had not entered its ken. They did not know, perhaps, that one named Callimachus stood upon our stem castle.

We backed from the wreckage, much of it flaming. The smell of pitch was in the air.

Dozens of ships, trying to come about, maneuvering, milling, struck by other ships, had been trapped against the chain.

There were hundreds of men in the water. Hundreds of oars, like sticks, had been snapped in the stresses involved, even against the hulls of their own vessels.

Archer shields, of heavy wicker, floated in the water, and ruptured posts and strakes, and parts of oars.

Vosk gulls dove and glided among the carnage, hunting for fish.

"Back oars! Reform our lines!" called Callimachus.

I saw a pirate galley slip under the water, near the chain.

"Back oars! Reform our lines!" called Callimachus. He was no fool. He would not risk open battle, not even on even terms, with ships such as those of the Voskjard.

"We have been fortunate," said a man.

"Yes," said another.

"The Voskjard will be angry," said another.

"I fear so," said another.

"There is still time to flee," said another.

Then the *Tina*, with the *Mira* to starboard and the *Talender* to port, lay to in our lines. The ships of Port Cos, now only the *Tais* and four others, resumed their station at our right flank. Had it not been for these ships of Port Cos it is difficult to know how we might have fared. They had taken heavy toll of the enemy before he had turned the wedge to face them, and then, as confused, he, struck by our unexpected attack, that of the independent ships and those of Ar's Station, had turned to face us, the *Tais* and her sisters had renewed their attack on his flank. I thought it not improbable that the Voskjard had lost in the neighborhood of thirty ships. Yet now we conjectured some fifty ships still faced us, for the chain, clearly, no longer provided a barrier north of his position. Those ships which we had for so long prevented from joining him had, by now, amplified his forces. I could not but think, bitterly, that if the Voskjard, truly, had had only some fifty ships, as we had gathered from the intelligences supplied to us by Callisthenes, we, if supplemented by the twenty ships of Callisthenes, yet to appear, would now have outnumbered him. In such a situation it was not unlikely that he would have come about and, at his leisure, still in strength, withdrawn to the west. We lay to, waiting. Now, in our lines, there were only seventeen ships, including those of Port Cos, on which we so crucially depended.

"The enemy fleet is marshaling," said a man.

"Is it again the wedge?" asked a man.

"One ship is astern and to the starboard of another," said a man.

"They will come with care, and hunt us in pairs," said a man.

"There is still time to flee," repeated a man.

"I recommend, Captain," said an officer above and behind me on the stem-castle deck, "immediate withdrawal."

"We must hold the line for Callisthenes," said Callimachus.

"Draw back to the south guard station. Join him there," pressed an officer.

"To be outflanked and trapped between the chain and the southern shore?" asked Callimachus.

"I counsel retreat," said the officer.

"Their ships are faster than ours," said Callimachus.

"Not faster than the *Tina*," said the officer.

"Am I then to abandon the fleet?" asked Callimachus.

The officer looked at him, angrily.

"You counsel not retreat, my friend," said Callimachus, "but rout, and slaughter."

"What, then, shall we do?" asked the man.

"Wait for Callisthenes," said Callimachus.

"Withdraw," said the officer.

"And leave Callisthenes to face fifty ships?" asked Callimachus.

"Forget about Callisthenes," said the officer.

"I will not forget about him," said Callimachus, "as he would not forget about me."

"Withdraw," said the officer.

"It is here that we are to be joined by Callisthenes," said Callimachus. "It is here that we will wait for him."

"Where is Callisthenes?" asked the man next to me.

"I do not know," I said.

I noted the approach of the Voskjard's fleet, the ships moving in pairs, with more than a hundred yards between the pairs. It is difficult, of course, for a single ship to protect itself against a brace of assailants. The members of the pair circle about, so as to attack at right angles to one another. It is thus impossible to protect oneself, if caught, against both. One's hull must be exposed to the strike of at least one ram.

"We must hold the line," said a man beside me, tensely.

"Yes," I said. "That is true."

Another fellow, near me, lifted his bow, an arrow fitted to the string. He bent the bow, drawing the string back, the arrow at a sharp angle. Then he relaxed the bow, but did not remove the shaft from the string. "They will soon be within range," he said.

"Withdraw!" begged the officer above and behind us on the stem castle with Callimachus. "Withdraw!" he begged.

"They would be upon us before we could come about," said Callimachus.

I heard steel leaving sheaths about me.

"Sound the battle horns," said Callimachus.

"Sound the battle horns!" called the officer beside him.

The bronze horns of battle then smote with their shrill trumpeting the air of the Vosk.

I withdrew my sword from its sheath.

V
_____

I SEE THE *TAMIRA*;
I CONSIDER THE *TUKA*

I kicked back, screaming, the face that thrust itself over the gunnels. With the blade I slashed down, cutting the rope taut on the grappling hook caught over the wood. I thrust twice, driving back pirates. One of my feet was on the *Tina*. The other was on the railing of the pirate vessel. Others, too, stood between the ships. Others stood on the decks of their own vessels, thrusting and cutting, stabbing, over the bulwarks. Men on the *Tina*, using loose oars as levers, were trying to pry the ships apart. There was a screaming of metal as shearing blades, locked together, protested the stresses imposed upon them by the shifting ships. The port shearing blade of the pirate vessel was torn, splintering strakes, from its hull. Our starboard shearing blade, that great crescent of iron, some seven feet in height, some five inches in width, was bent oddly askew. It had been turned like tin. A man next to me fell, reaching out, clutching, grasping, between the ships. He screamed. Then he was lost among the splinters of oars and the grinding of the hulls. The bowman, below me on the deck, and to my left, unleashed an arrow, at point-blank range across the gunnels. I could not follow its flight. Only the blood at the pirate's throat marked its passage. The shaft itself was lost somewhere behind, among the screaming men.

40

I leaped onto the deck of the pirate vessel, slashing about myself. A spear thrust from behind tore through the side of my tunic. I twisted away, hacking passage. Then pirates thrust forward and I felt them sweeping about me. They pressed toward the rail. I turned. They did not even realize, in the heat of battle, in the confusion, that I was not of their number. I nearly struck, by accident, an oarsman from the *Tina*, too on the pirate's vessel. As pirates swarmed toward our ship we cut at the backs of their necks. I saw the fellow I had nearly struck board the *Tina*, literally with the pirates. He struck a defender's pike away from himself. Then he cut at the pirates to his left and right. Then he was again on the deck of the *Tina*. Then he had turned and was fighting the pirates. I heard timbers creak. Pirates were at the stern castle of the *Tina*. We had ten or more men fighting on the pirate vessel in the vicinity of her stem castle. I cut two more of the ropes attached to grappling hooks. "Rogue!" cried a fellow. I turned to face him. We crossed swords five times. His blood was on me. With two hands, grunting, I jerked the sword from his body. Ribbing snapped. It had been a clumsy stroke. Callimachus would not have been pleased. I lifted my head, wildly. The ships were now drifting apart. They were held close only at the sterns. I smelled fire. I saw a man on the *Tina* plunge backward, his hands clutching at an arrow protruding from his forehead. In two steps I climbed the archer's platform and leaped behind the blind. I passed my blade into the fellow's body, and he fell, turning, from the platform, arrows spilling, like rattling sticks, to the deck. A pirate leaped toward me and I cut him from the platform. Arrows sped toward me, two of them, and caught, tearing, in the wicker. Behind me I could see another pirate vessel looming. Near the stem castle I saw some of my fellows cutting through pirates. Burning pitch flamed upon the deck.

"This way, Lads!" I called, leaping down from the archer's platform. An arrow struck into the deck at my feet.

We sped down the deck. The ship shuddered as the great catapult loosed a stone which shattered into the rowing frame on the port side of the *Tina*.

In moments I and the others, now some seven men, cutting at pirates, severing ropes, separated the two vessels and, as they slipped loose of one another, leaped onto the stern of the *Tina*, falling upon the pirates who had boarded her there.

The pirates, pressed by our defenders, and attacked now from their own vessel, fought for their lives. We forced them to the railing, and over it, those who were not cut down, into the Vosk.

"Are there no more?" I inquired.

"Are you disappointed?" asked a man.

"Our decks are cleared of the sleen," said a man.

"They fought well," said a man.

"They are men of the Voskjard," said another.

Our deck was run with blood. It was splintered. Arrows protruded from it. The port rowing frame was half struck away. Damage had already been incurred by our stern castle in an earlier engagement. Our starboard shearing blade was awry.

We sought our men in the water, throwing them ropes. "Aiii!" I cried.

"What is it?" asked a man.

"That ship," I said, pointing, to a vessel less than some hundred yards away, engaged in war. "That is the *Tamira!*"

This legend was emblazoned on her starboard bow. Doubtless it appeared, as well, on her port bow. The same legend also appeared on her stern. Gorean merchantmen are often identified at these three points.

"So what of it?" asked a man.

"She is not our ship," said another.

"She flies the pennons of the Voskjard," said another.

"She is the ship which, in the Vosk, east of the chain, with the *Telia*, captained by Sirnak, of the men of Policrates, took the *Flower of Siba!*" These things I had learned while held captive in the holding of Policrates.

"What of it?" asked a man.

"She is captained by Reginald, in the fee of Ragnar Voskjard," I cried. "She is the scout ship of Ragnar Voskjard."

"What of it?" asked a man.

"She came to clear the way for the passage of the Voskjard east," I said. "But," I said, anxiously, "was the rendezvous with the Voskjard's fleet at his holding or was it in the river?"

"What difference does it make?" asked a man. He threw a rope to one of our fellows, struggling in the water.

"Perhaps no difference," I said. "Perhaps no difference."

"Would you engage her?" laughed a man.

"She is supported by heavy galleys," said another man.

"That she is!" I said, elated.

"That pleases you?" asked a man.

"It suggests to me that the rendezvous was, indeed, made in the river, and not at the Voskjard's holding."

"Is that good?" asked a man.

"It could be splendid," I said. "But, too, it might make no difference."

"You are mad," laughed a man.

We then heard again battle horns. Swiftly I gave my aid to drawing two more men from the water. They were survivors from the *Claudia*, she of Point Alfred.

Fifty yards astern we saw the jury-rigged ram of the *Sita*, a converted merchantman of Jort's Ferry, take a ship of the Voskjard in the stern.

"To the benches!" called an officer. I, too, ran to the benches and seized an oar.

Behind us we heard the rending of strakes. The *Sita* herself, extricating herself from her victim, sluggish, half-listing, underoared, was stove in on the port and starboard sides by ramships of the Voskjard.

"Where are the ships of Callisthenes!" cried a man.

"Stroke! Stroke!" called the oar master.

"To starboard, hard to starboard!" cried an officer.

The helmsmen thrust against the tillers.

"Oars inboard!" cried the oar master. The great levers, scraping, were hauled inboard.

A ramship of the Voskjard, her ram missing our port bow by inches slid rapidly past. Arrows struck solidly into the rowing frame.

We heard oars of the enemy snapping against our hull. Then there was a crash and tearing astern as our port rudder was torn away.

"Oars outboard!" called the oar master, and we slid the wood through the thole ports.

The *Daphne* of Port Cos was in flames. The *Andromache* and *Aspasia* had already gone down.

Abeam on the starboard side we saw a ship bearing down upon us and then, suddenly, though it could have smote us, it veered away.

"It is a ship of the Voskjard!" cried a man.

"No!" said another. "It flies the pennons of Ar's Station!"

"Ar's Station has no such ships," cried a man.

"It did not strike us!" a fellow pointed out.

As the ship slipped past we saw, indeed, that it bristled with the helmets of Ar's Station.

"How can it be?" asked a man.

"It is reinforcements!" cried a man, elatedly.

"No!" said a man. "That is not a ship of Ar's Station. They do not have such ships. It is a ship of the Voskjard! It has been taken as a prize!"

"How could that be?" asked a man. "Ar's Station is unskilled upon the river. Their ships are undermanned!"

To be sure we had noted, earlier, the wreckage of at least four of the ships of Ar's Station, including two of her heavy-class galleys, the *Tullia* and the *Publia*. It seemed to me not unlikely that others of her galleys, as well, might by now have met a similar fate. It was not clear to me why Ar's Station had resorted to such vessels as she had. They were too squat and sluggish; their holds were too large; their lines were clumsy; they were too slow, too unresponsive to their helms; they seemed little other than fat merchantmen, fit less for war than for the placid transportation of weighty cargos. Did Ar's Station truly think to match such swollen, ponderous freighters against the swift, sleek menace of the Voskjard's warships? And to aggravate the situation the ships of Ar's Station seemed undermanned. What luscious fruit they must seem for picking. How attractive, how inviting, they must appear to the predators of the Voskjard!

A mighty rock, then, suddenly, not more than ten feet from my bench, plummeted through our deck, splintering the wood upward, exploding it upward, in a shower of sharpened fragments. We had not even seen from whence the stone came. A looping bowl of flaming pitch traced its trajectory off our starboard bow and fell into the water.

"Stroke!" called the oar master.

We began to nose our way among flaming and shattered ships.

Our benches vibrated as our own major catapult hurled a stone skyward.

The smell of burning pitch was in the air. I heard men crying out in the water.

"We must seek our sister ships, to stand with them!" called the oar master. "It is thus that Callimachus commands!"

"The *Portia* is off the starboard bow!" called an officer. "She is sorely beset!"

"Two ships approach her!" cried another man. "They will draw alongside of her! She is to be boarded and taken!"

"To the rescue of the *Portia*!" cried the officer on the stern castle. "Two points to starboard! Stroke!"

"Stroke!" called the oar master.

"Hold! Back oars!" cried the oar master, miserably. "Steady!" he called to the two helmsmen, now at a single tiller.

In the distance involved, at full strike, with the lost port rudder, we could not have come about in time to attain the attack course.

"Now, stroke!" called the oar master.

"Hold!" called the officer, miserably.

"Hold, hold!" cried the oar master.

In the delay a ship of the Voskjard had interposed herself between us and the *Portia*. Our rams, separated by some fifty yards, faced one another. We backed slowly away. No longer was the *Tina* alert to her helms. Even low and shallow-drafted she could no longer veer in a matter of yards. She had been designed for a double-helm system. The port rudder was now gone. Additional open water was now required in which she might maneuver. The ship of the Voskjard lay to. She did not attack. It may be that from her position she could not detect the missing port rudder. Or it might be that she was waiting for support.

"Shall we not attack?" asked a man.

"That will do little to aid the *Portia*," said another man.

The *Tina* lying to, several of us stood upon our benches, that we might observe the *Portia*'s fate.

"Can we not yet press to her aid?" asked a man.

"If we did so," said another man, glumly, pointing to the rocking galley of the Voskjard off our bow, "she would take us in the hull like a speared tarsk."

"The *Portia* is done for," said a man.

"Gone," said another.

Grimly we watched the efficient approach of the Voskjard's ships, one to the port of the *Portia*, the other to her starboard. On the deck of the *Portia* there seemed no more than fifteen or twenty figures.

"What are they doing?" asked a man.

"I do not know," I said.

Men on the masts of the *Portia* were unslinging the ropes which held the tops of the long, heavy planked constructions back against the masts. These constructions were mounted on platforms. When freed of the masts they leaned back against the platforms. Other men were busying themselves at the foot of the masts, where they were lengthening and playing out the chains that attached the platforms to the masts. When they had done this other men, with shoulders and levers, and hauling on ropes, moved the platforms, which were on long, solid rollers, with their planked constructions, away from the masts, one to port, the other to starboard. At this point the fellows who had been handling the chains adjusted them to the appropriate lengths. Still by these chains, of course, the platforms with their planked constructions, were held to the ship's masts. I saw the rollers then locked in position.

Pirates crowded to the rails of their ships. I saw grappling irons, on their lines, hurled over the bulwarks of the *Portia*.

But almost at the same time the planked constructions, on their platforms, were pulled downward by ropes. These constructions, some twenty-five feet in length, and some seven feet in width, as the pirates scattered back in their path, crashed downward, their great bent spikes shattering into the decking of the pirate ships, anchoring the ships together, yet holding them some seven or eight feet apart.

At the same time battle horns of Ar sounded from the galley and hatches were thrown open.

The pirates, startled, unable to reach the ship, stood confused along their railings.

"Infantrymen of Ar!" cried a man on the *Tina*.

Out of the opened hatches poured warriors of Ar, grimly helmeted, bearing great, rounded shields and mighty spears, bronze-headed and tapering.

Pirates rushed to the planked road bearing ingress to their ship, but a dozen spears, and then another dozen, hurled by running men devastated resistance, and then, on the run, swords drawn, their shields struck by arrows, buffeting, slashing, driving men into the water, the soldiers of Ar rushed over the bridges linking the ships. Half turned toward the stem of the vessel and half to the stern. The pirates' lines, thin, strung out for boarding, were instantly cut. Vicious and swift, clean, exact, merciless, was the steel of professional warriors. In moments had the decks of both pirate vessels been cleared. And still soldiers emerged from the hold. In all, I had little doubt that they outnumbered the pirates eleven or twelve to one. The spacious hold of the *Portia* had been crammed with men.

"It was an infantry battle," said a man beside me, in awe.

"But it was fought at sea," said another.

We watched the great planked constructions being pried up from the decks of the pirate ships. We saw flags of Ar's Station being run out upon their stem-castle lines.

"Ar knows what she does best," said a man.

"Yes," said another.

The ship of the Voskjard which had been lying to, preventing us from joining the fray, now backed away from us.

I think all of us, both friend and foe, had from that moment on a new respect for the ships of Ar's Station.

"Let us join our sisters!" called Callimachus.

We then made our way toward the *Portia* and her prizes.

"It will be dark soon," said a man.

"We can slip away under the cover of darkness," said a man.

"Callimachus will not abandon Callisthenes," I said.

"Where is Callisthenes?" asked a man.

"I do not know," I said.

"Surely we cannot last another day," said a man.

"Not without the support of Callisthenes," said another fellow.

"It would be the third day of fighting," said a man.

"Callisthenes will be here before morning," said a man.

"How do you know?" asked a fellow.

"He must," shrugged the fellow.

"We must rig a new port rudder," I said. "We can obtain materials from the wreckage."

"I will help," said a man.

"I, too," said another.

The thought of the *Tamira* crossed my mind. I had been within a hundred yards of her today.

"We shall seek permission to put down the longboat," said one of my fellows.

"Do so," I said.

The thought, too, of the *Tuka*, crossed my mind. She had been the lead ship of the Voskjard's first wedge attack. She now lay damaged, unmanned, stranded on a bar near the chain, not more than a pasang away. It was said that she was a well-known ship of the Voskjard. Too, she was a heavy-class galley, with a large hold.

"What are you thinking of?" asked a man.

"Nothing," I said. "Nothing."

VI

WE AWAIT SUPPORT FROM CALLISTHENES; IT DOES NOT COME; THE THIRD FLEET OF THE VOSKJARD; AGAIN WE SOUND OUR BATTLE HORNS

We saw the *Leda* of Port Cos taken full in the hull.

"Back oars!" cried the oar master.

The *Tina* shook in the water and, swerving, slid back. A medium-class galley of the Voskjard slipped past our bow, the tooth of her ram failing to feed, the water from her cleft passage, swelling away from her, forcing us to port. I saw one of her great eyes, that on her starboard bow, slide balefully by. Our own ram, as she passed, gouged a furrow, the length of a spear, the wet wood squeaking, in her flank. A man screamed on the stern of the *Portia*, to starboard, not more than forty yards away, and tumbling, reeling, like a torch, his clothing soaked with flaming pitch, fell into the water.

"Back oars!" called the oar master. "Steady! Hold!"

Many of our benches were empty. Blood was on the thwarts.

A set of javelins, five of them, from a springal, struck from their guides by a forward-springing plank, raked the interior wall of the starboard rowing frame.

There was a grinding astern and a dozen men from one of the Voskjard's pressing ships, close in the crowded waters, leapt aboard.

"Repel boarders!" I heard cry.

"Keep the benches!" cried the oar master.

Men fled past us to strike the visitors from the stern. I kept my bench, my hands on the oar.

"Back oars!" called the oar master.

"The decks are cleared!" cried a man.

"The *Portia* has been stricken!" cried an officer. I saw one of our archers, his chest transfixed with an arrow, tumble from the stern castle. A spume of water rose like a geyser from the water near us, marking the miss of a huge stone hurled from an enemy catapult.

I saw, peering through the thole port, the *Leda's* bow lift suddenly at a sharp angle from the water, the ram and hull dripping water, glistening, and then, in a moment, she slipped back, three-quarters below the surface. Her stern was in the mud of the river bottom. The bow, then, in the current, with men clinging to it, swung toward the chain.

"Back oars!" called the oar master.

The ram of a Voskjard ship smote the jutting bow of the *Leda*. Men leaped from it into the water, mixing in the water with the striking oars of the Voskjard's ship. Archers on the Voskjard's ship, leaning over her gunnels, fired down on the struggling swimmers. Elsewhere I saw men fighting in the water.

"Two points to port!" called an officer.

We swung to port. Our ram, now, threatened the Voskjard's ship. The archers scattered behind the bulwarks. Consternation held sudden sway upon her decks. Oars, like startled limbs, not in unison, unevenly, rose from the water. We saw rudder activity, not synchronized between the port and starboard rudders. Oars, one and two, and more, at a time, began to slash down at the water. She, too, swung to port. Then she had slipped away behind the shattered bow of the *Leda*. We had not charged her. Off the starboard bow lay a galley of the Voskjard, rocking on the water, seemingly somnolent, but we knew, in an instant, if we exposed our flank to her, she would come alive, springing to the attack. "Beware the sleen that seems to sleep," is a Gorean proverb.

A bowl of flaming pitch, streaming smoke behind it, looped toward us, flung by a ship near the chain. It struck in the water to the starboard side.

"Back oars, back oars," said the oar master. "Back oars, gently, Lads."

In moments we had drawn alongside of the *Olivia*, which had been the flagship of the fleet from Ar's Station, commanded by Aemilianus. She and the *Portia* had been the last of the original ten ships which had constituted that small fleet. The *Portia*, now, was gone. To the starboard side of the *Olivia* was the *Tais*, slender, scarred, indefatigable, valiant, of Port Cos, which held the center of our line. On her starboard side were the *Talender*, of Fina and the *Hermione*, a prize taken in battle, manned by soldiers of Ar's Station.

"We cannot take another attack," said a man.

We listened to the signal horns from the Voskjard's fleet.

"They are drawing back," said a man.

"Perhaps they will go away," said another.

"They are regrouping," said a man.

"There will be another attack," said a man.

"Of course," said another.

We had begun the morning with eleven ships. Of Port Cos, we had had the *Leda* and *Tais*; of Ar's Station, we had had the *Olivia* and *Portia*, and four prize ships; of Fina, we had had the *Talender*; of Victoria, we had had the *Mira* and *Tina*. Of these eleven ships, now only five remained, the *Tais*, *Olivia*, *Talender*, *Tina* and *Hermione*, which had been taken as a prize. It was a slender line which we had to present to the might of the Voskjard, surely still some twenty-eight or twenty-nine ships, now being marshaled off our bows.

"The *Tais* should make a run for it," said a man near me, a native of Victoria, a survivor of the *Mira*.

"She remains in the line," said a man.

"Who would have suspected it, of the sleen of Cos," said a soldier of Ar near me, one of several whom we had taken aboard, from the careening decks of the sinking *Alcestis*, which, yesterday, had been taken as a prize by the men of Ar. Without such men we could not have manned our oars.

"Interesting," said one of his fellows.

"Perhaps there is courage, other than in Ar," speculated another.

"The sleen of Cos have fought well," said another.

"Yes," said another.

"Where is Callisthenes?" inquired the fellow from the *Mira*.

"I do not know," I said.

"We are out of stones and pitch," said a man.

The sound of battle horns drifted across the water towards us.

I watched one of our archers, with a knife, removing an arrow from the wood of the stem castle. He worked carefully, in order not to damage it.

"They are running flags on their stem-castle lines now," I said.

"It will be soon," said a man.

"Their oars are outboard now," said a man.

Again we heard the sounds of battle horns.

"To your stations, Lads!" called an officer.

We hastened to our places.

"Oars outboard!" called the oar master.

We slid the wood through the thole ports.

"They are coming now," said the man behind me.

"Why is there silence?" called Callimachus from the stem castle. "Can we give no response?"

Men looked at one another.

Then, from the scarred, half-shattered, smoke-blackened stern castle of the *Tina*, first from one trumpet, lifted by a fellow who was little more than a boy, and then from another, and from another, there resounded notes of defiance. The trumpeters on the stern castle of the *Olivia*, too, seized up their instruments, and then, too, from the *Tais*, and from the *Talender* and *Hermione*, came the clear, unmistakable, brave sounds of men determined to stand together.

The hair on the back of my neck rose, and I was proud. I gripped the oar.

"Ready!" called the oar master. "Stroke!"

And the five ships of our small line sallied forth to meet the stately advance of the Voskjard's fleet.

"The *Hermione* is down," said a man.

"The *Talender* has been taken as a prize," said another.

We rested on our oars.

"I had not thought we could survive that attack," said a fellow.

On our starboard side was the *Olivia*, and on her starboard side was the valiant *Tais*.

"They are coming again," said a man.

"It will be the end," said another.

"There is shouting on the stern deck of the *Olivia*," said a man, rising at the bench.

I, too, stood up.

"There is commotion there," said another, standing now on his bench.

"What is it?" asked a fellow, his head down, leaning over his oar.

"There was then, too, a cry from our stern castle. "Ships! Ships astern!" cried an officer from the stern castle.

"It is Callisthenes!" cried a man.

I stood up on the rowing bench, clinging to the top of the rowing frame.

"Callisthenes!" cried a man.

"Keep your benches!" cried the oar master.

"Callisthenes!" cried other men.

On the horizon, astern, like tiny dots, sped toward us a flotilla of ships.

"Callisthenes! Callisthenes!" we cried. Hats were flung into the air. Rejoicing, we embraced one another. Tears of joy streamed down grizzled faces. Even soldiers of Ar, at our benches, crying out, seized up shields and bucklers, and smote them with the blades of spears and the flats of swords.

"The tide turns!" cried an officer. "The tide turns!"

Callisthenes commanded twenty ships.

"Keep your benches!" called the oar master. "The fleet of the Voskjard approaches!"

"Callisthenes!" we cried, joyfully. "Callisthenes!" Joy, too, reigned on the decks of the *Olivia*. We could hear cheering even from the *Tais*, alongside of the *Olivia*.

"We are saved!" cried a man.

Callimachus, alone on the deck of the stem castle, with a glass of the Builders, surveyed the fleet, flung out across the horizon, advancing astern.

I climbed, joyfully, to the top of the rowing frame. The galleys, I could see, stretched from horizon to horizon. Suddenly I felt sick. "It cannot be Callisthenes," I said. "There are too many ships."

A man looked at me, startled, disbelievingly.

"It can only be ships of the Voskjard," I said.

This insight was not unique to me. Almost simultaneously the cheering on the *Olivia* and on the *Tais*, too, ceased. Our three ships, silent, rocked on the water. We could hear battle horns, now, from not only the forces of the Voskjard moving towards us, off our bows, but we could hear, too, the notes of battle horns drifting across the water towards us from astern.

"It is the attack," said a man, reading the notes.

"We are trapped," said another man.

"To your stations, Lads!" called Callimachus.

I took my place at the oar. I was in consternation, and stunned. These ships, advancing from the south, were clearly ships of the Voskjard. But they could not approach from the south in such force, for the south was guarded by the fleet of Callisthenes. To bring a fleet in such force through the cut chain would seem impossible. Presumably it would have been brought, beached and on rollers, about the south guard station. This was the major danger we had anticipated in defending the river. It was for such a purpose that we had placed the twenty ships of Callisthenes at that point, to guard against this major weakness in our defenses. That the new ships of the Voskjard were bearing down now upon us, and in such force, suggested that they had not been opposed, that either they had been permitted to cut the chain and advance unmolested, or, more likely, perhaps, that they had been permitted to circumvent the chain by the use of the beach route about the south guard station.

"Ready!" called the oar master.

Callisthenes must have withdrawn his ships from their position. Too, his information on the power of the Voskjard had proved haplessly inadequate. The error in his intelligence on such matters must have been of the nature of a factor of almost three. His sources had been proved again, and even more seriously, unreliable. The ships of Callisthenes had been essential to our defense of the river. They had failed to support us in our fight at the chain. Now, it seemed, they had failed, too, even to prevent the third fleet of the Voskjard from making an unimpeded entry into the waters east of the chain, from which position, of course, they could take the defensive fleet in the rear. Callisthenes must have abandoned his post. He must have withdrawn his ships. He must, perhaps feeling battle fruitless, have retired to Port Cos.

Battle horns, then, from off our bows and astern, shattered the air of the Vosk.

"It is the end," said a man behind me.

Notes of answering battle horns, from our stern castle, and from the stern castles of the *Olivia* and the *Tais*, almost lost in the din of enemy signals, gave response.

"Stroke!" called the oar master.

The *Tina* shuddered in the water, and then, once more, with her sisters, the *Olivia* and the *Tais*, her oars catching at the water, her ram half lifting, dripping, from the Vosk, defiant and gallant, leapt forward.

VII

I AGAIN SEE THE *TAMIRA*;
I GO FOR A SWIM

"There is the *Tamira*," said a man, pointing to starboard, at one Voskjard ship among others.

I discarded my sword, and seized up a knife from the deck. I placed it between my teeth. I dove into the water, from the bow railing of the *Tina*.

I was then among slashing oars and swimming men. An arrow pierced the water near me, then bobbed to the surface.

Behind me I heard hulls grinding together.

Voskjard ships crowded about the *Olivia*, the *Tais* and *Tina*. Oh bloody decks men held discourse with steel. The twang of bowstrings rang in the air.

I clung to a piece of wreckage. A man clung, too, to the other end of the section of planks. I did not know if he were a pirate or not.

It was late afternoon.

It was like a lake of bloody wood in the center of the Vosk. The ships of the Voskjard so pressed about our three ships that they could not use their rams or shearing blades. More than one Voskjard ship had been set afire by flaming pitch cast from another. More than one, at the waterline, or on her decks, it falling among crowded men, had been smitten with stones cast from the catapults of their own ships.

Fusillades of javelins, struck from springals, hailed down on pirate ships as frequently as they did on ours. Even arrows, as often as not in the fray, in the mixings and shiftings of men, indiscriminately, to the consternation of pirates, found unintended targets.

There was a movement in the water behind me, and I twisted suddenly to the side, turning, and catching the arm, its knife in hand, striking toward me. "For the Voskjard!" hissed the man. We struggled, in the water. I dragged him to me. I got the knife from my teeth and, under the water, thrust it, edge up, into his abdomen, and then drew it, deeply in him, diagonally, upward and to the right. The smell came up through the water. I kicked him away from me and, half submerged, he floated backwards away from the wreckage.

I turned to the fellow who had been clinging to the wreckage with me. "I am from the *Mira*, from Victoria!" he said.

"No, you are not," I told him.

"I am!" he cried.

"Who was the commander of the *Mira*?" I asked him.

Swiftly then did the fellow, turning white, swim from the wreckage. I did not pursue him. Temus, who had been the captain of the *Mira*, had been taken aboard the *Olivia*, that he might, by his skills of seamanship, give aid to the men of Ar.

A longboat was some twenty yards away. Archers were in it. They were hunting the waters. Already the men of the Voskjard were killing survivors.

I saw a man stroking toward me, knife in fist. He was a bearded, vicious-looking fellow. "For the Voskjard!" he said.

I slipped beneath the water. I came up behind the fellow and took his neck, bending back his head, in the crook of my left arm.

Almost at the same moment I saw the fellow at the tiller of the longboat turn it towards us. Archers stood between its thwarts, arrows fitted to the strings of their bows.

I lifted the bloody knife in my right hand. I let the fellow I had seized drift away from me.

"For the Voskjard!" I grinned, brandishing the knife.

The archers lowered their bows. "Well done, Fellow," said the fellow at the tiller of the longboat.

I treaded water, and watched the longboat draw away. I heard, several yards behind me, the rending of strakes, taken by a ram. One of the Voskjard's ships, in the press of battle, had struck her fellow.

The *Olivia*, the *Tais* and the *Tina* were still afloat. They were protected from the rams and shearing blades of their enemies by the closeness of the quarters. They had managed, almost like a fortress of wood, three ships jammed together, surrounded, under fire, beleaguered, to repel assault after assault, pouring over the rails of enemy vessels. The infantrymen of Ar, in their numbers, inordinate for the vessels involved, and their skills in war, uncommon on the river, stiffened the resistance of the remnants of our small fleet. Because of the closeness of the quarters, and the ships about, we could not be easily approached, and those who could approach us, actually attempting to board us, must, toe to toe, make the acquaintance of the warriors of Ar. By the buffeting of those mighty shields, by the thrusting of great spears, by the swift, ringing flash of well-tempered steel, wave after wave of boarders was repelled, cut to pieces, swept back like rabble. Yet I knew that in the end even the mighty larl, if chained, must eventually succumb to the attack of endless streams of hissing urts. The tiny gnawings, the miniscule lacerations, the drops of blood extracted, must in their cumulative effect take their inevitable toll.

I looked at the sun. There was blood in the water about me. It was late in the afternoon. A ship of the Voskjard, a hundred yards away, back from the immediate press of battle, was aflame. A Vosk gull had alit on the wreckage to which I had earlier clung. I put the knife in my teeth and swam slowly toward the *Tamira*.

VIII

I CONDUCT BUSINESS UPON THE *TAMIRA*; I RETURN TO THE *TINA*, BRINGING WITH ME SOME THINGS WHICH I FIND OF INTEREST

I, knife between my teeth, in the water, clung to the starboard rudder of the *Tamira*. Then, lifting myself from the water, clutching at the rudder, I inched my way upward. It was some eight feet in length. I then had my feet on the broad blade of the rudder and grasped the upright shaft. The tarred cables, some four inches in width, moved. The rudder creaked. I looked over to the windows of the stern cabin. These were high, and formed of a lacing of wood and glass. The *Tamira* had once been an ornate, richly appointed merchantman. This guise, doubtless, still served her well in her work for the Voskjard. Her darker offices would not be evident from her respectable and stately exterior. I climbed upward, and swung on ornamental grillework, toward the windows. Then I stood beside the sill of the port window, back that I not be visible through it. This cabin, surely, would be that of Reginald, her captain. I had little doubt but what I sought, either it or a copy, would lie within. The *Tamira* shifted in the current. I reconnoitered, as I could, moving the side of my head slightly. I peered into the cabin. I saw a table, and charts. I could not see his berth. I could not see the entire cabin. I assumed the cabin was empty. Surely Reginald himself, captain of the *Tamira*, would be above decks and forward, presumably on the stem castle taking note of the course of the battle. On the other hand if he should be in the cabin, or if it should be otherwise occupied, I must enter swiftly and without warning, that I might, if necessary, strike before being struck. I wiped the knife on my thigh. The preservation of the life of Reginald, or of another within, was not essential to the pursuit of my objectives.

With a shattering of glass and wood I crashed into the cabin.

She screamed, suddenly rising to a kneeling position in the berth, clutching the scarlet sheet about her throat.

I stood between her and the door, half-naked, the knife in my hand.

"Who are you?" she cried.

I backed from her and then, turning, tried the door. She had been locked within, as I had speculated. From the inside, then, scarcely taking my eyes from her, I dropped the heavy bar into place, in its brackets, securing the door from the inside. I then, with its chain, and ship's lock, secured the bar in place.

"Who are you?" she demanded, holding the sheet high about her.

"Lower the sheet to your shoulders," I told her.

She looked at me, angrily. Then she obeyed. There was a close-fitting steel collar on her neck.

Seeing that she was a slave, no longer did I fear to compromise the modesty of a free woman. "Discard the sheet," I told her. She, kneeling in the berth, dropped it to her knees. "Completely," I told her.

She cast the sheet aside.

She was voluptuous, and blond, and blue-eyed. I saw that she would bring a high price in a slave market.

"I shall scream," she said.

"Do so, and I shall cut your pretty throat from ear to ear," I said.

"Who are you!" she demanded.

"Your master," I told her.

"I am the slave of Reginald," she said. "Captain of the *Tamira*."

"Are you aware that there is a battle going on outside?" I inquired.

"Yes," she said, uneasily, squirming, naked, in the berth.

I grinned. Gorean men sometimes order their women to await them, thus. Indeed, that sort of thing is done even on Earth, by men who own their women. Perhaps a telephone call instructs the woman to be waiting naked in bed for them when they arrive. She lies there alone, unclothed, under the sheets, awaiting her master. When he arrives, she is well ready to be touched.

"Reginald, I take it," I said, "anticipates victory."

She tossed her head. "Of course," she said.

"This is the scout ship of Ragnar Voskjard," I said.

"Perhaps," she said.

"Why are you aboard?" I asked.

"It pleased my master to bring me," she said.

"Are you a Luck Girl?" I asked.

She shrugged. "I am a female slave," she said.

I smiled. Many Goreans regard the sight of a female slave as good luck. Certainly, at the very least, they are joys to look upon. The presence of a free woman on a ship, incidentally, causes some Gorean sailors uneasiness. Indeed, some, superstitiously, and mistakenly, in my opinion, regard them as harbingers of ill fortune. This is probably, from the objective point of view, a function of the dissension such a woman may produce, particularly on long voyages, and of the alterations in seamanship and conduct which can be attendant upon her presence on shipboard. For example, knowing that a free woman is on board, and must be accommodated and protected, can adversely, whether it should or not, affect the decisions of a captain. He might put into shore when it would be best to remain at sea; he might run when he should fight; when he should be firm, he might vacillate; when he should be strong, he might be conciliatory and weak.

There have been occasions recorded when a free woman, usually one who has been haughty and troublesome, has been, by order of the captain, who is supreme on the vessel, simply stripped and enslaved on board. The reservations of Gorean seamen pertaining to the presence of free women on board, incidentally, do not apply to the presence of slave girls. Such girls are under effective discipline, and must be pleasing and obedient. If they are not, they know they may be simply thrown overboard. Similarly, they are commonly available to the crew, to content and please them. Their presence on board is a delight and convenience. The men are fond of them, regarding them with affection. They are, in effect, pets and mascots. A round of paga and a girl is a pleasant way to relax after one's watch on deck. Incidentally the reservations held by some Gorean seamen pertaining to free women on board, also, interestingly, do not hold of free women who are captives. Even the pirates of Earth found uses to which such women could be put.

"Are you available to the crew?" I asked.

"Only if I do not sufficiently please Reginald, my master," she said.

"Do you strive to please him?" I asked.

"Yes," she said, shuddering. "I do."

"This ship," I said, "in league with the *Telia*, captained by Sirnak, of the holding of Policrates, took recently upon the river a merchantman, the *Flower of Siba*." I had learned this in the court of Kliomenes, in the holding of Policrates. The loot had been divided. Part of that loot had been Florence, a curvacious, auburn-haired slave, who had belonged to Miles of Vonda.

"Perhaps," she said.

"Prisoners, then, from the *Flower of Siba*," I said, "are still on board."

"Perhaps," she said. I gathered from the nature of her response that this was, indeed, true. More importantly, I gathered from her response what I had been truly after, that the *Tamira* had made her rendezvous with the Voskjard's fleet in the western Vosk, and not at his holding. Had the rendezvous been made at the holding the prisoners, presumably, would no longer be on board.

"The captain of the *Tamira*," I said, "is an important man, and much trusted by Ragnar Voskjard."

"Yes," she said, proudly.

"The rendezvous of the *Tamira* with the fleet of the Voskjard," I said, "took place then not at his holding, but in the river." I recalled that in open battle the *Tamira* had been supported, and, indeed, convoyed, by two heavy galleys. This had further confirmed my suspicion that she carried a cargo more precious than many understood.

"Perhaps," said the girl.

"Has Reginald boarded the flagship of Ragnar Voskjard since the return from the holding of Policrates?" I asked.

"No," she said, "though signals were exchanged. Why?"

"Then what I seek," I said, "must still be on board."

"I do not understand," she said.

"Doubtless it is in this very cabin," I said.

"I do not understand," she said, uneasily.

"When Reginald returned from the holding of Policrates, doubtless you met him, either on deck, or in the cabin, as a naked, kneeling slave, licking and kissing at his sea boots, begging to serve him."

"Yes," she said, shrinking back.

"He would have been carrying an object, so precious that it would have been in his hands alone."

"No," she said.

"Then it would have been papers, in his tunic," I said. "You, in his cabin, undressing him, bathing him, serving him, would have seen what he did with them."

"No!" she said.

"Do not look to the place where he concealed them," I said.

I saw her glance wildly to my right, to the side of the cabin.

I smiled.

Then, knowing she had betrayed herself, she slipped, frightened, half crouching, from the berth.

"Were you not to remain in the berth until Reginald came for you?" I asked.

She looked at me, frightened.

"Do you not fear you will be slain?" I asked.

She glanced beyond me, across the cabin. I stepped back, that she might have free passage.

"But I do not object," I told her. "I did not order you to remain in the berth. I own you now."

I saw her tense her lovely body. I stepped further back. Then, suddenly, she darted past me, falling to her knees at the side of a great sea chest. She flung up its lid and, frantically, with two hands, rummaged in the chest.

I slipped my knife in my belt. I removed an object from the cabin wall.

Then she had leaped to her feet, wildly, clutching, holding over head, what appeared to be two, flat, rectangular sheets of lead, bound together. She ran to the windows of the cabin, those between and above the rudders, through which I, breaking the frames and glass inward, had entered. She drew back her arms, holding the bound lead sheets over her head, to hurl them into the Vosk.

The whip cracked forth, lashing, snapping, whipping about her startled wrists, binding them together, causing her, crying out with pain, to drop the leaden sheets. By her wrists, temporarily caught in the coils of the whip, I jerked her back and to the side, and she fell, stumbling, among the glass and wood, to my right. With my foot I spurned her to the side of the berth, on the cabin floor. The coil of the whip was then freed.

She whimpered.

I had gathered from the fact that the chest had not been locked, that it had been open to her, and that she had acted with such alacrity, that a charge had been placed upon her in the matter with which I was concerned. That charge, of course, could only have been to see to the immediate destruction of the documents in the event of an emergency. On shipboard, of course, it would be possible to immediately dispose of the documents only by casting them overboard. The lead weighting, of course, would carry them to the mud at the bottom of the Vosk. In a short time, then, the inks would run, and the papers held between the sheets, would disintegrate. My surmises in these matters had been correct. The girl had proved useful.

Whimpering, she was now on her hands and knees at the side of the berth. She extended her hand toward the leaden sheets. The whip cracked savagely and, quickly, she drew back her hand.

"I do not wish to become impatient with you," I told her.

"You do not own me," she said.

I smiled. I lifted the whip before her. "You are mistaken," I told her.

She eyed the leaden sheets. "Who are you?" she asked.

"Jason," I said, "of Victoria, your master."

"I am the woman of Reginald, captain of the *Tamira*," she said.

"No longer," I said.

She looked at me, angrily. "I am a captain's woman," she said.

"You are a mere slave," I said, "who must crawl to any man."

"No!" she said.

"Are you haughty?" I asked.

"If you like," she said.

I turned from her, to search for oiled cloth and wax, something, anything, with which to make a sealed packet.

I heard wood and glass suddenly move, as she scrambled across the cabin floor, on her hands and knees, toward the leaden sheets.

With a cry of rage I spun about and smote down with the whip. The stroke caught her across the back and buttocks and struck her to her stomach on the floor, amidst the wood and glass. Her extended hand was a foot from the leaden sheets. It had not occurred to me that she would attempt to reach the leaden sheets. Apparently she did not yet know who owned her.

I looked down upon her.

She lay there, on her stomach, in the wood and glass, absolutely quietly. She did not move a muscle. She had felt the whip.

"I am not pleased," I told her.

"No," she cried. "No!"

I then, displeased, her Gorean master, savagely lashed the slave. She tried to crawl from the whip, but could not do so. Then she tried to crawl no more, but knelt, her head down, her head in her hands, weeping, at the side of the berth, a whipped slave.

"Forgive a slave for having been displeasing, my Master!" she begged.

She looked up, and I held the whip before her. Eagerly, crying, she took it in her hands and kissed it, fervently.

"Fetch oiled cloth, a lantern, sealing wax, a candle, such things," I said.

She hurried to obey, and I replaced the whip on the wall. In Gorean domiciles, wherein serve female slaves, it is common to find a whip prominently displayed. The girls see it. They know its meaning. Too, displayed so, it is readily available for us.

I went to the leaden sheets and, with my knife, cut away the binding holding the sheets together. I took the envelope from within, and opened it. I examined the papers which I had extracted from the envelope. I smiled. They contained what I had expected.

The girl, from a shelf to one side, fetched a large candle,

some five inches in diameter. This candle was set in a shallow, silver bowl. She had lifted the bowl upward, off the shelf. In its bottom, protruding, was a spike. This spike had been sitting in an aperture cut in the shelf, that the bowl might sit evenly on the wood. There was a similar aperture, about a half of an inch in width, in the table. She set the spike into this hole and, again, the silver bowl rested evenly on wood. This prevents the movement of the candle in rough weather. The table, too, was bolted to the floor. For similar reasons ships' lanterns, in cabins or below decks, are usually hung from hooks overhead. Thus, in rough weather they may swing, but they are not likely to fall, scattering flaming oil about, with attendant dangers of fire. Most ships' furniture, of course, berths and such, are fixed in place. This prevents the shifting of position which, otherwise, of course, particularly in rough seas, would be inevitable. She lit the candle. On the table, too, in a moment, she placed waxed paper, and an envelope of oil cloth. Such things are not uncommon on ships, to protect papers which might be carried in the spray or weather, for example, on a longboat between ships, or between ships and the shore. Sealing wax, too, in a rectangular bar, she placed on the table. She then knelt beside the table. She kept her head down, deferentially, not daring to meet my eyes.

"Head to the floor," I told her.

She obeyed, swiftly.

I replaced the papers in their envelope, from with I had withdrawn them to examine them. I then wrapped the envelope in several thicknesses of waxed paper. Then, with the sealing wax, melted by the candle, drop by drop, then smoothing the drops into rivulets of liquid wax, I seamed shut the waxed paper.

The girl trembled, to one side, kneeling, her blond hair forward, on the dark, polished floor of the cabin. The collar was clearly visible on her neck, and the small, heavy lock, by means of which it was secured upon her.

"What is your name?" I asked her, while working.

"Luta," she said.

"Oh?" I asked.

"Whatever Master wishes," she said, quickly. "Please do not whip me further, Master," she begged.

"Your name now," I said, seaming shut the last opening on the waxed paper, "is Shirley."

" 'Shirley'!" she sobbed. "That is an Earth-girl name."

"Yes," I said.

Her shoulders shook with the indignity of what had been done to her.

"I was a captain's woman," she said.

"Do you not rejoice in your new name?" I asked.

"Yes, Master," she said, quickly, "I rejoice in my new name."

"Good," I said.

She began to sob.

I inserted the envelope, now enclosed in several thicknesses of sealed waxed paper, in the larger envelope of oil cloth.

"Master," she said.

"Yes," I said.

"Please do not whip me," she said.

"We shall see if you are sufficiently pleasing," I said.

"With such a name," she said, "will I be expected to be so abject, so low, as those hot, surrendered sluts of Earth, so obedient, so owned, so helpless, in the arms of their Gorean masters?"

"What is your name?" I asked.

"—'Shirley'," she said.

"What?" I asked.

" 'Shirley' " she said. " 'Shirley'!"

"Is the answer to your question not now obvious?" I asked.

"Yes, Master," she sobbed.

Earth girls have a reputation on Gor of being among the lowest and hottest of slaves. There are doubtless various reasons for this. Perhaps one is that Earth girls are alien to Gor and have no Home Stones. They are thus subject to unmitigated predation and total domination. They are slave animals, completely. Gorean men, accordingly, treat them as such. In turn, of course, their womanhood is reborn and blossoms, as it can only in a situation in which the order of nature both obtains and flourishes.

A second reason, however, I suspect, why Earth girls make such astoundingly desirable slaves, is their background. In their native environments they encounter few but psychologically and sexually crippled men, men whose merest intuitions of their blood rights are likely to be productive of conditioned, internally administered shocks and anxieties, or externally administered sanctions of censorship, suppression, ridicule and denunciation, imposed by those who are perhaps only a bit more rigid and fearful than themselves. In such a world, largely the ideological product of superstition and hysteria, it is difficult for manhood to exist, even dormantly. Accordingly, when an Earth female finds herself translated to Gor, she finds herself, for the first time, in the presence of large numbers of men to whom nature and power are not anathema. Moreover, she is likely to find herself belonging to them. Beyond this, of course, the culture itself, for all its possible defects and faults, is one which has been constructed to be congenial to the natural biological order, and neither antithetical to, nor contradictory of it. The culture has not suppressed the biotruths of human nature but found a place for them.

The culture is a setting which transforms and enhances the simplicities and rudenesses of nature, ennobling her and exalting her, lending her glory and articulation, refining her, fulfilling her, rather than a sewer and a trap, in which she is kept half-starved and chained.

An example of this sort of thing is the institution of female slavery. It is clearly founded on, and expressive of, the order of nature, but what a wonder has civilization wrought here, elevating and transforming what is in effect a genetically coded biological datum, male dominance and female submission, into a complex, historically developed institution, with its hundreds of aspects and facets, legal, social and aesthetic. What a contrast is the beautiful, vended girl, branded and collared, desiring a master and trained to please one, kneeling before her purchaser and kissing his whip, with the brutish female, cowering under her master's club at the back of his cave. And yet, of course, both women are owned, and completely. But the former, the slave girl, is owned with all the power and authority of law. If anything, she is owned even more completely than her primitive forebear. Civilization, as well as nature, collaborates in her bondage, sanctifying and confirming it.

It is no wonder that the institution of slavery provides the human female, in all her sensitivities and vulnerabilities, in all her psychophysical complexity, with the deepest fulfillments and most exquisite emotions she can know.

Briefly put, the second reason that Earth girls make such astoundingly desirable slaves is that they have been, in their Earth years, subjected, in effect, to sexual and emotional starvation. They have labored in a fruitless desert, often not even understanding the causes of their unhappiness, of their misery and frustration. Confused, they have lashed out at themselves and others, ultimately profitlessly and meaninglessly. Translated to Gor, encountering true men in large numbers, in overwhelming numbers, so different from the crippled males of Earth, finding themselves in an exotic environment, and participating in a culture markedly different from their own, and in many respects both fearful and beautiful, and founded on the order of nature, they find themselves, in effect, restored to love. The Gorean girl knows such joys can exist, though she may or may not have experienced them. The Earth girl, commonly, did not know that such joys, truly, could exist. Only in her troubled sleep, perhaps, did the Earth girl dream of the slaver's noose or the harsh, flat stones of the dungeon on which she might be forced to kneel.

There was a sudden, loud pounding on the cabin door.

The startled girl lifted her head, suddenly, fearfully, looking at me.

With a curt gesture I signaled she should flee to the captain's berth. She crawled rapidly into it. I accompanied her to the berth, and stood beside her. She knelt there, on the berth, frightened. If she were to speak, her voice must be recognized, through the door, as coming from the vicinity of the berth.

She knelt there, clutching the scarlet sheet. I did not speak.

Again came the pounding. "Luta," called a voice. "Luta!"

"Respond to the false name," I told the girl.

"Yes, Master," she called.

"Are you naked, and in the berth?" called the voice.

"Yes, Master," she called.

"Are you all right?" he asked, through the door.

I drew the knife from my belt and thrust its point a quarter of an inch into her sweet, rounded belly. She looked down at it, wincing.

"Yes, Master," she called.

"Who is it?" I whispered.

"Artemidorus," she whispered, "first officer."

"Are you certain that you are all right?" asked the officer, through the door.

I placed my left hand behind the small of her back, so that she could not pull back from the point of the knife. A plunging slash, she knew, might disembowel her.

"Yes, Master," she called.

"Are you keeping yourself hot for your master?" laughed the voice, roughly.

"Yes, Master!" she called. "Is the battle nearly over?" We could hear the occasional sounds of fighting outside, from some hundreds of yards off, across the water.

"Curiosity is not becoming in a Kajira," laughed the fellow.

"Yes, Master. Forgive me, Master," she said.

"Keep yourself hot," he said.

"Yes, Master," she said.

I then heard him laugh again, and then turn about and climb five stairs, which must have led to the main deck, from a short companionway.

"The battle must be nearly over," she said.

"Why do you think so?" I asked.

"My readiness for the master was being checked," she said.

"It is fortunate that he did not choose to check it by hand," I said.

"Yes," she said, shuddering. She looked down at the knife.

I was curious to know how the battle outside waged. I removed my hand from the small of her back, and the knife from its ready and threatening location at her belly. She respired in relief. I placed the knife in my belt again. I saw that her lower belly, so sweetly rounded, was beautiful.

"Lie down," I told her.

She lay on her back, and by the brass rings, some two inches in diameter, and by the leather thongs, near her shoulders, and at the bottom sides of the berth, tied her upon it.

I looked down upon her. She was beautiful, and secured.

I then went to the shattered window at the rear of the cabin. I did not make my surveillance obvious.

"May I inquire as to the situation, Master?" she asked.

"No," I told her.

"Yes, Master," she said.

Through a gap in the pirate fleet, I could see that the beleaguered, desperate ships of the defenders fought on, stoutly.

I was convinced that they, still active, pennons still flying on their stem-castle lines, could hold out until nightfall. Yet I did not think they could withstand the concerted attacks of the pirate fleets for another day. How nobly, and well, they had fought. I was bitter. I looked back to the berth. There, tied upon it, helpless, was she who had been the woman of a pirate captain, she who had been the woman of one of my enemies. I then looked again out the window. In the water, among the larger ships, were small boats, manned by pirates. Considering them I became furious. These were being used to hunt for survivors, luckless fellows, struggling in the water, fishing for them with attentive leisure, with arrows, and with spear and knife. They would also make it difficult to return to the *Tina*. I glanced to the table, to the packet, now in its oil-cloth envelope, which lay there. It had immense value, if only it could be exploited. I looked again, out the window, at the ships of the pirate fleet, and at the defenders, and then I returned to the table, and sat before it.

"Master," said the girl.

I did not respond to her.

"Forgive me, Master," she whispered.

That the defenders had lasted this long was a function largely of two factors, first, of the crowding of the pirate fleet which made it difficult for them to bring their rams and shearing blades into play, and, secondly, the unusually large numbers, and skill, of the soldiers of Ar who had been transported in the holds of the ships of Ar's Station, making boarding hazardous and costly.

The tactics which seemed to me obvious in such a situation the Voskjard had not yet employed.

I suspected then he might not be with his own fleet, that it might be under the command of a lesser man.

Carefully, with the sealing wax, I closed the oil-cloth envelope. I then folded it over, into a rectangular packet, and, with some binding fiber, cut from a coil of such fiber, looped at the bottom of the berth, tied it in this shape. I noticed that the girl was watching me. Accordingly, not speaking, I tore a broad strip from the scarlet sheet and, folding it five times, encircling her head with it, tied it tightly behind the back of her head, blindfolding her with it.

"Forgive me, Master," she whimpered.

I then broke loose a board from the wall, a shelf, some two

feet in length, with spike holes in it, to accommodate projections such as that on the silver candle bowl on the table. With binding fiber I tied the packet to this board. Then, with more binding fiber, I improvised a towing loop for the board. This board, then, with its towing loop, and its cargo, the packet in the sealed, oil-cloth envelope, I placed near the window.

It was at this time that I heard the signal horns of the pirate fleet. The orders, I thought, had been too long delayed. I looked out the window. As I had thought the pirate fleet was now drawing back. The self-frustrating futility of their attack, obstinate and unimaginative, had, at long last, apparently been brought home to its commander. The pirate ships now, sent forward judiciously, singly or doubly, supported as need be, no longer crowded together in useless attempts at boarding, could now bring their rams and shearing blades into play against the cornered, pathetically outnumbered barks of the defenders. But it was now quite late in the afternoon. Doubtless this attack would be postponed until morning, that the slaughter might lose nothing of its effect, some survivors perhaps being enabled, in small boats or in the water, to slip away under the cover of darkness.

I turned and slowly walked back to the side of the berth, on which the voluptuous slave was blindfolded and bound.

I looked down upon her. She knew I stood beside her. She trembled. Her sweet wrists and slim ankles moved in the leather bonds which, tied to the brass slave rings, confined them.

I removed the folded, scarlet strip of the sheet which had covered the upper part of her head, and cast it to one side.

She looked up at me, frightened. She shrank deeper, back in the berth. She had been the woman of Reginald, one of the captains of the Voskjard.

"Please, Master," she whispered, "do not hurt me."

She had been a woman of the enemy.

"Please, Master," she begged, "show me mercy."

How beautiful she was in her collar, close-fitting, and of gleaming, engraved steel, which she could not remove. How beautiful women are in collars. It is no wonder men enjoy putting them in them. How beautiful is the collar itself, and yet how insignificant is the beauty of the collar compared to the beauty and profundity of its meaning, that the woman is owned.

"You are well tied, Slave," I told her. "You are absolutely helpless."

"Yes, Master," she said.

"You are lovely," I told her.

"Thank you, Master," she said.

"A veritable delicacy," I mused, "which was to have been kept simmering on the stove, so to speak, awaiting the pleasure of her master."

"Yes, Master," she smiled.

"Why did Artemidorus, the first officer, when he inquired as to your readiness, not attempt to enter the cabin, and check you by hand?"

"None may touch me save Reginald, my master," she said, proudly, "unless I have displeased him.

"Oh," she cried. "Oh!"

"Have you forgotten, so soon," I asked, "pretty slave, to whom it is that you now belong?"

"To you," she said, "to you, Master! Oh!"

"It seems you are still simmering, little sweet, little delicacy," I said.

She looked at me, wildly. "Your touch!" she whispered. "What is it doing to me?" Then she lifted her body, piteously, the sweet, rounded centralities of her, to me. Then I took her by the hips, holding her, pressing my thumbs into the sides of her belly. She recoiled, frightened. "Show me mercy," she said.

"No," I said.

I pulled the portion of the wadded strip of scarlet sheet, wet and heavy, out of her mouth, a portion of the same, and still attached to it, that I had used earlier to blindfold her. I had thrust it in her mouth to muffle her cries. She was moaning softly, and kissing at me.

"I see that you are still simmering," I said.

"Simmering?" she laughed, ruefully, softly. "You brought me to a boil, and then, when you had well tasted of me, let me subside, and then again, when it pleased you, made me simmer, and then again brought me to a boil, and then again made me simmer, and then, once again, brought me to a boil."

I brushed back some blond hair from her face.

"You well know how to prepare a girl for your delectation,

Master," she whispered. "Surely you are a gourmet of slave use, a master chef well trained in the art of preparing delicious slave viands for the satisfaction of your lustful hungers."

"Be quiet, little delicacy," I told her.

She then thrust her body again against me, and I saw her need. Again I thrust the portion of the scarlet sheet, wadded, into her mouth. She could not protest. There were tears in her eyes. Again she pressed herself, as she could, against me.

The candle on the table had burned out. It was dark outside. I returned from the window of the cabin.

"Please, Master, once again," she begged.

"You are an amorous, passionate wench," I said.

"I cannot help myself," she said. "I am a female slave."

I smiled to myself. Slavery brings out the female in a woman.

I gently joined her on the berth. My knife was thrust, point deep, in the wood above the berth, and to one side, to my right, where I might reach it, if need be. It had been necessary only once to hold it to her jugular. I wadded the portion of scarlet sheet together in my hands and then, holding it between the thumb and fingers of my right hand, pushed it back in her mouth, deeply, behind her teeth.

I untied her and put her on her stomach, in the darkness, on the berth. The portion of cloth I had used to gag her lay to the left side of her head. Her head, too, was turned to the left.

"Am I not as low and passionate as the collared sluts of Earth?" she asked.

I took her wrists behind her back. "There is hope for you," I granted her. I then tied her wrists behind her back.

"Bah," she said, "a Gorean girl is a thousand times more passionate than an Earth slut."

"Perhaps," I said. I smiled. Let them compete with one another, to see who could please men more. Both Earth girls and Gorean girls, I knew, were marvelous. Both were women.

I then pulled the girl to her feet and stood her beside the berth.

"You have tied my hands behind my back," she said. "You

have stood me naked before you. What are you going to do with me?"

I regarded her.

I removed the knife from where I had wedged it in the wood above the berth, to one side and to the right. I held it to her belly.

"Please do not kill me," she begged.

I thrust the knife in my belt.

She shook with relief.

"It is late," I said. "Go to the window."

In the darkness of the cabin, barefoot, stepping softly through the glass and bits of frame scattered on the floor, she went, as commanded, to the window. She stood facing it. I fetched the wadding of scarlet silk which I had earlier used to gag her and put it in my belt. I also fetched the remains of the scarlet sheet from which, standing beside her, I tore what I needed, and then discarded the rest.

"Do you intend to take me with you?" she asked.

I blindfolded her. She would be absolutely helpless in the water.

"Yes," I said. I thought someone might want her. She was a hot and lovely slave. Perhaps I could give her to Aemilianus.

"Listen," I said, suddenly. There was a step on the stairs leading down to the companionway.

"It is Reginald," she said, lifting her head. I did not doubt this. Slaves, like many domestic animals, can often recognize the step of their master.

"Reginald," she whispered, frightened. Her lip trembled. The step had approached down the companionway, and halted before the cabin door. I heard a heavy key thrust complacently into a lock on the outside of the door. It was late. Reginald had come to enjoy his slave. Gorean masters may or may not knock before entering compartments occupied by their slaves. The decision is theirs, as is the slave. If he knocks it is usually only to make his presence known to the slave, and the knock is commonly authoritative and rude, often startling her, even though she expects it, signaling her in no unclear or ambiguous fashion that she is to prepare herself, and well, to greet him, her master, which she does then in a position of docility and submission, usually kneeling and head down.

I heard the padlock, on its chain, fall to the side of the door. "Flee!" whispered the girl to me. Her head twisted in the blindfold. Her small wrists fought futilely the thongs that confined them.

I heard the door push inward, but, of course, it could not move, as I had secured it from the inside, with a lock and bar.

There was a silence.

I took the towing rope, attached to the board and packet, and looped it, and put it through the girl's collar. I passed the lower end of the loop about the board and packet.

"What are you doing?" she asked.

"Is this door locked?" inquired Reginald, not pleasantly from the other side of the door. I smiled. Clearly it was locked.

I pulled the rope tight on her collar.

"Open this door!" said Reginald. He struck the heavy wood with his fist.

The girl moaned. As she moved, the board, on its towing loop, cracked against her legs.

"Open this door!" commanded Reginald. He struck it twice, angrily, with his fist.

"Can you swim?" I inquired.

"No," she said, "and I am bound!"

"Open the door," commanded Reginald. Then he shouted, "Artemidorus! Surtus!"

The girl moaned in misery, unable to obey. I thrust her a step toward the window, holding her by the arm. I looked out. I saw no small boats in the vicinity.

"Oh, no," moaned the girl, "please, no!"

I heard men joining Reginald, outside the cabin door.

"I cannot swim," she said.

"Good," I said.

"I am bound!" she protested.

"Excellent," I said.

I then took the wadding from my belt. "No!" she said. Then I pushed it, still heavy and damp, deep in her mouth. Then I secured it in place with a folded, twisted strip from the torn sheet. I had decided that she would not now, for the time, be permitted to communicate with me. I would remove the gag from her later, if I chose, at my convenience.

"Luta!" called Reginald. "Are you in there?"

I tossed the board and packet, on its towing rope, outside the window. It caught against her collar. I lifted the helpless girl in my arms.

"Luta! Luta!" called Reginald, angrily. "Are you in there?"

"No one called Luta is in here," I called back, cheerily, through the door, "but there is one here who once was known by that name, "one whom I have renamed 'Shirley,' giving her, as seemed fitting, the name of an Earth girl."

The girl squirmed in my arms, writhing in misery, but could not free herself.

"Who are you? Who speaks?" demanded Reginald.

"I am taking your slave, who is quite good," I said, "and something else, too, which I have found of interest."

"Who speaks? Who speaks?" cried Reginald.

"Jason," said I, "Jason, of Victoria!" Then I climbed to the shattered window and, holding the girl, crouched there for a moment. She was uttering small, muffled sounds, whimpering piteously. Then I leapt into the water. As I leapt to the water I heard the men outside the cabin begin to hurl their shoulders against the wood.

IX

I ACQUIRE ANOTHER GIRL;
I RENEW AN ACQUAINTANCE WITH
TWO OLD FRIENDS

"Who is there?" called the fellow from the gunnels of the *Tina*. "Speak, or we shall fire!"

"Jason," said I from the dark, cold water, "Jason of Victoria. Help me aboard!"

"It is Jason," said a voice. I recognized it as that of Callimachus. "Help him aboard!"

I was towing the girl by the hair, on her back, behind me, in the water. Attached to her collar, floating to one side, on its double rope, was the board and packet.

Hands reached down toward me. Two men, clinging to the gunnels, clambered down to assist me.

"What have we here?" asked one of the men.

"A female slave," I said, "and something else, which is of value."

The girl was lifted up, by her bound arms, by two men, and hauled over the bulwarks, the board and packet striking against the side of the ship, with her.

I climbed up, after her. In a moment I stood, shivering, on the deck of the *Tina*.

Callimachus seized me by the arms. "We had feared you were lost," he said.

"We must make ready to withdraw," I said. "We cannot withstand an attack in the morning."

"We were waiting for you," said Callimachus.

I bent down beside the girl and removed the board and packet, on its rope, from her collar. "Put this in the cabin of the captain," I said to a man.

"Yes, Jason," said he.

"What is it?" asked Callimachus.

"I shall explain later," I said.

"There seems light and consternation on the deck of the *Tamira*," said a man. To be sure, we could see ships' lanterns moving about on the *Tamira*, some two to three hundred yards across the water.

I smiled. I did not think Reginald would be quick to report his loss to the fleet commander.

"What have we here?" asked a man, lifting a lantern, indicating the girl, who was kneeling on the deck at our feet.

I jerked the blindfold down from her head, until it hung about her neck.

"A pretty one," said the man.

"Yes," said another.

The girl looked wildly about, frightened, a prize, among the enemies of her former master.

"You are in the presence of men, Woman," I said. "Put your head down, to their sea boots."

Immediately, kneeling, she put her head down to the deck.

"The *Tamira* is coming about," said a man. "I think she means to attack."

"She must be very anxious to recover whatever it was which you took," said Callimachus.

The girl lifted her head, startled.

"Not you, Pretty Slave," I told her, "that which was of value."

She looked at me, tears in her eyes, over the gag, angrily. "Tie her legs, and throw her below decks," I told a man.

"Yes, Jason," he said.

"Oarsmen to your benches," said Callimachus. "All hands to your stations."

"The *Tamira* must be mad to threaten three ships," said an officer.

"She is desperate," said another.

"Reginald may be ready to lose his ship," I said, "that his

loss may be covered, that it may have seemed unavoidable, a fortune of war."

"Surely he would have no orders to leave the line," said Callimachus.

"No," I said, grinning. A cloak was thrown about my shoulders, to warm me from the chill of the water. The girl, her ankles now bound, was carried backwards, her body over the shoulder of a man, to the nearest hatch, that amidships, leading to the hold. Her eyes were wild over the gag. She would be thrown in the hold, and the hatch would be secured. I realized that she would have to be beaten as she had, earlier, raised her head without permission. Such negligences on the part of a slave seldom go unnoticed on Gor.

"It is clear," said an officer. "The *Tamira* plans to attack." He seemed perplexed.

"It is as I had hoped," I said to Callimachus. "She will, thus, open a hole in their lines." To be sure, I had not expected Reginald to notice his loss so quickly. I had hoped to have more time to formulate my plans with Callimachus.

"I shall have the signal horns sounded," said an officer to Callimachus.

"No," I said, "no, Callimachus!"

"Do not sound them," said Callimachus to the officer. "It is not yet time to alert and confuse the fleet."

"Precisely," I said. Orders, at our proximity with the *Olivia* and *Tais*, could be, for the moment, verbally conveyed.

"Is it your intention to exploit that aperture in the enemy line?" asked Callimachus. "It will not remain long. The movement of the *Tamira* will be quickly noted."

"Not directly," I said. "That would be transparent Kaissa, as it is said. Yet the enemy will expect us to dart for that opening."

"Accordingly, they will shift to cover the position," said Callimachus.

"Producing numerous realignments of ships, and perhaps consternation," I said.

"The very wall may be dismantled," said Callimachus, "opened, in a dozen places."

"It will not be understood why the *Tamira* left her position," I said. "It may be assumed by many ships that the attack has been ordered."

"The *Tamira* is bearing down upon us," said an officer. "Shall we engage her?"

"No," cried Callimachus. "Helmsmen, hard to starboard! Oar Master, full stroke!" "Full stroke!" called the oar master. "Port oars inboard!" cried Callimachus. "Port oars inboard!" echoed the oar master.

The *Tamira*, her port shearing blade passing to port like a quarter moon of steel, slid past our hull, between us and the *Olivia*.

"There are lights on other ships!" called an officer. Across the water, here and there, we could see lanterns moving. We heard battle horns.

"Draw alongside the *Olivia*, Callimachus," I begged. "Orders must be swiftly issued, and unhesitantly obeyed."

"Do you plan escape?" asked Callimachus.

"I plan not only escape," I said, "but victory."

We could hear the shouting, as though of a pirate victory, coming from over the water.

My feet slipping on the sand bar I thrust my shoulder against the hull of the *Tuka*, which had been the lead ship in the first major attack against us three days ago. She had been rammed and wounded, and had been abandoned, left aground on the sand bar, near the chain, half in the water, half on the bar. It was a well-known ship of the Voskjard. Near me other men, with their shoulders, and using oars as levers, pried at the hull, its keel sunk in the sand. On either side of the bar, the *Tina* and the *Tais*, with stout ropes, four inches in width, strained, too, to free the *Tuka*.

The shouting carried over the water. There was a reddish glow to the east, from flames.

"They will soon realize they were tricked," said a man near me.

"Work, work harder," I said.

In the confusion and darkness, and in the movement of ships, we had set the *Olivia* afire, her sails set and her rudders tied in place; she was moving eastward, which would be the likely escape route toward towns such as Port Cos, Tafa and Victoria. Like a majestic torch she would sail into the midst of the enemy. Using this as a diversion the *Tina* and the *Tais*, with Aemilianus, and the crew and men of the *Olivia*, with captured pennons from prize ships taken earlier from the

Voskjard, had permitted other ships, like sharks, to pass them, following the light of the *Olivia*, taking that light for the locale of battle. Soon, of course, if it had not already occurred, it would be discovered that the *Olivia* was unmanned.

"Work harder!" I said.

We grunted, and pressed our weight against the hull of the stranded *Tuka*. The great ropes strained. Near me I heard the snapping of an oar, it breaking under the force of the four men using it as a lever. Other men, with spear points, scraped at the sand under the keel.

"I fear there is little time," called Callimachus from the rail of the *Tina*.

"It is hopeless," said the man near me.

The great weight of the *Tuka*, so dark, so heavy, so obdurate, so seemingly resistant and fixed in place, suddenly, unexpectedly, straining, with a heavy, sliding noise, the keel like the runner of a great sled, leaving a line in the sand, thrust by our forces, moved by the water, slipped backward, six inches.

"Work!" I whispered. "Push! Work!"

The *Tuka* slipped back a foot. Then another foot. There was a cheer. "Be silent!" I cried.

I left my position and, hurrying, ankle deep in sand and water, lowering my head to pass under the ropes between the *Tina* and the *Tuka*, made my way along her hull until I came to the river, and there entered the water, and swam about her stern quarters. I joined the men on the other side, on the bar, where the great rent had been torn in her side three days ago by the ram of the *Tais*. The splintered, gaping hole was easily a yard in height and width, the result not only of the ram's penetration but of the tearing and breakage in the strakes attendant upon its withdrawal. The strike had been well above the water line, when the vessel would ride on an even keel. Yet, in the rolling and wash of battle, it had sufficed, at the time, to produce a shippage of water sufficient to produce listing. Rendered unfit for combat her captain and crew had abandoned her, doubtless with the intention later, at their leisure, to repair and reclaim her. I peered into the rupture in the strakes. The ropes strained again and the *Tuka* slipped back another yard. She would soon be free of the bar. I considered, as well as I could, from my position outside the hull, what time and materials might be requisite to restore the

Tuka to seaworthiness. Such repairs, of course, must be made upon the river, and in flight. I did not wish to leave her as she was, of course, for she was important to my plans. She was, it was said, a well-known ship of the Voskjard.

"There is a ship approaching!" I heard a man cry.

"No," I cried out, angrily. "No!"

"It is a derelict," said another man. "She is dark. Her rudders are free!"

It must, then, be a ship drifting unmanned, lost, and carried by the current from the concourse of war. Even if it should be a trick, it was but one ship. Given the men of Ar we had, though only two fighting ships, and the *Tuka*, crews enough to man at least five vessels.

The *Tuka* slipped another yard back, toward the water. With two hands I hoisted myself through the rupture in the hull of the *Tuka*. I drew my sword. The men of the *Tais*, I knew, after her disabling, had briefly boarded her. She had, at that time, been abandoned. I did not doubt but what she was now, too, empty. Yet I did not know that. My sword was drawn. The *Tuka* is a large ship and I could stand upright within her first hold. I felt her move beneath me, impelled again by the ropes and men, toward the river. It was dark in the hold. As the *Tuka* slipped in the sand, being drawn backward into the river, water from the hold rushed about my feet, for a moment some six inches in depth. It then drained through the rupture. I could feel the wet wood beneath my bare feet. Beneath the first hold is the lower hold, but this is little more than a damp crawl space, containing the bilge, and sand, which, on Gorean vessels, commonly serves as ballast. I stood back from the rupture. I was uneasy.

I listened. The hold was dark. I seemed to hear nothing. It had been nothing. Surely it had been nothing.

I did not move. I was uneasy.

Suddenly in the darkness there was the rush of a body toward me. I stepped to the side. Steel slashed down. I heard it cut into the wood at my left almost at the same time that I turned and, in the darkness, slashing, cut at it. I knelt beside it. With my left hand I felt it. The neck, struck in the back, had been half severed.

I then rose to my feet. I stood there, in the darkness, and in the silence, my sword ready.

Then I felt soft lips press themselves against my feet. "Please do not kill me, Master," begged a woman.

I lowered my sword until the point of it was at the back of her neck.

"Please, do not kill me," she begged.

She was at my feet, on her belly, in the darkness.

"Cross your wrists," I told her, "palms facing one another, and touch your fingers to my ankle."

She did this, lying on her stomach. With her hands in this position, a girl can exert almost no leverage, and it may be determined, too, that her hands are empty. This is a simple Gorean procedure, not uncommon, for determining that a girl encountered in the darkness is both helpless and un-armed.

I reached downward and, with my left hand, closing it about her small wrists, pulled her wrists up, drawing her into a kneeling position, her hands, in my grip, held over her head. With my blade, I gently felt between her legs. Feeling the steel between her thighs, she shuddered. This pleased me, for it indicated that she was hot. I then, with the blade, felt along the outside of her thighs and belly. "Yes, Master," she said. "I am naked." I had determined that she wore no cords, or belts, from which a weapon might be suspended. I then touched the side of the blade lightly to her neck. There I felt it move against a steel collar. "Yes, Master," she said. "I am a slave."

"Who was he, he who attacked me?" I asked.

"Alfred," she said, "a man of Alcibron, captain of the *Tuka*."

"What was he doing here?" I asked.

"He was left here to kill those, not of the pirates, who might seek refuge in the hulk of the *Tuka*," she said. "He killed five," she said.

"And what were you doing here?" I asked.

"I was put here, that I might content and please him," she said, "that his duties might be made more enjoyable."

"Are you beautiful?" I asked.

"Some men have found me not displeasing to their senses," she said.

"Who is your master?" I asked.

"Alcibron, Master of the *Tuka*, was my Master," she said, "but now you are my Master, and you own me, fully."

"You sound familiar," I said. "Do I know you?"

"I was once a girl of Port Cos," she said, "one born free, but one who knew herself in her heart to be a slave. I fled Port Cos to avoid an unwanted companionship. He who desired me too much respected me, and though I muchly loved him, I knew that he could not satisfy my slave needs. He wanted me as his companion and I wanted only to be his slave. He wanted me in veils and silk, and wished to serve me. I wanted only to be naked, and collared, and at his feet, kissing his whip.

"I confessed my needs to him and he was scandalized, and that he was scandalized shamed and mortified me. Each outraged by the other we parted.

"I then decided that I would hate men, and do without them. I would be bold and insolent with them, and make them suffer, punishing them for their rejection of my womanhood. If they could not, or would not, understand me, then I would take my vengeance on them, making them miserable! Even in my hatred, of course, I could never forget that in a corner of my heart, kneeling, there languished a love slave. Our parents, naturally, knowing nothing of what had occurred between us, pressed us to intertwine our arms and drink the wine of the companionship.

"He, furious but resigned, cognizant of his expressed intentions and earlier proposals, became convinced that his duty lay in this direction. I had little doubt that if I were but once taken into companionship by him I should be sequestered, and left untouched, that that would be my punishment for having shamed him; he would keep me as his official 'companion' but he would not so much as put his hands on me; I would be forced to endure honor and freedom; respect and dignity would be forced upon me, like chains. I would lie alone, twisting in the darkness, while he reveled elsewhere, contenting himself, in the lascivious embraces of obedient slaves, painted, bangled girls, such as might be purchased in any slut market. How I would envy such girls their collars and the lash of his whip!

"It was thus that I fled Port Cos. I thought I did so, at the time, to make my fortune, but, as I understand it now, I did so to become enslaved. It was soon done to me. In the beginning, true to my resolves, I tried to be rebellious, but the impracticality of that was soon brought home to me. I soon learned that I was a slave. Gorean men allow women little latitude in this regard. She quickly learns she is a slave or she is slain. Yet I did not mind being a slave, truly, for it was what I was. I had known it for years, since my body had developed the contours and needs of a slave. It pleased me deeply that I had been given no choice in the matter, that my slavery, like the brand and collar, had been forced upon me. I had been given no choice but to be what I was. This pleased me. I have known many whips. I have had many masters, good and bad. My longest slavery was in Vonda, in a slaver's house, the House of Andronicus."

"I know who you are," I said.

"Master?" she asked. "Oh!" she said. "Master's grip is tight on my hands!" I was holding her hands over her head, together, she kneeling before me in the darkness. It pleased me to let her feel herself again in my grasp, helpless.

"By what name have you commonly been known, Slave?" I inquired.

"Oh!" she said. "Please, do not kill me, Master!" I had put the point of the blade I carried to her belly. I could feel her, through the steel, wince. She knew that even a slight pressure on that blade, Gorean steel, at that location and angle, could slit her open to the heat of her.

"By what name have you commonly been known, Slave?" I asked. It is sometimes useful to let a slave know that she may be easily killed.

"Lola, Master!" she said, frightened. "Lola!"

I released her hands. I sheathed my sword. "You may lick and kiss at my feet, Lola," I said.

She did so.

"Do you know who I am?" I asked.

"My Master," she said, "my Master."

"Stand, Girl," I said.

She did so.

"I am Jason," I told her, "Jason, of Victoria."

"Master!" she cried out, suddenly, tearfully. "Master!" She seized me in her arms, sobbing, pressing herself against me. I put my arms about her, permitting myself this tenderness towards her, though she was but a branded slave. "She sold me! She sold me!" she sobbed. "She took me to the wharves, while you were at work. She sold me!"

"She had no right to do so," I said.

The girl was sobbing, against me. I could feel her tears against my chest. "I was sold to a merchant from Tetrapoli," she said. "In Tetrapoli I was again sold, to an agent, who proved to be in the fee of Alcibron, one of the high captains of Ragnar Voskjard."

"He brought you along for his pleasure on the *Tuka*," I said.

"Yes, Master," she said.

I took her by the arms, and held her from me. "I have little time for you now," I said.

"Yes, Master," she said. "Oh, Master!" she said, as I pressed her back, and then put her on her back, on the wet boards of the hold. Swiftly I had her, for I had little time for her, then. She clutched at me, hot and shuddering. The *Tuka* was then free of the bar. I could hear feet on the deck over our heads. Men were taking their places at the benches. The ropes by which the *Tina* and the *Tais* had drawn the *Tuka* from the bar were being cast off. I could hear Aemilianus giving orders. I rose from the girl's side. I snapped my fingers. "On your feet," I told her. "We must board the *Tina*." "Yes, Master," she said. She groaned, gaining her feet.

I went to the rupture in the side of the *Tuka*. Through the jagged rupture I could see the *Tais*, and the river chain, behind her.

I tumbled the body of the fellow who had struck at me from the hold, into the water.

The girl joined me, at my side.

"Can you swim?" I asked her.

"No," she said.

I took her by the arm and, lowering my head and crouching, pulling the girl with me, leapt downward into the water.

"Turn about," I said, "lie on your back, relax, completely."

"Yes, Master," she said, frightened.

I then, my hand in the girl's hair, drawing her behind me, swam slowly about the bow of the *Tuka* and to the side of the *Tina*. In moments, helped by crewmen, we had attained the deck of the *Tina*.

"Welcome, Jason," said Callimachus. He grinned. "While we have been hard at work, moving the *Tuka*, it seems you have been trying chain luck."

"I did my share of the work," I laughed. "It merely chanced that she fell across my path."

We turned to regard the wet, shivering girl. Like most girls, either of Earth or Gor, she was short, curvacious and luscious, sweetly slung.

"She is nice," said Callimachus.

"She is a pretty bauble," I granted him. The girl put down her head, smiling.

"Bring a cloak," I said. I then put the cloak about her. She drew it closely about her, holding it with her small hands.

"Thank you, my Master," she whispered.

"Lock her in the hold," I told a sailor.

"Yes, Jason," he said, and conducted the lovely slave to her confinement.

"We must soon make away," said Callimachus.

"I shall find a place at one of the benches," I said.

"Sir," said an officer to Callimachus, "there is movement on the ship to starboard."

"Then she is not abandoned," said Callimachus. "I thought not."

I remembered, then, the ship I had heard of, shortly before entering the hold of the *Tuka*, that which had been identified as a derelict, one presumably drifting downriver, lost from the confusion of the night, illuminated by our diversion of the burning *Olivia*, a pasang or so to the east. She had perhaps been struck by one of the pirate ships, or perhaps, earlier, a casualty from a previous day, had come loose from one of the bars in the river.

Callimachus and I, with the officer, went to the starboard rail of the *Tina*.

We saw oars sliding outboard. The ship was not dead.

"Surely it does not mean to attack three ships," said the officer.

"Why has it not attacked earlier?" asked a man.

"Doubtless it has been waiting," I said, "hoping that other ships would join it."

"Why should it be preparing to attack now?" asked a man. "It is not supported by other ships."

"It knows the *Tuka* is free," said Callimachus. "If it is going to attack, it must now do so."

"But we are three ships," said a man.

"Two, if we do not count the *Tuka*," said a fellow.

"The odds, even so, are decisively in our favor," said a man. One ship, in oared battle, cannot well defend itself against two. One flank, at least, must be exposed.

"The captain is desperate," I said.

"Do you know the ship?" asked Callimachus.

"It was the first ship which left the line, the first ship to strike at us," I said. "In the movement and clashing of ships, in the confusion, in spite of the diversion, in spite of the Voskjard pennons which we have flown, she has not lost us. She has stayed with us. She has followed us, tenaciously."

"Ah," said Callimachus.

"Yes," I said, "it is the *Tamira*."

"She is moving!" said the officer.

"So, too, is the *Tais*," cried a man. I spun about. The *Tais*, dark, low in the water, beautiful, scarred and lean, fierce, one of the most dangerous fighting ships in the navy of Port Cos, under the command of Calliodorus, captain in Port Cos, swept about the stern of the *Tuka* and the bow of the *Tina*. She, too, had spotted the *Tamira*.

"She must not be sunk!" I cried. "Signal Calliodorus!"

"No," said Callimachus, grimly. "The horns would give away our position."

I watched the advance of the *Tamira*. She was an armed merchantman.

"Her captain must be mad," said a man.

"He has doomed his own ship," said another.

I did not even know if Reginald, on the *Tamira*, was aware of the *Tais*.

"She must not be sunk," I cried. "If anything, she must be boarded."

There was a rending of wood, a jarring and ripping of timber. I heard the screaming of men.

"It is too late," said Callimachus.

"Blood for Port Cos," said a man.

"To the *Tamira*," I begged Callimachus. "Please, Callimachus!"

"There is no time, Jason," said Callimachus.

"Other ships will be searching for us," said an officer.

"We must make away," said Callimachus.

I discarded my belt and sword and dove from the rail of the *Tina*. I heard Callimachus cry out behind me, "Come back, Jason!"

In moments I was at the side of the *Tamira*. The dark hull rolled toward me, and pressed me beneath the water. I felt her keel with my two hands, and pushed away, and again came to the surface of the water. My arm struck against an oar, unmanned, projecting downward from her side. I was aware of other men in the water about me. Some yards away I saw the dark shadow in the darkness which was the *Tais*. I pushed away a man in the water near me. My hand struck on a piece of wreckage.

"She is coming again!" I heard a man cry out in misery.

I turned in the water. The dark shape that was the *Tais* seemed almost upon me. I twisted to the side. Under the water I felt myself being lifted and flung back and to the side by the bow wave of the *Tais* and, at the same time, I heard the second impact. For the moment I could not think. I was aware only of the sound, my motion, and the pain. My head then again broke the surface, and I could once more breathe. I was at the side of the *Tais*. Men in the water were crying out about me. I put out my hand. I could feel the port shearing blade of the *Tais*. Then the blade moved back and the *Tais*, oars cutting at the dark river, with a ripping of strakes, extricated her ram from the hull of the stricken *Tamira*. Through wood and men I swam to the side of the *Tamira*. A dozen feet of planking, lengthwise, and some three planks vertically, had been lost.

I put my hand onto the breakage. The hole in the hull was some two feet in height. Water, as the hull shifted, would rush past me, flooding into the hold. I climbed into the hold. It was dark. A crate, loose in the water, struck against my legs. The water was then to my knees. I felt the *Tamira* shudder, and water rushed past me, aft. The floor of the hold tilted beneath my feet. Outside I saw the dark shape of the *Tais* swinging to starboard. Then, not hurrying, she withdrew. She had done her work.

The ship suddenly tilted sternward and I slipped in the hold, and slid aft, then struggling in the water. The breakage in the hull, through which I could see stars, was several feet away, and up the steep slope of the tilted floor of the hold. More water poured in through the breakage. Holding to the side of the hold I pulled my way toward the breakage. I got my hands on its edges and pulled myself through. I dove swiftly into the water.

I turned in time to see the *Tamira*, stern first, slip under the water. I fought back against the undertow. Then, again, the water was calm.

"Help!" I heard. "Help!"

My heart leapt. I swam toward the sound. I came to the two men struggling in the water.

"I cannot support him!" cried a voice.

"I shall help you!" I said.

I reached out and clutched the iron collar locked on the man's neck. "Do not struggle!" I told him. His hands, in manacles, on a single chain passing through a loop on the collar, thrashed at the water. Too, from the manacles, other chains disappeared beneath the surface of the water.

"Do not struggle, Master!" begged the other man.

"Can you stay afloat? Can you swim?" I asked them.

"Our feet are chained!" said the man who had spoken.

"Hold to your fellow," I said. "I can support you."

I then drew them through the water to a piece of floating wreckage. I drew the first man upon it. The second climbed painfully, hampered by the chains, to its surface.

"I had not thought to meet you thus," I told them. "Strange indeed can be the fortunes of war."

"We are alone, in the river," said the first man, he whom the second had addressed as 'Master.' "It is night. We are among enemies."

"Not all are enemies," I reassured him.

"What hope is there?" he asked.

"There is hope," I assured him.

A vessel, a lantern at her bow, nosed towards us.

"We are lost," said the first man.

"Jason, is it you?" inquired a voice from the bow of the vessel.

"It is," I said.

"Come aboard," said Callimachus. "There is little time. We must make away."

I helped the two chained men to stand on the wreckage, that they might be lifted aboard the *Tina*.

"Who are your friends?" inquired Callimachus.

"Krondar, the fighting slave," I said, "and Miles, of Vonda."

X

WHAT HUNG AT OUR PROWS;
HOW WE GREETED KLIOMENES

I crossed the wrists of Lola and, with the dark strap, bound them tightly together, before her body. I then tied the line about her wrists, that strung through the prow ring. I signaled the sailor and he lifted her from her feet and threw her over the bow rail. In a moment, caught and held by the line, she dangled, an exhibited prize, at the prow. In a river galley, of the construction of the *Tina*, her legs fell on either side of the heavy, wooden concave slope of the bow to the water and ram. Shirley, whom I had taken from Reginald, captain of the *Tamira*, said once to have been of Tafa, hung at the bow of our lead ship, the *Tuka*, that vessel said to be a well-known vessel of the Voskjard. Our *Tina* was second in our line. The *Tais*, which we feared might be recognized, brought up the rear. Both girls were naked. Both made lovely adornments to our ships. Preferably, of course, a stripped free woman hangs at the prow of the ship, that the degree of the victory may be made even more keen and manifest, but we were forced to make do with mere slaves. Free women are not often found in the vicinity of pirates. After a free woman has once been at the prow, there is nothing to do with her later, of course, but to make her a slave.

Our three ships made their way unhurriedly through the channel leading to the holding of Policrates.

"I would stand back," said Callimachus.

I did so. It would not do to be recognized. In my tunic, against my body, there was a mask of purple cloth. I had made it in Victoria before venturing west, there to join the *Tina* at the chain. It was identical to that which had been worn by the masked fellow who had tried to obtain the topaz from me in Victoria. I was certain that he had been the true courier of Ragnar Voskjard. I had thought that it might, in certain circumstances, prove useful. I did not, however, don it. I did not know if the courier would be expected to travel with the fleet of the Voskjard or not.

On the *Tuka* the rowers were singing, lustily. They wore an odd assortment of garbs. Insignia had been torn from clothing. Crests had been ripped from helmets, identificatory devices pried from the convex surfaces of shields. It was not a song of Ar they sang, but a river song, a song of pirates and brawlers, "The Ten Maids of Hammerfest," in which is recounted the fates which befell these lovely lasses. I was mildly scandalized that the stout fellows of Ar, soldiers and gentlemen, as Gorean gentlemen go, would even know these lyrics, let alone sing them with such unabashed gusto. I gathered that those of Ar's Station, as well as those of Port Cos and the other river towns, knew well what to do with women, providing, of course, they are put in collars.

I saw the flags run out on the stem-castle lines of the *Tuka*. The signals were those prescribed in the documents I had obtained from Reginald.

I saw answering flags run up on the walls of the holding of Policrates.

"Stay back," warned Callimachus.

I stepped back, further, but maintained still a position whence I might gauge the issuance of the action.

The *Tuka*, under the command of Aemilianus, lay to now, before the great sea gate of iron bars. Her rowers were now silent.

On the stem castle of the *Tuka* stood Miles of Vonda, one who was not of the river towns, and one who was almost certain to be unknown to the denizens of the holding. When freed on the *Tina* he had first expressed his desire to be put ashore, when possible, to make his way to Turmus, but, upon

learning that a certain slave, one called Florence, was confined within the high walls of the holding of Policrates he had
begged instead to be granted a place on a bench and given a
sword. These things had been granted him. He had permitted
his beard to grow and, over one eye, had placed a patch. I
did not think that even Sirnak, who was a captain of Policrates, he who, with Reginald, had waylaid the *Flower of Siba*,
should he still be in the holding, would be likely to be able to
identify him, to detect in the bearded ruffian on the stem
castle of the *Tuka* the former refugee landowner from
Vonda. We thought it otherwise with Krondar, the fighting
slave. It would be difficult, once seen, to ever forget the mas-
sively scarred, misshapen countenance of Krondar, a veteran
of many bouts with the spiked leather, and the knife gaunt-
lets, in Ar. Krondar, sword in hand, with many of Ar's Station, crouched below decks in the hold of the *Tuka*.

My heart leaped. I saw a figure emerging on the walls. It
was that of Kliomenes.

On the night of our escape from our encirclement on the
river, we had set afire the *Olivia*, our slowest and clumsiest
ship, and directed her eastward against the enemy's shifting
lines, opened and disarranged by the departure of the *Tamira*
from her position. This, we had hoped, would create a diversion, and lead the pirates, in the confusion and darkness, to
assume that we were moving eastward, and that the *Olivia*
had been set aflame by their own forces. We had then lain to,
in the movement of ships, pennons of the Voskjard on our
lines, should we fall within the light of passing lanterns. We
had then withdrawn west to the chain, where we had salvaged
the *Tuka*. At this point the *Tamira*, which had tenaciously
kept with us, and despairing of support, desperately attacked.
She had fallen prey to the swift *Tais*. Twice struck, she had
soon sunk.

I had managed to rescue Miles of Vonda and Krondar, his
slave, from the dark, wreckage-strewn water. Following the
Tuka and the *Tais*, by prearranged plan, we in the *Tina* had
then rowed southward along the chain until we came to the
point where the northward-moving portion of the Voskjard's
fleet, that which we had once mistaken for the support vessels
of Callisthenes, had cut the chain. We did not think that the
pirate vessels had been brought on rollers about the beach
south of the chain's terminal pylons to the south. It had

shown no sign of combat or damage. Thus, it had not been opposed by Callisthenes. Accordingly, unopposed, it would have cut the chain rather than engage in the arduous task of beaching and moving over fifty ships some two or three hundred yards overland.

Our speculations in this matter proved correct and we used this break in the chain to move to its western side. Before we had left the vicinity of the encounter between the *Tais* and the *Tamira*, I had called loudly, as though to Callimachus, "We have made good our immediate escape! Let us hasten now to Tetrapoli, where our safety most securely may be sought!" There had been an answering cheer from the crew of the *Tina*, to which cheer the men, upon our signal, gave vent. This ruse, of course, was for the benefit of survivors of the *Tamira*, still in the water about, clinging to wreckage. When picked up by the vessels of the pirate fleet, turning westward, having discovered the ruse of the *Olivia*, they would report what they had heard.

To be sure, I did not think this small, second ruse was truly necessary. It would be assumed by those of the pirate fleet that we, if we could make it west of the chain, would surely fly to one of the western towns for refuge. Tetrapoli is the first major town west of the chain. It would never occur to them, nor probably even to Reginald, captain of the *Tamira*, if he had survived the clash with the *Tais*, what might be the true nature of our intentions. At the least we would wish to garner a large force, one sufficient to exploit any possible advantage which might accrue to us in virtue of our possession of the documents stolen from the *Tamira*. By the time such a force might be raised in the river towns, of course, the fleet of the Voskjard would have reached the holding of Policrates, reinforced it, and participated in the development of new security arrangements. Too, I did not think Reginald would be eager to report that the documents had been stolen from his own ship, before its loss to the *Tais*. Now, if he had survived the clash with the *Tais*, he could always maintain that the documents had been lost with the ship, in his bold and ill-fated attempt to prevent our escape. I had little doubt that he would find it preferable to be commended for gallantry than cut to pieces for an inadvertent lapse or negligence.

Miles of Vonda, on the stem castle of the *Tuka*, and Kliomenes, on the walls of the holding, exchanged signals.

We had not, of course, struck out for Tetrapoli, nor any of
the other river towns. Instead of proceeding northwest toward
Tetrapoli, or toward any other of the western towns, we had,
under sail and oars, proceeded directly northward along the
chain. By dusk we had come to the northern break in the
chain, that produced by the second portion of the Voskjard's
fleet. Utilizing this opening, the first produced by the buccaneers' incursions, we turned east by southeast. We had little
doubt that we would be pursued first, mistakenly, northwest-
ward toward Tetrapoli. While vessels followed our putative
course, and the balance of the pirate fleet, regrouping and repairing injuries, waited upon their return, we sped, in alter-
nating shifts, day and night, toward the holding of Policrates.
My original plan, I was confident, had it not been for its be-
trayal, would have gained us admittance into the holding.

I could not hear the discourse which took place between
Kliomenes and Miles of Vonda, but I knew, and well, its
nature.

"What is it which becomes whole when stones are joined?"

"That ship which sails a topaz sea."

"Where might be found a topaz sea?"

"Within four walls of rock."

"And where might be found these walls of rock?"

"About a topaz sea."

"Who owns the Vosk?"

"Those who own the ship that sails the topaz sea."

There was a cheer from the pirates on the walls. Kliomenes spoke to someone beside him. That man signaled another man, near the west gate tower. He, in turn, called out
to another, apparently within the tower. Kliomenes stepped
back from the wall. My hair stood up on the back of my
neck. I heard the groan and the creak of the great gate. I saw
the chains grow taut and then, protesting, dripping water,
dark, wet and glistening, I saw the great bars lifting out of
the water.

Callimachus, near me, lifted and dropped his blade a bit in
his scabbard. It was a warrior's gesture. He may not even
have been aware that he did it. It was as natural as the curl-
ing of the lip of a sea sleen, anticipatory to the baring of a
fang, trembling, preparing to charge.

"Do not do that," whispered Callimachus to me.

"What?" I asked.

"Loosening your sword," he said. "That suggests that you expect to use it."

"I did that?" I asked.

"Yes," said he.

"I am sorry," I said. I smiled to myself.

I wondered how many of the hands of the fellows, mostly of Ar's Station, tensed on their oars in the *Tuka*, anticipating the reach below their benches to where their weapons lay concealed.

The sea gate rose. I was well aware of the force required to lift that weight.

Within the holding I could hear the sound of flutes, drums and kalikas. The melody, however, was slow and decorous.

Miles of Vonda had represented us, of course, as being the advance ships of the Voskjard's fleet.

I looked upward as we moved slowly, rowing, sail down, under the great gate. It was impossible to pass beneath it without a sense of apprehension. I remembered how, the last time, it had plunged downward. It had shattered the ship on which I had ridden in two.

Then, following the *Tuka*, the *Tais* behind us, we were within the holding's sea yard.

Kliomenes had descended from the wall. He was waiting on the broad walk, near the iron door leading within the holding, for Miles of Vonda. Lines were being cast from the *Tuka* to willing hands on the walk.

More than fifty slave girls, their hair coiffured high on their heads, clad in sleeveless, classic gowns of white silk, were aligned on the walk nearest the wall containing the iron door, that leading within to the halls of the fortress. To the music of the musicians, near the iron door, they performed a most decorous dance, slowly and gracefully lifting their arms and turning, facing first one side and then the other. In their hands they held baskets of flower petals. The dance was the sort that free maidens of a city might perform to honor and welcome visiting dignitaries, or the ambassador and his entourage, of a foreign city. Had their gowns not been sleeveless, and had they not been barefoot, and had their throats not been locked in collars, one might have mistaken them for free women. I could smell viands, too, cooking, the delicious

odors of them emanating from the holding. A feast was being
prepared.

I did not see either the slave, Beverly, or the slave,
Florence, among them. Doubtless they, like many of the
other slaves, were within the holding, preparing, under whips,
the feast for their masters. I regarded the slaves. Even in such
gowns and in the performance of movements so decorous I
found them maddeningly exciting. How excruciatingly beautiful and desirable are women! How difficult it is even to look
upon them and not scream with desire. One could scarcely
conceive of what such women would be later at the feast
when, stripped or clad in rags, or perhaps insulted with a bit
of silk, perhaps tied about their left ankle, they must, in the
full exposure of their slavery, present themselves before
strong men. I did not think their dances then would be so decorous, but would be such as to manifest the full sexual needs
of women, under the command of men. I could conceive of
them crawling on their knees, if so commanded, serving. I
could conceive of them, as I had seen them at other Gorean
feasts, their bodies stained with food and drink, caught by the
hair, thrown on the low tables and raped by masters, and
then raped again. They were naught but slaves. There was no
service, pleasure or intimacy so delicious, so profound, so
prosaic or so unexpected, that they must not render, and
swiftly, at the merest whim of a master. They were, after all,
naught but slaves.

I looked away from the girls. The door leading within the
holding, and the walls, must be taken, swiftly.

The *Tuka* now drew alongside the walk. Mooring lines
were now made fast. Miles of Vonda made ready to disem-
bark. Kliomenes waited to greet him. The girls had now
stopped dancing. In their left arms they cradled the baskets
of flower petals. With their right hands they reached into the
baskets of petals, to cast them on the walk, in the path of
Miles of Vonda and of the men disembarking from the *Tuka*.
The symbolism of the casting of such petals is perhaps reasonably clear. Feminine, and soft and beautiful, they are cast
before the tread of men. Is the token in this not obvious?
Men are the masters, the conquerors and victors. Beneath
their feet, theirs, surrendered, lie the petals of flowers. In this
we may see a lovely gesture, one of both welcome and submission, and one in which the order of nature is beautifully

and sensitively acknowledged. But, of course, there are many ways in which the order of nature may be acknowledged. Another is that in which the woman, naked and collared, branded, under a man's whip, writhes at his feet to the beating of drums.

"Welcome to the Masters," sang the girls.

Miles of Vonda stepped upon the rail of the *Tuka* and he, and other men, leaped to the walk.

"Welcome to the Masters. Welcome to the Masters, all!" sang the girls, casting their petals on the walk before the men emerging from the *Tuka*.

I saw Kliomenes seizing the hand of Miles of Vonda. Aemilianus and his men must move to the door. The halls must be taken.

"All is yours," sang the girls, "and we are of the all. Welcome, Masters, all!"

The *Tina* drew alongside the walk. We cast out our mooring lines. Scarcely were they fast when Callimachus, followed by myself, and others, leaped over the rail. Callimachus, and his men, must seize the walls.

"Welcome, Masters, welcome, all!" sang the girls.

Aemilianus, followed by men, moved swiftly, past startled pirates, toward the iron door.

"Hold, hold there!" cried Kliomenes, suddenly. He had seen Callimachus and myself. "There are spies among you!" he cried. Then the sword of Miles of Vonda was at his throat. "Order your men to throw down their arms!" said Miles of Vonda. My sword then, too, threatened him, at his belly. The arms of Kliomenes were pinned behind him by two men. Slave girls screamed. Baskets of petals fell to the walk. They shrank back against the wall, armed men moving past them. "Throw down your arms," called Miles of Vonda to the pirates on the walk, "or you are dead men." "Throw down your arms!" called Kliomenes, hoarsely. We saw Aemilianus, followed by a file of men, thrust through the iron door. Beyond it, almost instantly, we heard shouts, and then some swordplay, and running feet. Callimachus, followed by his file of men, raced up the steps toward the walls. I saw two pirates, cut from the steps, fall twisting and striking against stone to the sea yard below. A pirate leapt past me and fled down the walk. I pursued him. Then ahead of him another ship was at the walk's edge.

"The *Tais*!" cried the pirate. Men leapt from her rail, ahead of him. He threw down his sword. I moved past him, through the men of the *Tais*, toward the wall. No pirates must escape. I raced toward the wall's height. Swordplay there was sharp. I cut one man from the wall. I thrust a man through who was climbing through an opening in the parapet. I cut my way through men and swords.

I saw, to my alarm, pirates in the water, in the sea yard, swimming toward the gate. I forced my way into the west gate tower. I struck the sword from the hand of the pirate within and spun him about, seizing him by the neck. I thrust him toward the interior balcony, that opening into the chamber of the windlass.

"Order the lowering of the gate, the plunging lowering of the gate!" I said. "Lower the gate," he cried. "Loose the gate! Loose the gate!" Cries of dismay rose from the water below, within the sea yard. With a rattling thunder of chain and iron the huge gate splashed downward into the water, its bars entering and anchoring themselves in their deep, subsurface sockets.

"We surrender!" called the pirates on the wall. Swords were flung down. I put my prisoner with the rest. From the wall's height I could see the walk near the holding crowded with our men, emerged from the holds of the *Tuka* and *Tina*. The fleet of Policrates, as I knew, some forty ships, was abroad, to prevent reinforcements from the eastern towns, should they appear, from proceeding westward to assist at the defense of the chain. Accordingly, within the fortress, under the command of Kliomenes, only a small force had been left, some two hundred to two hundred and fifty men. These would have been sufficient to hold the fortress against a significant attack, but, once the enemy, in numbers, as we were, were within, the defense of the holding would be a lost cause.

From the wall, looking down and across the sea yard, Callimachus and I saw Aemilianus emerging from the holding. He looked upward, toward the wall. He lifted his bloody sword into the air.

"We have won," said Callimachus.

"This battle," I said.

"Yes," he said.

We would not raise over the holding of Policrates the flags of Port Cos, or of Victoria, or of Ar's Station.

XI

MILES OF VONDA AND I OBSERVE SLAVES, UTILIZING THE SCREENED BALCONY ABOVE THE CENTRAL SLAVE QUARTERS

"Would you care to join me, my friend, Miles of Vonda?" I asked.

"Yes," said he.

It was the night of our victory, that in which we had taken the holding.

I put the heavy key into the lock on the door, and opened it. It led onto a narrow balcony, screened by intricate grillework, which, some twenty feet above the floor, encircled the area of the central slave quarters.

The room below was lit by lamps.

We observed the girls through the grillework. It is so designed that they do not know when they are under observation, and when they are not. Anything that they might do or say, thus, for all they know, is being seen and heard by men. This is acceptable. They are slaves.

"Yes," I said, softly, "she is beautiful."

Miles of Vonda, I saw, could not take his eyes from one slave. She sat against the far wall, her hands upon her knees. She was auburn-haired, and luscious. She was clad in her collar, and a bit of yellow rag. She had once been the Lady Florence of Vonda. She was now the mere slave, Florence.

I saw the fists of Miles of Vonda clench.

"If we are successful," I said, "doubtless she, and the others, will be distributed." These girls, of course, like silver and gold, and rich cloths, were loot, and prizes. "You have thus far played a significant and handsome role in our business, Miles of Vonda," I said. "If you desire her, it is quite possible she will be allotted to you, as a portion of the spoils."

"If I want her," said Miles of Vonda, lightly. "There are doubtless numerous others captive below who are quite as beautiful."

"Doubtless," I granted him, "but, yet, she is quite lovely."

"Yes," he said, looking upon her, "she is." I smiled to myself. Did Miles of Vonda seek to conceal from me his affection for a mere slave? It was obvious that he cherished that slave. I had little doubt but what he would die for her.

"It seems that you, too," said Miles of Vonda, looking at me, "find one of these slaves of interest."

"Several are not displeasing to my senses," I admitted.

"What of that exquisite little brunet?" he asked.

"Which one?" I asked.

"That one," said he, indicating a collared girl in a scandalously brief bit of red rag sitting below and across from us, near the foot of the opposite wall.

"Her?" I asked.

"Yes," he said.

I shrugged. It was not impossible that my eyes had more than once strayed to her.

I saw her petulantly, impatiently, push another girl away from her, who had, apparently in her opinion, come too close to her.

"She apparently has a nasty streak in her," said Miles of Vonda.

"She is from Earth," I said. "The whip can take that out of her."

"Could you whip her?" asked Miles of Vonda.

"Of course," I told him. What woman could respect a man who is not strong enough to put her under the whip?

We continued to look downward into the central room of the slave quarters. Many such rooms are quite lovely, resplendent with multicolored tiles and rich hangings, and beautifully appointed with baths and columns, but this was not such a room. This was more in the nature of a gloomy, forbidding, ill-lit, stoutly secure incarceration chamber for females. The walls were high and stern; the tiles were large and dark. In the center of the room there was a cistern. To one side there was a trough for wastes. Scraps of food were commonly thrown to the girls through a window in the grillework on the side of the room to our left. It is not common on the part of pirates to pamper their slaves. All the girls in the holding we had placed in this one room, that they might, for our convenience, be located in a single place. Among them, too, we had placed Shirley and Lola, who had been at the prows of the *Tuka* and *Tina* when we had entered the sea yard. Before we had put them in with the other girls we had given them brief slave tunics, that they might have some prestige among their new fellow slaves. When the fellow had thrust Lola into the room, earlier in the afternoon, I had, from the concealment of the balcony, wishing to keep my presence in the holding unknown to the brunet, observed what had ensued. Seeing the small, exquisite brunet in the bit of red rag, Lola had shrieked with pleasure. "You sold me!" she cried, delightedly, more of her body covered by her brief slave tunic than was covered of the body of the brunet by the scrap of red cloth she had been allotted. "You sold me!" she cried. "Now, you, too, wear a collar!" The brunet, terrified, had shrunk back against the wall. The fellow who had brought Lola to the central room of the slave quarters took her by the hair and shook her head. "She is not to be attacked, or blinded," he told her. This warning I had instructed him to issue to Lola, anticipating her hostility, which was only too understandable, against the brunet. "Yes, Master! Yes, Master!" had wept Lola. She had then been locked inside, with Shirley, and the others. I had instructed Lola, clearly and firmly, prior to her confinement in the central room of the slave quarters that she was to mention to no one that I was present in the holding. A similar injunction was imposed upon lovely Shirley. These girls would keep this secret. They were slaves. They did not wish to be fed to sleen. Accordingly, though the brunet would know that, to her woe, she, now in her own collar, was confined with a girl to whom she had once been almost as Mistress, she would not begin to know or suspect that one named Jason, of Victoria, a free man, resided now within the same holding as she.

"How beautiful are slaves," said Miles of Vonda.

"Yes," I said.

I watched Lola moving toward the brunet. She had, I gathered, seen the brunet push the other girl away, earlier. She sat down, apparently indolently, next to the brunet, and stretched her body languorously, as a slave girl. Though Lola seemed thoughtless and unconcerned in what she did, neither I nor the brunet could be under any delusion as to what was transpiring. She then, as though wearily, and paying no attention, intruded herself even more closely to the brunet. Would the brunet push her away, as she had the other? If so, Lola would not, strictly, have attacked her. The first blow would have been struck by the brunet. Lola, it could then seem, could only be defending herself. I smiled to myself. Lola's defense, I was certain, might leave the little brunet half torn to pieces. I saw the shoulders of the little brunet shake, and then she sobbed, and leaped to her feet, fleeing. She ran across the room. Lola, then, lay down in her place, and curled up, cat-like, to sleep. The brunet then sought another place. "Go away!" said a girl pushing at her. Weeping, the brunet then went to another place. "Go away!" said another girl. The brunet then went and knelt, head down, her dark hair to the floor, before a girl. "Yes," said the girl, "you may rest here, there is enough room for two." It was the girl whom the brunet, earlier, had pushed away. "Thank you," said the brunet, and lay down there. That, then, would be her section of the tiles for the night. It would be there that she would, this night, sleep. I saw her briefly rise up on the palms of her hands, and, furtively, regard Lola. Then, quickly, she lay down again. She trembled. She feared Lola. This pleased me. I smiled to myself. There was another, too, whom she would soon learn to fear, and well, he who would be her master.

"I count eighty-nine," said Miles of Vonda, "including those two, both yours, whom we brought in at the prows of the *Tuka* and *Tina*."

"That is correct," I said.

"An exquisite lot," said Miles of Vonda.

"Pirates have excellent taste in slave flesh," I said.

"Have the barred alcoves and the cell blocks, and the kennels, been emptied?" he asked.

"Yes," I said.

"They are all here?" he asked.

"Yes," I said.

"What of the pens," said he, "those deep below the fortress?"

"They, too, have been emptied," I said. "See those in the corner, those naked, and in close chains?"

"Yes," said he.

"They are the ones from the pens of which you have spoken," I said.

"Were they in close chains in the pens?" he asked. He did not inquire pertaining to clothing. It is common to keep girls naked in the pens. Not only is this excellent for discipline, but it is more sanitary.

"No," I said. "We put them in close chains only upon bringing them to this room. That they were in the lower pens suggested that they might be being disciplined, or were perhaps not well trained, or were new to their collars."

"The close chains, then," said he, "are in compensation for their being brought to an upper level."

"Yes," I said. "They must soon learn that their new masters are stricter than their old."

"Excellent," said Miles of Vonda.

Close chains, even after only two or three Ahn, build up a considerable amount of body pain. Girls confined in close chains soon beg to be released, that they may then strive to better please their masters.

"There is quite a diversity in the garbing of these slaves," remarked Miles of Vonda.

"We brought them in as they were," I said. The clothing worn by the girls ranged from the long, classic gowns worn by the girls from the walk, who had welcomed us with song, flowers and dance, on our entry into the holding, to the cruel, heavy scantiness of the close chains, and their brands and collars, of the girls brought up from the lower pens. Most of the girls, however, wore one or another of a recognizable variety of slave garments, such as tunics, camisks or the scandalous Ta-Teeras. Some, however, had been put in little more than twists of torn rags, such as those on the body of the auburn-haired beauty in which Miles of Vonda had seemed to take an interest and on the body of the small, exquisite brunet of whom I had deigned to take note. I gathered that the pirates had enjoyed setting off their beauty in this fashion. Their decision met with my full approval.

The dressing of slaves, incidentally, is an interesting and

intricate pastime. The slave is almost never totally nude. Her body is marked almost always with some token of her condition, which is bond. This is usually a collar, but it may also be an anklet, sometimes belled, or a bracelet. Her brand, of course, fixed in her very flesh, deep and lovely, is always worn. There is no mistaking it. The iron has seen to that. Beyond these things, much depends on the individual girl and on her particular master of the time. Individual taste is here supreme. To be sure, there are natural congruences and proprieties which are generally observed.

For example, although one may see a girl in the streets, naked save for, say, her brand and collar, or a bit of chain, this is not common. This sort of thing is done, usually, only as a discipline. Free women tend to object, for the eyes of their companions tend almost inadvertently to stray to the exposed flesh of such girls. Perhaps, too, they are angry that they themselves are not permitted to present themselves so brazenly and lusciously before men. Needless to say it is difficult for men to keep their minds on business when such girls are among them. Perhaps this is the reason that magistrates tend to frown upon the practice. After all, Goreans are only human.

In a family house, of course, girls are almost always modestly garbed. Children of many houses might be startled if they could see the transformation which takes place in their pretty Didi or Lale, whom they know as their nurse, governess and playmate, when she is, in their absence or after their bedtime, ordered to the chamber of one of the young masters, there to dance lasciviously before him, and then to be had, and as a slave.

Context determines much. If a young man is giving a proper and refined dinner, his girl, modestly attired, will commonly serve it, shyly and deferentially, quietly and self-effacingly, as befits a slave. She may even draw commendations from his mother, pleased that he has purchased such a modest, useful girl. In a dinner given for his rowdy male companions, of course, in which even unmixed wines might be served, she, obedient, writhing and sensuous, is quite a different girl. Perhaps he has even purchased her some training, from local slave masters. His guests, uncontrolled in their desire, driven half mad with passion, will mightily envy him his girl. Perhaps he, in Gorean hospitality, will share her with them, but, in the end, when they have gone, it is at the foot of his own couch that she, licking and kissing, and begging, will be chained.

The most common Gorean garment for a slave is a brief slave tunic. This tunic is invariably sleeveless and, usually, has a deep, plunging neckline. It may be of a great variety of materials, from rich satins and silks to thin, form-revealing, clinging rep-cloth. Camisks are favored in some cities. The common camisk is a simple rectangle of cloth, containing, in its center, a circular opening. The garment is drawn on by the girl over her head and down upon her shoulders; it is worn, thus, like a poncho; it is commonly belted with binding fiber or a bit of light chain, something with which the girl may be secured, if the master wishes.

One city in which the common camisk is favored, generally, is Tharna. The Turian camisk is a bit like an inverted "T," the bar of which has beveled edges. It goes about the neck, down, low, and is drawn up, and snugly, usually quite snugly, between the legs, the beveled bar ends of the "T" then being folded closely forward about the girl's flanks and being tied, tightly, at her belly. In the common camisk the girl's flanks, and her brand, are bared. In the Turian camisk, because of its snugness and adjustment cords, it is easy, as you might well imagine, to leave little doubt as to the girl's beauty.

Needless to say, the camisk most commonly found in great Turia, the Ar of the south, is that camisk which Goreans, generally, know as the "Turian camisk." Interestingly, in Turia itself, it is known simply as the "camisk," and what I have called the common camisk is, in Turia, referred to as the "northern camisk."

One of the most exciting slave garments, if the slave is permitted clothing, is the Ta-Teera, or, as it is sometimes called, the slave rag. This is analogous to the tunic, but it is little more, and intentionally so, than a rag or rags. In it the girl is in no doubt as to whether or not she is a slave. Some cities do not wish girls in Ta-Teeras to be seen publicly on the streets. Some masters put their girls in such garments only when they are camping, or in the wilds. Others, of course, may prescribe the Ta-Teera for their girls when they are within their own compartments.

There are many types of slave garments, of course, other

than such obvious categories as tunics, camisks and Ta-Teeras. Pleasure silks, in all varieties, and swirling, diaphanous dancing silks might be mentioned. The leathers forced on the slave maidens of the Wagon Peoples, taught to care for the bosk and please their masters, too, might be called to mind.

Sometimes, too, it is controversial as to what constitutes a garment and what a bond. For example, is a slave harness a garment or a bond; objectively, I suppose, it is both. So, too, I would suppose, are the tunic chains of Tyros. A girl may be "set off," of course, and beautifully, even if, technically, she is not clothed. She may be garbed, for example, in netting, as the "Hunter's Catch"; or she may be bedecked in jewels and leather, and shimmering chains, dancing under a whip in a tavern in Port Kar; or she may have flowers intertwined in her chains, as when she is awarded to a victor in public games in Ar.

Interestingly, what counts as slave garments and what does not, is apparently a culturally influenced phenomenon. Goreans, unhesitantly, regard such things as the brassiere and panties, or panty hose, as slave garments. This may be because such garments have been associated with Earth females brought to Gorean slave markets, garments which are sometimes permitted the girls during the early portions of their sale, or, perhaps, independently, because they are soft, sensual and slavelike. Earth girls who don such garments might be interested to know then that that they are putting things on their bodies which on Gor are taken to be the garments of slaves.

The main purpose of slave garments, of course, is not particularly to clothe the girl, for she need not even be clothed, as she is an animal, but to, as I have suggested, "set her off." In this sense slave garments may be as resplendent and complex as the robes of an enslaved Ubara, to be removed by the general who has captured her upon a platform of public humiliation, or as simple as the cords on a girl's wrists and a piece of rope knotted on her throat.

Additional functions of slave garments, of course, other than those of displaying the girl and making it clear to all how desirable she is, are to remind her, clearly, that she is a slave, which is useful in her discipline, and, also, interestingly, to stimulate, intensify and deepen her sexuality. It is impossible for a woman to dress and act as a slave, and be enslaved, in full legality, and not, sooner or later, understand that she is really what she seems to be, a slave. The master, meanwhile, of course, keeps her under discipline, uses her frequently and often casually, and forces her to undergo the abuses proper to her degraded condition. At a given moment of tenderness, sooner or later, she yields herself to him, fully, and as his slave. This moment is usually accompanied with tears of joy, and love. This is experienced by the woman as a moment of marvelous liberation.

Gone then are the thousand frustrations and conflicts; released then, in a flood of tears and joy, is her fundamental womanhood; the hypocrisies are then at an end; the long shams are done; she melts into his arms, kissing and sobbing, his. But enough of the wonders, and astonishments and pleasures, of slave garments. Their nature, their varieties and types, and their meanings, are limited only, as you might expect, by the widely ranging imaginations of the lovely slaves and their strong masters.

Miles of Vonda and I continued to look downward, into the central room of the slave quarters, upon the confined inmates.

"The feast tonight," said Miles of Vonda, "would have been more pleasant, had it been served by these."

"We must, for the time, deny them to ourselves," I said. "There is the work of men to be done."

"When do you think the fleet of Ragnar Voskjard will arrive at the holding," he asked.

"Tomorrow," I told him.

We then looked, one last time, upon the fair slaves so securely incarcerated below us. I think he looked upon the auburn-haired beauty, in the bit of yellow rag. I myself regarded the small brunet, so frightened and exquisite, in the bit of red rag, curled pathetically, a slave, on the tiles below. I smiled to myself. "It would not be unpleasant to own her." I would teach her her condition well. We then left the balcony, locking the heavy door behind us.

XII

WE BID WELCOME TO THE VOSKJARD'S FLEET; THE COURIER OF RAGNAR VOSKJARD; THE FLEET OF POLICRATES

"There must be fifty ships in the channel," said Callimachus, snapping shut the glass of the Builders.

"Bring Kliomenes to the wall," I told a man. "And see that he is well attired, fit to welcome his friends from the west. Some there, doubtless from the crew of Reginald, or Reginald himself, may recognize him."

"Yes, Jason," said the man, hurrying downward from the wall. Kliomenes had spent a good part of yesterday, and the night, with certain other pirates, chained, in rags, at the windlass. His appearance on the wall, Callimachus and I had speculated, might allay suspicions in the advancing fleet.

"How many ships will the sea yard hold?" inquired a man.

"Surely fifty or better," said Callimachus, "but I doubt that so many will enter the holding."

The *Tuka*, the *Tina* and the *Tais* had been removed from the sea yard.

"Is the Tassa powder ready, and the goblets of welcome?" asked Callimachus of a man.

"Yes, Captain," he said, grimly, "but there is far too little for so many."

"The pits in the fortress have been prepared?" inquired Callimachus of one of his officers.

"Yes, Captain," said the man. More than one hundred captured pirates had been drafted to this work, after which, in chains, they had been thrust, packed, with others, into cells below the holding.

"The fleet approaches," said a man. "Their identificatory signals emerge now upon their lines."

"Run up the flags of welcome," said Callimachus.

"Yes, Captain," said a man, signaling to others.

"Have the fire jars been prepared?" asked Callimachus.

"Both those upon the walls, and those along the channel, my Captain," said a man.

I saw the flags of welcome, narrow, triangular and yellow, run up on their lines.

A smoke bomb, trailing smoke, was lofted upward from a catapult on one of the lead ships. It arched gracefully upward and then fell into the marshes lining the channel.

"Return the signal," said Callimachus.

In moments an answering smoke bomb, from a catapult on the walls, describing its graceful parabola, ascended and then seemed to pause, and then looped downward, to splash into the marshes.

We watched the oars of the approaching ships. There was no hesitation or vacillation in their unison.

"They approach with confidence," said a man.

"Good," said Callimachus.

There was a sound of chain near us and Kliomenes, his ankles shackled, was thrust to the parapet. He was clad in a scarlet robe. A yellow, tasseled baret was upon his head. "Smile, Kliomenes," I encouraged him. He winced. The point of my dagger was in his back.

In moments had the first of the galleys reached the vicinity of the sea gate. Kliomenes, at our suggestion, climbed to a place behind the wall where he might be the more easily seen. Crossbows, the fingers of men on their triggers, were trained on his back. He smiled. He lifted his hand, and waved. I did not think it would be necessary to kill him, at least immediately. From the stem castles and decks of the galleys below the shackling on his ankles could not be seen.

Cautiously, from behind the parapet, I surveyed the stem castle of the lead galley. Three individuals stood upon it. Only one of them was I certain that I knew, and he, interestingly, was masked. That one, however, in spite of the mask, was, in his way, not unknown to me. I had met him on the wharves of Victoria, late at night. He had wanted the topaz. He had tried to kill me. It was he who was the true courier of Ragnar Voskjard. The other two men wore the garb of captains. Neither, however, seemed to me to possess the suggestion of power, or the presence, that I would have expected of Ragnar Voskjard. The Voskjard, I suspected, was not with the fleet. I had, indeed, earlier speculated from pirate strategies, that the fleet had been under the command not of the Voskjard, but of a lesser man. The Voskjard, I suspected, during the battle, would have contented himself with reigning in his holding. He would not have seen fit, I conjectured, to concern himself with the travail of personally conducting the immediate and pedestrian affairs of an unimportant battle which, in his opinion, would have had a foregone conclusion. Such a task might be left to subordinates. He himself could join the fleet later.

"Who is on the deck of the stem castle?" I asked Kliomenes.

"Reginald," said Kliomenes, "who was the captain of the *Tamira.*"

"Who else?" I pressed. I had never seen Reginald, though I had, to be sure, been on his ship. He seemed a tall, impressive man.

"The courier of Ragnar Voskjard," said Kliomenes, "he in the mask."

"Who is the other man?" I asked.

"I do not know," said Kliomenes.

"Is it Ragnar Voskjard?" I asked.

"I do not think so," said Kliomenes.

Reginald hailed Kliomenes. Signals could not properly be exchanged. It seems the sealed documents pertaining to these signs and countersigns had been lost with the *Tamira,* that they were now in the mud at the bottom of the Vosk. The *Tamira,* we were informed, had been sunk while valiantly defending herself against an attacking fleet of a dozen ships. Naturally Kliomenes, quarrels trained on his back, saw fit to accept these explanations. Besides, strictly, surely, such signs were not necessary in the present circumstances. Reginald himself was recognized. He had conducted business in the holding before, with Policrates and Kliomenes.

We gave orders and the great gate began to rise. This time,

in the room of the windlass, however, it was pirates who labored to lift that mighty weight. I regretted only that Kliomenes was not sweating with them, in rags, under a whip, chained to a windlass bar. The identity of the third man on the deck of the stem castle of the lead galley, we learned, in the exchange of identifications, was Alcibron, who had been the commander of the *Tuka*. I was much pleased that we had removed the *Tuka*, as well as the *Tina* and *Tais* from the sea yard. Alcibron, and, doubtless, many others, might have immediately recognized her. Alerted thusly to their danger they would have attempted to withdraw. Our trap, presumably, would then have been fruitlessly sprung. Something else which had been Alcibron's, too, was not far away, a wench I had taken from him and made my own slave. She, Lola, with another of my slaves, Shirley, I was keeping, for my convenience, in the central room of the slave quarters, with the captured beauties of the pirates. These latter girls, such as the auburn-haired beauty in whom Miles of Vonda was interested, and the small brunet in whom I had some interest, were in ignorance as to what their disposition would be. This was appropriate. They were slaves.

I saw the lead galley drawing alongside the walk near the fortress wall, across the sea yard. Mooring lines were made fast. Pirates disembarked.

"You will never be successful," snarled Kliomenes.

"Stand back on the ramparts," I said, "that the stern impediments locked upon your ankles not be visible."

He stepped back a foot.

"Smile, and wave," I encouraged him, "unless you wish to die."

He smiled and waved.

I saw Reginald and Alcibron wave to him, from the walk across the sea yard. He who had been the courier of Ragnar Voskjard looked about himself, suspiciously, and then, with the others, entered the holding. Inside, in a previously prepared room, on a great table, were aligned two hundred goblets of wine. Each contained Tassa powder. When the pirates, unsuspecting, were within, and giving themselves to the wine, the door would be locked. Other vessels, too, were now being moored at the walk, and others, following them, were being tied up alongside the first. In a short time the sea yard, if all went well, would be almost filled with vessels. In such

close harborage it would be possible to walk across the sea
yard, moving from deck to deck. More than two hundred pirates had now been welcomed and encouraged within the
holding. Later crews, now, in smaller groups, in single file,
would be conducted deeply within the holding. There, by
larger numbers, the smaller groups would be disarmed,
beaten and hurled into waiting, smooth-sided capture pits,
prepared earlier by the captured pirates of Kliomenes. Narrow corridors, too, and blind passages, suddenly shut off by
barred barricades, through which arrows might be fired by
our men, served a similar purpose. Caught within, as helpless
as penned vulos, subject vulnerably to the pleasure of our archers, pirates would surrender, stripping themselves and submitting themselves, one by one, to our chains.

"There must be twenty ships in the yard," I said.

"It goes well," said Callimachus.

Suddenly, reeling, his sword bloody, I saw he who had
been the courier of Ragnar Voskjard, his clothing torn,
emerge wildly from the interior of the holding.

"Go back! Go back!" he screamed. "It is a trap!"

Pirates looked at him, puzzled.

"Go back!" he screamed. "Go back!" There was then a
confusion of oars. One galley tried to come about. Another,
entering, grated against it. Men began to run about on the
decks of the ships. There was consternation. The fellow who
wore the mask, then, shouting, waving his sword, distraught,
began to leap from ship to ship, trying to make his way
toward the gate. Shouts of alarm now arose from the sea
yard, though, I think, most were more perplexed than
alarmed. Another vessel entered the sea yard.

"I do not wish to lose that man," said Callimachus, grimly.
He lifted and lowered his hand. This signal was rapidly
relayed to the west gate tower and, as the fellow below leapt
into the water, to swim for the gate, it, with a thunderous
rattle of weight and chaining, shaking and sliding, crashed
downward, smiting and dividing a galley just aft of amidships, and then anchored itself in place. The courier of Ragnar Voskjard would not escape.

"Fire bombs!" called Callimachus. "Signal our fellows in
the marshes! Let the attack flags be raised!" There was a
cheer upon the walls. Men rose up on the walls, lighting fuses
of oil-soaked rags, thrust into oil-filled, clay vessels; a smoke

bomb, trailing red smoke, was lofted from a wall catapult high over the marshes. Red attack flags, torn by the wind, snapped on their lines. Vessels of clay, spreading broad sheets of flaming oil, shattered on the decks of the vessels in the yard. Soldiers of Ar's Station, emerging from the marshes on the left and right, screaming, hurled, too, such flaming missiles against the ships in the channel. Our men emerged through the iron door of the holding to command the walks lining the sea yard. They then began to board the moored vessels. A melee took place, even upon the flaming decks. Our men, too, from the wall, streamed down the steps to assist their fellows.

"Watch this man," I told a fellow, indicating Kliomenes.

"Onto your belly, Urt," said the man, "and cross your hands behind you."

Swiftly Kliomenes obeyed.

I hurried downward.

Already pirates, their weapons discarded, were kneeling before our men.

I went to the walk, near the great gate. "You there," I said, gesturing with my sword, "climb to the walk, and kneel."

The courier of Ragnar Voskjard, then, bedraggled, his weapon gone, still masked, knelt before me.

Callimachus, come down from the wall, joined me on the walk. "It goes well in the marshes," he said. "Ships are aflame. Pirates attempt to flee." He looked at the man kneeling, at the point of my sword. "So you are the courier of Ragnar Voskjard," he said, grimly. "Now you are where you belong, on your knees at the feet of honest men." The voice of Callimachus was heavy with rage. I feared he was going to run this fellow through. "It was to him, or to an agent of his," said Callimachus, "that we were betrayed by Peggy, the traitorous Earth slut, the paga slave of Tasdron."

I was silent.

"What do you think should be her punishment?" asked Callimachus of me.

"If she is guilty," I said, "whatever you wish, as she is a slave." This was in full accord with Gorean law. Indeed, anything, for whatever reason, or without a reason, may be done to a slave."

"If she is guilty?" inquired Callimachus.

"The Earth beauty," I said, "by our intent, in her servings

of us, was seldom so placed as to be able to overhear our deliberations." Usually we had kept her at the far side of the room, where she might not hear, but might be immediately summoned, had we desired aught. "Though, doubtless, that we conspired was not unknown to her, I suspect she knew little or nothing of the specifics of our plans."

"Who, then, could it have been?" asked Callimachus.

"Too," I said, "I do not think she would betray you, for, in her heart, I believe her to be your slave."

"Impossible," said Callimachus.

"Buy her from Tasdron," I said, "and put her in your collar, and see."

"Who, then, could it have been?" asked Callimachus.

"Another," I said.

"But, who?" asked Callimachus.

"He," I said, drawing the mask from the head of the courier of Ragnar Voskjard.

The man looked up, angrily, his features exposed.

"Callisthenes!" cried Callimachus.

"Certainly," I said.

"How long have you known this?" asked Callimachus.

"I have suspected it for some time," I said. "I was attacked by him on the wharves. In defending myself I injured him. That night, in our meetings, he appeared with an injured shoulder, claiming to have fallen. In spite of this, and his resemblance to the courier of Ragnar Voskjard, I dismissed the possibility of his guilt. He was well known to you, and you vouched for him. He was, too, one of us, and a high officer of Port Cos. Then, again, when we were betrayed, because of the small number of individuals who knew of our plans, and his resemblance to the courier of Ragnar Voskjard, and the injury, it seemed it must be he. But then, again, because of his high position, and the confidence which you placed in him, I rejected this possibility. I decided that the traitor must be Peggy, the Earth-girl slave. It could only have been she. But, later, when the southern fleet of Port Cos did not support us in the battle, continually denying us her succor, in spite of our desperate need, I became at last fully confident of the justice of my suspicions. All things, then, fell into place."

"Why did you not speak to me?" asked Callimachus.

"The burdens of command were much upon you," I said.

"Little would have been served by my burdening you with cruel and unproven conjectures."

"You were wise," said Callimachus, sadly. "Doubtless I would not even have considered them."

"Nor would I, doubtless, in your place," I said. "But now, incontrovertibly, the proof kneels before you."

"What were done with the ships of Port Cos, your fleet?" asked Callimachus of Callisthenes.

"They are safe," said he. "I withdrew them to Port Cos, on the pretext of fending a threatened attack on the town. On the ruse of undertaking a mission of reconnaissance I then joined the fleet of the Voskjard."

"Where is the Voskjard?" asked Callimachus.

"He is journeying east on the river, in his black ship, *Spined Tharlarion,* to rendezvous with Policrates here, and then to take command of their joint forces in the control of the river."

"Captain," said an officer, coming up to report to Callimachus, "in the marshes the battle is done. Fifteen pirate ships have been destroyed. Many pirates have been killed or captured. Some twelve to fifteen ships escaped. Too, other pirates have fled into the marshes."

"Victory is yours," I told Callimachus.

"Had we ampler forces," said Callimachus, "our victory might have been more complete."

"Do not rise to your feet," I said, warningly, to Callisthenes.

He looked up, at Callimachus. He smiled. "Do not forget that we are friends, Callimachus," said he. "The affection that I bear to you remains unchanged. As children we played together in Port Cos. We have been brother officers."

"You are crying," I said to Callimachus.

"It is the wind," he said. Then he said to the officer nearby, indicating Callisthenes, "Put him in chains."

We watched Callisthenes being led away, between two soldiers, the officer following.

"Would you rather that the traitor had been the slave, Peggy?" I asked.

"No," he said.

I thought that an interesting response on the part of Callimachus. I had, however, little time to ponder it.

"The fleet of Policrates!" we heard, from the height of the

wall. "The fleet of Policrates is at the mouth of the channel!"

"Bring our forces, and their prisoners, within the holding!" called Callimachus.

"Policrates cannot retake the holding," I said. "We would hold it against ten thousand men!"

I followed Callimachus up the stairs to the height of the wall. There was no possibility of our tricking Policrates, of course, as we had Alcibron and Reginald, and the others. Escaped pirates would only too quickly inform him of what had occurred. Too, smoke from burning ships, from the sea yard, and in the channel, climbed skyward.

Callimachus and I, on the wall, regarded the fleet of Policrates at the mouth of the channel. He had returned from his work on the eastern river. He had returned for his rendezvous with the Voskjard.

"We have nothing to fear from Policrates," I said.

"You do not know Policrates," he said.

XIII

CALLIMACHUS AND I ARE PASSENGERS ABOARD THE FLAGSHIP OF POLICRATES; POLICRATES WILL VENTURE TO VICTORIA

My arms were taken far behind me. The ropes on my wrists were tight.

"Secure him well," said Policrates.

I winced, my back arched over the port shearing blade of Policrates' flagship. Involuntarily I cried out with pain. Then the ropes were drawn even tighter. My legs were then drawn back, ropes tight on my ankles. Ropes were adjusted. Lying as I was, bound upon the blade, looking to my right, I could see the port rail of Policrates' flagship. I put my head back. I could see blue sky and clouds. I could not see ahead. On the other side of the ship, similarly secured, fastened to the starboard shearing blade, as I understood it, was Callimachus.

The ultimatum of Policrates had been clear. Callimachus and I must be surrendered to him, Callisthenes, Reginald and Kliomenes must be freed, else Victoria would be subjected to fire and the sword. Defenseless Victoria, we had vowed, must not perish. We had, against the protestations of Miles of Vonda, whom we left in command of the fortress, surrendered ourselves.

"Put about!" I heard Policrates call to his helmsmen. I felt my body move with the blade, as the ship came about in the channel.

"Though you cannot see ahead, surely you can hear," said a voice at the port rail.

I looked upward and to the right. There, at the rail, stood Policrates.

"It is my hope," said he, "that we shall have an engagement."

"Whither are you bound, Captain?" I asked.

"Victoria," he said.

Momentarily, in rage, I struggled. Then I felt blood running at the blade. In frustration, moaning, I ceased struggling.

I heard him laugh. Then he turned away from the rail.

In misery, in fury, I lay bound, not moving, over the blade. I felt the steel, hard and narrow, in my back. The ropes were tight. I felt the motion of the ship. I saw the blue sky and clouds. I was absolutely helpless.

XIV

RAGNAR VOSKJARD MEETS POLICRATES; RAGNAR VOSKJARD LEARNS THAT HE IS NOT FIRST ON THE RIVER

Bound over the great, curved shearing blade I could see little but the sky. But I heard another ship nearby.

"It is *Spined Tharlarion!*" I heard cry. We must now be in the vicinity of Victoria. *Spined Tharlarion,* I knew, was the personal ship of Ragnar Voskjard. He had come from the west on the river to rendezvous with his fleet and the ships of Policrates. The rendezvous was supposedly to have taken place, we had learned from Callisthenes, at the holding of Policrates. Scout ships, however, had been left at the channel's mouth, that he might now, rather, be directed to Victoria.

"You are Policrates?" I heard call.

"I am," answered Policrates.

"He is," called another voice, from my right. "He is Policrates." That was the voice of Reginald, who was known to them both. I remembered it from earlier, from outside the sea gate, at the holding.

"Where are my ships?" demanded the first voice, from my left. The voice was furious. Only recently, I gathered, surely only with a few Ahn, had the Voskjard become apprised of the fate of so many of his ships. The wings of the Voskjard had been cruelly clipped. Of his original three fleets, number-

121

ing in the neighborhood of some one hundred and fifty or sixty ships, he must now retain less than twenty. It would take time to rebuild such power on the river.

"Ask the Vosk, and your captains, the sorry lot of them," responded Policrates.

"Do you test me, Captain?" inquired the voice from my left.

"Be tested or not, as it pleases you," said Policrates.

"How is it that they were not supported?" demanded the voice from my left.

"I did my part," said Policrates. "I defended the eastern river, upholding my portion of our bargain."

"Not one ship of yours shows a scratch!" cried the voice from my left.

"Men knew war against me would be fruitless," said Policrates. "My presence alone guaranteed the security of your flank."

'In your holding were my men ambushed!" called the voice from the left.

"I was not there," said Policrates. "Guile was employed. My men were tricked."

"Your men are fools!" cried the voice.

"So, too, then are yours, who entered the holding like verr trotting into a pen," said Policrates.

"How is it that the signs and countersigns came to be known?" demanded the voice from my left.

"I do not know," called Reginald. "It could not be from me that they were obtained. The *Tamira* went down. It went down at the chain. I was fortunate to have escaped with my life."

"Two who were involved in this miserable business," said Policrates, "surmount now, as stripped and helpless prisoners, the shearing blades of my vessel."

"Good," said the voice from my left. "I shall see that they are rewarded well for their pains, lengthily and at my leisure." The voice now sounded mollified. I felt the eyes of men upon me.

"They are my prisoners," said Policrates. "They are mine to do with as I please."

"As you wish," said the voice to my left. I saw that Policrates wanted Callimachus and myself for himself. We were precious to him. He would not see fit to surrender us to another. I did not care to consider what projected vengeance he might care to impose upon us.

"Convey now to me the flags of command," called the voice to my left.

"I am first upon the river," said Policrates.

"I am Ragnar Voskjard!" called the voice to my left.

"And I am Policrates," said Policrates.

"I am first!" said Ragnar Voskjard.

"You retain, at most, no more than twenty ships," said Policrates. "I command forty."

"There is our agreement!" cried Ragnar Voskjard. "The pledge of the topaz!"

"I have revised the provisions of that agreement, my dear Captain," said Policrates.

"By what right?" asked Ragnar Voskjard.

"By the right of forty ships," said Policrates.

"I shall withdraw to my holding," said Ragnar Voskjard.

"Do so, should it please you," said Policrates.

"I did not come east upon the river to return with empty coffers," said Ragnar Voskjard.

"There is more than enough for all of us in Victoria," said Policrates.

"I shall join you," said Ragnar Voskjard.

"I am first upon the river," said Policrates. "Should you care to contest that, we shall do so, ship to ship."

"I do not care to contest it," said Ragnar Voskjard, bitterly.

"Then I am first upon the river," said Policrates.

"Yes," said Ragnar Voskjard, bitterly, "you are first upon the river."

XV

VICTORIA

"It is quiet," said Kliomenes.

He stood upon a wharf in Victoria, to the left of the blade upon which I was bound. Mooring ropes were still being made fast.

"It is as I had anticipated," said Policrates, beside him. Pirates, disembarking from the flagship, filed past them. I heard jokes about the women of Victoria, and how they would please the pirates this night.

"Not even the alarm bar rings," said Reginald, who had been the captain of the *Tamira*.

Other ships, too, were nosing into the numerous wharves lining the water front of Victoria, and were being tied to mooring posts, and to one another.

"Surely they should come forth, with gifts, and their daughters garlanded, with songs of welcome, to pacify us," said Callisthenes.

"Soon their daughters would wear only their garlands and our chains," said Kliomenes.

Reginald laughed.

"They fear even to do that," said Policrates.

I struggled on the blade. Then I felt blood at my back. Then I felt the point of a sword in my side.

"Do not struggle," said Policrates. My fists were clenched. The ropes were hot and tight on my wrists and ankles. I could feel sweat under the coarse fibers, and the rope burns where I had sought to free myself. I could see the blue sky, and the white clouds. Overhead a Vosk gull was soaring in the wind. I winced, feeling the blade enter a bit more deeply into my side. It was Gorean steel. It does not require great pressure to thrust it through a man's body. I then lay back on the blade quietly, bound. "That is better," said Policrates. I felt the point of the blade withdrawn from my side. I heard it enter a sheath.

"Unfortunately we did not meet resistance," said Policrates. "Had we done so it might have been pleasant to observe you on the shearing blade. Tonight, in chains, perhaps we will permit you to serve wine to our newly collared slave girls, the women of Victoria. Tomorrow, as a participant in our naval exercises, in our projected maneuvers, designed to celebrate our victory, perhaps we shall permit you to return to your post upon the shearing blade." I shuddered. "That should be interesting," said Policrates. I then heard him turn away from me, and with him, too, the others. He, and some of the others, I gathered, then strode down the wharf, away from the ship. Some others, at least, however, remained momentarily behind.

"It is quiet," said Kliomenes, uneasily.

"I had hoped there would be resistance," said Callisthenes.

"There has never been resistance in Victoria," said Kliomenes.

"Nor is there now," said Callisthenes. "The people cower in their houses."

"But never has it been this quiet," said Kliomenes.

"And never before," said Callisthenes, "have the cowards of Victoria had this much reason to be so fearful. Policrates is not pleased with them. When the town is suitably sacked, emptied of anything of interest, he will have it burned to the ground."

"It will be a valuable lesson to all the towns on the river," said Kliomenes.

"Yes," said Callisthenes.

"Let us join Policrates," said Kliomenes.

"Precede me," said Callisthenes.

I then heard them, and the rest, leave the side of the
moored vessel, moving down the wharf toward the concourse.
I sensed, then, that I was alone. In fury, in rage, unobserved,
I tore at the ropes. Tears of frustration were in my eyes.
Blood ran at my back. I was able to move some inches down
the blade, but could not free myself. Again and again, wincing, I tried to pull free. I could not have struggled in this
fashion when under the observation of my captors, of course.
I hoped I might be able to loosen the ropes. They were thick,
and coarse. They were not binding fiber, designed for the perfect holding of prisoners and slaves, nor chains. Too, they
had not been knotted by trained warriors or guardsmen. Too,
I was strong. Too, the metal back of the blade, though not
sharp, was narrow, and rectangular. I had not been bound to
a large, rounded metal ring. I was sure that, given time, I
could free myself. Then, angry, miserable, I again hung helplessly on the blade, scarcely moved some inches upon it. I
could not free myself. It was hopeless. I was covered with
sweat. I had lost blood from the blade at my back. I feared I
might bleed to death.

I sobbed in frustration, bound upon the great, curved
blade. I had underestimated the skills of my captors. Though
the ropes were thick and coarse, they were tight, and well-
knotted. The pirates had not intended me to escape. Thus,
they had tied me well. Such men, I realized, angrily, were experienced in the tying of men, as well as women. Yet they
were neither warriors nor guardsmen; they had not used binding fiber; and I was strong. Again I struggled and then, again,
ceased struggling, sick, gasping and held.

I had, in my struggles, moved my body down some inches
on the blade. By lifting my head I could see ahead, painfully,
to the concourse. There the pirates, at the edge of the concourse, some hundred yards from the office of the wharf master, set back on the concourse, had gathered, preparatory to
their attack on the town. I could see the broad, lateral width
of the concourse behind them. It was empty. The docks
seemed deserted. Victoria, I then suspected, had been abandoned, left to the wrath of the vengeful reavers of the river.

XVI

THE LONGBOAT

"Have you a taste, Lads," called Policrates, "for precious wines and delicate viands?"

"That we have, Captain," called a man.

"Have you a taste for well-tooled leather and fine cloths?"

"Yes, Captain!" called men.

"Have you a taste for more gold and silver, and jewels, than you know what to do with?" called Policrates.

"Yes, Captain!" called dozens of men.

"Have you a taste for luscious slaves, to train with whips to your pleasure?" demanded Policrates.

"Yes, yes, Captain!" called hundreds of men. I heard weapons unsheathed and clashed. "Yes, Captain! Yes, Captain!" shouted hundreds of men.

"Then, Lads," cried Policrates, "take Victoria! She is yours!"

Then, at that very instant from atop the frame building housing the office of the wharf master the alarm bar began to ring. I saw a single man on the roof, striking it with a great hammer. It rang again, and again. The pirates turned, startled, puzzled, to regard the source of the sound. Almost at that very moment, from the seemingly deserted buildings of Victoria, running and screaming, charging, brandishing an incredible assortment of chains, tools and weapons, there issued hundreds of the outraged citizens of Victoria. Archers sprang into view on the rooftops. Showers of arrows sped like dark, linear hail over the heads of the charging citizens, striking into the startled, suddenly reeling, disordered crowds of pirates at the foot of the concourse. But a moment later the charging citizens, like thundering, horned kailiauk, like uncontrolled, maddened, stampeding bosk, pikes and spears leveled, chains flailing, swords flashing, boat hooks, and axes and shovels upraised, struck the dumbfounded, disarrayed throngs of astonished buccaneers.

A cheer rose spontaneously from my throat.

"Fight!" I heard Policrates scream. "Fight!"

I saw a pirate being strangled with a chain. I saw a flailing chain, doubled, tear a pirate's head half from his body. Shovels slashed down at pirates. Pikes stabbed and cut. Spears thrust. I saw a pirate fall over the body of another pirate, who had been struck with an arrow. An outraged citizen thrust down, driving the vertically mounted point of a boat hook into the fellow's face. An instant later he had caught another pirate by the neck, with the horizontally mounted hook on the staff and pulled him backward. Another citizen thrust his sword into the fellow's belly. The archers had now left the rooftops to hurry to the melee, that they might, at point-blank range, pick targets. I saw some five pirates thrust back off the edge of the concourse into the water. An ax split the side of the hamlet open of another pirate. Still more citizens were running forth, from buildings, from further down the wharves, with spears and swords.

"On!" I cried. "On for Victoria!"

"Fight! Stand! Fight!" screamed Policrates.

I saw a dozen pirates break and run for their ships.

I struggled on the blade. In a frenzy I tried to free myself. But I could not do so. I was helpless. I had been tied by Gorean men.

A man ran past me, hurrying to the ship.

"Stand, fight!" I heard Policrates screaming. I saw him strike a pirate in the back of the neck with his sword, cutting his head half from his body, who had turned to run. "Stand, fight!" he screamed.

A dozen more pirates, here and there, in their ragged lines, turned about and broke for their ships. Then a dozen more!

"Withdraw!" shouted Policrates. "Back to the ships!"

"Back to the ships!" called Ragnar Voskjard.

"Back to the ships!" called Kliomenes.

"Back to the ships!" called Callisthenes.

Men were now hurrying past me. Some were bloody, and wounded. Swords slashed down at the mooring ropes. I felt the flagship of Policrates shift in the water. Men were fighting on the wharf now. Men behind me, I heard clamber aboard. I did not know whether or not they could board a crew. Policrates himself ran past me, and Kliomenes and Callisthenes. I heard them leaping to the bulwarks of the ship and clambering aboard. "Poles!" shouted Policrates. "Oars outboard!" I could see the pirate ship to my left, across the wharf, moored on the opposite side, its mooring ropes cut, backing away from the wharf. Then the ship on which I was bound, poles thrusting against the wharf, slid to my right and backward. A pirate running for the ship missed the bow rail and fell into the water. He began to thrash and scream in the water, attacked by eels. I looked down, into the water. Below me the water was swarming with eels. The blood from my back, I realized, running down the blade and dripping into the water, had attracted them.

The wharves, now, were crowded with men. Pirates fell into the water. Others, in the rearward ranks, who could turn, did so, and fled toward the ships. Some ran past me and apparently leaped to oars, trying to hold them and use them to clamber aboard. I heard a man scream, struck, behind me. "Do not encumber the oars!" cried Policrates. I heard a body slide into the water behind me. An outjutting oar struck against the wharf. I heard another body strike the water. Then the ship was out from the wharf. I saw pirates throwing down their weapons, and kneeling on the wharf. There was cheering from the men of Victoria.

"Well done, Lads!" I called. "Well done!"

"We shall return!" screamed Policrates to the wharves. "You have not heard the last of us! We're coming back, you sleen! We're coming back!"

Then the stern of the ship struck against another pirate galley, trying to extricate itself from the press of ships. "Get that fool out of the way!" screamed Policrates. Arrows, wrapped with oil-soaked, flaming rags, struck against the ship. The bow swung about, eccentrically. Below me, swirling in the water, I could see eels.

"Back oars!" screamed Policrates. "Back oars!" cried Kliomenes. "Extinguish the fires!" cried Callisthenes. There was another heavy, grating noise as the stern of the ship was struck again, by another pirate vessel. Blood flowed down the blade to which I was bound, yet I was almost uncognizant of this, so elated I was. On the wharves I could see kneeling pirates, being stripped and bound. They were, too, being roped together by the neck. I did not think that they would find the citizens of Victoria indulgent captors. They would be treated little better than slave girls.

"Well done, Lads!" I called to the men of Victoria. A spear blade from the bulwarks, thrust down, struck down at me, but glanced off the metal, flashing sparks near my right cheek. I could smell smoke. The flagship of Policrates seemed jammed among the ships, each trying to escape. "Well done, Lads!" I cried. "Well done!"

"Get those fools out of the way!" Policrates was screaming. The flagship of Policrates moved backward a dozen feet or so, and then again, striking against another ship, or the same, came again to a stop. "Well done!" I cried. The spear blade thrust down again, but again, came short of its mark. I heard a man curse. Then he left the rail.

"Well done," I cried. "Well done!" I was elated. I could scarcely feel my pain, or the burns of the ropes. I was only dimly conscious of the wetness of my back. Then something wet and heavy, slithering, leapt upward out of the water, and splashed back. My leg felt stinging. It had not been able to fasten its jaws on me.

I looked downward. Two or more heads, tapering, menacing, solid, were emerged from the water, looking up at me. Then, streaking from under the water, suddenly breaking its surface, another body, some four feet in length, about eight or ten pounds in weight, leapt upward. I felt the jaws snap and scratch against the shearing blade. Then it fell twisting back in the water. It was the blood which excited them. I strove again, then, to escape, pulling against the bonds, trying to abraid them against the back of the blade.

I was now, suddenly, alarmed. My struggles had done nothing more than to lower me a few inches on the blade. I now feared I might be within reach of the leaping eels. I tried to inch upward on the blade. Pressing my legs and arms against the blade I could move upward to my original position, but no further, because of the ropes on my ankles, catching on the bottom side of the blade fixture, and it was extremely difficult and painful to hold myself that high on the blade.

I was sweating, and terrified. Then the flagship of Policrates, responding to another impact, lurched to starboard, and, terrified, I slipped back down the blade. My feet, bound back, on each side of the blade, were little more than a foot from the water. Again, frenzied, in terror, I tried to struggle. But, to my dismay, I was again held perfectly. I could not even begin to free myself. I was absolutely helpless. I had been bound by Gorean men.

I felt another stinging bite at my leg, where another of the heavy, leaping eels tried to feed. Again I inched my way painfully, by my thighs and forearms, higher on the blade. If we could get to free water I did not think the eels would pursue us far from the wharves and shore.

Then suddenly I realized I might have but moments before the ship managed to free itself and back into the river. Suddenly I allowed myself to slide down the blade. "Are you hungry, little friends?" I inquired. "Can you smell sweat and fear? Does blood make you mad? Leap, little brothers. Render me service." I looked down at several of the heavy, tapering heads projecting from the water, at the eyes like filmed stones. "Taste blood," I encouraged them. I thrust back against the blade. I tried to abraid my ankles against the steel.

I knew that the fastening of those jaws, in a fair bite, could gouge ounces of flesh from a man's body. Too I knew that the eel seldom takes its food out of the water, that such strikes, in all probability, had not been selected for. Accordingly, the only inward compensation for the refraction differential would presumably have to be learned by trial and error. More than one of the beasts had already struck the blade and not my body. But, too, they might not understand that the blood source was my body; they might understand, rather, only the point at which blood was entering the water.

The waters beneath me now fairly churned with activity. The ship moved backward a yard. "Help me swiftly, little friends," I begged. "Time grows short!" A large eel suddenly

broke the surface tearing at the side of my abraided leg. I felt
the teeth scratching and sliding along my leg, its head twisted
to the side. Then it was back in the water. "Good, good," I
called. "Nearly, nearly. Try again, big fellow!"

I watched the water, giving it time to swirl and circle, and
then again, aligning itself, leap toward me. My left ankle, cut
deliberately on the back of the blade, oozed blood, soaking
the knotted ropes that held it. With the small amount of play
given to me by the ropes on that ankle I must manage as best
I can. Then, almost too quickly to be fully aware of it, I saw
the returning shape erupting from the water. I thrust, as I
could, my ankle towards it. Then I screamed in pain. The
weight, thrashing and tearing, must have been some fifteen or
twenty pounds. It was some seven feet in length. I threw my
head back, crying out. My left ankle was clasped in the
clenched jaws, with those teeth like nails. I feared I might
lose my foot but the heavy ropes, doubled and twisted, and
knotted, like fibrous shielding, muchly protecting me, served
me well, keeping the teeth in large measure from fastening in
my flesh.

The beast, suddenly, perhaps puzzled by the impeding
cordage, shifted its grip. It began to tear then at the ropes. Its
mouth must have been filled with blood-soaked, wirelike
strands of rope. The blood doubtless stimulated it to continue
its work. Its tail thrashed in the water. It twisted, and swal-
lowed, dangling and thrashing. Then, its mouth filled with
rope, pulled loose, it fell back into the water. Again I
struggled. Again I was held. I struggled yet again, and this
time heard the parting of fibers, ripping loose. I twisted against
the blade, my ankles free, and, by the ropes on my wrists,
swung myself up and behind the blade, getting my right leg
over the upper part of the blade fixture.

"Ho!" cried a voice, angry, above me and to my right. I
saw the spear blade draw back to thrust. I clung to the blade,
crouching on the flat blade mount. Ropes were on my wrists,
but my hands were separated by, say, a foot of rope, as I had
been bound on the blade. When the spear struck toward me,
I seized it, behind the blade, at the shaft rivets, and jerked it
toward me. The fellow, unable in the moment to release the
weapon, was dragged over the rail. He struck against the
blade and, screaming, half cut open, slid into the water. The
spear shaft was twisted from my grasp. The water churned

beneath the blade. Bubbles exploded to the surface. It seemed scarlet. "Feed, little friends," I told them. "Feed well, and be thanked."

The flagship of Policrates was now, unimpeded, backing into open water. I sawed apart the rope joining my wrists on the cutting edge of the great blade. I heard battle horns. I did not understand this. On the wharves and along the water front I could see hundreds of citizens of Victoria. They were waving and brandishing their weapons. Pirates, naked and bound, roped together by the neck, lay on their bellies before them.

A ship to my left, *Spined Tharlarion*, the flagship of Ragnar Voskjard, was aflame. I heard a ram strike a ship nearby, with a great splintering of wood. This made no sense to me, for the pirate ships, so closely packed, so struggling, could not, even by accident, have achieved the momentum for such an impact.

Smoke stung my nostrils. I clung to the blade. The flagship of Policrates was now swinging about. I heard more battle horns, from both upriver and downriver. I heard the devastating impact of yet another ram pounding into a hull somewhere. There was screaming from pirate ships.

I leaped from the blade mount to the port rail and, struggling, pulled myself upward. In a moment, crouching, I was on the deck of the ship. A man lunged toward me, with a sword. I dove under the blade and, seizing his ankles, utilizing his momentum, threw him upward and over my shoulders. He disappeared over the rail, grasping at it, screaming. Another man struck down at me and I, slipped to the side, seized him about the chest with my right arm and hurled him back against the forward wall of the high stem castle. He grunted. With the heel of my right hand under his chin I smashed his head back into the wood of the stem castle. He slumped to the deck. His sword was mine.

I heard, from somewhere to starboard, the splintering of another hull. Policrates was crying out orders on the height of the stem castle above me. I thrust the sword into the wood above me, where I could seize it, and, putting my feet and hands into the ornate carving of the stem castle, climbed a yard and a half from the deck. My heart leaped.

The river seemed alive with ships. I saw the *Tais*, captained by the indomitable Calliodorus, and other ships of

Port Cos. They must needs be the fleet which Callisthenes had commanded, and had withdrawn to Port Cos, not permitting them to engage in the battle at the chain. With them, too, I saw ships with the banners of Tafa, Ven, Tetrapoli and even distant Turmus. They had come from the west, from downriver.

To starboard, from upriver, the river bristled with armed merchantmen. I saw the colors, there, of more than a dozen towns. The banners and pennons of Victoria were there, and of Fina and Hammerfest, of Sulport, Sais, Siba and Jasmine, of Jort's Ferry and Point Alfred, of Iskander, of Tancred's Landing and Forest Port. Too, among other pennons, I saw colors hailing from so afar east as White Water and Lara, at the very confluence of the Vosk and Olni. The patience of the honest men had at last been exhausted.

I drew the sword from the wood and leaped down to the deck. The flagship of Policrates rocked, struck by another pirate ship, it lurching to port. I lost my footing, and then regained it. I ran to the starboard rail and leaped down to the starboard shearing blade.

"Jason!" cried Callimachus, bound upon it.

In an instant I had severed the bonds which held his ankles and, holding his arms, cut apart the ropes that bound his wrists. He drew himself, trembling, to the blade mount. "You are free," he said. "What is going on?"

"The towns are rising," I said. "They come from the east and the west, from upriver and downriver, with men and ships. In their heart is war. Policrates and the Voskjard are finished!"

"Get me a sword!" said Callimachus.

"Are you strong enough?" I asked. "There is little you need do."

"A sword!" said Callimachus. "I must have a sword!"

I grinned. "Doubtless one may be found on deck," I said.

Scarcely had we climbed to the deck than the pirate ship to starboard, shifting, grated laterally along the flagship. The shearing blades locked and we felt timber being torn from the sides of the ships.

"Back oars!" screamed Policrates, on the stem castle. "Back oars!" We heard a pirate ship, somewhere to starboard, being boarded. Callimachus strode to an oarsman. Oarsmen, of course, face the stern in rowing, for greater leverage. Callimachus drew the fellow's sword from his sheath. He looked about and then, white-faced, hurled himself over the rail. Callimachus looked up the stairs to the height of the stem castle. It was then that Policrates saw him. Behind him was Callisthenes. Two men rushed down the steps toward Callimachus. Policrates and Callisthenes drew their swords. I saw the two men fall, one to each side of Callimachus. I had scarcely seen his blade move. He was not unskilled with the weapon. Policrates and Callisthenes, white-faced, regarded him. "I am with you," I told him. "No," said Callimachus, "these are mine."

I regarded him. He smiled. "Fetch Ragnar Voskjard," he said. I grinned, and turned away from him. Behind me, in a moment, I heard the sound of swords.

I looked over the port rail. Some forty yards away, across the water, some hundred yards or so out in the river, off the wharves, half afire, I saw the ship of Ragnar Voskjard. Timbers and wreckage strewed the waters between the ships. I could almost cross to his ship on the debris between us. More battle horns sounded. Not far off I could hear the clash of weaponry betokening yet another fierce ingress of boarders upon the deck of some vessel of hapless buccaneers. A dozen ships off the wharves must have been in flames.

I bit at the leather binding on the handle of the sword I carried. I tore loose a strip of it and, with this cordage, improvised a wrist sling. If it were necessary to use my hands in the water I did not wish to risk losing the weapon. Then, clutching the weapon, the sling about my wrist, I vaulted the rail and, feet first, entered the water. I swam to a raft of planking. There is commonly little danger of eels near Victoria, save near the shadows and shallows of the wharves themselves.

Scarcely had I ascended the heavy planking then, approaching rapidly, bearing down on me, I saw a medium galley, thrusting itself between the flagship of Policrates and *Spined Tharlarion*, the flagship of Ragnar Voskjard. It flew the banners of Tafa. I dove to the port side of the vessel. In a moment I was caught in its bow wave and, lifted, hurled toward *Spined Tharlarion*. Sputtering, lifting my head, spitting water, trying to clear my eyes, I saw another shape approaching. I struck out for the hull of *Spined Tharlarion*.

The encroaching shape seemed to veer toward me, and

then I realized, to my horror, that she intended to shear the starboard oars of *Spined Tharlarion*. I was now between the two vessels. There was a grating, shearing noise and snapping oars. I put out my hand and touched the strakes of the shuddering *Spined Tharlarion*. I saw the shearing blade sliding toward me. Scarring and ripping timber, snapping oars, it scraped and scored its way toward me. I dove under the ship. The greatest danger to a swimmer, incidentally, is not the blade itself, for its lower curve is usually at least a foot out of the water, and it is not difficult to avoid it. Indeed, one may even go between the blade and the ship on which it is mounted, if one wishes. The greatest danger to a swimmer, usually, is the grating together of hulls, behind the blades. Few captains are so skillful as to manage a clean, parallel shearing. Both ships are moving, and the angles vary instant by instant.

Looking above me, up through the water, I saw the long, lean hull of the attacking vessel pass overhead. Then there was a rending noise as it gouged the starboard strakes of *Spined Tharlarion*. It had come in at too sharp an angle. The hulls then, grinding, swung together. When I saw the light of open water between them I surfaced. I found myself in a welter of debris and splinters. Oars were thrusting out from the attacking vessel, to force the ships apart. I seized a broken oar from *Spined Tharlarion*, its blade gone, its shaft swinging loose in the thole port. I climbed on the oar, the sword dangling from its wrist sling. I got my hand to the wood beside the thole port. I could see the bench inside had been abandoned. I gathered many of the crew of *Spined Tharlarion* had abandoned the vessel.

Using the oar and thole port I drew myself upward. In a moment I was over the rail and on the deck of *Spined Tharlarion*. The stem castle was empty. The few men on the decks did not attack me. I saw the attacking vessel moving backward, trying to maneuver. She would try to come in with her ram, and, doubtless, later board. The stem castle was empty. There was a figure on the stern castle. His back was to me. I saw him ripping away the insignia of the captain from his robes. Two pirates leapt overboard, on the port side. I hastened down the deck and raced up the stairs to the stern castle. He spun to face me, the golden cordage of the captain

in his right hand. "Greetings, Ragnar Voskjard," I said to
him, "I have come to fetch you."

He reached for his sword, but the point of my sword was
in his belly. He removed his hand from the hilt of his blade.

"That is better," I said. "Now, on the deck, on your belly,
to be stripped and bound."

He looked at me, in fury. I grinned, and, loosing the wrist
sling of the sword, flung it into the deck beside me.

He looked at the sword, upright in the deck beside me.

"Now," I told him.

His eyes glinted.

Swiftly he attempted to draw his blade. Instantly I was before him and caught him with a balled fist, driven upward
into his gut. He looked at me, sick, bent over. I then
measured him, and, at my leisure, from the balls of my feet,
with the full force of my shoulders and arm, struck him,
spinning, from his feet. I walked over to where he had fallen.
I dragged him back by his ankles to the center of the small,
high deck of the stern castle, where I put him on his belly.

"You would be troublesome," I told him. I knelt across his
body. "I was once a fighting slave," I told him. With strips of
cloth cut from his garments I tied his hands behind his back.
"Perhaps you even, at one time or another, have bet upon
fellows such as I was." He moaned. "It is amusing, is it not,"
I asked, "that the great Ragnar Voskjard is now naught but
the prisoner of an ex-fighting-slave?"

"Free me," he begged. I tightened the knots that confined
him. "I will pay you much," he said. "What pay could com-
pare with the pleasure of taking the Voskjard prisoner?" I
asked. "Mercy," he said. "No," I said. "You need not have
tied me so tightly," he said. "It amused me," I told him. I
smiled to myself. It was a Gorean answer.

Suddenly the ship shook with a great impact. "We have
been rammed!" cried the Voskjard. "It is the ship which
sheared your starboard oars," I told him. "She flies, as I
now see, the colors of Turmus."

"We shall sink!" cried the Voskjard. "Not immediately," I
told him. I stood up, the bound Voskjard between my feet.
"They are preparing to board, as I see," I said. "Surrender me
to the men of Turmus," he begged. I, with the sword, then
cut his garments from him. He was then naked between my
feet. "You are my prisoner," I told him. From the straps of

his sword belt I improvised a short leash for him. "Do not permit me to fall into the hands of those of Victoria!" he begged.

"You would have sacked their town. You have seen them fight," I said. "Keep me from the men of Victoria," he begged. "They are boarding now, many of them, the fellows of Turmus," I observed. "Give me to them," he begged.

"On your feet, Sleen," I told him. I dragged him to his feet by the leash. "Give me to the men of Turmus!" he begged. "And let them cheat me of my prisoner?" I asked. "Who are you?" he asked, frightened. "Jason," I told him, "Jason—of Victoria."

"No!" he cried. I then threw him from the lofty stern castle of *Spined Tharlarion*, bound, into the water. I then thrust my hand through the wrist sling of the sword and, seizing it, withdrew it from the wood. I waved to the fellows of Turmus, swarming onto the already listing deck of *Spined Tharlarion*. I then, feet first, leaped downward into the water, landing near the floundering Ragnar Voskjard. In a moment I had my hand on the short leash I had devised for his throat and, he on his back, helpless, my prisoner, was towing him toward the flagship of Policrates.

The battle, I gathered, was muchly over.

The Voskjard grunted, and half choked, as I hauled him, partly by the neck leash, partly by his arm, over the rail of the flagship of Policrates. I threw him on his belly, on the listing, awash deck, at my feet. The flagship of Policrates seemed deserted. She had been rammed. I did not think she would stay long afloat.

The waters off the Victoria wharves seemed crowded, but many of the ships were aflame.

The alarm bar was ringing in Victoria, but now in token of victory. There were crowds upon the concourse. Garlanded, white-clad maidens could be seen. At the front edge of the concourse, near the wharves, pirates, in rows, stripped and bound, lay on their bellies. Maidens cast flowers upon them, and some of these maidens, from their own heads, placed garlands upon the brows of the victors.

Ragnar Voskjard tried to rise, but my foot, thrust between his shoulder blades, pressed him rudely back to the deck. "Free me," he begged. "Be silent," I said. I then stood with my left foot on his back, holding him in place. I had thought that I had heard a noise. I then dragged him, half strangling him, up the sloping deck to the starboard rail, where, with a swift knot, I tied him to one of the uprights supporting the rail. He turned on his side, to regard me. "If the ship sinks," he said, hoarsely, "I am helpless." "Yes," I said.

I turned about.

Forty feet away, down the deck, amidships, sword in hand, half crouching, blade ready, slowly approaching, I saw Kliomenes.

"You must have hidden," I told him, "perhaps in the lower hold. Then, when the ship was rammed, when the hold began to fill with water, you were forced upward, as an urt."

He continued to approach. I observed the point of the blade. The eyes of a man can lie. The point of the blade cannot.

"Where are Policrates and Callisthenes?" I asked.

"I do not know," he said.

"Free me. Free me!" cried Ragnar Voskjard.

"It is every man for himself," said Kliomenes. He then rushes fiercely upon me. I demended myself in four exchanges. Then he stepped back.

"Do not permit your arm to grow weary," I told him. "Perhaps you would give me your tunic," I said. "I do not wish to become chilled. The air on the river is cooler now."

With a cry of rage he again rushed upon me and, again, I merely defended myself.

Sometimes we were ankle-deep in the water on the deck and, sometimes, near the port rail, we fought in water to our knees. Twice he slipped, but I did not strike him.

Then he stood, knee deep in the water, soaked, gasping. "Remove your tunic," I told him.

With two hands holding the sword he stumbled toward me, exhausted, striking downward. I slipped to the side and my blade's point was then entered into his right side. He shuddered, bent over, his head over the water. "Discard your blade," I told him. He released the weapon. I stepped back, my blade ready. "Go to the starboard rail," I told him.

He waded to the starboard rail, and I followed him. A single stroke could have severed his spine.

"Kneel down," I told him, "facing me."

He did so.

"Remove your tunic," I told him.

He did so.

"You are my prisoner," I said.

"Don't strike me," he suddenly said.

"Perhaps, perhaps not," I said. "Turn about," I ordered him.

Frightened, he did so.

"Will I strike you?" I asked him.

"I do not know," he said.

"On your belly," I told him, "and place your hands, crossed, behind you."

He did this. "Will I strike you now?" I asked him.

"I do not know. I do not know!" he said.

I thrust the sword into the deck. "I have placed the sword in the deck," I told Kliomenes. "If you wish to attempt to escape, this would be an excellent time to do so." Kliomenes tensed. "You must consider such things as whether or not, should you do this, you could rise to your feet before I could, say break your neck or back, or take the sword and cut your head away. I leave such speculations, and decisions, to you."

Kliomenes moaned, and lay still. I picked up the tunic from the deck and, unhurriedly, tore some strips from it. I looked over the port rail. It was considerably lower now, given the listing of the ship, than the starboard rail. "I see that the fellows from Turmus have drawn away from *Spined Tharlarion*," I informed them. I threw the strips, torn from the bottom of the tunic onto Kliomenes. "Those are what I am going to bind you with," I told him. "They will be quite sufficient to hold you. Once you are bound with them you will have little opportunity for escape. I am now going to put on your tunic." I slipped the tunic over my head. Kliomenes lay quietly, trembling. He did not move. I laughed, and then knelt across his body.

"Listen closely, Kliomenes," I told him. "You will be able to hear, from the wharves at Victoria, the ringing of a hammer, pounding on iron, on an anvil. Do you hear it?" "Yes," he said. "They are curving collars of iron, with chains attached, about the throats of your fellow pirates." He was silent. "Such collars are heavy and uncomfortable," I said. "I know. I have worn such collars. There is this to be said for them, however. They hold a man, perfectly." I then, with the strips of cloth torn from the tunic, bound Kliomenes' hands behind his back, tightly. He winced. "Are you bound well enough?" I asked. "Yes," he said. "Do you think such bonds will hold you?" I asked. "Yes!" he said. "Yes, what?" I asked. "Yes," he whispered, "—my captor."

I laughed, and stood up. *"Spined Tharlarion* has gone down," I said. At that moment the deck of the flagship of Policrates gave a lurch in the water. I almost lost my footing. Kliomenes slid downward, toward the port rail. I seized him by the hair and pulled him again toward the starboard rail.

"We are sinking!" cried Ragnar Voskjard. He tried to free himself, but succeeded in doing little more than squirm choking on the deck, a stripped, tethered prisoner. I then freed his leash from the upright but then, to his dismay, passed it again about the upright and, holding Kliomenes' head close to the upright, fastened him to the other end of the leash. Both men, then, were tied by the neck, and closely together, about the stanchion.

"We are sinking!" said the Voskjard. "I believe you are right," I said. "And we are helpless!" cried the Voskjard. "I know," I said. "I have seen to it." "Mercy, mercy!" cried the Voskjard. "Mercy!" cried Kliomenes, suddenly terrified, pulling his legs up, as water lapped about them. I stood by the rail. "Do you both beg for mercy?" I asked. "Yes, my captor!" cried Ragnar Voskjard. "Yes, my captor!" cried Kliomenes.

"Greetings," I called down, cheerily, to Callimachus and Tasdron, in a longboat, with other men, which had drawn alongside. The approach of the longboat had been visible to me, of course, for some time, from my standing position by the rail. It had not been visible, of course, to either Ragnar Voskjard or Kliomenes.

"Did I hear someone beg for mercy?" grinned Callimachus, looking upward.

"It is not impossible," I admitted.

"What have you up there?" he asked.

"A pair of neck-harnessed urts," I told him. "Do you think you might find collars for them?"

"Ashore," said Callimachus. "We will put them with the rest of the catch."

With the sword blade I slashed the strap that bound the two men about the stanchion. Then I pulled them to their feet and knotted together the two loose ends of the strap, thus again effectively putting them on a common leash. I then thrust them overboard, headfirst, into the arms of oarsmen who took them and, not gently, threw them to the bottom of the longboat.

I looked down into the longboat. "I see that you have found a tunic somewhere," I said.

"Policrates was kind enough to give me his," said Callimachus, gesturing to the floor of the longboat, near the bow. I grinned. There, lying together, stripped, bloody and trussed, were Policrates and Callisthenes.

"Will they live?" I asked Callimachus.

"I did not make their wounds lethal," said Callimachus. "Thus they may be saved for the quarries or the galleys."

I did not envy Policrates or Callisthenes, nor Kliomenes, nor Ragnar Voskjard. In the quarries and on the galleys the chains are heavy and the whips are swift.

"Come aboard," said Callimachus. He extended his hand to me. I slipped over the rail of the flagship of Policrates, and entered the longboat.

"The day is ours," I said.

"It is ours," said Callimachus. We embraced. I took my position on a thwart amidships, between two oarsmen, and he took his place on a thwart near the stern, before the helmsman. "Put in to shore," said Callimachus to the helmsman. "Yes, Captain," said he.

The oars entered the water. The bow turned toward Victoria. There the alarm bar was ringing in victory. I could hear, too, the shouting of crowds and the singing of maidens. Looking aft I saw the flagship of Policrates subside beneath the surface of the river. The drag of its subsidence pulled momentarily against the headway of the longboat and then, after churning ripples, the narrow, shallow-drafted ship gone, the waters were smooth. I looked to the bottom of the longboat. There, naked and bound, at our feet, lay our enemies. I could hear, too, from the wharves of Victoria, the ringing of the hammer, closing links of chain and curving collars of iron about the throats of helpless pirates. I lifted my head, and looked ahead. Victoria lay ahead. I was pleased.

XVII

THE COIN GIRL;
I DISMISS HER

It is called the Street of the Writhing Slave. It is dark and narrow, and not far from the wharves. It has its name from the fact that most renters of, and dealers in, Coin Girls in Victoria, keep their kennels on this street. The girls of the day, designated by a coiled whip pressed against their left shoulder, wearing their neck chains, with the attached bell and coin box, are sent into the streets in the late afternoon and expected to return before the nineteenth Ahn. And woe to the girl who does not return with a jangling coin box on her neck chain! Some girls, once designated, and locked in their accouterments, kneeling, weeping, scratch even at the insides of the stout gates of their masters' houses, hoping to be sent into the streets early, that their chances of turning a profit for their master, and thus avoiding a beating or torture, may be enhanced. Such a lenience, however, is seldom shown to the girls, as it is against an agreement binding the entrepreneurs engaged in this trade. Sometimes the girls are sent into the streets with their hands braceleted behind their backs. Sometimes they are sent into the streets with their small hands free, that they may use them to please their master's customers. Sometimes a new girl is sent into the streets on a leash, with an older girl, that she may learn how a Coin Girl behaves. I recalled that once, long ago, when I had purchased, and freed, Miss Henderson, we had encountered a Coin Girl on the way back to my inn. "Get away, you filthy thing," had said Miss Henderson. "Disgusting! Disgusting! Terrible! Disgusting!" she had said. I smiled. The girl had been half naked, in a brown rag. I had thought she had been superb. To be sure, Coin Girls are usually regarded as the lowest form of Gorean street slave.

I continued to walk up the Street of the Writhing Slave. Such girls, now, as it was late, past the nineteenth Ahn, would surely, at least for the most part, be chained in their basement kennels, lying on their straw mats, trying to sleep, clutching their thin blankets about their nude bodies.

The Street of the Writhing Slave winds tortuously upward from the wharves, threading its narrow way through a commercial district upward towards a hilly residential district. Free women, incidentally, tend to avoid the Street of the Writhing Slave. It frightens them, it seems, to walk upon it. I supposed I could not blame them. What free woman would dare to walk upon such a street, particularly at night? Her throat might suddenly feel the capture loop of a slaver and, by morning, branded, gag-hooded and chained, she might be fifty pasangs downriver, on her way to a market in Ven or Turmus.

By putting out my hands I could almost touch the walls of the facing houses.

I thought I heard the sound of a bell. I smiled. It was late, of course, for the sensuous peregrinations of a Coin Girl. Would they not all, now, be secured in their kennels, safe even from fruitless dreams of escape?

I continued on my way. The street was twisting. I could not see far ahead. I heard again the bell. I smiled.

I paused, near a tiny tharlarion-oil lamp. It was about a yard above my head, recessed in a small niche. It was by means of such that the street was lit. Families alternate in the fueling and tending of such lamps. As in many such matters, as in cleaning and repairing streets, Gorean responsibility tends to devolve on the individual and not on the polity. His taxes, in this sense, in such matters, are applied directly, and by himself, to the affairs with which they are concerned. Third parties, thus, in such matters, are not involved, and he knows precisely, at least in such instances, how much money is involved, and where it is being spent.

I heard the bell again. Again I smiled. I then proceeded further, climbing, up the street. Through the soles of my sandals I could feel, clearly, the street's harsh, rude cobblestones. I was pleased by this.

I turned a corner in the street, and it was then that I saw them, some fifty yards away, approaching, descending, nearing the location of one of the small tharlarion-oil lamps. Near the lamp the girl who was on the leash was jerked up short. I heard the flattish bell on her neck chain. It has a distinctive note. Then she stood still. She must stand in the light of the lamp, to await my approach. Both girls wore brief slave tunics. Both were barefoot. My step was casual, unhurried. It did not even seem, then, that I saw them. I might be anyone, returning late, say, from a tavern or from the visiting of friends. The meeting, surely, was one of mere chance.

"Oh," I said, pausing, stopping, suddenly, a few yards from them. It seemed that I, lost in thought, had just then noticed them. I regarded them. It seemed then that I looked at the leashed girl intently, as though trying to place her, at the distance, in the light, and then I reacted, as though I might then have placed her, or feared that I might have placed her, feared, dismayed, that I might have recognized who she might be. Swiftly she put her head down, hiding her face in her hands. This made a note sound from the bell. An abrupt command was spoken to her by her fair companion, and she quickly put her hands down, at her sides. Another command was spoken, and the leash jerked taut. She lifted her head. I approached her. Tears were in her eyes. Her lower lip trembled.

I regarded her, in the yellowish, flickering light of the tiny tharlarion-oil lamp, late at night, on the rude stones of that dark, narrow street in Victoria. She stood before me, small, slim, exquisite, beautiful. Her binding-fiber-belted, wraparound tunic was brown, and of clinging, thin rep-cloth; it was sleeveless and had a plunging neckline; it was slave short. About her neck there was a chain. From the chain there hung two objects; the first was a narrow, bronze bell, flattish and tapering, with a flat top and ring; when she moved it would sound, calling attention to her whereabouts; the second was a metal coin box, which contained a slot for the deposition of coins; the coin box was locked. I had not heard coins sound, from within the coin box. Too, about her neck, under the chain, with its dangling articles, there was a high, tight leather collar. Her leash, in the hands of the other girl, was attached to a ring at the back of this collar. The leash, too, was of leather, and long. It was coiled four or five times in the hands of the other girl. More Gorean leashes are long. There are two advantages to the long leash. It may be used, if one wishes, to bind the slave, and its long end, if one wishes, may easily serve as a whipping strap.

"Beverly," I whispered. "Is it you?"

She did not respond. Her eyes were filled with tears. Her lip trembled.

The girl who held her leash then jerked twice on the leash.

"May I serve your pleasure, Master?" asked the leashed girl.

"I thought you were a Coin Girl," I said.

"She is a Coin Girl," said the girl who held her leash. Then she jerked the leash once, against the collar ring.

"I am a Coin Girl," said the leashed girl, before me.

"Interest him," said the other girl.

"I am yours for a tarsk bit, Master," said the leashed girl.

"Open your tunic," said the other girl.

The girl then slipped loose the binding-fiber belt, letting it fall against the two belt loops in the back. Then, with her left hand and her right hand, parting the tunic, holding it open, she showed herself to me.

She was the most beautiful, and attractive, woman I had ever seen.

"It is my hope that I please Master," she said.

"Beverly," I said.

"She has no name," said the girl who held her leash. "Her master has not yet given her one. But once, it is true, that she was known as Beverly. For that reason I suggest, if you are interested in her, that you give her, for your use of her, another name."

I regarded the beautiful girl. She trembled. She did not close her tunic.

"She is an Earth slut," said the girl who held the leash. 'Some men like them."

"I could call her 'Linda'," I said.

"An Earth-slut name," said the girl who held the leash.

"Excellent!" Then, suddenly, viciously, loosening the coils of the leash, she lashed the girl across the back of the thighs with the long end of the leash. "Do you not realize you are standing in the presence of a free man, Linda?" she said.

And then she who had once been Miss Beverly Henderson, of New York City, of Earth, and was now Linda, knelt before me, on the rude stones of that narrow street in Victoria. "Forgive me, Master," she whispered.

"Earth girls are so stupid," said the other girl, wearily.

"Many are not stupid," I said. "It is only that they are ignorant."

"Perhaps they may be taught," mused the other girl.

"Any woman may be taught," I told her.

"That is true," she smiled. Then she jerked the leash of the kneeling girl.

"Have me for a tarsk bit, Master," cried the kneeling girl, her tunic parted, looking up at me.

She who had been Miss Henderson, now kneeling before me, had asked to be had by me, and for a tarsk bit.

She looked up at me, piteously.

"You are a female, and he is a man," said the girl who held the leash. "Interest him."

"Please, Mistress," begged the girl.

"Bite at his tunic, and lick at his legs and feet," commanded the girl who held the leash.

Softly then did the bell of the Coin Girl sound, and the chain and coin box on her neck, as she who had once been Miss Henderson turned her head to the side, and began, with her small, fine white teeth, to bite and nibble at the hem of my tunic. I felt these small tugs, piteous and delicate, and then she, with her lips, pressed the wet tunic against my thigh and through the wet cloth, kissed me. She then, putting her head down, began to lick and kiss at my legs and feet. She performed this submission behavior for several minutes, piteously, desperately, beseechingly, entreatingly. Then, at last, her head down, over my feet, she whispered, begging, "Please have me for a tarsk bit, Master. Please have me for only a tarsk bit, Master."

"No," I told her. "Of course not."

She looked up, startled, dismayed.

"Do you think I respect you so little?" I asked.

"You have failed to interest him," said the girl who held

the leash. She shortened the leash and, her fist almost at the girl's collar, jerked it taut, pulling the girl's head up and back straight. Women are very beautiful kneeling in this position.

"But I am a slave," protested the kneeling girl, looking up at me.

"I can see that," I said.

"Have you not wanted to have me, many times?" she asked. "Was I so wrong in sensing that?"

"No," I said.

"Then have me," she said. "I am half-naked before you. I am yours for a tarsk bit. Take me!"

'Surely you would not expect me to press myself upon you, with you at your present disadvantage," I said.

"Disadvantage!" she said. "I am a slave! You are free, but I am a slave. I am a slave girl!"

"Yes," I said.

"Look upon me," she said. "Do you think I am to be freed?"

"No," I said.

"Gorean men will always keep me in a collar," she said.

"Yes," I said. I wondered if she knew how truly she spoke.

"Take me," she begged. "Take me!"

"Surely you do not think that I am a bounder, or a cad?" I said.

She sobbed suddenly in frustration.

"On your feet, Slave," said the girl with the leash, giving her a yard of strap, that she might rise. "You have failed to interest him."

"Please let me try further, Mistress!" begged the kneeling girl. "Please!"

"On your feet," said the girl with the leash, jerking on the leash. Sobbing, the beautiful, leashed slave rose to her feet. Fumbling, she closed her tunic, and tied shut the binding fiber which belted it. It seemed she could hardly stand. She trembled, and wept.

"What is wrong?" I asked.

"She is a worthless slave," said the girl with the leash. "Look!" She shook the coin box on the girl's neck chain and shook it. "Empty!" she said, scornfully. She then struck the grl twice about the legs with the strap. "We have been out for Ahn," said the girl with the leash, "and we have passed many masters, not one of whom would deign to have her."

"Why is she crying?" I asked.

"She fears, rightfully, her master's displeasure," she said.

I nodded. It is very natural for a slave girl, who is completely at the mercy of her master, and is owned by him, to be very sensitive as to whether or not he is pleased with her.

"Perhaps he is a lenient fellow," I suggested.

"He is a merciless brute, who has more girls than he needs," said the girl holding the leash.

"What will be done with her?" I asked.

"At the least she will receive a severe beating," said the girl with the leash. "If he is in an ugly mood, she may be tortured and slain."

The leashed girl, sobbing, fell on her knees before the girl who held her leash. She put her head to her feet. "Please, Mistress," she begged, "do not take me in yet!"

"It is late," said the girl with the leash. "It is past the nineteenth Ahn. That you should be out now is even against the agreements of the renters of Coin Girls."

"Please, Mistress!" begged the girl.

"On your feet," said the girl with the leash. "You are now to be led back to your master, as a failed slave."

"Wait!" I said.

The kneeling girl, turning, regarded me wildly.

"Yes, Master?" said the girl with the leash.

"I have a tarsk bit here," I said, opening my pouch. "She need not return with the coin box empty." I smiled at the leashed girl. "It is the least I can do," I said to her, kindly. She was looking up at me, frightened. I went to deposit the coin in the coin box on the kneeling girl's neck chain, but the hand of the other girl, she who held the kneeling girl's leash, interposed itself. "There can be no payment, without the rendering of services," she said. "The honor of my Master must not be offended."

I drew back, holding the coin.

The kneeling girl, she who had once been Miss Beverly Henderson, once a graduate student in English literature at a major university in the New York City area, eyed the coin, fearfully. She feared I would replace it in my pouch.

"I will endeavor to be worthy of the tarsk bit, Master," she whispered.

"A Coin Girl," said the girl with the leash, "will struggle to please a man as much for a tarsk bit, as a high paga slave for a thousand gold pieces, to be paid by her master's customer for her use."

"I see," I said.

"The levels of skill in the Coin Girl, of course," said the girl with the leash, "are commonly much lower." This was true, of course. Yet it must be mentioned that sometimes Coin Girls are extremely skillful. Too, it is not unknown for a master to sometimes send even an exquisitely trained, beautiful high slave into the streets, usually as a joke or a discipline. Such a girl knows that she must perform superbly. Some of the men she falls in with may have been hired by her master, to report back on the quality of her services.

The girl with the leash drew back her hand, it then no longer shielding the opening on the coin box. "You understand the conditions?" she asked.

"Yes," I said.

"Please, please, Master," said the kneeling girl, tears in her eyes, "put the coin in my coin box. You will not regret it."

I hesitated. I looked at her.

"I beg to please Master," she said clearly.

"You," I asked, as though disbelievingly, "you beg to please a man?"

"Yes, Master," she said.

"Whom?" I asked.

"You, my Master," she said. "I beg to please you, my Master."

"As a slave?" I asked.

"Yes, Master," she said, "I beg to please you—as a slave."

I dropped the coin into the narrow, metal coin box. I thought the girl would almost faint with relief, and pleasure. Too, I saw another emotion in her eyes, which was harder to fathom.

The girl with the leash bent down to a nearby slave ring. Such things are common in Gorean streets. They are usually mounted in a wall, a foot to a yard above the walk or pavement. This one was mounted about a foot above the street, and was ahead of me and to my right, a bit behind the kneeling girl, and to her left. "There," said the girl, knotting the end of the leash about the ring. Usually, at such rings, slaves are on a short leash or chain, and are fastened to them on their knees. If the slave is braceleted to the ring and the ring is in the neighborhood of a yard high her hands are braceleted before her face, and her belly faces the wall, or behind the back of her head, and her back or side faces the wall; with the lower ring her hands are braceleted before her lower body if she faces the wall or has her side to it, and roughly at the small of her back, if she has her back to the wall. But the girl who had controlled the kneeling girl's leash had left her a good deal of slack. She might lie, fully, on the stones, and be moved about on them, if I chose.

"I shall withdraw," said the girl who had controlled the leash. "But understand clearly," she said, meaningfully, "that when I return her body will be closely examined."

"I understand," I said.

The girl who had controlled the leash then withdrew.

I looked at the girl, kneeling on the stones before me. I crouched down, before her.

"You know that you must use me fully," she said. "My body will be carefully examined, for the signs of your use."

"I know," I said.

She then, demurely, unbelted her tunic, and brushed it back.

"You must have me, and fully," she said. "You have no choice."

"I know," I said.

She dropped her tunic behind her, on the stones. "It is my hope," she said, "that I may please my Master."

I grinned. "Who are you?" I asked.

"Your Linda," she said.

"If I choose to have you by that name," I said.

"Yes," she said. "You may have me by any name you care to fix upon me, or nameless, if it pleases you."

"I know," I said.

"In all this time," she said, "you have never had me."

"No," I said.

"You wanted to, didn't you?" she asked.

"Yes," I said.

"And now I am only a leashed slut before you," she said, "one for whom you have paid your tarsk bit."

"Yes," I said.

She leaned forward, and kissed me, softly. "I will endeavor to be worthy of my tarsk bit, my Master," she whispered.

"Have no fear," I told her. "I shall see that you are."

"Master?" she asked, drawing back.

I then put my hands on her arms.

She winced, in pain. She looked at me, disbelievingly. "That is not the grip of a man of Earth," she said, "that of one who treats women with respect." She squirmed.

"You are a slave," I told her.

"It is the grip of a Gorean male," she said, "of one who is the master of a woman."

"Is it?" I asked.

"Yes!" she said. "Release me! I mean, 'Please release me, my Master!' "

"No," I told her.

"No?" she asked. "But you are a man of Earth! You must do whatever a woman asks!"

"Why?" I asked.

"I do not know," she cried. "I do not know!"

"Do you wish me to release you?" I asked.

"Yes," she said. "Yes!"

"Lying slave," I sneered.

"Please do not punish me, Master," she whimpered.

"The brutes of Gor have their way with you, as it pleases them," I said, "and you serve them well. Do you think the men of Earth should be content with less?"

"No, Master," she whimpered.

"If the men of Earth choose to surrender the birthright of their dominance, to exchange it for the garbage of a political perversion; if they should choose to deny their genes; if they should choose to subvert and violate the order of nature; if they should choose self-castration to manhood, that is, I suppose, their business."

"I do not know, Master," she said.

"Provided, of course, that they are willing to accept such penalties as anxiety, guilt, misery, frustration, sickness and shortened life spans."

"I do not know, Master," she said.

"A subverted nature cannot be expected not to retaliate," I said.

"No, Master," she said.

"Does a man have a right to be a man?" I asked.

"I suppose so," she said. "I do not know."

"And are there not hierarchies among rights, and some which take priority over others?"

"Be kind to me, Master," she begged.

"And is not the right of a man to be a man the highest right of such a sort that man possesses?"

"Yes," she said.

"What right takes precedence over that?" I asked.

"None, Master," she said.

"Has man," I asked, "the right to bring about his own downfall, to destroy himself."

"He has the capacity, Master," she whispered, "but I do not think he has that right."

"He does not have that right," I told her, "for it conflicts with the higher right."

"Yes, Master," she said.

"Rather," said I, "he has, beyond rights, duties, and high among his duties is his duty to be true to himself, his duty to be a man."

"Yes, Master," she said.

"The denial of his manhood, then, by a man, is not only irrational, but morally pernicious. Men have not only a right to preserve their manhood, but a duty to do so."

"Perhaps there is no such thing as manhood," she whispered, "or womanhood."

"Tell that," I said, "to strong men and yielding women, and history."

"Perhaps there are no such things as duties, and rights," she said, "perhaps there are only the words, used as the instruments of manipulative rhetorics, devices of conditioning, cheaper and more subtle than guns and whips."

"That is an interesting and profound possibility," I said, "but then there would still remain needs and powers, forces and desires, and the facts of the world, that certain courses of action lead to certain results, and that other courses of action lead to other results. And in such a world who will argue with the larl as to whether or not it should feed, or with a man as to whether or not he should be a man? In such a world the larl hunts, and the man is a man."

"Gor, I fear," she said, "is such a world."

"It is," I told her, "Slave Girl."

"I'm frightened," she said.

"As well you might be, rightless slave," I told her.

"Rightless slave?" she asked.

"Of course," I told her, "you are a rightless Gorean slave girl, leashed and ready for having."

"Is that all I am?" she asked.

"Yes," I told her.

"To you?" she asked.

"Yes," I told her.

She shuddered.

"What is wrong?" I asked.

"I dare not speak," she whispered.

"Speak," I said.

"I am aroused," she said.

I continued to hold her right arm with my left hand, and placed my right hand on her body. She squirmed. "It is true," I told her.

She tried to pull back. "You do not handle me like a man of Earth," she whispered.

"I am not a man of Earth," I told her. "I am Gorean."

I then pressed her back to the stones.

"What are you doing?" she cried.

"I have been patient," I told her. "I have waited a long time for you."

She squirmed. Her strength was as nothing, compared to mine. I brushed the flattish bell and the coin box over her left shoulder, and to the side of her neck. I heard the bell, and the coin, my coin, in the small, narrow metal box on her neck chain.

"What are you going to do?" she asked.

"I am now tired of waiting," I told her.

"Then you will truly have me?" she asked.

"Of course," I told her.

"But with dignity, and respect!" she begged.

"I have waited too long for that," I told her.

She struggled, unavailingly.

"Be gentle, solicitous and tender!" she begged.

"No," I told her.

"No?" she asked.

"No," I said.

"Oh!" she cried.

"When I finish with you," I said, "you will not have any doubts, as you might with a man of Earth, as to whether or not you have been had."

"Oh!" she cried.

"You will know," I assured her.

"This cannot be you," she wept. "It cannot be you!"

"It is," I told her.

"What are you doing?" she cried.

"Treating you as the slave you are," I told her.

"But I am a woman of Earth!" she cried.

"No," I told her, "you are only a leashed slut, a rightless Gorean slave girl, who is soon to learn something of the meaning of her collar."

"Yes, Master!" she cried, suddenly, helplessly.

"Do you admit that you are a slave?" I asked.

"Do not ask me, a woman of Earth, to admit to a man of Earth that I am a slave!" she begged. "It would be too shameful!"

"You would admit it swiftly enough to the brutes of Gor, would you not?" I asked.

"Yes, Master," she wept. "Yes, Master!"

"Admit it then to me," I said, "for now you are no longer a woman of Earth, nor am I now any longer a man of Earth."

"I am a slave, Master," she said. "I admit it." I recalled then the time that we had dined in the small restaurant on Earth, so long ago. Her hair had been bound back in a severe bun. She had worn an off-the-shoulder, svelte, white satin-sheath dress. She had carried a small, silver-beaded purse. She was now in my arms, sweating, naked and leashed. "I am a slave, Master," she said. "I have always known it."

"Now you speak the truth," I said.

"Yes, Master," she said.

"Do you now feel shamed, that you have made this confession?" I asked.

She looked up at me, startled. "No," she said.

"How do you feel?" I asked.

"It is strange," she said. "I feel exalted, glorious. It is strange. It is as though I had come home to myself."

"The only true liberation," I said, "is to become what one truly is."

"Oh!" she cried.

"Does a slave object to being treated as a slave?" I asked.

"No, Master," she said. "I regret only that I never admitted my slavery on Earth."

"There would have been little point," I said. "There are few masters on Earth."

"There is no dearth of masters on Gor," she said.

"No," I smiled.

She shuddered in my arms. "I admit to you that I belong in a collar," she whispered.

"It is true," I said.

"I long to be taught its meaning," she said.

"You will be," I assured her.

"Teach me my collar," she begged. "Make me the slave I long to be."

"I shall," I said.

"Linda is now ready to serve her master," she said. "Master," she said, "what is wrong?"

I looked down at her, locked as a hot, leashed slave in my arms. "I shall have you under the name of 'Beverly'," I said.

"That was my name on Earth, long ago, when I was free," she said.

"I put it on you now, for my use of you, as a slave name," I told her.

"Yes, Master," she said.

"You were once of Earth, were you not?" I asked.

"Yes, Master," she said.

"Are you now of Earth?" I asked.

"No, Master," she said.

"Of where are you now?" I asked.

"Gor, Master," she said.

"Once you were a free woman, were you not?" I asked.

"Yes, Master," she said.

"Are you now free?" I asked.

"No, Master," she said. "Please, Master!"

"What are you now?" I asked.

"I am now naught but a Gorean slave girl!" she wept. "Please, Master!"

"What is your name," I asked.

"Beverly," she said. "My name is 'Beverly'. That is the name which my master has seen fit to put upon me."

"It is a pretty name," I said.

"Yes, Master," she said. "Thank you, Master. Please, Master!"

"You appear to be sexually aroused, Beverly," I said.

"I am, my Master," she said. "Please, please!"

"Speak, Slave," I said.

"Beverly begs to serve her master," she said.

I then took her, and, in moments, in helpless spasms, sobbing, in joy, she cried out her slave's submission to me. "I am now naught but a Gorean slave girl! I am now naught but a Gorean slave girl!" she cried. "And I am yours, my Master! I am yours! I am yours!"

The girl who had held the leash of the girl whom I had just enjoyed, having now returned, removed her hand from the docile, supine slave's body. She tasted, and smelled, her fingers. "I see that you have earned your tarsk bit," she said.

"Yes, Mistress," said the girl, happily.

The girl who was the Coin Girl's leash holder then bent to untie the leash from the slave ring.

"Please, Mistress," begged the girl whom I had just enjoyed, scrambling to her knees and putting her head to the feet of the other girl, "do not yet untie my leash!"

"It is well past the nineteenth Ahn," said the girl who was apparently the new girl's slave supervisor and trainer.

"But the pleasures of the master are not to be interfered with," said the kneeling slave. "That I was told in the house!"

Then, on her knees, she turned and looked pleadingly at me.

I took out another tarsk bit, and held it out. The girl came then near to me, and leaned forward, that I might, from my reclining position, be able to reach the coin box chained on her neck. I put in another tarsk bit. The kneeling girl then turned and looked, pleadingly, at the girl under whose orders she was.

"Very well," said the girl who was standing, looking down upon the kneeling slave. "I shall wait up the street." Then she looked at me. "When you are through with her," she said, "send her to me."

"Very well," I said.

Beverly knelt happily beside me, and I lay back, on my back, on the tunic, on the stones of the street. I felt her small hands, lovingly, timidly, touching me about the shoulders and chest. "I did not know you could be like this," she said. "I have never seen you before like this."

"A woman looks differently at a man when she is a slave," I said.

"Yes, Master," she smiled. "What must you think of me?" she asked, ruefully.

"I do not understand," I said.

"How I behaved, how I acted," she said.

"I do not understand," I said.

"How can you respect me?" she asked.

"I do not," I said.

"You do not respect me?" she asked.

"No," I said, "of course not, for you are a slave."

"Yes, Master," she smiled. She kissed me, softly, on the right shoulder. Then she knelt back, on her heels, beside me. Her knees were spread, in the position of the pleasure slave. "You think little of slaves, don't you?" she asked.

"Yes," I said.

"Then you must think little of me?" she asked.

"Yes," I said.

"Am I good?" she asked.

"Yes," I said.

"I am glad," she said. "Master," she said.

"Yes," I said.

"What if I were not good?"

"Then I would not have put another coin in your coin box," I said.

"What if I were not good the first time, after you had put a coin in the coin box?" she asked.

"Then I would have beaten you," I said.

"Could you beat me?" she asked.

"Yes," I told her.

"Would you, truly, had you not been satisfied with me, have beaten me?" she asked.

"Yes," I said.

"I am pleased that you found me pleasing," she said.

I smiled.

"Too," she said, "you would have been entitled to a refund, though I myself could not have given it to you, for the coin box is locked. You could have obtained it, however, later from my master."

"I know," I said.

"But then, too, I would be again beaten," she said, "doubtless whipped."

"Yes," I said. The satisfaction of Coin Girls, in its way, is guaranteed, or one can receive one's money back. It is not surprising, then, that the girls, under the conditions obtaining, strive to be pleasing.

"I put a second coin, did I not, in your coin box?" I asked.

"Yes, Master," she said.

"Address yourself to my pleasures," I said.

"Yes, Master," she said, and bent forward, over my body. I felt her sweet lips, and her small teeth and tongue, those of a slave, on my body. In a few moments I ordered her again to her back.

She lay beside me.

Then I pulled her by the neck chain closer to me. I thrust another coin into the small metal box on the chain. She kissed me. "Again, Master?" she asked. I took her by the arms and flung her beneath me. "Do you know the name of this street?" I asked.

"The Street of the Writhing Slave," she said.

"Writhe, Slave," I said.

"Yes, Master," she said.

It was an Ahn later.

She lay beside me, pressing her softness against me, kissing at my arm, my shoulder and chest, softly, piteously. "Very well," I said.

"Oh, yes, Master!" she breathed. "Yes, yes, Master!"

I then put her beneath me, and looked down into her eyes. "Yes, Master," she said. "Yes, yes, yes, Master!"

I was preparing to have her when suddenly I saw fear come into her eyes. "Oh, no, Master!" she cried. "No! No!"

"What is it?" I asked.

"The coin!" she cried, in misery, "the coin. You have not paid the coin!"

I smiled.

"I am a Coin Girl!" she cried, miserably. "I may not be had without the coin!"

"Oh," I said.

"Please," she begged. "Please pay the coin!"

"Do you beg it?" I asked.

"Yes, Master," she said. "Yes, Master!"

"Very well," I said. I put another tiny coin in the coin box.

"Thank you, Master," she breathed, lifting her lips to mine. "Now have me, have me, have me!"

"Very well," I said.

"It must be near dawn," I said.

"Yes, Master," she whispered, softly, frightened.

"We must think about having you returned to your master," I said.

"Oh, please, Master, not yet," she begged. "Let me stay beside you for but a little more time."

"Very well," I said, "for perhaps a moment more."

"I never want to leave your side," she said. She clutched me.

"Who owns you?" I asked.

"I do not know," she said, "doubtless some renter of Coin Girls. I was apportioned to him in the division of the spoils taken from the holding of Policrates."

"What does he look like?" I asked.

"I do not know," she said. "I have never even seen him."

"What manner of man is he?" I asked.

"He is harsh and cruel, uncompromising and merciless," she said. "He keeps me well as a slave."

"Do you fear him?" I asked.

"I fear him terribly," she said. "I am his girl."

"Perhaps he is not such a bad fellow," I said.

"He keeps me chained in a basement, in the darkness," she said. "He throws me scraps of food for which I, on my chain, must search, or starve."

"Perhaps he merely wishes you to learn that you are a slave," I said.

"He has taught it to me well," she said.

"He does not sound like such a bad fellow," I said. "If I owned you, I might treat you similarly, at least at first."

"Until I had learned well to whom I belong?" she asked.

"Yes," I said.

"And what if a girl is incapable of learning her lesson?" she asked.

"She may always, then," I said, "be fed to sleen."

"She will learn her lesson, and well," said the girl.

"Of course," I said.

"But he has never once summoned me to his couch, to abuse me, or caress me, or order me to serve his pleasures."

"I see," I said.

"If you owned me," she said, "you would have used me by now, would you not have?"

"Yes," I said, "if I owned you, doubtless, by now, I would have put you, and well, to my pleasure."

"Perhaps he does not find me attractive," she said. "Perhaps he has many women. Perhaps he does not even find me a curiosity to exploit."

"Perhaps," I said.

She then lay closely against me, her head at my hip, trembling.

"I am afraid to be a slave," she whispered.

"As well you might be," I said.

"I can be bought or sold, or given away," she said. "I may even be slain, on the least whim of a master."

"Yes," I said.

"Master," she said.

"Yes," I said.

"Masters do not respect their slaves, do they?" she asked.

"Of course not," I said.

"But might they not, sometimes, feel other emotions toward them?" she asked. Her voice was very soft, and frightened. I gathered that she feared she might be struck.

"Yes," I said.

"What emotions?" she asked, timidly, beggingly.

"Irritation," I said, "desire, lust."

"But is there no other emotion that a master might, sometimes, feel towards his slave?" she asked.

"What emotion did you have in mind?" I asked.

"Please, Master," she sobbed, "do not make me speak!"

"Very well," I said.

I felt her tears, and hair, at my hip. Doubtless it is hard, I thought, to be a slave girl. One is so helpless.

"It is light now," I said.

"I hear a bell," she whispered.

"It is not the bell of a Coin Girl," I said. "It is the bell of a vendor of bosk milk. He is making his rounds, coming up the street."

"Do not send me from your side," she said.

"Would you be seen here," I asked, "as a naked slave, leashed, lying upon the street?"

"Slaves have no pride," she said.

"On your knees," I told her.

"Yes, Master," she said, getting to her knees. I stood up, and looked down upon her, kneeling on the stones, in the gray light of the Gorean dawn.

"Use me but once more," she begged, "before you send me away."

I looked down at her.

"Shorten my leash," she said. "Tie my hands before my body. Fasten me closely at the slave ring."

"The vendor of bosk milk approaches," I said.

"I care not," she said. "Take me before him."

I pulled her back by the leather collar, and leash, not gently, to the slave ring. There I untied the leash and then re-tied it, considerably shortening it. She knelt there, then, against the wall. The tether, from the heavy metal ring to the stout ring at the back of her collar, taut, holding her head up, was about eighteen inches in length. She held out her hands to me, wrists crossed. With the free end of the leash I bound them together, tightly, before her body.

I looked down at her. "You are now tied, or muchly so," I said, "as was the girl on the walk, outside the shop of Phile-bus, in Ar."

"Yes, Master," she said, happily.

"I had brought her a drink of water," I said. "I had set the price for this favor as my having of her." This had occurred long ago, when I had been a silk slave, owned by the Lady Florence of Vonda. I had, myself, later captured my mistress, and sold her into slavery. She belonged now to Miles of Vonda, who had helped us in our work with the pirates, part of the spoils, as many other slave girls, taken from the hold-ing of Policrates. My former mistress was now naught but the obedient and joyful love slave of the proud Vondan.

"You were a beast, of course, my Master," she said.

"Yes," I said.

I looked down upon her, she who had once been Miss Bev-erly Henderson, of New York City. She looked well, naked and bound, tethered at the slave ring.

"You accused me of raping her," I said. "You were furi-ous."

The palanquin of Oneander, a salt and leather merchant of Ar, had been passing. To the rear of the palanquin, in a dou-ble coffle of briefly tunicked beauties, display slaves, their hands braceleted behind their backs, had been the girl who now knelt before me. Then the palanquin had stopped, as Oneander had chosen to pass the time of day with another fellow, he, too, in a palanquin, with display slaves. When I had withdrawn from the girl at the ring I had seen her, she who had once been Miss Henderson, among the display slaves. It had been the first time that I had seen her as a slave. I had never forgotten that first glimpse of her as a slave. It had been one of the most exciting moments of my life.

"Yes," she said, "I was furious."

"I was only making her pay for the drink of water," I said.

"But making her pay as a slave," she said.

"Of course," I said. "She was a slave." "As you are," I added.

"Do you know why I was furious?" she asked.

"You felt pity and indignation seeing the abuse of one of your sisters in bondage?" I asked.

"No," she said, "I was furious because it was she, and not I, whom you forced, with such casual audacity, to serve your pleasure at the ring."

I smiled.

"I wanted to be at the ring, not she," she said.

"I see," I said.

"I am now at such a ring, before you," she said.

"And well tethered there," I said.

"Yes, Master," she said.

"That girl," I said, "was not, truly, raped at the ring. She was only paying for a drink of water." I looked down at her. "It is you, rather," I said, "who will be raped at the ring."

"Yes, my Master!" she said.

I crouched down before her. I heard the bell from nearby, that of the vendor of bosk milk. "The vendor of bosk milk approaches," I said to her.

"Take me, take me!" she begged.

"Are you shameless?" I asked.

"Yes," she said, "I am a slave. Take me!"

I looked at her. She regarded me wildly. Then I placed the tiny coin, a tarsk bit, into the coin box on her neck chain. Then, straining against the leash and collar, she tried to press herself forward, against me. I took her by the ankles, her right ankle in my left hand, and her left ankle in my right hand, and pulled her to a sitting position. I then drew her toward me, and then thrust her bound hands up and over her head. I then threw apart her ankles. "Yes, Master!" she cried. I heard the bell, and the creak of the narrow, wooden wheels of the cart of the vendor of bosk milk, nearby. Then, rather behind us, and to my right, it stopped. "Yes, Master, yes,

Master," the girl was sobbing. When I had finished with her I
stood up. She lay there at my feet, on the stones, on her side,
breathing deeply. She turned to look at the vendor of bosk
milk, and then again lay on her side, the right side of her
head on the stones, her eyes, half glazed, regarding the surface of the street.

"She is a hot one," said the vendor of bosk milk.

"Yes," I said.

He then, ringing his bell, leaning into the traces, attached
to two wooden handles, drawing his two-wheeled cart behind
him, proceeded up the street.

"How you had me!" said the girl. "Surely there is nothing
left in you of the weakling of Earth."

I untied her hands, and untied the leash from the ring. "Do
not disparage the men of Earth," I said. "Some, perhaps one
day, wearied of their suppression, may assume their manhood."

"It is against the law," she said.

I shrugged. "Antibiological legislation may be repealed," I
said. "Political forms may be replaced."

"The men of Earth are lost to manhood," she said.

"Perhaps," I said. "I do not know."

"It would require a revolution," she said.

"Perhaps," I said. "I do not know." Then I said, sharply,
"Kneel."

Swiftly she knelt.

"In the position of the pleasure slave," I said.

She then knelt before me in the position of the pleasure
slave, back on her heels, her knees widely spread, her back
straight, her hands on her thighs, her head up. A woman is
very beautiful in this position, proud, exciting, submitted,
displayed.

"No such revolution is required on Gor, Master," she said.

"No," I said.

I then turned the collar, slowly, carefully, on her neck, for
it was high, thick and close-fitting. The stout collar ring was
then in front of her throat, with its long, dependent leash. I
looped the leash. She eyed the loops warily. Such loops serve
quite well as a set of lashing surfaces.

"Have you ever kissed the whip?" I asked her.

"Other than in training and in the hands of an auctioneer,
when I was being sold?" she asked.

"Yes," I said.

She looked down.

"Well?" I asked.

"I was once given for the night in the holding of Policrates to he whom we, at that time, thought to be the courier of Ragnar Voskjard," she whispered. "He forced me to kiss his whip."

"Look up, Slave," I ordered her.

"Yes, Master," she said.

"This fellow in the holding of Policrates," I said.

"Yes, Master," she said.

"Did you yield to him?"

"Do not make me answer such a question, not to you, please," she pleaded.

"Look into my eyes," I told her.

"Yes, Master," she said, in misery.

"Speak," I told her.

"Yes, Master," she said, "I yielded to him."

"Fully," I asked, "and as the degraded slave you are?"

"Yes, Master," she said. "I yielded to him fully, and as the degraded slave I am."

"Did you yield to him more fully, or as more of a slave, than you did to me?" I asked.

"No, Master," she said, tears in her eyes. "You two are the mightiest of the masters who have used me."

"I see," I said.

"Yes, Master," she said.

"What does he look like?" I asked.

"I do not know, Master," she said. "In the feasting hall of Policrates he wore a mask. Later, in the chambers, when he used me, I was blindfolded."

"I see," I said.

"It was he who first taught me, fully, what it was to be a female slave," she said.

"Are you grateful to him?" I asked.

"Yes, Master," she said.

"Kiss the whip," I said.

She took the coils of the leash in her small hands and, putting down her head, covered them with kisses. She then lifted her eyes to me, in which there were tears. "Now, too, my Master," she said, "I have kissed your whip."

"Perhaps someday you may come again into his possession," I said.

"No, Master," she said, "doubtless he has high and beautiful Gorean girls to serve him. I am only a miserable Earthgirl slave. Doubtless he has already forgotten about me. I was only a novelty, and a pleasure, for a night to him."

"I see," I said.

"He made me a spasmodic and submitted slave, and then abandoned me."

"You have not yet seen your master, you have told me," I said. "Perhaps, unbeknownst to you, it is that very fellow who owns you."

"No, Master," she smiled, ruefully. "I know such a man. By now he would have used me, richly and fully. Muchly, by now, would I have had to crawl to him and serve him."

"Do you love him?" I asked.

"Yes, Master," she sobbed, "but I am the most miserable of slaves!"

"Why is that?" I asked.

"For I love two men!" she wept.

"Who is the other?" I asked.

She looked at me, suddenly terrified. There were tears in her eyes. "Please do not make me speak," she begged.

I shrugged. "Very well," I said.

A householder emerged from a nearby door. He paid us little attention. The woman was obviously only a branded, stripped slave, and a mere Coin Girl at that. He had doubtless seen many such girls, and many who, doubtless, in his opinion, were of much greater interest. He carried a small ladder and, on it, climbed to the tiny tharlarion-oil lamp, and pinched it out. In a moment, carrying the short ladder, he had returned inside. To him, doubtless, the former Miss Henderson was only another little, meaningless, exquisite enslaved wench.

I dropped the leash. It fell between her breasts, and then to the stones of the street. "Get up," I told her, "and put on your tunic."

She looked up at me, agonized.

"Must a command be repeated?" I inquired.

"No, Master," she said. She then got to her feet, the long leash falling before her. She picked up her tunic and drew it on, but did not tie it shut.

She looked at me. "You are sending me away?" she asked.

"It is time for you to be returned to your master," I said.

"So simply as that?" she asked.

"Of course," I said.

She fell on her knees before me, and put her head down. She clasped me about the right leg, and began, sobbing, to kiss at my knee. I took her by the hair and pulled her head up, to where she must look at me. "Master," she sobbed.

Casually I inserted another coin in the coin box. She looked at me, with horror.

"Are you obedient?" I asked. I crouched before her, and tossed the leash over her shoulder.

"Yes, Master," she whispered.

I then, casually, jerked apart the sides of her tunic.

"Master," she said.

"Lie down," I told her.

"Yes, Master," she said.

She then lay back on the stones before me, obedient, agonized.

I brushed back the bell, and coin box, and they lay then on the stones, beside the left side of her neck.

"Master," she said.

I entered her, and held her.

"Master," she wept.

"What is wrong?" I asked.

"Nothing," she said.

"Will it be necessary to whip you?" I asked.

"No, Master," she wept.

In a moment she cried out, "Is it all that I am to you, a Coin Girl?"

"What else could you be?" I asked.

"Nothing," she wept. "Nothing." Then she clutched me, desperately, sobbing. "Buy me," she begged, "buy me! Keep me! Keep me! I never want to leave you! Buy me, Master, I beg you! I will be a good slave to you! I will strive to please you as might a thousand girls! I want to be your slave! I beg you, my Master, I beg you to buy me!"

Finished with her, I stood up. She lay shattered at my feet, weeping.

I looked down upon her. It was pleasant to see her thusly.

I drew on my tunic.

I kicked the sobbing figure with the side of my foot. "Kneel," I told it.

"Yes, Master," she said. She knelt.

"Adjust the bell and coin box," I told her.

"Yes, Master," she said.

"Too," said I, "tie shut your tunic. Free women may soon be about. We must not scandalize them."

"No, Master," she said. Kneeling, shuddering, her head down, she closed her tunic, and tied it shut.

I heard the long, horizontal shutters of a shop being flung upward, over the counter. This opens the shop to the street. It was the shop of a leather worker.

The girl looked up at me, agonized.

I then, by the leash, pulling it forward, jerked her to her feet. The collar cut the underside of her chin. I coiled the leash and put the coils in her own hand. "Hold the leash taut," I told her. "Yes, Master," she whispered. She would, thus, her hand about six inches from the ring, lead herself on her own leash. "Seek out now the girl who held your leash last night," I said. "She will be waiting up the street. Find her, and beg her to return you swiftly to your master."

"Yes, Master," she whispered.

I regarded her.

"Please, Master," she begged, "please!"

I pointed up the street.

"Yes, Master," she said, and then, turning about, stumbling and crying, the bell of the Coin Girl sounding, the coins jingling in the box on her neck, she fled up the street.

XVIII

THE GAG AND HOOD

The small, exquisite, dark-haired slave, naked, knelt on the tiles before the large mirror, trembling, trying to apply, with the tiny brush, the bluish eye shadow.

I watched from behind a dark curtain, one bearing, on both sides, in gold embroidery, an intricate design incorporating cursive Kefs, one larger and several smaller.

"I am afraid," said the kneeling girl, with the small brush.

"As well you should be," said the girl standing behind her, who carried a long, supple leather switch, "for you are soon to be presented to your Master."

"He has treated me with such cruelty," said the kneeling girl.

"You have been treated precisely as you have deserved," said the standing girl.

"Yes, Mistress," said the kneeling girl. She was quite beautiful under the light of the three, dangling tharlarion-oil lamps, depending from an erect, tall iron stand near the mirror. She replaced the tiny brush and the small, blue, round box which contained the eye shadow on the cosmetics tray on the tiles.

"More eye shadow," said the standing girl.

"Mistress!" protested the kneeling girl.

"Remember that you are a slave," said the girl with the switch.

"Yes, Mistress," said the kneeling girl. Then, she again took up the brush and the tiny box. She applied the eye shadow more heavily then, more sensuously then, in a manner more befitting what she was. Her protests in the matters of her lipstick and perfume, and certain other cosmetics, had been similarly overruled. In a few moments she replaced the materials in the small, oblong tray and leaned back on her heels. She surveyed herself. Her long, dark hair had already been combed with an antique, yellow, stained comb of kailiauk horn.

She regarded herself in the mirror. "I am a slave," she said.

"Yes," said the girl with the switch. She poked the kneeling girl with the switch. "Do not cry," she warned.

"No, Mistress," said the kneeling girl.

"Are you truly disappointed?" asked the girl with the switch.

"No, Mistress," she said. "It is only that I am not used to seeing myself like this."

She had been forced to make herself up to be maddeningly sensuous.

"Surely you would prefer for your master to see you in terms of desire and not in terms of discipline," said the standing girl.

"Yes, Mistress," said the girl at the mirror, fervently.

"Do you object," asked the girl with the switch.

"No, Mistress," said the kneeling girl.

"Are you not, rather, pleased to see how you look?" asked the girl with the switch.

"I did not know I could look like this," said the kneeling girl.

"How do you think you look?" asked the girl with the switch.

"Sensuous, and exciting," said the kneeling girl.

"Yes," said the girl with the switch.

"How could a man see me as aught but a slave, like this?" asked the kneeling girl.

"But you are naught but a slave," said the girl with the switch. "Do you doubt that?"

"No, Mistress," said the kneeling girl.

"And a pretty one," said the girl with the switch.

"Yes, Mistress," said the kneeling girl.

"Look in the mirror, closely," ordered the girl with the switch.

"Yes, Mistress," said the kneeling girl.

"What do you see?" demanded the girl with the switch.

"A slave," said the kneeling girl.

"Say, 'I am a slave,' " said the girl with the switch.

"I am a slave," said the kneeling girl, regarding herself in the mirror.

"Do not forget it," said the girl with the switch.

"No, Mistress," said the kneeling girl.

"Look now again into the mirror, little slave," said the girl with the switch.

"Yes, Mistress," said the kneeling girl.

"Men will make that girl serve them well, will they not?"

"Yes, Mistress," said the kneeling girl.

"And that is fitting, is it not, for she is a slave?"

"Yes, Mistress," said the kneeling girl.

"And she is very beautiful."

"Thank you, Mistress," said the kneeling girl.

"And are you not pleased to be she?" inquired the girl with the switch.

"Yes, Mistress," said the kneeling girl, "I am pleased to be she."

"Then what is wrong?" inquired the girl with the switch.

"I am afraid," said the girl kneeling before the mirror, trembling. "I am afraid to be presented before my Master."

"A suitable fear for a slave," said the girl with the switch.

"What does he look like? What manner of man is he?" asked the kneeling girl.

"You will learn, Slave," said the girl with the switch.

"But what if he does not find me pleasing?" she asked, fearfully.

"You are a slave girl," said the girl with the switch. "It is up to you to see that he finds you pleasing."

"What shall I do?" begged the kneeling girl, looking piteously up at the girl with the switch.

"Be beautiful, and humble," said the girl with the switch.

As the light was arranged I could, through the curtain, see the girls easily; they, on the other hand, because of the same arrangement of light, and because I had set no light behind

me, in the room within which I stood, were totally unable to
see me. They were, so to speak, visually at my mercy. This,
incidentally, is not an unusual arrangement in a Gorean
house, particularly in rooms where slaves might be kept or
found. This represents a convenience for the master. Also it
is thought to be helpful in the management of a woman, that,
when the master wishes, she can be brought secretly under
observation. Too, it might be noted that only a curtain separated the cosmetics room from the rest of the house. This
sort of thing, too, is not that uncommon where rooms which
may be occupied by slaves are found. Such curtains, without
ceremony, may be thrust aside, startling the slave and revealing the keeper or master.

Slaves, of course, being mere articles of property, are not
entitled to privacy. They may be entered upon as often, and
however, one wishes. The Gorean master does not require the
permission of a slave to enter a room, no more than the man
of Earth requires the permission of his dog to enter a room.
This lack of privacy, to be expected, given the lowly condition of the slave, is revealed even in details so obvious as almost to be taken for granted, such as the fact that slave
kennels and slave alcoves are almost invariably barred, rather
than given opaque portals, say, with observation apertures
closed by sliding metal panels, the opening of which might
warn the slave of the presence of those under whose gover-
nance she finds herself.

She knows that she is exposed to the view of masters, or
available for their viewing, whenever they might please to do
so, at any hour, either of the day or night. She may be
looked in upon, she knows, and is sometimes certain that she
is, even when she sleeps. This is similar, too, of course, to the
situation of the man of Earth and his dog. He, too, may look
upon his dog whenever and however he pleases, even when, if
he wishes, the animal, curled in its place, is asleep. That is his
privilege.

The analogy, incidentally, between the dog of the man of
Earth and the slave girl of the Gorean male is a quite close
one. Of course, the analogy is not perfect. It is, for example,
far more delicious to own a slave girl than a dog. To be perfectly candid, however, the slave girl is a lovely, vulnerable,
highly sensitive organism; the rational master commonly,
unless she chooses to be troublesome, handles her with deli-

cacy and affection; if she is displeasing, of course, even in small ways, she must expect to be shown little or no mercy; on the other hand, if she is obedient and loving, her life is likely to be a joy almost incomprehensible to the neurotic, masculinized, egotistical women of Earth.

The slave girl, subject to male domination, surrendered to service and love, branded and collared, serving and kneeling, is, under the institutional enhancements of a civilization, fixing her condition upon her with uncompromising clarity, in effect, the primitive woman, the biological woman, the selected-for woman, the woman in her place in nature, the fulfilled woman. It is little wonder then that slaves, in a situation where their condition is scarcely unique, and in a supportive, appropriate cultural matrix, where they are free, without being subjected to envious, vicious, hysterical criticism, to be themselves, tend, once the right master is found, to be relieved and happy. The collar, in effect, has returned them to themselves. They have become women. And, to be sure, the Gorean men will have it no other way.

"Am I to be presented to my Master clothed?" asked the kneeling girl.

"At least in the beginning," said the girl with the switch.

"I see," said the kneeling girl.

"Stand," said the girl with the switch.

Immediately, gracefully, the girl stood.

The girl who was serving as keeper went to a large chest at the side of the room. She hung her switch on a hook on the wall and opened the chest. "When your Master wishes you to enter his presence," she said, "you will be summoned by the sound of a gong."

"Yes, Mistress," said the girl standing near the mirror. She had not been given permission to turn about.

The girl who was serving as the small brunet's keeper withdrew from the chest, and shook out, a flimsy, tiny, diaphanous snatch of yellow pleasure silk. It was the sort of garment which, commonly, would be worn only by the most lascivious of dancing slaves writhing before strong, rude men in the lowest taverns on Gor. Free women had been known to faint at the sight, or touch, of such cloth. In many cities it is a crime to bring such cloth into contact with the flesh of free women. It is just too exciting, and sensuous.

As the girl before the mirror shuddered the garment was

brought forward and placed upon her. The girl regarded herself in the mirror. She smiled, wryly. "Is this the 'clothing,'" she asked, "in which I am first to be presented to my Master?"

"Yes," said the other girl.

"It is like being more naked than naked," said the girl before the mirror.

"In the presence of your Master," said the girl who was serving as her keeper, "you will find yourself grateful for even these few threads."

"Yes, Mistress," said the girl.

"Feel them," ordered the larger girl, sternly.

The girl, between her fingers, felt the cloth that clung about her body. I saw her tremble.

"It is a slave's reflex," sneered the girl who was serving as her keeper.

"It is so exciting," said the girl before the mirror.

"It is nearly time for you to be belled," said the girl who was serving as her keeper.

"When this garment is removed from me," asked the smaller girl, "am I then to be whipped?"

"That is the Master's decision, is it not?" asked the larger girl.

"Yes, Mistress," said the exquisite, small, ravishing brunet.

The girl who was acting as the lovely slave's keeper then went again to the chest and, with a sensuous jangle, withdrew from it bellings suitable for a slave. Before the mirror, then, was the exquisite slave belled. Her ankles were belled, and her wrists, and, lastly, about her neck, was closed a belled collar.

"I am now ready to be presented before my Master," said the exquisite brunet.

"Yes," agreed the other girl.

"When will I be presented before him?" asked the exquisite brunet.

"When the gong sounds," said the other girl.

"But when will the gong sound?" asked the exquisite brunet, in misery.

"When the Master wishes," said the other girl, "and, until then, you will wait, as befits a slave."

"Yes, Mistress," whispered the small brunet, in misery. When she moved there was a sensuous jangle and rustle of the slave bells locked upon her body. I resisted the impulse, almost overwhelming, to thrust aside the curtain, declaring myself to her, seizing and throwing her to the very tiles of the cosmetics room, there subjecting her to delicious slave rape. I controlled myself. I conquered my impulses, not that they might be unhealthily and indefinitely suppressed and frustrated, in the manner of Earth, but, rather, in the manner of Gor, that they might later be the more sweetly and fully satisfied. "Before the feast, go hungry." So say the Goreans.

"You will kneel now, head down and knees widely spread, to await the summons of your Master," said the girl who had held the switch.

"Yes, Mistress," said the exquisite brunet, obeying.

Silently I withdrew then from my position behind the curtain. I would leave the house and, at a paga tavern, purchase supper. I would return after my repast, later, sometime in the early evening, at my leisure.

I sat upon a great curule chair, on a broad, three-stepped, carpeted dais in the house which I had borrowed from a friend, a citizen of Victoria, for the past few days.

I wore a mask identical to that which I had worn when I had first gained admittance to the holding of Policrates, when I had, long ago, pretended to be an agent of Ragnar Voskjard, he who was the bearer of the topaz. I remembered well the feast at which I had been entertained. The slaves in the holding, as I recalled, many of them former free women, had been quite beautiful. I well remember one of them, in slave steel, a small, exquisite brunet, who had knelt before me, lifting fruit cupped in her hands for my delectation, and, in this, of course, as the pirates wished, presenting herself as well for my survey and consideration. Later she had been sent to my room.

I had amused myself thoroughly with the small beauty. Indeed, in that night, I gathered, she had been, for the first time, taught the full meaning of her collar. When she had entered the room she had been a woman who had been enslaved; when I had left the room she knew herself to be a woman who was a slave. She had piteously begged to be bought, and to be taken with me, and kept as my own. I had learned later in the holding, when I had been captured, that she was owned in her heart by that brutal, anonymous master who had so abused her, that her love, the helpless love of a tormented, yielding slave, was his. How she had contrasted the audacity and glory of that unknown Gorean master with the timidity and weakness of the males of Earth, such as, at that time, she took me to be.

Then, last night, on the rude stones of the Street of the Writhing Slave, she helpless in my arms, locked in the chain collar of a Coin Girl, with the flattish bell and coin box, I had instructed her, and thoroughly, in the respect due, did he but assume his mastery, to one who was once of Earth. By morning she had learned this lesson well. We did not relate to one another in the perverted modality of unisexual identicals but in the order of nature, she as woman, and slave, I as man, and master. When I, finished with her for the time, had sent her fleeing from me, she had been riven with conflict. Two men, it seemed, she loved, he whom she had served in the holding of Policrates, he who had treated her with the insolence commonly accorded an Earth-girl slave by Gorean masters, and he whom she had served on the stones of the Street of the Writhing Slave, he who had treated her as a full and lowly slave, who once, perchance, had been an Earth girl.

I reached to my left and, from the rack on the gong frame, picked up the slender stick which reposed there. On this stick was mounted a rounded, fur-wrapped head. I struck the gong once, smartly, replaced the stick, and leaned back in the curule chair.

Before the reverberations of the gong had subsided I heard, hurrying towards the room, from deep within the house, the sound of slave bells.

A curtain was thrust aside at the end of the long room, and I saw her in the threshold, barefoot, her ankles belled, her feet almost lost in the piling of the deep carpet leading to the dais.

She seemed startled, stunned. How beautiful she was in the bit of yellow pleasure silk.

The other girl, who was serving as her keeper, and had now retrieved her switch, thrust her forward.

Timidly, and as though she could scarcely believe what was occurring, the girl in the yellow pleasure silk approached the dais.

She could not, it seemed, take her eyes from the mask which I wore.

Then she stopped at the foot of the dais, trembling, belled, looking up at me.

"A slave, Master," explained the girl with the switch, standing behind her.

Immediately the girl in the yellow pleasure silk fell to her knees and put her head to the carpet at the foot of the dais.

I gestured to the girl behind her, she with the switch, that she might leave. She smiled, and withdrew. I, too, smiled. Lola had done a good job with her. Lola, too, of course, had been her keeper as a Coin Girl when I had, as Jason of Victoria, by apparent accident, encountered her on the Street of the Writhing Slave. I was pleased with Lola. She had served me well. Perhaps I could reward her, by giving her to a suitable master.

I snapped my fingers and the girl kneeling before the dais lifted her head.

Furtively she looked about. She then realized that she was alone with me. She looked up at me.

"Is it you, my Master?" she whispered. "Is it truly you, my Master?"

I did not respond to her.

"If I may not speak," she said, "by your least gesture or movement of irritation, warn me to silence. I have no wish to displease you in the slightest."

I indicated, with a movement of my fingers, that she should discard the pleasure silk. She did so, dropping it behind her.

"You won my heart in the holding of Policrates," she said. "Since that time I have been yours. Never did I dream that my fortune would be such that you would even remember me, let alone see fit to bring me into your own house. Thank you, my Master! Thank you, my Master!"

I looked down upon her.

"It is my hope that you will find me pleasing," she said. "I will endeavor to be a good slave to you."

I smiled.

"Of course I must, I know," she said, "for I am your slave. I am not a fool, Master. But it is more than that. It is not only that I am afraid of being fed to your animals, or of being whipped and tortured, if I am not pleasing. No, it is more than that." There were tears in her eyes as she looked up at me. "You see, my Master," she said, "your Earth-girl

slave loves you." She put her head down. "She has loved you
ever since that night in the holding of Policrates. She is thus,
my Master, more your slave than you could ever know." She
lifted her head. "Did you make me love you that night, or
were you only such that I could not help loving you. It does
not matter, for I loved you then, and love you now, with the
total helplessness of a slave's love for her master. You are my
Master, and I am your slave, and I love you." She brushed a
tear from her eye. It smeared the mascara-type compound
which had been put on her lashes, making a dark smear on
her cheek. "I love you, my Master," she said.

I looked down upon her. It pleased me to hear the former
Miss Henderson confess her love for me, in my guise as her
Gorean master.

"I do not ask that you love me, even a little, my Master,"
she said, "for I am nothing, and a slave. I know well, and
need not be taught, that I am owned. I know that I am only
an article of your property." She put her head down. "Just as
you own some piece of clothing, or the thongs to your sandals, so, too, do you own me. To you, too, I am doubtless of
far less value than a pet sleen. I do not ask, accordingly, nor
would I be so presumptuous or bold as to ask, or beg, that
you care even a little for me. No, my Master. I am only your
slave." She then lifted her head again. Tears were in her eyes.
"But know, my Master," she said, "that my own love, unde-
sired though it might be, worthless as it doubtless is, that of a
slave, is yours."

With my finger I indicated a place upon the mask I wore.
With her fingers she reached to her own face. She touched
her face, beneath her left eye. On her fingers, she saw, was
the stain of the smeared cosmetic. She looked at me,
frightened. She rubbed her cheek and then, her head down,
rubbed her finger tips on her right thigh.

From beside the curule chair I picked up a five-stranded
Gorean slave lash. I threw it to the carpet, in front of the
girl.

She looked down at the lash and then, frightened, up at
me. "Am I to be whipped, my Master?" she asked.

I gestured that she should return the whip, and then,
briefly, placed four fingers, downward, on the arm of the
curule chair. The whip would be returned, then, in the manner of the naked slave.

"Yes, my Master," she whispered.

She fell forward, to her hands and knees, with a jangle of slave bells, and put her head down. She took the staff of the whip, which is about an inch and a quarter to an inch and a half in diameter, gently between her teeth, and looked up at me. The staff of the whip was crosswise in her mouth. Her mouth, by the whip, was held widely open. I snapped my fingers. Head down, then, on all fours, to the small sounds of the slave bells on her wrists and ankles, and collar, she slowly ascended the three broad steps of the carpeted dais. She was then before me, on all fours, the lovely, obedient slave, the former Miss Henderson, before the curule chair on which I reclined. She lifted her head, and, extending her slender, closely collared neck, delicately tendered the whip into my grasp. I took the whip from her, and she looked at me, frightened. Was she now to be whipped? The decision, of course, was mine. I folded the blades of the whip back against the staff, and held out the staff and blades to her. Suddenly, gratefully, tears in her eyes, sobbing, and half gasping and choking with relief, kneeling before me, grasping my calves, her head over my thighs, she covered the whip, that symbol of masculinity, and of the authority of men over her, and specifically of my own authority over her, with kisses.

"I kiss your whip, my Master," she said, gratefully, continuing to kiss the brutal, uncompromising blades and staff. "I submit to you a thousand times! Thank you for not whipping me! I am your slave, and I love you!" She then looked up at me, joyfully. "I love you, my Master," she said. "I love you!" Then, joyfully, kneeling before me, she put her left cheek down upon my right thigh. "I love you, my Master. Command me," she begged. "I am eager to serve you I will do anything." I smiled to myself. Of course, she would do anything. She was an owned woman. Such must do anything, and superbly, and unhesitantly, upon the least wish of the Master. They are slaves. And yet it pleased me to hear the former Miss Henderson, of her own free will, beg to please me. This was a gratification which few men of Earth had obtained, I speculated, from the women of Earth. But then few men of Earth had had the illuminating experience of seeing their precious women, their sexuality liberated by Gorean males, returned to the primitive natural state of biological women, crawling, collared, to the feet of masters. Woman in her place in nature is perfect and delicious. Out of her place in nature she is a deviant and a freak.

"Master has not commanded me," said the girl, keeping her cheek down upon my right thigh.

I hung the whip, by its handle loop, over the arm of the curule chair.

"It is my hope that I am not displeasing to him," she whispered. "Perhaps he will command me later. It is my hope that he is saving me for his own pleasure, and not for the pleasure of another." She looked up at me, frightened. "I know well the power of your desire, and the strength of your arms, from the holding of Policrates. And yet in these days that you have owned me, you have used me not once. I trust that I have not lost my charm for you. I hope that it is for yourself that you are keeping me, and that you are not keeping me for another. I know that my will means nothing but it is to you that I wish to belong, and not to another. Keep me, I beg of you. I will struggle to be worthy of your decision."

I reached to the side of the curule chair and took from a bronze dish on the carpet a small leather sack. It contained some tiny scraps of meat, remnants which I had saved from my supper.

Bit by bit I fed these to the slave.

"The Master feeds his slave," said the girl. "It is thus my hope that he is not wholly dissatisfied with me."

When I had finished feeding her I gently dabbed her mouth with her hair, being careful not to disarrange the slave's lipstick with which her sweet, full lips had been adorned. It was crimson. It was, by design, kissably sensuous, designed to arouse men and provoke the lust of masters; some girls are terrified to wear such lipstick; they know how it enhances their loveliness and proclaims them well as slaves; they understand well its intention and are seldom left long in doubt as to its effectiveness; had they originally entertained doubts as to its efficacy these doubts are often dispelled rapidly, as they squirm, naked and collared, perfumed, in the arms of a strong man, as it is being ruthlessly kissed from their lips. Yet, of course, it is not simply the lipstick, but the entire appearance and ensemble of the slave, and perhaps mostly simply that she is a slave, which so enhances her desirability, which so drives men wild with the desire to have her.

I extended my fingers to her and she, gently, licked the grease from them. I then dried my hands on her hair, and she knelt back, kneeling on the broad carpeted dais before me, in the position of the pleasure slave.

"Thank you, my Master, for feeding me," she said. I nodded. Many slave girls, of course, cannot even take their food for granted. And, strictly, of course, every slave girl depends, ultimately, on the master's decision, as to whether or not she is to be fed.

"I am happy that it is you who owns me," she said. "I cannot tell you how happy it makes me, I, a slave, to belong to one such as you. In my deepest heart of hearts I desire to obey, to serve and love. I know, too, full well, that you, and ones like you, will require, and, nay, even enforce, uncompromisingly, these lovely exactions upon me. I shall then, in my womanhood, be fulfilled. How I pity the unfulfilled, frustrated women of my old world whose sex and dispositions, meaningless and largely useless in the bleak labyrinths of an artificial world, must be thwarted, suppressed and denied, in the interests of economic and mechanistic exigencies. How far are the barren, dismal corridors of such a world from our native countries. How long my people have been lost. How far we have drifted from our own hearts. How far we have wandered from home. What can any journey profit us, if it is ourselves whom we have left behind?

"But I speak foolishly, my Master," she said, "for what can such nonsense mean to one such as you, one skilled in the mastery, Gorean in blood and power? How little has your own world prepared you to comprehend such lamentations. How meaningless they must seem to you. But suffice it to say that I, who was brought to Gor, and put in a collar, and am an abject slave, am here a thousand times more free than ever I was upon my native world. The thousand trammels of my captivity on Earth I have here shed. As a slave I am more free here than ever I was there. In coming here I have found myself, for the first time, in a world such as that for which I, thousands of years ago, was bred. Here I am a woman. Here I am happy."

I looked down upon her. I did not speak.

"I kneel before you, your slave, yours to do with as you

wish. Command me, and I shall obey. I am yours." She looked up at me, smiling. "Whip me, or terrify me," she said. "I must accept. I must endure. I am a slave. But I wish to please you. That is what I really wish to do. You can probably never know how much I wish to please you."

I regarded her. I did not speak.

"I am before you, and you have not dismissed me. I gather then that I may remain as I am, for the time, kneeling before you." She smiled. "I gather that it pleases you, for some reason, to have me kneeling before you, naked, and as your slave. I suppose that if I were a man it would please me, too, to have a woman so situated before me. And I shall tell you a secret, my Master, for we slaves may not keep secrets from our masters. It pleases us women, too, to kneel thusly before men, especially if we are slaves, for their perusal and inspection. And it is our hope, too, that we will be found attractive by our masters. It is they who own us, and we wish them to find us pleasing. How scandalous we slaves are!" she laughed. "Oh, Master," she said, "if my girlish prattle should displease you in the slightest, please indicate this by some gesture or expression. I will then remain silent until I sense that it may, again, be acceptable for me to speak. I know well who is master here."

But I displayed to her no disapprobatory sign.

"Do you like my bells?" she asked, happily. "They have been put upon me for your pleasure. It excites me to be belled." She lifted her left arm, and turned it. There was a shimmer of sound from the glinting rows of tiny bells locked on her wrist. "Are they not pretty?" she asked. "They mark my movements well, and as those of a slave," she smiled. Then she lowered her arm, and knelt back again, on her heels, in the position of the pleasure slave. "How happy I am yours," she said. "Thank you for bringing me to your house, my Master."

I looked down upon her, so exquisite and desirable, kneeling before me, perfumed, naked and belled. Her knees and the bells on her ankles were almost lost in the soft, deeply piled carpet before the curule chair.

"My Master licks his lips," she said. "Perhaps he sees before him a morsel which he would like to devour?"

I did not speak. '*Go hungry to the feast*,' I thought, '*so say the Goreans*.' And what a slave feast knelt before me!

"I gather that I may continue to speak," she said. "It seems to please my Master to hear me speak." This is not unusual, incidentally, among Gorean masters. High intelligence is highly valued in a female slave. One of the great pleasures in owning a girl is listening to her. It is a great pleasure to become intimately acquainted with her expressions and thoughts, from the most casual and trivial to the most delicate and profound. She must always, of course, be kept strictly in her place.

The contrast here between the man of Earth and the Gorean male is illuminating. The man of Earth subscribes to the thesis that he prizes a woman's mind but, considering his behavior, it seems reasonably clear that, on the whole, he does not. In his conversation, and in his advertising, and such, it seems his attention, almost exclusively, interestingly, is occupied with little more than the extents and distributions of planes and masses. Indeed, some men of Earth seem more interested in parts of women, than in women. Goreans, it might be pointed out, would find this almost incomprehensible. They would not even regard it as a perversion. They simply would not understand it.

The Gorean, incidentally, does not subscribe explicitly to the thesis that he values a woman's mind. Similarly he does not subscribe explicitly to the thesis that he values a woman's foot. It would not occur to him to propound such peculiar theses. Such theses are evidence of cultural schizophrenia and an alienation from nature. He does, however, value women, whole women, and this interest is richly documented in his sayings, his songs, his art, and his behavior. Indeed, he values them so highly that he is fond of owning them. To be sure, let us not appear to blame the man of Earth. He labors, usually, in a desert of sexual starvation. Some of his most basic physical needs are often frustrated, cruelly and systematically. In such a world, where he is seldom granted more than the appearances of women, it is natural for him to become, sadly, preoccupied with mere appearances. Often he knows little more of women than these appearances, with which he is expected, culturally, to make do. The Gorean, on the other hand, who might buy a woman, or have a lovely slave in a paga tavern for the price of a drink, has little trouble with the satisfaction of his basic sexual needs. These needs satisfied he can then attend to the latent richnesses of the prizes he can command.

Let us suppose that the Gorean youth buys his first girl. Before this, of course, he may have used house slaves or the girls in the paga taverns. Indeed, in gangs of roaming youths, he may have caught and raped slave girls on errands in his own city. Some young men regard this as an interesting sport. If a magistrate should chance upon them in some alley he will commonly say, "Thigh," to them, and they will turn the girl, so that he may see if she is branded or not. If she is branded, he will commonly continue on his rounds. The unauthorized rape of slave girls, without the permission of their masters, is officially frowned on in most cities, but, too, it is as often winked at.

There are thought to be two major advantages to the custom of permitting, and, sometimes, of even encouraging, the practice. First, it provides a way of satisfying the sexual needs of young men who may not yet own their own girls, and, secondly, it is thought to provide a useful protection for free women. Free women, incidentally, are almost never raped on Gor, unless it be perhaps a preparatory lesson preceding their total enslavement.

There seem to be two major reasons why free women are seldom raped on Gor. First, it is thought that they, being free, are to be accorded the highest respect, and, secondly, slave females are regarded as being much more desirable. There is little difficulty, commonly, incidentally, in distinguishing between the free woman and the slave. The garment of the slave is usually brief, distinctive and sexually exciting; it is designed to show her to men; the garments of the free woman, on the other hand, are commonly multitudinous, concealing and cumbersome; they are designed to protect her modesty, and hide her from the eyes of men.

In many cities it is a capital offense for the slave girl to don such garments. They are not for her. She is only a slave. Similarly, free women will almost never touch the garment of a slave. They would be scandalized to do so. Such garments are just too sexually exciting. On the other hand, there have been cases when a free woman, boldly, has donned such a garment and dared to walk in the streets and upon the bridges, masquerading as a mere slave upon an errand for her master. She will not be recognized for, commonly, when she goes out, she is veiled.

On the streets, now, of course, she will be taken for only another slave. She revels in this new-found freedom; she exults in the bold appraisals to which she now finds herself subjected, those which free men may fittingly bestow upon a slave; she inclines her head submissively as she passes free men; should they stop her, perhaps to question her, or inquire after directions, she falls to her knees before them; then, later, aroused, excited, trembling, breathless, she returns to her home and enters her compartment, perhaps there to throw herself on her couch, to bite and tear at the coverlets, sobbing with unrelieved passion.

The excursions of such women, commonly, grow more bold. Perhaps they take to walking the high bridges, under the Gorean moons. Perhaps they fall to the noose of a passing tarnsman. Perhaps they attract the attention of a visiting slaver. His men receive their orders. She is brought to him and subjected to rude assessments. If she is found sufficiently comely she is gagged and hooded, and slave iron is locked upon her body. When this caravan leaves the city she is carried away with it, another girl, another piece of merchandise, in chains, bound for a distant market, and a master.

One of the most interesting examples of such a case occurred in Venna some years ago, in the vicinity of the Stadium of Tharlarion, where tharlarion races are held. Several young men captured for their sex sport what they took to be a slave girl, and thrust her, gagged, her hands bound behind her, into the corner of one of the giant tharlarion stables behind the stadium. They discovered only after her thorough and lengthy raping and their own apprehension that they had been lavishing their predatory attentions not upon a slave but upon a young and beautiful free female who had been masquerading as a slave. Obviously the case was complex. The decision of the judge was generally regarded as judicious. The young men were banished from the city. Outside the gate, lying in the dust of the road leading from Venna, bound hand and foot, was the girl. She was clad in the rag of a slave. The young men were seen leaving the vicinity of the city leading the girl behind them, her hands bound behind her, on a neck-rope.

Suffice it to say, in one way or another, the Gorean male

finds his sexual satisfaction. Now let us suppose, again, that he has now bought his first girl. This girl will generally mean much more to him, of course, than one who might be bought for him by, say, his parents. Every young man wishes to buy a girl who will appeal, personally, to him. Mothers, in particular, can be nuisances in such respects. The young man will wish to buy a helplessly passionate, hot-eyed slut whom he can whip-train, on her belly, kissing at his feet, to his every disposition and pleasure, and the mother will wish to buy him a "sensible girl." It is sometimes difficult for the Gorean mother, as for the Earth mother, to realize that their little boys have at last become men.

The young Gorean male, we shall suppose, now brings his girl home. This is now his own domicile, of course. There he is totally alone with her. There he puts his collar on her. She will wear it. It marks her as his. She looks up at him. She is at his feet. Let us suppose he gives her a few initial rapings, if only to get the feel of her body. He then orders her about, to cook for him and to serve him. Now, having had her, and having had her serve him, and owning her, fully, he can begin to get to know her. The same girl whom he bought as a mere piece of slave meat from a sales block, for his pleasure, we shall suppose, when brought home, and put in a collar at his feet, turns out to be a highly intelligent, sophisticated vulnerable and delicate organism.

In short we shall suppose that he discovers that he has purchased, as is often the case, not a mere slave, but a treasure. And she belongs to him! What a fortune, and joy, to own such a woman! He will want to watch her, to observe her least movements, to know her smallest thoughts. He will want to talk with her, and listen to her, and know her with a depth and fullness far beyond anything that might be accorded to a mere contractual partner. She is not merely a person who is living with him. She belongs to him, literally, and he prizes her. But he will take care to be strict with her. He will keep her in his collar; at night he may chain her at the foot of his couch. Her least insolence she knows may be rewarded with exact, swift punishment, such as the whip or close chains, nudity in the streets or public rental, or the deprivation of food. She understands clearly, and unmistakably, who is the master and who is the slave. She is happy.

How different are the relationships of the men of Earth

with women. On Gor I see, on the whole, contentment and love; on the Earth I see, on the whole, discontentment and misery. Who shall say which is best? Perhaps discontentment and misery are superior to contentment and love. Who knows? Goreans, however, we might note, whatever be the truth in these matters, have chosen contentment, and love. Let each choose, perhaps, that which is best for him.

"I shall, therefore, unless warned to silence, continue to speak," she said. She smiled wryly, and lifted her belled wrists from her thighs. "But I did not think, in the room of cosmetics, that I would be summoned before you, merely that you might hear me speak." She returned her hands, palms down, to her thighs. She lowered her head. "I thought that you might have other interests in me." She lifted her head. "I am ready for love, and with the abject helplessness of a slave," she said. "Will you not touch me, or caress me?"

I said nothing. But it pleased me mightily to know that the slave, the former Miss Henderson, was aroused before me. I remembered her from the restaurant, so long ago, in the candlelight, in the svelte, off-the-shoulder, white-sheath dress, so chic and lovely, carrying the tiny, silver-beaded purse. She now knelt before me, a slave girl on Gor.

"Alas!" said the girl. "What a poor slave I must be! I have been made-up for love, and I have been scented and belled, and my master does not deign to so much as touch me. I trust that I am not fully displeasing to him."

I regarded the girl. In the restaurant her wrists and ankles had not been adorned. Here they wore heavy circlets of sensuous bells. In the restaurant she had worn golden pumps, with a golden wisp of straps. Here she was barefoot, as if befitting for a female slave.

"What does it mean, my Master," she suddenly cried, "that you have not used me? Does it mean that I am not pleasing to you? Does it mean that you are only playing with me, and are saving me for another? Please do not let that be, my Master!" Then she put her head down, fearfully. "Forgive my outburst, my Master," she begged. "I am only a girl, and a slave." Then, again, she looked up. "You are not angry with me," she said. "Thank you, my Master." She tossed her head, the gesture, almost, of a free woman. "Doubtless you have had other women beg to grovel before you," she said. "Doubtless I am not the first. I wonder if you Masters scorn us for our needs. Scorn us if you must. We cannot help ourselves. We are slaves!"

I continued, of course, to remain silent.

"Not once have I seen your face, my Master," she said. "Either, as at the feast of Policrates, or now, you have been masked, or, in your chambers, in the holding of Policrates, when you forced me to so thoroughly and intimately serve you, I must do so in the darkness of the blindfold. You know me well, for you have stripped me not only of my clothing, but of my inmost thoughts. And yet, of you, I know nothing. I do not know your name. I do not know your face. I have never even heard your voice. Not once have you even spoken to your slave. But I know that curiosity is not becoming in a Kajira. Forgive me, my Master."

I did not speak.

"If you wish," she said, "put me under your whip. You may then see if I writhe well."

I said nothing.

"It is my hope," she said, "that you will not have me chained in the basement again tonight. That you have let me appear before you indicates that perhaps I may now be permitted a kennel on an upper floor. It is cold in the basement, and dark there. And it is hard to find the bits of food on the floor. Too, there are urts there. And I scream in the darkness, frightened, hearing them. They take the food, often before I can find it. I am afraid to sleep there, so cold and chained. Sometimes, too, the urts run across my legs, or nibble at them. I scream then, and I am frightened. Please, my Master, if it pleases you, may I have a blanket and a kennel. As I am the most miserable and lowest of your slaves, let it be, if it pleases you, the smallest and meanest of your kennels. I do not care. Only I beg a kennel. Forgive me, Master, if I am presumptuous. I want only to be pleasing to you."

I gave her no response, by voice, or expression or gesture. She would, thus, not know where it was that I would choose for her to spend the night.

"I shall wait to see, of course," she said, "what will be my Master's pleasure."

I fingered the slave whip, thoughtfully, hung by its handle loop on the arm of the curule chair.

"Forgive me, if I have displeased you, Master," she said, nervously. She eyed the whip. At my least whim she knew it could be used upon her. No woman who has felt the whip, even so much as a single lash, scorns it. It is a most useful disciplinary device for women.

She put her head down, swiftly, to the deep piling of the carpet, her hands beside her head. "Yesterday," she said, "sent forth from the house as a Coin Girl, I made six tarsk bits for you, my Master. I hope that you are pleased." She lifted her head. "Perhaps that is why you have let me be admitted to your presence this evening," she said. I snapped my fingers, and indicated to her that she should resume the position of the pleasure slave which she did, immediately and beautifully. "Perhaps you may like to hear me speak of the matter," she said.

I smiled.

"I take it that your attitude is favorable, and that I may speak on this subject," she said. "I shall proceed to do so, fully cognizant that the lovely slave who serves as my keeper in this house has doubtless already made you a full report."

I nodded. It was true.

I gestured that the girl should continue.

"Yesterday afternoon," she said, "locked in the chain collar of a Coin Girl, with the bell and coin box, on the leash of my keeper, I was conducted forth from the house. I thought that I was incredibly beautiful, and must be repeatedly raped. I learned swiftly, as men passed me, that I must be only a common girl. This brutal intelligence dismayed me. It seemed that I, who had been so vain of my beauty, must now learn to strive to please men."

I smiled inwardly. To me, of course, the slave before me was the most beautiful woman on all Gor. I was sufficiently objective, of course, to recognize that in the common appraisals of slave flesh, and its gradings, and in the prices commonly commanded by such flesh in the markets, she would count as only being somewhat above average. That would doubtless be hard for her to accept, but it was true. On the other hand, that she, who was, after all, exquisite, was subjected to such casual negligence in the streets was largely of my doing. I had sent men ahead of her, requesting that she be spurned and ignored, that as a favor to Jason of Victoria, dozens of men, my friends and fellow citizens of Victoria, good-naturedly cooperated in this ruse. In the streets it was the merry jest of the day.

"No one wanted me," she said. "And I grew ever more desperate. I knelt before men. I licked at their feet. I bit at their tunics. I groveled before them on my belly, begging them to consent to touch me. But for my troubles I was only ignored, or kicked and thrust aside. Then I would feel the leash stinging against the back of my legs and my keeper would order me up, and ahead, to try harder, warning me of the displeasure of my master, should I return with an empty coin box. I grew ever more frantic. Ahn passed. Dusk came. No men would touch me. Then it grew dark. Still no man would touch me. They would not even strip me, under a street lamp, to see if I might be of interest to them. Then it was time to be returned to the house. I began to fear for my very life."

I continued to regard her. The slave was to be permitted to continue speaking.

"Then," she said, "late at night, on the Street of the Writhing Slave, I encountered one whom I had once known on Earth, one once called Jason Marshall. The irony of it! I scorned him. I held him in contempt. I despised him as a weakling from Earth, so different from the masters of women, from men such as you, my Master, but now I must needs try to please him, and as a slave and Coin Girl! I opened my tunic to him. I knelt before him. I bit at his tunic. I licked and kissed, piteously and submissively, at his feet and legs. I begged him to be interested in me. I pleaded. I groveled. I did all that I could before him, as a piteous and lascivious slave, one begging his least touch, one helplessly his, should he but pay his coin, only a girl at his feet, one begging to be had, one supplicating her rape on the stones of the street. He, however, of course, a true man of Earth, extending me much respect, and according me courtesy and gentleness, declined to rescue me from my plight. I was to be returned to a stern Gorean master as a failed slave. But even he seemed soon to understand the consequences to a girl of that. He then was ready to place, in effect, as a gift, a coin in my box. My keeper, of course, would have none of that. There must be no payment without services rendered. Further, it was made clear to him, and to me, that my body would be physically examined for the explicit signs of his victory. He must then have me, truly. To this he reluctantly consented."

She put her head down. I did not hurry her. I listened to

the sound of the torches in the hall. Then, with a small sound of bells, those on her close-fitting collar, she lifted her head.

"I expected to be handled as though by a weakling of Earth," she said. "But I was not," she said. "Instead I found myself in the arms of a man of Gor, for that was what he had become. Too, though he knew that I had once been of Earth, he did not handle me as a woman of Earth, with respect and dignity, as I expected, but rather as what I now am, a Gorean slut, an imbonded, rightless slave. I could not believe it." She put her head down. She shuddered. "I was used with the full authority of the Gorean master," she said.

Again I did not hurry her. Two or three Ehn passed, I think, before she again lifted her head. She was trembling. There were tears in her eyes. "You see, my Master," she said, "I had loved him, even on Earth, but, too, I had despised him, for he was too weak to satisfy my needs. On Gor, too, he had never had me, even though we had shared a domicile. I had never permitted it." She straightened her back, smiling. "How amusing that must sound to you. 'I had not permitted it.' I, a natural slave, recognized by any slaver as such, had not permitted my rape! But remember, Master, that I was not then legally imbonded. How confused, and quaint and tragic, is a natural slave who has not yet been put in her collar!"

She paused and then, again, after a time, began to speak. "Later," she said, "courting slavery, for which I yearned in my heart, I went to the tavern of Hibron in Victoria, called the Pirate's Chain. I fell in there with one called Kliomenes, who was a lieutenant to the pirate Policrates. He got me drunk. Then, my senses reeling, I found myself, to the laughter of men and slaves, as I tried futilely to resist, being stripped and bound. I was carried to his galley. I was thrown to its deck, near the foot of the steps leading up to the height of the stem castle. My feet were tied to one ring and my neck to another. I lay there, cold and helpless, sick, exposed to their rude examinations. I could not even roll from where they had seen fit to put me. The oars were put outboard. I was taken to the holding of Policrates. There I was made a slave. There, at last, I was put in a proper collar.

"When the holding of Policrates fell his goods were divided among the victors. In the distribution of the goods I came to your house. It seems that at least a portion of your income is derived from the earnings of Coin Girls. In any event yesterday, I found myself put into the streets, under a keeper's watch, to earn coins for you, my Master. It was there that I met he whom I had loved and despised, Jason of Victoria. Consider my feelings, Master. He had never had me, and now he must have me! Too, I was completely at his mercy as an exposed slave. I loved him. I was prepared to yield to him, as a woman of Earth. I was certain of his tenderness, his gentleness, his solicitude. But what did I discover! What was done to me! Conceive of my feelings! He handled and treated me as a slave girl, one who might be any slave!" She put down her head, her face in her hands, weeping.

"Six times he had me," she wept, "six times, and he was merciless with me, casual and merciless! Then, when he was finished with me, he sent me from him, banishing me from his sight, our dealings done, the coins in the box on my neck." She wiped her eyes, and then put her hands, palms down, on her thighs. Still she did not lift her head. I listened to the crackle of the torches.

"I could not believe what had occurred," she said. "I had thought that I might be everything to him, and that he would be grateful for my least smile, but I discovered that I was nothing to him, and that he took merely for granted the most intimate services that I could conceive of delivering to him, they being no more than his due from a rented girl. Then, as though I might be a total stranger, he sent me from him." She threw back her head, and sobbed. Then she again put her head down.

"Forgive me my feelings and emotions, my Master," she whispered, "but there is more in this than you can know. There is in this more than you have been told. But how can I, a slave, stripped and helpless before you, conceal these truths? Doubtless my very body speaks them." There was much in what she suggested. It is extremely difficult for a woman naked and kneeling before a man to lie. Body-language cues make this almost impossible. "Let me therefore explicitly speak these truths," she said, "and hope that thereby my life may be preserved."

I took the whip from where it hung by its handle loop on the arm of the curule chair and placed it, its blades folded back against its handle, across my lap.

She raised her head, looking at the whip. She trembled. "Must I speak?" she asked.

She saw my grip tighten on the whip.

"Of course I must speak!" she said. "Forgive me, Master."
She looked down. "I submitted to him," she whispered, suddenly. "I submitted to Jason of Victoria. I yielded to him. I could not help myself!"

I smiled and she, looking up, saw me smile. She feared
then that I might have misunderstood her. "No, my Master,"
she said, "I do not mean merely that I submitted to him as
must any slave to any man to whom her master gives or rents
her." She saw that I still smiled. "No, my Master," she whispered, "I do not mean either merely that he induced in me the
spasm submissions of the bond girl, or that he enforced upon
me the fullness of the humiliating, ecstatic slave orgasms, so
far beyond anything attainable by the free woman, to which
any free man may subject the slave in his arms. No, rather
I mean something quite different. I mean that I yielded to
him as I had never before yielded to any man, save yourself,
my Master. As I had yielded to you, so, too, did he make me
yield to him."

I stood up, as though angry. With the whip I gestured her
to her belly on the soft, deeply piled carpet. She trembled, lying transversely on the carpeting near the edge of the dais,
before the curule chair, her hands beside her head, her fingers
clutching at the piling. "*He* conquered me, fully, and as a
slave," she said. "I confess it!" I examined her form dispassionately, and found it not displeasing. I then, with deft
touches of the whip, indicated that she should turn to her
back and lie in a certain position. With the sound of slave
bells she did so. She then lay on her back, before me. Her
body and left leg lay on the dais. Her right leg, and her right
arm and hand, were on the broad stair, leading to the height
of the dais. Her hands were below her hips, both that to her
left, and right, which was on the stair. The palms of both
hands were turned upwards, exposed to me.

"Yes," she wept, "he conquered me! Forgive me, Master! I
am only a female, and a weak slave!" I examined her beauty.
It was that of a slave. It was ravishing. '*How fortunate is this
fellow, Jason of Victoria,*' I thought to myself, smiling inwardly, '*to have conquered himself such a prize.*' Some men
conquer themselves. Others conquer women. "I love you,
Master," she said. "I love you. I love you!" She lifted her
belled wrists, her small hands, supplicatingly, piteously extended to me. "Forgive me, my Master," she said. "Do not

kill me. I do not wish to die. Let me placate you! Let me placate you!"

Things had preceded precisely as I had planned. Given sufficient time, and the obligation to speak, through natural associations and continuities she had confessed her love for Jason of Victoria to me. Let her now be terrified of the wrath of her Gorean master.

I cast aside the whip and, with two hands, seizing her by the waist, I lifted her foot from the dais; she was bent backwards in my hands, her head and feet down. "Forgive me, my Master!" she begged. Then I threw her back upon the dais. She pulled her legs up, frightened, and turned to the side.

"Please do not kill me, Master," she begged. I then, with two hands, seized her ankles and threw them widely apart, with a jangle of slave bells. I then ruthlessly had her. Later, I had her again, more methodically, her head hanging down, over the dais, on the broad stair leading to its height. Then, later, I pulled her supine to the height of the dais, and, not hurrying, spending much time looking into her eyes, and studying her expressions, had her before the curule chair.

I then, at last, with a cry of angry pleasure, withdrew from her, and stood up. I looked down upon her. There had been little sound save that of our breathing and of her bells. "I hope that I have pleased my Master," she said, frightened. As though angry I strode to the frame within which hung the small gong. With the fur-wrapped striking surface of the wand, removed from its rack, I smote the gong, once, smartly, decisively.

Swiftly, in a matter of moments, Lola ran into the room. The slave whom I had so richly used knelt, frightened, confused, on the height of the dais. "Quickly, Slave," commanded Lola, "come stand before me, at the foot of the dais, your head down." Swiftly the girl obeyed, trembling. Lola had brought with her the objects which I had specified in my instructions to her, issued even before the slave had been ordered to report to the cosmetics room.

The first object was the key to the slave's bells and collar. Lola removed the bells from her left ankle, putting them on the rug. "What is wrong, Master?" inquired the dark-haired slave. Lola then removed the bells from her right ankle, placing them, too, on the rug.

"I am sorry if I have displeased you, Master," said the dark-haired girl, frightened. Lola then removed the bells from the girl's left wrist. "Forgive me, Master," wept the girl. "I will try to be a better slave!" The bells, then, were removed from her right wrist. "Please, Master," wept the girl. "Please!" The key was then inserted into the small, heavy lock on the back of the girl's collar. "Please, my Master," begged the girl, "have mercy on me!"

Then the collar was removed from her, and placed with the belled anklets, and wristlets, on the rug. The beautiful slave, not daring to raise her head, shuddered visibly. It can be an extremely frightening thing for a slave girl to be between collars. What is to be done to her?

I then took the second object which Lola had brought into the room, an eighteen-inch length of Gorean binding fiber. Such fiber does not slip. It is designed for the binding of slaves and prisoners. The girl winced as I bound her wrists tightly behind her. I then took from Lola the third object which she had brought into the room. The slave regarded it with horror. It was a slave hood, with a gag attachment, common in many such hoods. "Do not kill me, Master!" begged the slave. "Please do not kill me!"

I thrust the thick, curled wadding of the gag deeply into her mouth. In her mouth it expanded. Then, using the cord and eyelets, I laced the two ends of the broad, flat binding surface, to which, in the front and the center, the wadding was attached, tightly together behind the back of her neck. She moaned. She was well gagged. She looked at me, wildly. It was a fitting gag for a slave, I thought. Then I took the attached hood and pulled it up and over her head, and then jerked it down, that her head be fully covered. Then, using its strap and loops, I tied the hood in place, securely shut, under her chin.

I then regarded her. The slave was well bound and hooded. I then removed the mask which I had worn, and thrust it in my pouch. I then threw her to my shoulder, her head over my back. She moaned. I then left the house of my friend. I was grateful for its use. The girl on my shoulder would know nothing of our destination. For all she knew she was being taken to a butcher shop, there to be dismembered for sleen feed. Such may be done to a girl, if it be the will of her master.

The former Miss Henderson, who had been so excruciatingly troublesome, and so tantalizingly beautiful, was now over my shoulder, hooded and bound, my slave. Lola would follow, in an Ahn. I was well pleased.

XIX

I WILL PLAN A PARTY;
A SLAVE IS TO BE INCLUDED
IN THE ENTERTAINMENT

In the Gorean streets I attracted little attention. It is not that unusual, in such streets, for a man to carry a naked slave, bound and hooded, over his shoulder. To be sure, such girls are often tied in a slave sack. The children that we passed in the streets, playing at marbles or stone toss, scarcely glanced up. Two children, however, one boy and one girl, did run and strike the slave. She started, and squirmed, on my shoulder under the blows.

I did not admonish the children. First, it was nothing to me that they had struck her, for she was a slave. Secondly, they were free persons, and free persons on Gor may do much what they please. It is slaves who must be careful of their behavior, lest free persons find it displeasing. The boy who had struck her, I believe, had been in a fit of ill temper. I think he had just lost at stone toss.

The girl, on the other hand, I think, had had far different motivations. She had not been involved in the game, but had only been watching it. Yet she had struck the slave by far the cruelest blow. Already she had learned, as a free woman, that female slaves are to be despised and beaten. The hatred of the free woman on Gor for the female slave is an interesting phenomenon. There are probably many reasons for this.

Among them, however, would seem to be a jealousy of the female slave's desirability and beauty, a resentment of the interest of free men in imbonded women, and an envy of the slave girl's psychological and biological fulfillments, and emotional freedom and joy. Something of the same hatred and contempt tends to be felt by masculine women on Earth towards feminine women. Perhaps they hate what they are not, and perhaps cannot be. The Gorean slave girl, incidentally, can be terrorized by the mere thought that she might be sold to a free woman. I glanced at the girl who had struck the slave. She was comely. I wondered if she might one day fall slave. If so, she, too, in her turn, would surely learn to fear free women.

I took a circuitous route to my house, with many twistings and turnings. The slave, in the darkness of the hood, bound and helpless, would have no idea of where she was being taken. This was the same house which we had earlier occupied together, when I had mistakenly permitted the slave the dignity and status of the free woman. I was fond of the house, as it was fit for my needs, and, indeed, I had made it more fit, by certain additions, for my pleasure, and for the work and holding of a slave. Too, I now owned this house, having purchased it with a few gold pieces, a small portion of my share of the spoils, taken from the holding of Policrates. Riches, too, there had been to distribute, of course, not merely females.

Indeed, as Goreans went, I was now a rich man. I could have afforded a hundred girls of the sort I now carried on my shoulder. But I wanted only this one. This one, alone, I had decided, would be ample to my needs. This slave, whom I recollected from Earth, long ago, was my selection.

The house, with its walled garden to the side, is set back, and on a small hill, into which it is partially built. I approached the house from the side, climbing the hill from the side, rather than frontally. Too, of course, I did not use the steps, which might have been counted. On the stone landing, before the heavy portal of the house, I stopped. I felt her squirm in terror on my shoulder. She knew we had arrived somewhere. But where? She knew only that we had climbed to a height.

I slid her from my shoulder into my hands and, turning her, took her by the back of the neck and the left thigh and lifted her high over my head. I held her that way for a moment. She moaned piteously, helpless and trembling. Was she to be cast from this height into a pit of sleen or perhaps into the cold waters of the Vosk? Then I lowered her again to my shoulder, her head this time forward. I could feel her shuddering in relief. Slowly I began to lower her, head first. Sensing her orientation she tried, desperately, to press her gagged mouth, beneath its binding and the leather of the hood, against my body, piteously attempting to please me.

I put her on her knees, on the stone landing, at the side of the door. She knelt with her knees widely apart, and then, piteously, opened them even more. She was in terror, desperate to appease and placate the master. I thrust the key into the door and unlocked it, and then replaced the key in my pouch. I looked down at my slave. I was pleased. I thrust the door open with my foot, and then bent down and picked up the slave. I held her in my arms. Then I crossed the threshold, carrying her. As a capture, a prize and a slave, in my arms, was she carried into the domicile of her master.

Within I put her on her knees, beneath the large beam, with the ring, chain and bracelets. The chain and bracelets had already been lowered. In moments I had untied her hands from behind her and locked her small wrists, before her belly, as she knelt, in the close-fitting steel of the bracelets. I then drew the chain back and through the ring, hauling her to her feet. She then stood with her hands high above her head. Her heels were just a quarter of an inch off the tiles.

In my house I saw fit to honor the customs of Victoria. No longer now did the girl seem frightened. Though she seemed apprehensive, now, as any slave in her position might well be, she had, as she had been pulled into position, shuddered with relief. She knew that she had been carried across a threshold as a slave, and had now been placed in a standard whipping position. This told her that her life would be spared, at least for the time, if she were sufficiently pleasing. And I had little doubt but what she would strive to be sufficiently pleasing.

I untied and loosened the slave hood, thrusting it up so that I might reach the gag. I unlaced the tight thongs, from behind the back of her neck, that held the gag binding in place. I then, carefully, little by little, extracted the curled, leather wadding of the gag from her mouth. She could now speak. I then thrust the binding and wadding, unrolled, up and under the slave hood, and readjusted the slave hood on her. I tightened it. She winced. But this time I had left her mouth uncovered. I had decided that it might please me to see her mouth, to note the trembling and movement of her lips as she spoke, and to be able to kiss those lips, or be kissed by them, if I should choose to permit this.

"I will be a good slave, Master," she said. "It will not be necessary to whip me."

I strode around her, to stand before her. She could not see me, of course, because of the slave hood, tight on her, which covered most of her face. This was, of course, by my intent.

"You may do with me as you please, of course, my Master," she said, quickly. "I am completely subject to your will." I saw her knees flex. There was a sound from the links of chain above her head as they suddenly drew against one another, for a moment suspending her full weight. She desired to kneel before me, but, of course, could not do so. The chain held her in place, perfectly. Then, again, she stood as she had before, her heels a quarter of an inch off the tiles. This is a discipline fastening, but it is not as cruel as that in which the girl is fastened on her toes.

"I meant no harm, my Master," she said. "I meant no harm!" I stood quite close to her, before her. She could doubtless feel my breath upon her body. A slave has no private space. "I meant no harm, my Master," she whispered. She lifted her chin, and extended her head towards me, pursing her lips. I gently touched them with my own. Then, delicately, we kissed. With my right hand I held her face so that she could not press her lips more fervently on mine. "I love you, my Master," she whispered. "I love you, my Gorean master."

I went from her to the side of the room, where was the wheel which controlled the chain and, nearby, on its hook, the disciplinary Gorean slave lash.

"Of course, my Master," she cried suddenly, delightedly. "I have been carried across the threshold. And now I have been put in whipping position! I am being introduced into a house, in which I am to be a slave. My mysterious master must, thus, be of Victoria, or of some other city in which are practiced the customs of the capture carry and the initiatory whipping!" The point of these customs, of course, is clear.

The girl knows that she is carried into the house as a

helpless slave, and then, in the initiatory whipping, learns that it is a house in which she is under discipline. These are thought to be salutary lessons for a new girl, when she is first introduced into a new house. To be sure, whether in Victoria or not, or in a city with comparable customs, new girls, in one way or another, are usually reminded, promptly and effectively, that their slavery is uncompromising and actual, and that they are fully at the disposition of their masters.

The former Miss Henderson, of course, had been in this house before. This was, however, the first time she had been brought into it as a slave. The slave girl, of course, sees a house much differently than does a free woman. Most simply she sees it as a house, and knows it, as a house in which she is a slave, whereas the free woman sees it and knows it as a house in which she is free. The houses are, accordingly, experienced quite differently. The free woman looks into a slave kennel but she, presumably, has never occupied it, the helpless prisoner behind its bars; the free woman may see chains but she, presumably, has never worn them; she may see the whip but she, presumably, has never felt it. She sees the door, a device by means of which she gains access to her dwelling, but can it have the same meaning to her as to one who has been helplessly carried through it, as a slave? Similarly, the free woman passes through that door whenever she wishes. She does not give it a second thought. It is only a door. To the slave, on the other hand, it is the portal to her master's house. It is, thus, a significant border in her world. Commonly, if the master is home, and she is not under orders, as in, say, running an errand, or conducting regular business, such as shopping or gardening, she must, on her knees, beg his permission to leave the house, usually specifying her itinerary and when she expects to return.

Similarly a free woman may look upon a wall and see there merely the side of a room, but the slave girl may see there an obdurate barrier, beyond which she cannot run, against which she could be thrown and stripped, a barrier at the foot of which, crouching in terror, she would have to await the pleasure of her master. The free woman may look upon the smooth tiles flooring a room but, presumably, she has never felt them on her naked flesh, on her belly, as she has kissed the feet of her master. Too, presumably, she will never have been beaten upon them, or forced, as a discipline,

to clean them, prone, her hands bound behind her, a small
brush held in her teeth. The free woman looks upon a stairwell. She sees a stairwell. The slave girl may also see a
place where she, if her master wishes, may be conveniently
tied to a railing and raped. Much sex between a master and
his slave is spontaneous and casual, occurring whenever the
master wishes, and not unoften when the slave begs for it.
The sweetness of these sometimes sudden and transient rav-
ishings, of course, does not replace the lengthy feasts of love
of which the Gorean is fond; rather, they merely supplement
them. They are, in their way, merely another attestation of
the condition of the girl, that she is truly a slave and must be
ready, at any time, and in any place, to serve her master's
pleasure. The same girl who, fed by hand, is lengthily ravished
over a period of Ahn, or even of a day or two, may, at another time, be merely told to stretch herself over a table. She
will do so, immediately, unquestioningly. She is a slave.

And how wonderously different does the bedroom of the
male seem to the free woman than it does to the slave. She
looks upon the couch of the male. She sees the slave ring at
its foot. She sees the furs of love, rolled against the side of
the wall. She sees the lamp. She sees, coiled beneath the slave
ring, a chain, with a collar or shackles. She sees the whip.
But these things, as she is free, mean little to her. Imagine,
however, if you will, her emotions if she entered that room as
a slave girl, stripped and rightless, bearing on her upper
thigh, just under her hip, the mark of bondage, her throat
clasped in the light, gleaming, close-fitting, locked circlet of a
slave. How different, then, would that room seem to her! She
is ordered to spread the furs of love. She does so, beneath the
slave ring.

She must light the lamp. She does so. She returns then to
the furs of love, and kneels upon them. She is then fastened
by her master to the slave ring. Perhaps this is merely done
by a single ankle ring, on her left ankle, or perhaps both of
her ankles are shackled, the length of chain running through
the slave ring. If this is done, of course, the chaining is such
that her ankles may be thrust widely, even painfully apart. Or
perhaps the collar is locked upon her, with its dependent
chain. She, then, feels the drag of the chain against her collar, and the chain, with its heavy links, between her bared
breasts; she knows well that she is chained.

Though the light of the lamp is soft and sensuous, it is quite adequate, by design, to illuminate her; she is under no delusion on this score; her tiniest movements and her subtlest expressions, she knows, will be fully visible to her master. This is as it should be; she is his slave. Some free women, incidentally, insist on making love in the dark, because of their modesty. If such a woman should be enslaved, however, she must learn to perform in full illumination, whether it be in the soft light of a common ravishment lamp or on a dock at midday.

We shall now suppose that the girl is kneeling before her master, on the deep furs, in the position of the pleasure slave, in the soft light of the lamp, chained to the slave ring. Do you not think that she will find that room different than would the free woman? The master walks about her, whip in hand. She tries to hold herself as beautifully as she can, that he will be pleased. Perhaps she lowers her head, frightened, submissively. She feels the butt of his whip under her chin, lifting it up. She must hold her head properly. She sees the master shake out the blades of the whip. Is she to be whipped, or raped, or both? But he folds back the blades and holds the whip before her. She kisses it, fervently, in token of her slavery and submission. He then drops the whip to the side, but where it may easily be grasped, should he wish to do so. He then lifts the chain and throws it to the side, over her left shoulder. He then begins to caress her, with the full and possessive caresses of the master, sometimes even holding her in place with her left hand behind the small of her back. She begins to moan. Then, when he wishes, she is thrust on her back on the furs. "Please, be gentle, my Master," she begs. But he will, or will not, as it pleases him. She lies before him, a slave, his to do with as he pleases. It is little wonder, then, I think, that the female slave experiences the bedroom of the male in a manner quite different from that of the free woman.

I observed the former Miss Henderson, chained in whipping position in my house, the tight bracelets holding her hands high above her head, at the termination of the chain, her heels a quarter of an inch from the floor, most of her face covered by the tightened slave hood. I felt moved to tenderness. Then I removed the Gorean slave lash from the wall. She was a slave.

I walked to a position behind her and to her left. Gently I slid the whip, the blades folded back, against her, moving it from her left thigh to her waist, and thence upward against her left side. "Yes, Master," she said. I walked about her. The slave was beautiful, and exquisitely figured. I then stood behind her, and slightly to her left. I shook out the blades of the whip, with a gentle loosening of the leather, so that she would know they were free.

"Yes, Master," she said. "I am a new girl, who is being introduced into the house."

Then I gave her ten strokes. This seemed to me a suitable number for such a purpose. She shook, gasping, in the bracelets. I timed the blows mercifully, and uniformly. I did not use a random timing, nor did I use a customized timing, in which the blows are indexed to the particular psychological and emotional condition of the individual slave. There are many ways to beat a girl. Against several of them there is no way that a woman can maintain resistance. I did not strike her with my full strength.

"Master kissed me earlier," she gasped, happily. "And Master did not strike me as hard as he might have!" She drew in a deep breath, and put her head back, delightedly. "I think that Master might care a little for his slave!" she laughed.

Angrily I went to the wheel at the side of the room, that to which the chain was attached. I put the whip on its hook, and angrily disengaged the wheel, and then turned it. "Oh!" she cried, suddenly drawn, painfully, to the very tips of her toes under the chain. I then locked the wheel in place, and seized again the whip from its hook. "Please, forgive me, Master!" she cried. "I am nothing! I am only a slave!" I then struck her ten times, savagely, with the unrestrained strength of a man. "Forgive me, Master!" she cried. "Oh!" she screamed. Then, sobbing, fighting for breath, she could only endure. After the tenth blow she hung helplessly in the bracelets, her full weight on the chain. I examined the beaten slave. I did not think she would soon again be presumptuous. Such presumptions, she had now learned, might entail penalties. Too, after this beating, I thought her position in the house might be clearer to her.

I tapped her on the back of the left shoulder with the whip. One more blow was to be struck.

"Yes, Master," she said, "that blow which is to remind me that I am a slave."

I then stood again behind her, and to her left. I grasped the handle of the slave whip with two hands. Then again, with unrestrained force, the hardest blow of all, was she struck. She cried out in pain. Then, again, sobbing, she hung in the bracelets, a whipped slave. This last blow is often, though not invariably, added to a slave's whipping. It is sometimes referred to as the *gratis* blow, or the mnemonic blow. Often it functions as little more than a stroke for, say, good measure. To be sure, whatever its purpose, it makes it very clear to the slave that she is fully under discipline, and that the master may, if he wishes, beat her how, when and as much as he pleases.

I went then to the side of the room. I replaced the slave whip on its hook. I released the wheel. With a rattle of chain the girl fell to her knees beneath the ring. I removed the bracelets from her and, by means of the wheel, returned the bracelets and the chain to their original positions. In place, overhead, rather toward one side of the room, they were visible, but not obtrusive. A girl, in her labors, might pass to and fro in the room many times a day, and not think of them, or notice them. But if she were to look for them, she would see them.

I looked to the girl who, naked, her face almost fully covered by the slave hood, knelt under the ring, on the tiles. I went and stood before her. Sensing my nearness she timidly put out her small hands, touching my calves and ankles. Then she put herself on her belly before me, her lips over my feet. "Forgive me for having displeased you, my Master," she said. I felt her lips upon my feet, kissing them. It is pleasant to have a beautiful slave at one's feet, thusly. "I am your slave, my Master," she said, "and I love you. I love you." Slowly she drew herself to her knees, still keeping her head down, kissing at my feet and ankles. "I love you, my Master," she said. "I love you." Then, slowly, kissing at my feet and legs, and holding them, she straightened her body before me. She lifted her head, in the hood. I saw her lips tremble. "I am totally yours, my Gorean master," she said. "I submit myself to you, fully, in all things, as your total and abject slave. Do with me as you will. I am yours."

I then disengaged her hands from my legs, and stepped

back. She extended her hands, piteously. "Master," she said, "have I displeased you?" She seemed small, forlorn and lost, on the tiles. "I shall try to overcome whatever might linger of my Earth-girl frigidities," she said. "I will try to be a full Gorean slave to you." I smiled to myself. An Earth woman brought to Gor and properly imbonded often proved to be among the hottest of slaves. "Have mercy on me, Master," she begged. "Please do not kill me!" I removed from its peg on the wall an opened slave collar. It was a standard collar, of a sort worn by many girls on Gor. It was both attractive and efficient. It would look well on a girl's throat, and it would hold, perfectly.

"Please do not kill me, Master," whimpered the girl. She put out her hands.

"A collar!" she cried, touching the metal. "A collar!" She reached out, holding my wrist, and kissed at my hand and the collar it held. She lifted her head to me, it mostly concealed in the tightened slave hood. "Do you deign to put me in your collar, my Master? Oh, thank you, my Master! Thank you! I want your collar! I beg your collar! Oh, please, Master, put your collar on me! Collar me! I am yours!"

It pleased me to have the former Miss Henderson, who had been such a haughty wench on Earth, naked before me, as a Gorean slave girl, begging my collar.

"Collar me, Master," she begged. "I am yours!"

I thrust her head back and, rudely, put the collar on her.

"Thank you, Master!" she breathed. "Thank you!"

I lifted her up, by the upper arms, half lifting her from her knees. Her head was back. I had collared her! She wore my collar! I shook her, in savage elation. She wore my collar!

"Master?" she gasped, frightened.

I then, wanting to scream with joy, twisted her and threw her on her belly to the tiles at my feet. She lay there, frightened, breathing heavily, her hands at the sides of her head. "Master?" she asked, frightened.

I looked down upon her, prone at my feet. She who had once been the haughty Miss Henderson, of Earth, now lay before me, on her belly on the tiles of my house, only a stripped slave on Gor. I saw the collar on her neck. It was mine, and locked. I had collared her! I owned her!

"Master?" she asked. What pleasure it gave me to see her as my collared slave!

I went to her and, with my foot, rolled her to her back. She whimpered, and threw apart her ankles. I smiled. What a little slave she was!

I stepped back from her, going to the center of the room. I then snapped my fingers and she crawled to me, and then, putting out her hand to determine my position, knelt before me.

"If I have annoyed or offended my Master," she said, "please permit me to appease or placate him, in the intimate manners of the female slave."

I said nothing.

"I thank my Master for his collar," she whispered. "I rejoice to wear it. I shall struggle to be worthy of it, the collar of such a man." Collars, incidentally, can be experienced quite differently by different girls. New girls, in particular, first finding themselves helplessly fastened in them, may find them distressing. For example, they cannot remove them. They are made to stay on their neck. The girl, seeing herself in the mirror, sees that her throat has been locked in what she, at the time, may take to be a shameful and degrading, even horrifying, symbol of bondage. This can distress, or dismay, her. Some girls even fear to leave the house in their collars, fearing that on the streets, unveiled, scantily clad and collared, they might die of shame. They are sometimes, mercifully, whipped from the portals.

In the streets they meet other girls in collars. Of course, they wear collars. They are slaves. Then, returning to her master, she is no longer so ashamed, and, in time, she will think little or nothing of the collar. Of course, she wears it. It is appropriate for her. She is a slave. It is undeniable, of course, that the collar is a symbol of bondage. That no one will dispute. On the other hand, how the collar is experienced is quite another matter.

Most girls, in fact, sooner or later, wear their collars with pleasure and pride. First, the collar is extremely attractive, setting off and enhancing, as it does, their beauty. Secondly it is almost dazzlingly seductive. It can excite men, and drive them wild. Few women object to this, though, to be sure, sometimes slaves fear the power of their collars, knowing, as they do, what effect their sight can have on men. Too, they know that the collar marks them, and they cannot remove it, as the helpless and fit objects on which may be practiced the predations of the mastery. Similarly, the collar often has an interesting "releasing effect" on the sexuality of the female.

A girl in a slaver's tent, for example, stripped and freshly collared, will often rage and sob, and cry out, and attempt to tear the collar from her throat. But when she finds she cannot remove it, she will often crawl on her belly, across the rugs, to the slaver's feet, begging to be had as the slave she now is. If she is comely perhaps the slaver will use her. If she appears less comely or clumsy, he will presumably order her out of the tent, to appeal to first one of his men, and then to another, to find one who is willing to use her. When she has learned something, he may then permit her to serve him.

If he has only a few girls he may "try her out" before putting her on sale. This could make a difference in the price he asks for her. The "releasing effect" of the collar on female sexuality is interesting and complex. Perhaps a word or two pertaining to the matter would be in order.

Wearing the collar, the girl knows that she is a slave, and, accordingly, that the fullness of her sexuality, in all its helplessness, delicacy and profundity, is now subject to the imperious beck and call of men. She knows, too, that she may now be summoned to perform sexually, and fully, by as little as the merest snapping of the master's fingers. Further, she knows that she will not be permitted the least restraint or inhibition, of any sort whatsoever, on her sexuality. Such things are simply not permitted to her. She is a slave. This condition tends, with its vulnerability and helplessness, as might be expected, to be an extremely arousing one for the female. She knows that she must be ready to serve, even on an instant's notice. This tends to keep her, as the Goreans say, rather vulgarly perhaps, "ready in her collar."

One would not say to a free woman, for example, when one had a moment to spare, "Strip, and run to the furs," but one, of course, would not even think twice before ordering a slave to do so. Furthermore, the slave knows that when the master arrives at the furs, she is to be waiting there for him, vulnerable and soft, eager, luscious and loving, his. To most women the very thought of being a female slave is fearfully fraught with sexual significance. They know very well the sorts of things that would be required of them. And, of course, they are not mistaken. If they had any doubts about it, these doubts will be swiftly dispelled, once they find themselves in the collar. They are not long left in doubt as to what it is to be a man's slave, totally.

It must be understood, of course, that the slave's sexuality is imbedded in an entire matrix of obedience, love and service. In her heart and mind these things are inextricably, and delicately and beautifully, intertwined. Her sexuality, commanded of her by her master, by the whip, if necessary, is, in one sense, but one aspect and expression of her total bondage; she serves fully, and in all things; yet, in another sense, her entire condition is, in its way, an expression of the depth, complexity and beauty of her sexuality. She ties her master's sandals; she looks up at him; she loves; she serves; she is the female. The slave girl, it might be mentioned, in connection with the "releasing effects" of the collar, is relieved of many social pressures to which the free woman, because of her freedom, must remain subject. The free woman, for example, may fear that men will learn of her sexual vitality. It would not do for her for them to know that she, that lofty creature, on the couch, is a helpless, panting, licking she-sleen. The slave girl, on the other hand, does not have this problem. She knows that she belongs to a category of women toward which respect need not be shown, and will not be shown. She, a slave, she knows, is expected to be an obedient, lascivious animal in her master's furs or, if permitted, on her master's couch. Indeed, she will be punished severely, if she is not. She is thus free, irreservedly, joyfully, gloriously, to revel in her sensuality. Furthermore, she knows that her most intimate performances and qualities are likely to be discussed openly and with candor by her master with others, perhaps even in her presence. Accordingly, rather than becoming ashamed of her sexual nature, she becomes quite proud of it, and often becomes competitive with her imbonded sisters, vying with them to become the most desirable slave in the house, or in the circle of her friends.

The slave girl, of course, will usually have many friends. These are, of course, almost always wenches collared like herself. Friends of her master will often bring their own girls with them, in visiting, and with these, after the men have been served, she may make friends, perhaps chatting in the kitchen. These girls may be exchanged among the men, but commonly they are not. Most masters are rather possessive about their slaves, particularly if they are fond of them. She may also, of course, meet girls in the streets, encountered in the neighborhood, or on her errands. The slave girl, almost always, has no dearth of friends. To be sure, they are likely only to be mere slaves like herself. Women desire, in their hearts, to be beautiful, helpless, conquered animals, owned and dominated by masters. The collar makes it clear to them that their dream has been enacted upon them; that, indeed, their dream, to their joy, has become their reality. They know that they are now in their place, and will be kept there. They are happy.

The "intensification effect" of the collar, incidentally, might also be briefly mentioned. Not only does the collar serve often to release the female's sexuality, and deeper nature, but it tends to deepen and intensify them. Knowing herself as an owned animal, rightless, one forced to submit, one who must obey in all things, who must yield wholly to the master, holding nothing back, she can be driven to almost excruciatingly ecstatic orgasmic heights, experiencing sensations and raptures, perhaps enforced cruelly upon her, of which the free woman, in her freedom, cannot even begin to dream.

A third reason why girls tend to wear their collars with pleasure and pride, aside from the attractiveness of the collar and its seductiveness, is seldom mentioned. That is, that the collar, in its way, functions as a symbol of interesting differences among women. It, like a wired seal of quality, attests to the value of the merchandise upon which it is fastened. "Beautiful enough to be collared" is a Gorean compliment, though perhaps a rather rude one, and one that one would not be likely to hear addressed openly and to the face of a free woman. "She has legs pretty enough to be those of a slave girl" is another such compliment. If the free woman should hear such compliments she will be scandalized. But she may also wonder if, indeed, she is beautiful enough to be collared, and if, indeed, her legs are as pretty as those of a slave girl. If, at some later time, she is collared, she will then, for all practical purposes, have the answers to her questions. Normally it is only the finest, and the most feminine and desirable of women who are enslaved. This makes sense.

There can be many dangers involved for the slaver in the capture of women for slave markets. Accordingly, generally, at any rate, he wishes to take no risks which are not justified.

Too, of course, he has his reputation to consider. When he leads his chain to market he wants it to be a chain of beauties. Too, of course, obviously, he is out to make money on these women. It is thus in his best interest to put up for sale the highest quality merchandise he can obtain. The collar, thus, particularly statistically, is a symbol of excellence and quality, of value, among women. It says, in effect, "Here is a woman whom men have wanted. Here is a woman whom men have found beautiful enough, and desirable enough, to enslave." The slave girl, in her tunic and collar, trembling, kneels in the street before the ornately robed, arrogant, imperious free woman. Perhaps she is even struck or kicked by her. But who, truly, is the superior woman? Many Goreans believe that it is the girl who kneels on the stones.

But, "officially," of course, the functions of the collar are simple. It serves to mark the girl as a slave, and identify her master. The true momentousness here, of course, is not the collar, but what it signifies, the condition of bondage. This condition, also, of course, could be signified in many other ways, for example, by such devices as a bracelet or anklet, or even a ring. But I think that there is no real competitor to the collar.

It is the bondage device, particularly on a girl, *par excellence*. It is beautiful, and the throat seems the perfect place for mounting the bondage symbol. On the throat it is prominently displayed, for all to easily see. One may see at a glance that she is slave. Too, the throat is beautiful, and soft and vulnerable. How appropriate then that it should be here, in this delicate, prominent and defenseless place that the steel, or the leather or chain, should be placed. Too, where else on the body, that the impossibility of escaping it could be more obvious, could it be placed? Surely the physics of widths dictates such a mounting. But, too, psychologically, where could it be more advantageously placed? Where else on the body might it be placed that its security, its effectiveness and its meaning could be more clearly brought home to its lovely captive.

The collar also, of course, has other utilities. For example, it can be useful in leading her about, either because of its ring, to which a leash may be attached, or in connection with a leash with a snap lock, which can be placed about the collar itself; similarly it is useful, in connection with various

forms of hardware, in fastening her to such things as trees
and slave rings; her hands, too, can be tied at her collar,
making it impossible for her to defend her beauties from the
master's assault. Lastly, of course, many animals wear collars;
in animals the throat seems a natural place in which to place
such an identificatory control and guidance device; the slave
girl, too, of course, is an owned animal. Thus it seems appropriate that she, too, wear her device in the same place.

I looked down on the slave before me. She lifted her head
to me. It was almost entirely covered by the tightened slave
hood. "I thank you for my collar, my Master," she whispered. "I am yours, and I love you." I took her hands in
mine and I crouched down, and, lifting them, touched their
small fingers to my face. "My Master has removed his mask!"
she said, surprised. "But then it does not matter," she laughed,
wryly, "for I am well and effectively hooded."

I then released her hands and stood before her. Immediately she assumed the position of the pleasure slave.

I looked upon her, at length. She was quite beautiful, the
former Miss Henderson, now only a rightless, nameless slave
at my feet.

With my hand under her chin I then indicated to her that
she should draw herself up from her heels. She did so, this
action bringing her body upward and forward, and bringing
her knees more closely together. "Master?" she inquired. I
then untied the straps of the slave hood. "Am I to be
unhooded?" she cried. "But Master is not masked!" I
loosened the hood. I might then remove it from her. "Am I
to be permitted to see the face of my Master?" she whispered. She put her hands on mine. Her lips trembled.
"Truly?" she asked. "Truly?" She felt my hands at the edges
of the slave hood. "But wait a moment, Master," she begged.
"Let me first kiss your feet!" I permitted this. She put her
head down, the slave hood loose on her head. I felt her lips
kissing my feet. "I love you, my Gorean master," she said. "I
love you, and I am yours." She then lifted her head, the slave
hood loose upon it. "Now unhood me, or not, as you will, my
Master," she whispered.

I took the hood with my two hands, and, keeping the edges
under, getting a good grip on the sides, rolled it an inch or so
upward on her face. I could now lift it from her with one

motion. Still, of course, as it was placed, she could not see. I looked down upon her. "I love you, and I am your slave, my Gorean master," she whispered.

I flung aside the slave hood and, quickly, holding my left hand behind the back of her neck, covered her mouth, pressing it tightly shut, with my right hand. I feared that she might cry out my name, and that it might then be necessary to put her again under the whip, for such an insolence. Her eyes, over my hand, were wild, and incredulous. I held her mouth pressed shut for some time, that she might collect herself and make her adjustments. Then, when her breathing was calmer, though still deep and swift, I released her mouth. I stepped back from her. I saw consternation in her eyes, and confusion and uncertainty. She did not speak. She did not know what to do. She did not know how to relate to me.

To make it easier for her I went to the wall and removed the slave whip from its hook.

"You?" she said. "You are my Gorean master? It was you who did those things to me?"

"Yes," I said. I shook out the blades of the Gorean slave whip.

"The strength, it was yours?" she said.

"Yes," I said.

"And it was you who forced slave yieldings from me?"

"Yes," I said.

"I am unclothed," she said.

"Of course," I said. I saw that she thought of turning from me, and covering with her hands, as best she could, her nakedness. But she did not do so. She still did not know how she must behave with me.

"I was whipped," she said. "Did you do that?"

"Yes," I said.

"I was well whipped," she said.

"Of course," I said.

"This collar?" she said, touching it.

"It is mine," I said.

"Yours?" she said.

"Yes," I said.

I saw that she had not yet called me "Master," but, too, I noted that she had, as well, carefully refrained from using my name. She was a highly intelligent girl.

"Surely you will now take the collar off me," she said.

"No," I said.

"Surely you know the meaning of such a collar on Gor," she said.

"Yes," I said.

"I cannot take it off myself," she said.

"I suppose not," I said.

"Then how am I to get it off?" she asked.

"You are not," I told her.

"It designates bondage!" she cried.

"Yes," I said.

She drew back, and looked at me. Then she laughed, with rather an uneasy, forced merriment I thought. "What a joke!" she laughed. "What a little fool I was! I thought for a moment that you were serious, that you might have an actual intention of keeping me as a slave!"

I did not bother responding to her.

"It is a joke!" she cried.

"You have been stripped, and collared and whipped," I said. "Does that seem to be a joke to you?"

"No," she said, suddenly, angrily, "it does not!"

"Do you object, in the least?" I inquired.

"No, no," she said, quickly. "Of course not!" I smiled inwardly. How uncertain she was as to her position, and condition. Slaves, of course, are not permitted to object to what is done to them.

She looked at me. "Now you have made me speak to you as though I might be a slave," she chided.

I did not speak.

"Your joke has gone far enough," she said, uncertainly, "now, please, please, let me rise, and take off my collar and bring me clothes."

I did not move. She remained on her knees.

"You cannot be serious about keeping me as a slave," she said.

I did not speak.

"You did not keep me as a slave before," she said.

"No," I said.

"See!" she laughed.

"I have no intention of repeating that mistake," I said.

"You cannot keep me as a slave!" she cried.

"Why not?" I asked.

"Because I am a woman of Earth, and you are a man of Earth!" she said.

"Men of Earth have often held women of Earth as slaves," I said. "Surely you are aware of this. Historically, slavery has been one of the most widespread and successful of human institutions. Most of the admired civilizations of the past have, in effect, been founded on slavery. Even today, on Earth, slavery is openly practiced in many parts of the world, and, in other parts of the world, it is known that there are men who keep their women secretly as slaves. Seeing a woman on the street it is often difficult to know whether, in the secrecy of her house, she is a slave or not. Too, who knows what will be the future course of civilizations on Earth. It is not impossible that slavery may again become a widespread and significant component in social fabrics, even in those of technological societies. The future is hard to read."

"Then the fact that I am a woman of Earth and you are a man of Earth need not protect me," she said.

"Of course not," I said, "no more than it has protected other women of Earth who, over the long ages, have found themselves placed in bondage."

"I see," she said.

"Incidentally," I said, "I reject not only your contention as being false, and obviously false, but its supposition, as well."

"Its supposition?" she asked.

"That I am a man of Earth, and you a woman of Earth," I said.

"Surely we are of Earth!" she said.

"It is true that our planet of origin is Earth," I said. "Is that all you have in mind?"

"No," she said.

"What else?" I asked.

"I do not know," she said. "It is hard to speak to you when I am stripped and kneeling!"

"Our realities have now changed," I said. "We are now of Gor."

"No!" she said.

"You lost the entitlements and prerogatives of the woman of Earth when, in a Gorean slave pen, your lovely thigh was branded."

"Please do not speak so explicitly of my body," she said.

"I shall do as I please," I said.

She put her head down, not responding.

"You were then only a girl of Gor, and a slave," I said.

She looked up, angrily. "And I seem to recall," I said, "that on the Street of the Writhing Slave, you cried out, confessing to me, that she in my arms was now naught but a Gorean slave girl."

She looked at me, angrily. She bit her lip.

"And, as I recall," I said, "she cried herself mine."

She looked at me, in fury.

"Have you forgotten?" I asked.

"No," she said. I was pleased to see that she was too shrewd to lie to me.

"But however you are pleased to view these matters," I said, "it makes little difference to me, whether we think of ourselves as being of Earth or Gor." I looked at her, naked before me. I fingered the slave whip. "Our realities, in either case," I pointed out, "remain much as they are."

"As an Earth man could own an Earth woman, you could own me on Gor?" she asked.

"Yes," I said.

"May I get to my feet?" she asked.

"No," I told her.

"You cannot own me!" she cried.

I did not deign to respond to so foolish an assertion. Did she not know that she was a branded, collared Gorean slave girl.

"Oh, I know you could own me," she laughed, uneasily, "but I know that you will not choose to own me."

"Why not?" I asked.

"You knew me from Earth," she said.

"That will make the owning of you all the more delicious," I said.

" 'Delicious'?" she said.

"Yes, 'delicious'," I said, "my beauty."

" '*Your* beauty,' " she asked.

"Yes," I said, " '*my* beauty.' "

"You speak of me as though I were a slave," she said, resentfully.

"You are a slave," I told her.

"But you will free me!" she cried.

"If that were my intention," I said, "it seems strange that I have just put my collar on you."

"But that was surely a joke, a cruel jest," she said.

"Feel the collar," I said.

She lifted her hands to the collar.

"Is it heavy or uncomfortable?" I asked.

"No," she said.

"It is a woman's collar," I said. "But it is close-fitting, of inflexible steel, and securely locked."

"Yes," she said.

"You have worn such collars before, have you not?" I asked.

"Yes," she said.

"You are familiar with them, and their effectiveness?" I asked.

"Yes," she said.

"Have I offered to remove it from you?" I asked.

"No," she said.

"Can you remove it?" I asked.

She looked at me.

"Try," I said.

Pathetically she struggled with the collar. Then, after a moment, she ceased her useless struggles. "No," she said, her fingers still hooked within the locked, obdurate band, "I cannot remove it."

"You may then fairly assume," I suggested, "that it has been fastened upon you."

"I know it has been fastened upon me," she cried. "I cannot get it off!"

"What sort of collar is it?" I asked.

"A slave collar!" she cried.

"Precisely," I said.

"Is it not a joke?" she whimpered.

"No," I said.

She looked at me, frightened.

"I am beginning to grow impatient with you," I said. "Perhaps you should be lashed."

She shrank back. "But you have brought me to our house," she said.

"Not our house," I said, "*my* house."

"You would keep me as a slave in the very house where once I was free?" she asked.

"Yes," I said. "But I have made certain improvements, bars and certain security devices, for example. Also, I have put in a new and stouter kennel for you and a new slave ring at the foot of my couch."

She looked at me, aghast.

"It is my hope that you will like them," I said.

"What sort of man are you?" she asked.

"One who will own you, fully," I told her.

"Then I am to understand," she said, "that it is possible that you might, in all seriousness, choose to keep me as your slave?"

"The choice is already made," I said. "It was made long ago."

"And what did you choose?" she asked.

"Are you stupid?" I asked.

"I am not stupid," she said.

"You speak as though you are stupid," I said. I wondered if, truly, she was stupid. If so, it would lower her value, considerably. I was growing weary of her fencings, her inanities, her protests. Did she think she was a free woman? Perhaps she must soon be reminded that she was a slave. That could be easily done.

"This is Gor," she said. "The choice, of course, is yours, totally." She looked at me, angrily. "What did you choose for me?"

"What do you think?" I asked.

"Freedom," she said, "respect, honor, dignity."

"No," I said.

"—Slavery?" she asked.

"Yes," I said.

"—Full slavery?" she asked.

"Yes," I told her, "total and complete slavery."

"I see that you must be taught the character and will, and the intelligence and power, of a woman of Earth," she said. She rose to her feet. "Take this collar off my neck, fellow," she said. "Do it now!"

I looked at her.

"I am calling your bluff," she said, "—Jason." Then suddenly she screamed, struck by the Gorean slave lash, her body stripped, stumbling across the room, striking against the wall, at whose foot she fell. She looked up at me, in terror, from the foot of the wall.

"Crawl to the center of the room, and lie there on your belly," I said.

Swiftly she did so.

"It is your bluff which has been called, little slave," I said.

She lay at my feet, shuddering, prone, her hands at the sides of her head.

"I will let you kiss me," she said. "I will even let you make love to me!"

I looked down upon her. I was furious. She had been an insolent slave.

"Let me be your employee," she said. "I am willing, even, to be your love employee! You do not need to pay me much. You do not need to pay me anything at all! I will work for nothing for you! Let me be your love servant! Sometimes I will even serve you as might a slave girl!"

"What did I ever think I saw in you?" I asked her. "What possible interest could I ever have thought I had in you?" I ran the whip along her side, and she shuddered. "To be sure," I said, "you are rather pretty, in a trivial and servile fashion." I continued to move the whip on her body, and she whimpered, helpless on the tiles before me. "I wonder what I could get for you," I said, "such a petty, stupid, worthless, meaningless, stinking little slave." She was whimpering. "Oh!" she said. "You do have the reflexes of the slave though," I said. "That would surely improve your price." She cried out in shame, putting the side of her head down to the tiles, her fingers scratching at them. "I think I shall put you up for sale, you pretty, meaningless little brute," I said.

"Oh, oh," she cried.

"Are you hot in your collar, little brute?" I asked, angrily.

"Oh!" she cried. Then she began to sob. Her tears fell to the tiles.

"But before you could be put up for sale," I said, "you must learn certain lessons, which apparently you have earlier failed to master, on the position, and condition, of the Gorean slave girl."

She shuddered with fear. She saw now, on the tiles before her, gently swinging, the shadows of the five loosened blades of the Gorean slave lash.

"You will not whip me," she said. "Surely you will not whip me!"

I then, furious with her, savagely laid the whip to her beauty. She writhed, and screamed, and twisted, and turned beneath the whip, from her belly to her back, and to her sides, and to her back, and to her sides again, and back, trying to fend the blows. She had displeased me. She had dared even to speak my name.

Then she lay before me, on her back, her legs drawn up, her hands extended. "Please, Master," she wept, "do not beat me further."

"What did you call me?" I asked.

"Master," she said. "Master. Master!"

"Why?" I asked.

"Because you are my Master!" she said. "Because you are my Master!"

"Are you sure of that?" I asked.

"Yes, Master," she said.

"Have you any doubt of it?" I inquired.

"No, Master," she said. "No, Master!"

"What are you?" I asked.

"A slave!" she cried.

"Whose slave?" I asked.

"Yours," she wept, "yours, Master!"

I then permitted her to scramble to her knees and she knelt before me, kissing at my feet. "You seem not as vain and arrogant as you were before," I said.

"No, Master," she said.

"Perhaps you have learned a little more of your slavery now," I said.

"Yes, Master," she said.

"What do you wish to do?" I asked.

"Please my Master," she said.

"The answer is suitable," I said.

"Thank you, Master," she said.

"Lift your head," I said.

She did so, fearfully, looking at me.

"Drop to your hands and knees, to all fours, and turn away from me," I said.

"Yes, Master," she said.

"You spoke my name," I said. "It is strange that you, a Gorean slave girl, should have made that mistake."

"Yes, Master," she said, "but I have been well whipped."

I then struck her again with the lash. "Oh!" she cried.

"Perhaps you should have been slain," I said.

"Forgive me, Master," she said. "Please, no, Master."

"Oh!" she cried out, in misery, the lash again swiftly falling upon her.

"And you were lax in your deference," I said.

"Yes, Master," she said. "Forgive me, Master."

Again I struck her.

"Did you think that such things would go unnoticed?" I asked her.

"No, Master," she said. "Forgive me, Master."

Again I struck her.

"And you were insolent," I said.

"Yes, Master," she said. "Forgive me, Master!"

Again I struck her.

"Did you expect your insolence to be overlooked?" I asked.

"No, Master," she said. "Please, please, forgive me, Master!"

"Oh!" she cried, in pain, once more well lashed.

Her head was down. Tears were upon the tiles.

"What shall I do with you?" I asked.

"I am your slave," she said. "You may do with me whatever you wish."

"That is known to me," I said.

"Yes, Master," she said.

"Why were you insolent?" I asked.

"It is difficult to speak in this position," she said.

"Speak," I said.

"When I saw that it was you, and remembering you from before, I sought to exploit your weakness, and conquer you. There is some gratification in this for a woman, for she is then a little bit like a man, a master, which she knows in her heart she is not. Too, it pleases her to torture weak men, men too weak to put her in the chains she longs to wear. But these gratifications, ultimately, are shallow and empty, and we, in our hearts, know that. Each sex has its place, and neither will be happy until it occupies that place. The place of man is master; the place of woman is slave. Gorean men, of course, do not see fit to tolerate our nonsense. They put us promptly in our places. They make us slaves. Had you not been from Earth, I would not have dared to behave as I did. Seeing you, remembering you from before, it did not even occur to me that I might be kneeling before one who had become, truly, a Gorean male. I wish that I had understood that, clearly. I could have saved myself much pain. Women engage in

battles which they yearn to lose. We wish to be overwhelmed
and conquered. That is why we fight. If we do not protest
and fight, of what value to a man, we ask ourselves, will be
our conquest? But, of course, I should not have fought you. I
am only a slave girl, a girl already collared and conquered. I
am not a free woman. It was presumptuous of me to indulge
myself in the vanities of a free woman. I am a slave. I should
have submitted myself to you, immediately and fully. Forgive
me, Master. It is my hope that you will permit me to live."

I regarded her. She was pretty, in my collar, and on all
fours.

"May I explain my behavior further, Master?" she asked.
"It may make you regard me less harshly."

"Do so," I said.

"I want to be a slave," she said. "I feared you would free
me. It was thus that I challenged you. It was thus that I tried
to incite you to my conquest. It was thus that I tried to make
you angry, that you might make me your slave, and keep me
as such, uncompromisingly."

"That was not necessary," I said.

"I am now well aware of that, Master," she said. "I did not
know it at the time, however."

I said nothing.

"My behavior, however foolish it might have been, was
motivated by a desire to be kept in bondage," she whispered.
"Perhaps now you will think more understandingly, more
pityingly, of your girl."

"So you desire to be a slave?" I said.

"Yes, Master," she said, "fervently."

"And you are a slave," I said.

"Yes, Master," she said, "completely."

"Do you think that you are free, or that you have any
rights whatsoever?" I asked.

"No, Master," she said. "I know that such delusions are
not permitted to a Gorean slave girl."

"Do you not fear your bondage?" I asked.

"Yes, Master," she said, "and sometimes we fear it terribly,
the uncertainty and the terrors of it, knowing that men can
do with us what they please, but these things heighten our experience, adding zest and spice to it, making it more meaningful, and, too, without them, we know that we would not

truly be in bondage, which is the condition for which we yearn."

"So you accept the miseries and terrors of bondage?" I asked.

"Willingly, and gladly, Master," she said, "and did we not do so then unwillingly and tremblingly must we accept them, for we are slaves."

"Do you like being a slave?" I asked.

"Yes, Master," she said.

"You are worthless, aren't you?" I asked.

"Yes, Master," she said, "except in so far as I might have some small value as a man's slave. I do not know my current market value."

I, too, did not know her current market value. Such things can shift from day to day. They are subject to considerable variance, being functions of many factors, such as the girl herelf, her intelligence, and training and beauty, the money in the economy, the conditions of supply and demand, and even the market in which she is sold and the time of year that she is put upon the block. A girl who is sold in a prestige market and, in the afternoon before her sale, placed with other lovely inmates within the chromed, ornate bars of an exhibition cage, has moved and posed upon the instructions of prospective bidders, is almost certain to bring a higher price than another girl, who by the hair, is pulled from a crowded, wooden, bolted cage and thrown upon a sales platform, or who, say, is sold from one of the cement, public viewing shelves of a common street market. Too, generally girls bring higher prices in the spring. I have little doubt that there is some intensification of the slaving done on Earth at a certain time of year, that the captured girls may be brought to the spring markets. Many Earth-girl slaves, on Gor, comparing notes, discover that they were sold in the spring. The more intelligent among them realize that this is not likely to have been a coincidence. They then have a deeper and more active appreciation of the intelligence, methodicality and organization of the men who saw fit to bring them to Gor.

Suddenly, angrily, I lashed her with the whip. She shuddered, struck. "Do you like that?" I asked.

"No, Master," she said, "but I love it that you can do it to me, and will, if I am not pleasing to you."

I walked around, before her. "Worthless little trollop," I said.

"Yes, Master," she said.

"Are you conquered?" I asked.

"Yes, Master," she said, "I am conquered."

"Totally?" I asked.

"Yes, Master," she said, "totally."

"Can a man respect such a conquered woman?" I asked.

"No, Master," she said. "But perhaps I might have the interest of the conquered slave for him."

I crouched down before her. She was still on all fours.

"You are a poor slave," I said.

"Yes, Master," she said.

"Yet," I said, lifting her chin with the whip, "you are pretty."

"In a trivial and servile way," she smiled.

"Yes," I said. "And, too," I said, "you have good slave reflexes."

"Which you have not seen fit to exploit, my Master," she whispered.

"I wonder if I should sell you," I said.

"Please do not sell me, Master," she said.

"I will if it pleases me," I said.

"Of course, my Master," she said.

I lowered the whip, and, crouching before her, continued to regard her.

"Is Master truly thinking of selling me?" she asked.

"Yes," I said. She had displeased me this evening. Too, I thought I saw her this evening more objectively than ever before I had seen her. I saw her now as little more than a pretty triviality.

"I would bring so low a price," she whispered, "that perhaps Master might keep me."

I stood up, whip in hand. I looked down upon her, on all fours before me. There was something in what she said. She would probably not bring a high price. Perhaps she might as well be kept, at least for the time. There did not seem much point, at least at the moment, in sending her to a market. Too, she was pretty, if only in a trivial, servile way. Too, she had good slave reflexes. Surely I could find uses for her around the house.

"Master?" she asked.

I walked around, behind her.

"Master?" she asked, frightened. She knew she might now be unexpectedly lashed.

"I shall keep you, at least for the time," I said, "to see if you work out."

"I shall endeavor to work out, Master," she cried, joyfully.

"Am I to be kept in full slavery?" she asked, not daring to look around.

"Yes," I said.

"In what slavery, or slaveries, will Master place me?" she asked.

I looked at her position. "Perhaps in the slavery of the she-quadruped," I said.

"Master may do so, if he wishes," she said, "if it pleases him, or amuses him."

In this form of slavery, which is commonly used for disciplinary purposes, or for the amusement of the master, the woman is not permitted to arise from all fours; similarly she is not permitted human speech, though she may signify needs and desires by such means as cringing, and moaning and whimpering. Not permitted the use of her hands, save as a means of locomotion, she must also eat and drink from pans set on the floor, or, sometimes, to satisfy her thirst, she must lap the water permitted to her from puddles or lick pillages from the tiles; too, it is not uncommon to chain her near her master's feet, while he dines, that he may, if he wishes, throw her scraps of food. She will also be taught tricks, through which paces she may be put for the entertainment of her master's guests, such things as begging, lying down, rolling over, and fetching his sandals in her teeth. And, needless to say, when her master wishes to use her sexually, it will be in a position common to the she-quadruped.

This form of slavery, incidentally, is often imposed on captured Ubaras. After a time, it is not unusual for the Ubara, on her belly before her master, given an Ehn in which to speak, to beg, in lieu of the slavery of the she-quadruped, that she be taught the salacious arts and lascivious dances of the female slave, that she may then be less a mere amusement for her master than a feast of slave pleasure for him. Her plea is usually granted. Such women tend to become superb slaves. They know, of course, that they may be, at any moment the master pleases, returned to the slavery of the she-quadruped.

I walked around, before the girl. "You may kneel," I said.

"Thank you, Master," she cried, joyfully. She was not then, at least, to be put into the slavery of the she-quadruped. She looked up at me. "I love you. I love you, my Master," she said.

"Kiss the whip," I told her.

"Yes, Master!" she said. She kissed it, fervently, again and again. The former Miss Henderson, of Earth, kneeling naked before me, now knowingly my collared slave, kissed my whip.

She looked up at me, happily.

"Do you think that you are much of a slave?" I asked.

"No, Master," she said.

"You need a bath," I said.

"Yes, Master," she said.

"Your body smells," I said.

"Yes, Master," she said.

"It stinks," I said.

"Yes, Master," she said. "Forgive me, Master." To be sure, her pretty little body stank. This was little wonder, considering what her experiences had been, and the beatings I had put her through. Too, it was covered with dirt and sweat, much of the dirt in small, fine rolls on the fairly complexioned, exposed flesh.

There were tears in her eyes.

I heard then a sound at the door.

"On your belly," I told her.

Swiftly she fell to her belly on the tiles before me, her hands at the sides of her head.

"Master!" she said, then hearing someone at the door.

"Lie quietly, Slave," I said, "or you will be whipped."

"Yes, Master," she said.

"Who is it?" I called.

"It is I, Lola," I heard. "I have brought your things." She had followed me, dallying according to my instructions, to give me time to introduce the new girl into my house.

I went to the door and, opening it, admitted Lola. She entered, carrying my gear, that which I had taken to the other house. She knelt deferentially before me. "I kneel before my Master," she said. "You may arise," I said. "Thank you, Master," she said. "Put my gear to the side," I said. "And lock the door." "Yes, Master," she said. She did these things, and then walked to the center of the room. She looked down at the prone slave. "Well, what have we here," she asked, "a well-tamed, well-whipped slave?"

The prone slave was silent, trembling.

"Well?" asked Lola, suddenly, viciously, kicking the girl in the side.

"Yes, Mistress," cried the girl, "I am a well-tamed, well-whipped slave!"

"My Master knows well how to handle a woman," said Lola.

"Yes, Mistress," said the girl.

"Do you remember that, when you were free, you once took me to the docks and sold me?" asked Lola.

"Yes, Mistress," said the girl, "but now, I, too, am only a slave."

"Do you think you will make a good slave?" asked Lola.

"I will try, desperately, Mistress," said the girl.

"Who is first girl?" asked Lola.

"I do not know, Mistress," cried the slave.

"Lola is first girl," I informed her.

"You are first girl, Mistress," cried the slave, "you are first girl!"

"Have you ever seen your collar?" asked Lola.

"No, Mistress," said the girl. "When it was fastened on me, I was hooded."

"Would you like to see it?" asked Lola.

"Yes, Mistress," said the girl.

Lola, from a chest near one wall, fetched forth a mirror, which she held close to the tiles, that the prone slave might for the first time see the collar in which she had been placed.

"It is beautiful," breathed the slave, touching it, "it is beautiful!" I smiled. It was only a common collar, of a sort which many girls on Gor wore. Yet, to be sure, it was attractive. It, like most slave collars for women, was designed for both beauty and security.

"You know the meaning of a slave collar, don't you?" asked Lola.

"Yes, Mistress," said the girl.

"You look well in one, don't you?" asked Lola.

"Yes, Mistress," said the girl.

"You belong in one, don't you?" asked Lola.

"Yes, Mistress," said the girl.

"There is writing here on the collar," said Lola. "It says, 'I am the property of Jason of Victoria.' "

"Yes, Mistress," said the girl.

"It will well serve to identify you, will it not?" she asked.

"Yes, Mistress," said the girl.

"Is what it says true?" asked Lola.

"Yes, Mistress," said the girl, "it is true!" I thought I saw her shudder with pleasure on the tiles.

In a moment Lola had replaced the mirror in the chest, and closed the chest. She then came to where I stood. Together we regarded the prone slave. "She is a pretty little thing," said Lola.

"I think she will prove satisfactory," I said, "for the purposes for which I require her, those of a common slave, a low slave, one to be set chores about the house, and one from whom full domestic services will be required."

Lola looked at me.

" 'Domestic services' in the Gorean sense," I said.

Lola laughed. Certainly the former Miss Henderson, of Earth, should have her sensuous possibilities exploited. How absurd it would be to permit those conquered curves to languish.

"What are your commands, Master?" asked Lola.

"In two days, in the evening," I said, "I shall have a small supper here, nothing pretentious, just something for a few friends. Substantially the affair will be catered by the tavern of Tasdron, but there will be much shopping and cooking for you, too, to do."

"I understand, Master," said Lola.

"The house, of course, is to be spotless," I said.

"Yes, Master," she said.

"And I shall also depend upon you for decorations, that the house may appear festive, lamps and ribbons, and flowers, and such."

"Yes, Master," she said.

"Too, see to it that some small, tasteful entertainment is provided."

"Yes, Master," she said.

"If things are not perfect," I said, "I shall not be pleased."

"Master will be pleased," she said.

"It is late now," I said.

"What of her?" asked Lola, gesturing with her head toward the prone slave.

We walked over to where the former Miss Henderson lay. I turned her over with my foot, and looked down upon her.

"She does not even know how to lie at a man's feet," said Lola. She then crouched down and turned the girl's hands so that their backs rested on the tiles, and the soft, open palms were vulnerably exposed to me. Also she lifted her left knee, that it might be flexed. "There," she said, "that is better." There are many ways, of course, for a woman to lie at a man's feet. Lola had selected, however, one of the loveliest.

The girl looked up at me, frightened.

I walked about her and, with my foot, turned her again to her stomach.

"What is to be done with her?" asked Lola.

"Clean her stinking slave's body," I said, "and then kennel her for the night."

"Look," said Lola, suddenly, "she is unconscious." She bent down beside the girl. "She has fainted," she laughed.

"It has been hard on her," I said. "She had to learn much this evening."

"In a collar a girl must learn quickly," said Lola.

"It is true," I said.

I turned away. I was weary.

"Master," called Lola.

"Yes," I said.

"How is she to be treated?"

"You are first girl," I said. "You hold switch rights over her. See that she is worked well."

"Full discipline?" asked Lola.

"Of course," I said.

"Excellent, Master," said Lola.

I hung the slave whip on its hook, and then went to the stairs, and, wearily, began to climb them. "Master," called Lola. When I reached the height of the stairs and stood upon the landing before my bedroom door, I turned to look down upon Lola. "Yes," I said. "Are you certain that, when I have cleaned her, you do not want me to send her to your room?" she asked. "No," I said. "I do not even want to see her until the party."

"Yes, Master," said Lola. "Master."

"Yes," I said.

"You mentioned entertainment."

"Yes," I said.

"Is this pretty little slave," asked Lola, indicating the unconscious former Miss Henderson, "to be included in the entertainment?"

"Of course," I said.

XX

THE PARTY;

AFTER THE PARTY

"Another bit of larma, Master?" asked the slave, kneeling behind me and to my left. I turned and, from where I sat cross-legged behind the low table, removed a small, crisp disk of fried larma, with a browned-honey sauce, from the silver tray. I regarded the slave. She put her head down, deferentially. She wore a tasteful garment of bluish gauze, in three layers, which fluffed about her. It came high on her thighs. I could see that her breasts in the garment, as she knelt, were exquisite. Her arms and feet were bare. Her hair was quite dark. My collar was lovely on her throat. I then turned my attention again to the dancers.

There were three of them in blue silk and golden collars. Lola had been fortunate enough to make arrangements for their rental only this morning. They belonged to a fellow who was en route to Port Cos, and thence to Turmus, and thence to the island of Cos itself, where it was his intention to exhibit and vend them. She had found them in holding cages, near the spice wharf. The address of their master, who was residing in an inn nearby, was given to her by their keeper. They were due to be shipped west to Port Cos at noon tomorrow. Tonight, however, he was pleased to make some coins on them.

"They are beautiful," said Glyco, the merchant of Port Cos to whom we owed so much. It was he who, in effect, had organized the resistance of the river towns to the pirates, and had had the good sense and fortune to recruit the redoubtable Callimachus of Port Cos as his field commander, a man without whose military skills and reputation on the river our projects might have been doomed to failure.

"Thank you," I said.

I looked about the table. Seven men, including myself, were present, Glyco, high merchant of Port Cos; Tasdron, Administrator of Victoria; Aemilianus, leader of the naval forces of Ar upon the Vosk; Calliodorus, captain of the *Tais*; and my friends, Callimachus and Miles of Vonda, who had brought with him his slave, Florence. Earlier, as a portion of our entertainment, she had played on the lyre, and sung for us. She had been warmly applauded, which, I think, pleased muchly both the shy slave and her master. Miles of Vonda had had her trained in these skills. As a free woman she had been, in effect, without accomplishments. Now she had additional ways in which to please her master. She now knelt behind her master. She wore a yellow tunic, and her collar.

I watched Shirley, the blond, voluptuous slave whom I had taken from Reginald, of the *Tamira*, in the battle on the river. She was one of three women whom I had had following our victory over the pirates, the other two being Lola and the former Miss Henderson. For this night Lola, who was first girl, had dressed Shirley much like the other slave, save that the gauze of Shirley's garment was yellow. For the last few days I had been boarding Shirley at a kennel in Victoria, but I had had her brought home this evening that she might help with the serving, and for another reason. She, kneeling, poured wine from a narrow, long-spouted silver vessel into the cup of Aemilianus, of Ar's Station. At the kennel, incidentally, I had arranged for Shirley to receive the whipping which had been due to her for having lifted her head without permission on the deck of the *Tina*. Gorean masters seldom forget such details, and their girls know it. This helps in the maintenance of their discipline. Lola was in the kitchen, supervising the food and service. She was not to be permitted to present herself until later, and then she would do so in the manner of my choosing. She knew only that she was in some way to be involved in my entertainment.

I again turned my attention to the dancers. Their movements were graceful and decorous. One would scarcely know that they were slaves, save, of course, that they wore collars and danced their beauty for men. Their movements were lovely, and refined. Free women might even have been present. This was suitable for the type of party which I had planned. This was not the type of party at which, say, the women of the enemy are forced to dance naked and, afterwards, are to be allotted to the victors as slaves, according to the whim of the commander or according to the fall of the dice. Similarly it was not one of those parties in which a given number of slaves must dance within a circle of free men, of equal number, with whips, stripping themselves to the strokes of the whips and then dancing towards the men. The man who does not accept the woman whips her back from him; similarly the woman who does not dance toward a man is whipped until she does. It is common in this form of dance to make each woman, dancing to each man, go about the circle at least five times. In this way the men have a chance to inspect the women, and consider which ones interest them. Needless to say, it is not long before the women are striving desperately to please the men. Only when she has sufficiently pleased a man is she permitted to crawl from the dancing circle to the cushions of her master for the Ahn.

The lead dancer reminded me somewhat of the slave, Melpomene, who had once been the Lady Melpomene, of Vonda. She was similarly figured to Melpomene; similarly, she had the same dark hair, complexion and high cheekbones as Melpomene. She was not Melpomene, however. I smiled to myself. I doubted that Melpomene, whose slave heat had been ignited, could have managed to dance in such a refined fashion before men. Even had she striven to do so I think that small expressions and subtle movements would have betrayed her, to the detriment of the type of dance which she was supposed to be performing. I regarded the dancers. I supposed that if, at some time in the future, their passions were to be ignited, then they, too, would be ruined for this particular type of dance. I was fortunate, thus, to have been able to obtain them when I did. Too, of course, doubtless their master would keep a close eye on them, at least until he had managed to get a good price for them. After that, what would it be to him if they learned, in the arms of a strong master, what it was to be a full slave.

I wondered where Melpomene was now. Having seen her dance I had little doubt but what she would be being used as a dancer. It takes a long time, of course, for a woman to become a good dancer. She might spend years in low taverns, or as a carnival dancer, or even as a street dancer, for provocation and use, on her leash, before her skills develop to a point at which she is good enough, as it is said, "to be permitted to dance before a Ubar."

"More, Master?" inquired the slave in bluish gauze, in the gleaming collar, kneeling behind me and to my left.

"Yes," I said.

With a serving prong she placed narrow strips of roast bosk and fried sul on my plate.

"Enough, Girl," I said.

"Yes, Master," she said.

There were seven musicians, who furnished the music for the dancers, a czehar player, their leader, two kalika players, three flutists and a kaska player. Tasdron kindly had brought these fellows from his tavern. Too, with him he had brought a girl, the former Earth girl, Peggy, who was one of his slaves. She was in a brief, white tunic, and collar. She hovered in his vicinity, waiting upon him. I noted, however, that she could hardly take her eyes from the mighty Callimachus. Tasdron and I had, together, agreed on the pertinence of her presence at the feast.

There was then a swirl of music and the dancers had finished. We well applauded them. They had been superb. They stood before us in their blue silk and golden collars, their heads down. Then, smiling, to another swirl of music, they turned and hurried from the room, going to the kitchen, where their master would be waiting for them. They were barefoot. There were golden bangles on the left ankle of each. In the kitchen they would be stripped of their costumes, which were not to be soiled. They would then kneel and be fed by hand. When they were finished they would be put naked in slave cloaks and, fastened together in throat coffle, conducted back to their holding cages near the spice wharf. Tomorrow, at noon, on the same ship on which their master had booked passage, they were to be shipped to Port Cos, and from thence, via Turmus, eventually to the island of Cos, in some city of which, probably Telnus, they would be put up for sale. The musicians now played unobtrusively in the background.

"She is a pretty one," said Glyco, indicating the slave in bluish gauze, barefoot and bare-armed, who was deferentially serving us. She put down her head, blushing. "You have been commended," I said to her. "Thank you, Master," she said to Glyco, kneeling, head down. "A girl is grateful, if she has been found pleasing by a free man." "What is her name?" asked Glyco. "I have not yet given her a name," I said. "I see," said Glyco. "You may continue your serving," I said to the girl. "Yes, Master," she said.

"I propose a toast," said Aemilianus, rising.

"A toast," we called. Shirley hurried about, making sure there was wine in the goblets. Callimachus drank water, but he permitted a drop of wine to mix in the water, that the ceremony of the toast might be one in which he fully shared. Wine, incidentally, is often mixed with water in Gorean homes. This is primarily because of the potency of many Gorean wines. The wines I was serving, however, were such that, sensibly, they could be served undiluted. An alternative with the potent wines is to serve very small amounts of them. We stood. The musicians stopped playing.

"To the Vosk League!" said Aemilianus, commander of the naval forces of Ar's Station.

"To the Vosk League!" we said, fervently.

Two of the men at the table had been signatories to the treaty of the Vosk League, solemnly signed under festive canopies on the wharves of Victoria yesterday at the tenth Ahn, Glyco, who had signed on behalf of Port Cos, and Tasdron, Administrator of Victoria, who had signed on behalf of Victoria. In all, nineteen towns had become members of the League, Turmus, Ven, Tetrapoli, Port Cos, Tafa, Victoria, Fina, Ragnar's Hamlet, Hammerfest, Sulport, Sais, Siba, Jasmine, Point Alfred, Jort's Ferry, Forest Port, Iskander, Tancred's Landing and White Water.

"To Ar's Station!" said Callimachus, lifting his goblet to Aemilianus.

"To Ar's Station!" we said.

"I am grateful to you all, for your generosity," said Aemilianus. "I regret only that I was not permitted to sign the treaty on behalf of Ar's Station." Well did we know his bitterness in this matter. Evnoys from Ar, though present at the signing of the treaty, extending felicitations to the league, and commending its intent, had refused to permit Ar's Station to become a party to the signing of the document. Though this was a great disappointment to Aemilianus, and to others of Ar's Station, who had fought with us, it came generally as no surprise on the river. Ar had had difficulties enough with the Salerian Confederation, to the east, not to welcome the formation of a new league along the Vosk. And, surely, such a league would prove detrimental to Ar's ambitions on the Vosk and in the Vosk basin. Port Cos, of course, had had no similar difficulties in joining the league. She was an independent town, and sovereign in her own right. Interestingly, envoys neither from Cos herself nor from the Salerian Confederation attended the formation of the league. They would wait, it seemed, to see whether or not the league became an effective, practical political reality upon the Vosk. If it did, that would be time enough, we supposed, for them to concern themselves with it.

"To Port Cos!" said Tasdron, lifting his cup.

"To Port Cos," said we all, and that toast was well drunk.

"To Victoria!" said Glyco, reciprocating the honor that Tasdron had shown his city.

"To Victoria!" we said, and well and heartily drunk, too, was this toast. Downing it, I found, startled, that there were tears in my eyes.

"What is wrong?" asked Callimachus, smiling.

"It is smoke," I said, "from the lamps."

"No," he smiled, "it is because Victoria is your city."

"Aemilianus!" I said, huskily, that I might drive this emotion from me.

"Yes?" said he.

"I have been meaning for days to give you a gift, one I have been saving for you."

"Oh?" he asked.

I looked at Shirley. "To his feet, Slave," I said.

Swiftly Shirley, startled, putting down the wine, knelt before Aemilianus.

"I took her from Reginald, captain of the *Tamira*," I said.

"That is known to me," said Aemilianus.

"Do you like her?" I asked.

"Yes!" said Aemilianus.

"She is yours!" I said.

Swiftly the slave put down her head and began to kiss the feet of Aemilianus. "My Master," she said, acknowledging him as her new master.

"My thanks!" said Aemilianus.

"It is nothing," I said. "She is only a slave."

"She is worth at least ten silver tarsks," speculated Tasdron. This heartened me, for Tasdron was quite skilled in the assessment of female slaves. As the owner of a paga tavern, he had bought and sold many, of course. It was a form of merchandise with which he was quite familiar. It seemed to me not impossible, upon reflection, that the voluptuous Shirley, put upon the block, exhibited by a skilled auctioneer, might bring the very fine sum of ten silver tarsks.

There was applause for me about the table, the striking of the left shoulder in Gorean fashion. One of the nicest gifts one can give a man, of course, is a beautiful woman.

"But, mercifully," I said, "let her continue to serve. You may then take her home with you tonight when you go."

"Very well," he grinned.

I threw him a narrow, eighteen-inch black strap. "This is for when you take her home with you tonight," I said.

"Thank you," he said. When he left tonight, of course, she would not be wearing a collar, and, presumably, she would be stripped. The strap would be useful in tying her hands behind her back. There would be no danger, of course, of her being mistaken for a free woman. She would continue to be well marked as a slave by her brand, which was small and fine, and burned deeply into her left thigh.

"Where are you supposed to be now, Girl?" asked Aemilianus.

"In the kitchen, I think, Master," she said.

"Well, then," he said, "run now to the kitchen."

"Yes, Master," she said and, leaping up, ran to the kitchen. She was closely followed by the lovely little slave in the bluish gauze. Doubtless both of them were soon to bring forth the next course of the meal, which I took to be assorted desserts, to be followed by black wine and liqueurs.

"Let us sit down," I said. Then I signaled to the musicians to begin once more to play.

I turned to Miles of Vonda. "What are your plans?" I asked.

"I shall venture to Turmus," he said, "where I have contacts. There I shall arrange a loan and with this money return to Vonda, there to rebuild the burned buildings of my ranch."

I glanced to Florence. In her yellow tunic and collar she knelt quite close to him.

The tunic and collar, of course, were all she wore. Slaves were permitted little clothing.

"What of your wench?" I asked.

"I will keep her on my estates, near Vonda," he said. "There will be no problem. She has been properly branded and collared."

"Will you board your slave in Victoria," I asked, "while you venture to Turmus?"

Florence looked frightened, suddenly.

"No," he said, "I will take her with me."

She then looked relaxed, and happy.

I grinned.

Florence then looked at me, reproachfully, and then smiled. Then she put her head against her master's shoulder.

"Was it your intention, earlier, to give Shirley to Aemilianus?" asked Callimachus.

"Yes," I said.

"But you would have done it later in the evening?" he asked.

"Yes," I admitted.

"Do not fear your sentiment," he said. He had detected that I, embarrassed by the tears which had formed in my eyes, following our toast to Victoria, had sought to divert attention from this putative weakness by making that moment in which I would give a gift to my friend, Aemilianus.

"I have carried weapons," I said. "I have fought."

"Tears are not unbecoming to the soldier," said Callimachus. "The soldier is a man of deep passions, and emotion. Many men cannot even understand his depths. Do not fear your currents and your powers. In the soldier are flowers and storms. Each is a part of him, and each is real. Accept both. Deny neither."

"Thank you, Callimachus," I said.

"Ah, chained slaves!" called Glyco, delightedly.

Two girls emerged from the kitchen, the girl in bluish gauze, whom I had not yet named, and the girl in yellow

gauze, whom I had called Shirley, who was now owned by
Aemilianus. I did not know what name he would choose to
give her. Each girl carried a tray of desserts, and each wore
two light, graceful, gleaming chains, one of which, some
twenty inches in length, by means of ankle rings, joined her
ankles, and the other of which, some eighteen inches in
length, put confinement on her wrists, each fair wrist being
clasped snugly in one of its locked wrist rings. They approached, beautiful and enslaved, carrying their trays, that
they might serve us, their movements, graceful and feminine,
measured to the permissions of their chains. There was a
murmur of pleasure and appreciation about the table. Chained
beauties were being looked upon by strong men.

The girls, carrying their trays, knelt before the table.
"Desserts, Masters," announced the girl in bluish gauze.
Then, rising, they began to serve, one on each side. On one
tray were assorted pastries; on the other was a variety of
small, spiced custards.

"Pastries, Master?" asked the girl in bluish gauze.

I looked at her. Her small hands held the tray. On her
tiny, lovely wrists, inflexible and close-fitting, were wrist
rings, each securely locked. Chain, under the tray, dangled
between the rings. Behind her, as she knelt on the tiles, there
lay the chain which confined her ankles.

"You may now serve another," I said. I had taken a small
pastry from the tray.

"Yes, Master," she said. "Thank you, Master."

She then rose, to serve Miles of Vonda.

Diagonally across the table and to my right the new voluptuous slave of Aemilianus knelt tremblingly before him, serving him. He was licking his lips. And I suspect it was not the
custards on her tray which so moved his interest. Rather it
was the first time that he had seen how beautiful she was in
chains.

"Thank you for the pastry, Master," said Florence to Miles
of Vonda.

In their serving the girls, of course, had ignored Peggy and
Florence. It was as though they were not present. They were
only slaves. But, of course, Miles of Vonda and Tasdron, of
Victoria, their masters, had given them food from their
plates. Florence had eaten well but Peggy had eaten hardly
anything at all. She could hardly take her eyes from the

mighty Callimachus. Sometimes her hand moved towards him but she, an Earth-girl slave, dared not touch him.

The pastry was quite good.

I was very pleased with the way Lola had handled the meal. All was simple, tasteful and unpretentious.

"Excellent," said Tasdron, lifting a small pastry.

"Thank you," I said.

I looked upwards, and about the room. The multicolored ribbons were festive; the lamps were lovely; and the flowers, abundant and colorful, mostly larma blossoms, veminia and teriotrope, were beautiful and fragrant. Lola had done well.

"The dancers were lovely," said Glyco, pausing, a spoon lifted in the air over a small yellow, spiced custard. "Perhaps I can rent them for a supper of my own in Port Cos, before their cages are ticketed for Turmus, and thence to Cos."

"It pleases me," I said, "that you found them not displeasing."

"It is an interesting mode of dance," he said, plunging his spoon again into the custard, "one of which women are capable before men have taught them their collars."

"Yes," I said.

I then watched the two slaves, in their chains, continuing their serving. They, too, serving in their chains, were a part of the entertainment, as much as the music of Tasdron's musicians in the background. The Gorean's concept of entertainment is perhaps simpler, or more subtle or broader than is that, doubtless, of many individuals in many other cultures. For example, he can enjoy watching a slave putting on her tunic or taking it off; he can enjoy seeing a woman chained, and rechained, many times, in many ways, each time being exhibited in her helplessness; and he can enjoy watching his slave working naked in the kitchen, or cleaning, or doing laundry or sewing; I think this is probably because he enjoys being with her, and finds her precious and beautiful. I had informed Lola that the little slave, now clad in bluish gauze, was to be included in the entertainment. And how delightfully and subtly had Lola complied with my directive! Even she had had the little slave announce the desserts to the guests. I observed the chains on the little slave in bluish gauze. How beautiful they were on her! I wondered if she even realized that she, thus, was now not only serving but was also now a pleasant portion of our entertainment. But of course she must understand this. Surely she had heard the murmur of pleasure and appreciation which had coursed about the table, greeting the appearance of herself and her fellow slave. In more sophisticated Gorean banquets, incidentally, the serving slaves often change costume and jewelry, and sometimes chains, with each course of the meal, their ensembles and accessories being matched to the various courses. I smiled to myself. Lola had put the two slaves in chains for the dessert course. That seemed a delightful and subtle touch. Slave girls know that to some men, and perhaps to any man some of the time, they are, in effect, and will be treated as, only meaningless, delicious desserts. They are, after all, slaves.

"Master?" asked the small, chained slave in bluish gauze.

I took another pastry, and, with a movement of my hand, dismissed her.

She went then, again, to Miles of Vonda.

"Please, Master, that one," begged Florence.

He took the indicated pastry from the tray, gave it to the slave, and continued his conversation with Tasdron.

"Thank you, Master," said Florence, and, kneeling behind her master, began to eat the pastry.

The chaining on the two slaves did not much restrict their movements, nor was it intended to. Like much chaining on Gor their chaining was primarily aesthetic and symbolic. On a world such as Gor chains are used far less for holding purposes than might be expected. For example, the girls are branded and collared, and their world is one in which the institution of slavery is accepted and respected; there is, in effect, no place for them to run, no place for them to go. On the other hand, chains do hold, and this is one of the major reasons for their symbolic effectiveness. The girl knows, for example, that her chains will keep her exactly where the master has chosen to place her; she is going to stay there; she has been chained there; it is his will which has determined this; she is only his slave.

Just as a woman may be chained in many ways, and Goreans can be ingenious in chaining their females, so, too, there can be many reasons for chaining her. Security against, say, escape or theft, is only one reason. She may also be chained for instructional purposes, that she may be taught, or reminded, that she is a slave. She may also be chained, particularly in certain positions, to humiliate her. She may also be chained as a punishment or discipline. She may also be chained for so simple a reason as that her master merely chooses to do so.

There are many reasons for which a woman might be chained. The women tonight, for example, were chained largely for purposes of beauty. Chains, as is well known, often enhance, and incredibly so, the beauty of a female. This matter is doubtless partly aesthetic and partly emotional and intellectual. The contrast of the unbreakable, merciless, interwoven metallic links, with their tasteful shackles, or cuffs and rings, with the confined, helpless softness of the slave is aesthetically interesting, providing, as it does, a lovely study in surfaces, textures and materials; too, of course, it is only fair to note that the meshed linkage of the chain, with its weight and harshness, with its metallic simplicity and solidity, with its uncompromising, unyielding, inescapable efficiency, merciless and unbreakable, contrasts with, calls attention to, and accentuates remarkably the vulnerability and softness, in all its beauty and curves, of its captive. But the greatest beauty of the chain, like that of the brand and collar, doubtless lies in the realm of the intellect and emotions, in its meaning, and how it makes the girl feel.

The brand and collar, though mighty in their significance, offer little actual impediment to a girl's action, unless, perhaps, she desires to pass alone and unchallenged through a city gate. Chains, on the other hand, permit her only certain latitudes of movement or keep her fixed in a given place. They, by actually putting a physical bond on her, and one which she knews she is powerless to break or escape, one in which she is absolutely helpless, bring her slavery home to her in a clear and unmistakable manner. They well teach her that she is a slave and owned. How could it be made more clear to her, that she is his to do with as he pleases, than when she actually wears his chain?

It is difficult to describe the subtle and exquisite emotions, so profound, and helpless and feminine, which may be felt by the chained woman. "You are chained, and a slave," the chains say to her. "He has chained you, and he is your master. He may now do with you as he pleases. You are now in your place. Choice is gone. Now you can be only, and wholly, a woman. Prepare now to serve your Master, beautiful chained slave."

It is a well-known fact that the mere sight of chains can make many women, even free women, sexually uneasy. Imagine if they were put in them! The chain, like the rope and the strap, and the whip, even when they have no reason to believe they will ever be used on them, speak on some profound level to women. Imagine, then, that a woman, falling slave, suddenly realized that she was now, in effect, subject to them! Consider her fears, her curiosity, her arousal! A woman, often, particularly if stripped, seeing a chain and knowing that it is to be placed upon her, will feel uncontrollable sexual desire, her body opening like a humid flower in its receptivity. That response can characterize even a free woman. Imagine, then, if you will, that now the woman is not free, but has fallen slave! She now knows that she is subject, categorically and in all ways, to the full domination of the master. No longer does she have even the theoretical option of offering a token resistance. Open, enraptured, joyful, she writhes moaning and crying out on the furs of love, a conquered slave, a fulfilled woman.

"There must be levies of men and ships, from the signatory towns," Glyco was saying to Callimachus, "rotations of men, and perhaps, too, of ships. Patrols must be organized. Communications and signals will be of great significance."

"You are now first captain in Port Cos, are you not?" I asked Calliodorus. He had been captain of the valiant *Tais*. I assumed, with the fall of Callisthenes, that the mantle and helmet of the first captain would surely devolve upon him.

"I am acting first captain," said Calliodorus. "But it would be my hope that Callimachus, who was once first captain, may be prevailed upon to resume that post."

The two slaves had now left the pastries and custards upon the table, and had returned to the kitchen. They would there presumably be relieved of their chains and would return with the black wine.

"The citadels of Policrates and Ragnar Voskjard have been burned, I heard," I said.

"Yes," said Tasdron. The citadel of Ragnar Voskjard had been fled by its defenders, after the news of the battle at Victoria reached them, they knowing themselves too few to defend it against a concerted siege.

"They might have been useful as bastions for the Vosk League," I said.

"The Vosk League," smiled Tasdron, "is a simple league, whose intent it is merely to control piracy on the river."

"That was the original intent, too, as I understand it," I said, "of the league on the Olni, which became the Salerian Confederation."

"We did not want trouble with Cos and Ar," said Tasdron.

"Not while we are weak," said Glyco.

"I see," I said.

"Not only have they been burned," said Tasdron, "but they will be dismantled. We have taken proposals on this work from stone merchants."

"And salt will be cast upon the ashes," said Glyco.

"Salt," I said, "can be a sign of life, and luck."

"True," smiled Tasdron.

"The headquarters of the Vosk League, as I understand it," I said, "is to be located in Victoria."

"Yes," smiled Tasdron. "The choice seemed judicious."

"Victoria was centrally involved in the resistance to the pirates," said Aemilianus.

"And it was here that the decisive victory was won," said Calliodorus.

"And in this fashion," grinned Aemilianus, "the headquarters of the league is not in Port Cos."

"And, similarly," smiled Calliodorus, "it is not at Ar's Station."

There was laughter at the table.

The two slaves, their chains removed, now returned, and began to serve the black wine. The voluptuous slave of Aemilianus, whom he had not yet named, placed the tiny sliver cups, on small stands, before us. The lovely little slave in bluish gauze, whom I had not yet named, holding the narrow-spouted, silver pouring vessel in a heavy cloth, to retain its heat and protect her hands, poured the scalding, steaming black fluid, in narrow, tiny streams, into the small cups. She poured into the cups only the amount that would be compatible with the assorted sugars and creams which the guest might desire, if any, these being added in, and stirred, if, and as, pertinent, by Aemilianus' slave, who directed the serving.

"Have the pirates been disposed of, suitably?" I asked Tasdron.

"Yes," said Tasdron. "We divided them among various wholesalers, with the understanding that no more than one of them will be sold in any given market, in any given city or town, or village or fair. Thus they will be well scattered, and distributed, over all known Gor."

"I see," I said. Policrates, Kliomenes and Callisthenes, and such men, branded and collared, would soon be owned slaves, laboring for masters. There are many uses for such slaves. They can be purchased for work chains, to be rented out by their masters, sometimes marched between cities, depending on the seasons and the work available. They can serve, too, in such places as the mines, the quarries and great farms.

"Master?" asked the girl in yellow gauze, who had been Shirley and now belonged, for the moment nameless, to my friend Aemilianus, of Ar's Station.

"Second slave," I told her, which, among the river towns, and in certain cities, particularly in the north, is a way of indicating that I would take the black wine without creams or sugars, and as it came from the pouring vessel, which, of course, in these areas, is handled by the "second slave," the first slave being the girl who puts down the cups, takes the orders and sees that the beverage is prepared according to the preferences of the one who is being served.

"Second slave," said the slave of Aemilianus.

"Yes, Mistress," said the girl in bluish gauze. She was extremely careful not to spill a drop. Black wine, except in the vicinity of Thentis, where most of it is grown on the slopes of the Thentis range, is quite expensive. Also, of course, clumsy slave girls are often whipped. The expression "second slave," incidentally, serves to indicate that one does not wish creams or sugars with one's black wine, even if only one girl is serving.

"Where is Krondar?" I asked Miles of Vonda.

"On his way to Ar," said Miles.

"To Ar?" I asked.

"He fought well with us," said Miles. "I freed him."

"Excellent," I said, "he is a splendid fellow."

"And I gave him portions of my share of the spoils, from the holding of Policrates."

"Excellent," I said.

"Do you remember that luscious little brunet, Bikkie, from the holding?"

"Of course," I said. "She was allotted to you, with Florence, in the division of the spoils."

"I gave her to Krondar," said Miles.

"Superb," I said. "He will make her writhe well."

"That is certain!" laughed Miles.

"How you men speak of us!" protested Florence.

"Be silent, Slave," said Miles.

"Yes, Master," she said, putting her head down, shyly. I smiled. Obviously she, too, was not averse to being made to writhe by her master.

I saw the two slaves returning now to the kitchen.

"Why is Krondar going to Ar?" I asked.

"He intends to purchase fighting slaves," said Miles, "and then free them, and organize matches among free men. Have you ever heard of such a thing?"

"There are perhaps places where such things are done," I said.

"Free men fight with weapons," said Miles. "They are not animals."

"Warriors are trained in unarmed combat," I said.

"But only as a last resort, only for emergencies," said Miles.

I shrugged. There were surely those at the table who knew more of such things than I.

"It is difficult to kill a man with your bare hands," said Miles.

"There are several ways in which it may be done, easily," said Callimachus.

"Yes," I said.

"Yes," said Calliodorus.

"Yes," agreed Aemilianus.

"Oh," said Miles of Vonda.

"Are you enjoying your supper?" I asked Calliodorus, who had been rather subdued most of the evening.

"Yes," he said. "It is very nice."

"I see that you have brought no slave with you," I said.

"No," he said.

Calliodorus, as we knew, had once wooed a maid in Port Cos. The companionship, however, had never materialized. The maid, it seems, before the ceremony, had fled the city.

"You should have a slave," I said. "They are marvelous in contenting a man."

"There is only one woman," he said, "on whose lovely throat I ever wanted to lock a slave collar."

I lifted the tiny silver cup to my lips and took a drop of the black wine. Its strength and bitterness are such that it is normally drunk in such a manner, usually only a drop or a few drops at a time. Commonly, too, it is mollified with creams and sugars. I drank it without creams and sugars, perhaps, for I had been accustomed, on Earth, to drinking coffee in such a manner, and the black wine of Gor is clearly coffee, or closely akin to coffee. Considering its bitterness, however, if I had not been drinking such a tiny amount, and so slowly, scarcely wetting my lips, I, too, would surely have had recourse to the tasty, gentling additives with which it is almost invariably served.

"Master, may I have that pastry?" asked Florence, indicating the one she desired.

"No," he said.

She knelt back.

But I noticed that, in a moment, he had given it to her, and she knelt back on her heels, her knees closely together, holding it with two hands, eating it.

I watched Aemilianus' slave emerging from the kitchen. I listened to the unobtrusive music of the musicians, who were sitting on a rug a few feet in front of, and to the left of, the table. I took another sip of the black wine.

The voluptuous blond slave began to lower certain of the lamps.

"What are you doing?" I asked her.

"Forgive me, Master," she said. She then hurried again to the kitchen. As she had done this work the light in the room was romantically softened, but an area, soft as well, of greater illumination had been left before the table. When she had left the room, the musicians, too, had stopped playing. This seemed interesting.

"What is going on?" asked Miles of Vonda.

"I do not know," I said.

"Is it an entertainment?" asked Glyco.

"Perhaps," I said.

The blond slave of Aemilianus then re-entered the room. She placed a large, folded square of sparkling white linen at the bottom of the table. She then lit a wide, large, low candle and placed this candle, on a plate, on the soft, wide square of folded linen. She then withdrew to the side.

I looked at the white linen, and the candle, in the half darkness.

I was startled.

What memories this stirred in me!

The musicians then began to play, softly. The girl emerged from the kitchen.

There were sounds of pleasure, and surprise, from those about the table.

"She is beautiful," said Tasdron.

"What manner of garments are those?" asked Glyco.

The dark-haired girl, exquisite and lovely, stood in the light, on the tiles, back from the foot of the table, that we might well see her. Her hair was drawn severely back on her head. She wore what seemed to be a svelte, satin, off-the-shoulder, white sheath gown. Twisted about her feet, over and under, were golden straps.

"I do not understand this," said Miles of Vonda. "Is this meaningful?"

I was almost overwhelmed. "It is very meaningful to me," I said. "Permit me, my friends, to explain. First, Glyco, in answer to your question, the garments she wears are much like, and are meant to suggest, the garments which a free woman may wear on Earth."

"But they are slave garments," said Glyco. "See! The arms and the shoulders are bare!"

"Nonetheless," I said, "on Earth free women may wear such garments."

The girl then turned gracefully before us, displaying the garments. I saw that her hair, severely drawn back on her head, was fastened behind the back of her head in a bun. I had known it would be. I had not forgotten.

"They are slave garments," said Glyco.

"True," I said, "but to understand what she is doing, you must understand that such garments, on Earth, are understood to be exquisite and lovely free-woman's garments."

"Very well," said Glyco.

"Too," I said, "they are, in this case, meant to remind me of, and resemble, the garments which she once wore, as a free woman, to a meeting with me. That is important."

"I understand," said Glyco.

"They would also be the garments in which, for the first time, to my knowledge, she had ever dared to explicitly express her femininity."

"Do the women on Earth not dare to express their femininity?" asked Glyco.

"Many fear to do so," I said.

"What of the men of Earth?" asked Glyco.

"Many of them encourage the women to pretend to be pseudo-men," I said.

"What sort of men are they?" asked Glyco.

"I do not know," I said.

"Observe the hair," I said.

"It seems severe, tight, rigid, constricted, constrained," said Glyco.

"That is part of the costume, so to speak," I said, "of many male-imitating women. The straight lines and severity are supposed to suggest, I gather, efficiency and masculinity."

"Interesting," said Glyco. "It is incongruous, of course, with the garment, which seems rather feminine."

"Such incongruities," I said, "are not uncharacteristic of many Earth women. They can indicate ambiguities in self-images and confusions, in particular, as to their sexuality. There might, of course, I suppose, be many other reasons for them. For example, in some cases, they may represent that a transition is in progress toward femininity."

"The cloth on the table and the candle," said Miles of Vonda, "are supposed to suggest to you the place of this meeting of which you spoke."

"Yes," I said. "It was a place where food was served, and where one might engage in pleasant conversation."

"A tavern?" asked Tasdron.

"Not exactly," I said. There is no precise Gorean expression for a restaurant. "There were no paga slaves there, and no dancers."

"Why would one go to such a place?" asked Miles of Vonda.

"She went there that she might engage in delicate and intimate discourse with me," I said.

"That she might offer herself to you as your slave?" asked Glyco.

"If so," I said, "that was not clearly understood at the time."

"She appears then now before us," said Glyco, "much as she appeared then before you?"

"Yes," I said, "though there are, of course, differences. For example, at that time, her throat was bare." The girl now wore a light white scarf twisted about her throat, the ends over her left shoulder. "Too," I said, "at that time she carried a small silver-beaded pouch."

"I see," said Glyco.

The girl did not now, of course, carry a purse. Slave girls are not permitted to carry such things. When shopping she carries the coins usually in her mouth or hand. Sometimes she ties them in a scarf about a wrist or ankle. Sometimes her master places them in a bag, which is then tied about her neck. Gorean garments, generally, incidentally, except for the garments of craftsmen, do not have pockets. Coins, and personal items, and such, are usually, by free persons, carried in pouches, which are usually concealed within the robes of a free woman, or slung about the waist, or shoulder, of a free man.

The girl, then, to the music, moved gracefully, turning, her hands held out, about the table, displaying herself and her garments for us. She then returned to her place on the tiles, at the foot of the table.

I regarded her. How beautiful she was! She looked at me. Then, gracefully and decisively, to the music, she unbound her hair.

There was applause for this at the table, the gentle striking of left shoulders, for she had done it well, and the significance of a woman's unbinding her hair before a man is well understood on Gor.

"You see now," I said, "how beautiful can be a woman of Earth."

"We know that from our slave markets," laughed Glyco.

She then, reaching to the left side, beneath her arm, of what seemed to be a white sheath gown, undid a fastening, and then others, at the side of her body, her waist, her thigh, and knee, and then, gracefully, the Gorean music unobtrusive but melodious in the background, removed the garment. I saw then that a rectangle of white cloth, cleverly tucked and sewn, had been used to simulate the off-the-shoulder, white sheath gown on Earth. Such an actual gown, of course, had not been available to her on Gor.

There was gentle, appreciative applause.

She now stood before us in what seemed to be a brief, silken, off-the-shoulder slip.

"Now that is a slave's garment, obviously," said Glyco.

"True," I admitted. But I smiled to myself, for I knew that such garments, on Earth, might be worn by free women. To be sure, on Earth, they were usually worn as undergarments, whereas, on Gor, such a garment, silken and smooth, with nothing beneath it, would be regarded as quite acceptable for a slave's street wear, particularly in warm weather. To be sure, of course, the color of the garment, on Gor, would not be likely to be white, but, commonly, red or yellow. White, on Gor, is a color commonly associated with virginity. It is, accordingly, worn by few slaves.

The girl then sat on the tiles before us, but back a bit, where we, sitting cross-legged at the low table, could well see her. She extended her right leg, gracefully. It was flexed and, as her foot was placed fully upon the floor, her toes were pointed. These two things, respectively, curved her claf deliciously and extended the line of her beauty. Her left leg was back, its ankle beneath her right thigh. She looked at me, and then, bending forward, removed the golden straps wound about and under her right foot. In the restaurant she had worn golden pumps, with wisps of golden straps. She looked at me. Well did she, and the others, know the significance of removing footwear before a free man. She cast aside the straps she had taken from her right foot. Then, putting her hands back, swiftly and smoothly, beautifully, to the music, without rising, she changed her position on the tiles. Her left thigh now faced me. Her left leg was now gracefully extended, flexed and toes pointed. Her left thigh, and calf, and ankle and foot were marvelous. Her right foot, as her left previously had been, was back, the right ankle now beneath her right thigh. She then removed the golden straps from her left foot, and cast them aside. She looked at me. She had bared her feet before a free man. The golden straps she had used to simulate the footwear which she had worn on Earth were golden binding straps. They were the nearest thing she could find, within her limited resources, I gathered, to what she had worn in the restaurant. I did not object. They resembled somewhat, and well suggested, that footwear. Such straps, incidentally, are commonly used to bind the hands and feet of women. Sometimes, if it amused me, I could tie her in them.

There was gentle applause for the girl, and murmurs of appreciation. The footwear had been well removed.

She then rose to her feet and stood again before us, but now barefoot upon the tiles.

She then reached again to her left side, and undid a fastening there, below her left arm, and then another below it, and then one at her hip. She then unwrapped the brief sliplike garment from her body, and dropped it to one side.

"Ah," said more than one man. "Interesting," said Glyco.

"The garments in which you now see her," I said, "are supposed to represent typical undergarments of an Earth female."

"I see," said Glyco.

The brassiere had been simulated cleverly with soft white silk. Her beauty, soft, and almost as though protesting its confinement, strained against this silk. Too, between her breasts, this silk had been twisted and knotted, this making even more evident the sweet contours of her beauty, and the sturdy, silken restraint placed upon it. The panties, too, were simulated with white silk, which, in a narrow rectangle, had been wrapped twice about her hips and tucked in at her waist. There was no nether closure to this silk, of course. The Gorean slave girl is not permitted to shield her intimacies without the explicit permission of her master.

Besides these two garments, intended, respectively, to suggest the brassiere and panties of an Earth girl, she still wore, of course, the light, narrow white scarf, this twisted and wound twice about her throat, the ends thrown over her left shoulder.

The girl then, to the music, put back her head and put her hands behind her back, and, reaching high behind her back, this lifting her breasts beautifully, strained for a moment, and then, one by one, twisting slightly, undid the hooks on the confining, tight silk.

Our eyes met.

The silk was then dropped to one side.

"Superb," said Glyco.

She then reached to the white scarf on her throat and, beautifully, to the music, undid it one turn. She then, to the music, drew it beautifully, slowly, from her throat, and, gracefully, dropped it to one side. She wore, of course, now revealed, a close-fitting, gleaming slave collar.

She lifted her head, and, with her fingers, delicately indicated and displayed the collar.

She then stood before us as a barefoot, half-naked, collared slave.

Gorean applause, and murmurs of appreciation, greeted this aspect of her performance.

Our eyes met again.

She then reached with her right hand to her waist and undid the tuck in the silk which was wrapped about her hips. Slowly and beautifully then, to the music, with both hands, she unwound the silk, and then dropped it to the tiles.

"Superb!" said Glyco.

She then crawled to me, on her hands and knees, her head humbly down. Then, when she reached me, she lowered herself to her belly and, extending her right hand, touched me on the knee. She lifted her head. "You are my master," she said, "and I am your slave, and I love you!"

"Superb!" said Glyco. "Superb!" Those at the table, even including the slaves, Florence and Peggy, unable to restrain themselves, applauded. She who had been Shirley, too, now the slave of Aemilianus, applauded.

I took the small slave by the upper arms, and held her, half turned, on her side, near me. I looked down into her eyes. She was breathing heavily. She was shaken with emotion. Her eyes looked up at me, pleadingly.

The voluptuous slave of Aemilianus was now attending again to the lamps, this time restoring the room to its original illumination.

I then drew the slave more closely into my arms, and again regarded her, looking deeply into her eyes. I had never suspected that she would have performed as she had. I had, of course, specified to Lola that she was to be included in the entertainment, but never had I expected anything of the nature or beauty of what I had seen. That the girl had helped to serve the dessert course in display chains would, in itself, have fully contented me. Informed by Lola that she was to be a component of our entertainment doubtless the girl herself had suggested and devised this performance, abetted, of course, by Lola. Of many things in the performance, such as the restaurant, Lola could have known nothing. The idea of

the performance, then, as well as most of the details involved
in its presentation, must have been that of my little dark-
haired slave. It was a most beautiful gift which she had given
me.

The room had now been restored to its normal illumination. The candle, blown out, and the white cloth, too, had
been removed. I saw that Florence, flushed, kneeling behind
Miles of Vonda, was biting at the back of his tunic, and putting her hands on his hips. "Get back, Slave," he said to her.
"Yes, Master," she sobbed, and knelt back. She had been
aroused by the performance of the dark-haired slave. I saw
that Peggy, too, in her white tunic, was flushed. She was
breathing deeply. It seemed she could not take her eyes from
Callimachus.

I looked down into the eyes of the little slave. She looked
up at me, pleadingly. "Master," she whispered.

"It is time to serve the liqueurs, Slave," I told her.

"Yes, Master," she whispered. She then rose to her feet
and hurried toward the kitchen.

"Slave," I called.

"Yes, Master," she said, stopping, turning, and falling to
her knees.

"You will serve as you are," I told her.

"Yes, Master," she said, and then, rising up, turned and
hurried to the kitchen, there to render aid to Lola and the
slave of Aemilianus.

A small whimper escaped Florence.

"Be silent, Slave," said Miles of Vonda.

"Yes, Master," she said.

"She is not the only one," said Tasdron, jerking a thumb at
Peggy, who, blushing crimson, put down her head, looking
away from Callimachus.

"Ah," said Glyco. "The liqueurs!"

First from the kitchen, bearing her tray, came the voluptuous slave of Aemilianus. Behind her, too with her tray, came
the little dark-haired slave. In a moment both were deferentially serving. The collared softness of the dark-haired girl
well set off the metal of the tray, and the small, multicolored
glasses and bottles upon it. It is not unusual, at a Gorean
meal, where free women are not present, for one or more of
the slaves to serve naked. At ruder meals, this makes it easier
for one of the guests, should the urge strike him, to use them.

"A free woman!" suddenly exclaimed Glyco, startled.

I smiled.

From the kitchen there had emerged, in the robes of concealment, the figure of a woman.

The men, save I, rose as one to their feet, for Gorean men commonly stand when a free woman enters a room.

The voluptuous slave of Aemilianus swiftly knelt, making herself as small as possible, putting her head to the floor. The little dark-haired slave, too, swiftly knelt, also putting her head to the floor. Too, she shuddered, trying to cover her nakedness with her hands. Peggy and Florence, too, now had their heads to the floor. Slave girls, as I may have mentioned, fear free women, terribly.

The woman in the robes of concealment seemed timid, frightened. She approached the table hesitantly, diffidently. She did not understand, fully, what she was to do.

"A free woman is present," whispered Glyco to me.

But I did not get up.

"You!" she suddenly said, from behind her veils, seeing Calliodorus, of Port Cos, captain of the *Tais*. "You?"

He seemed startled. He leaned forward, as though he might peer through the veils themselves.

"You are Calliodorus," she said, "of Port Cos!" I had not told her, of course, that Calliodorus was to be a guest at our supper.

"You!" he cried, suddenly. "Can it be you? No! It cannot be you! It cannot! Not after all these years!"

"It is I," she said, trembling.

"Gentlemen," said Calliodorus, huskily, "this is the free woman, Lola, of Port Cos!"

Suddenly the girl, sobbing, wildly tore away her veils and the robes of concealment, revealing that she wore a slave tunic and collar. "I am not a free woman," she cried, throwing herself to the feet of Calliodorus, "I am a slave girl!"

"And she is yours!" I cried.

Calliodorus, stunned, looked down at the beauty at his feet.

I rose to my feet.

She looked around at me, wildly. "Master!" she cried.

"You are now his," I said, indicating Calliodorus.

"Thank you, Master!" she cried. "Thank you, Master!" She rose to her feet, and ran to me, falling to her knees before me and putting her head down to my feet. She kissed my feet in gratitude. "Thank you, Master," she sobbed. I was pleased with her pleasure. She was a superb slave, properly handled, and I was quite fond of her. She had served me well. I thought it not unfit that she be rewarded. Accordingly I had given her to Calliodorus.

She rose to her feet and ran to kneel before Calliodorus. She looked up at him, tears in her eyes, her hands on his legs. "Will you accept me, Master?" she asked.

"In Port Cos," said he, "long ago, I wooed you with all the honors and dignities to be accorded to the free woman. Well did we grow acquainted, and many were the long and intimate conversations in which we shared." His eyes then grew hard. "And in one of these," he said, "you uttered an unspeakable confession, acknowledging your slave needs."

"I was so ashamed," she said, turning her face away.

"How could I take to my bed in honor one who had dared to confess her slave needs? Such girls I could buy at the market. We parted, naturally. But our families, desiring the companionship, pressed us for explanations. That our honors might be protected, of course, yours that you had dared to confess your slave needs, and mine, that I had been the scandalized auditor of so shameful an admission, we remained silent."

"But," said she, moist-eyed, "that our courtship not appear to have failed, and that our families not be disgraced, you agreed to proceed with the companionship, this in accordance with your conception of your duty as an officer and a gentleman."

He looked down at her, not speaking.

"I did not wish to languish, scorned and neglected, in a cold bed, while you contented yourself with market girls. I fled the city."

"You are mistaken in at least one thing," he said. "I had not determined to proceed with the companionship because of family pressures. I am not so weak. Similarly, my duties as an officer and a gentleman were not implicated in the matter."

"But, why then?" she asked.

"I wanted you," he said.

"But I have slave needs," she said.

"I thought long after our conversation," he said. "You had

dared to confess your slave needs, and this had shamed you, and it had scandalized me. But, why, I asked myself. Should not, rather, one be more ashamed by deceit than the truth? Can there truly be a greater honor in hypocrisy than in honesty? It does not seem so. I then realized how bravely you had trusted me and revealed this to me. My outrage gave way to gratitude and admiration. Similarly, I asked myself, why was I scandalized. Was this not connected with hidden fears of my own, that I might discover complementary needs within myself, the needs to own and be a master? Your confession, so expressive and poignant, tended to undermine a deceit of free persons. You had dared, it seemed, to break the code of hypocrisy. Had the gate to barbarism been left ajar? I regretted, for a time, the loss of the lie. We grow fond of our myths. Yet our myths are like walls of straw. Ultimately they cannot protect us. Ultimately they must perish in the flames of truth."

"You would have taken me," she asked, "knowing that I had slave needs?"

"Your slave needs," he said, "made you a thousand times more desirable. What man does not want a slave?"

She looked at him, startled.

"It was thus my intention to take you into honorable companionship," he said, "but, in the privacy of our quarters, away from the sight of the world, to put you in a collar, and keep you as a slave, even to the whip."

She looked up at him, disbelievingly.

"But," he said, "such a farce will not now be necessary."

"I do not understand," she said.

"Strip," he said.

"There are others present," she protested.

His right hand, in a backhand blow, lashed forth, fierce and powerful, striking her from her knees to her side on the tiles. She rose to her hands and knees and, blood at her mouth, regarded him, disbelievingly.

"Must a command be repeated?" he inquired.

Swiftly she tore away the slave tunic, stripping herself. He snapped his fingers and pointed to his feet. She crawled to his feet on her belly. She looked up at him.

"I gather that you accept the gift," I said.

"I do accept it," he said, "and I thank you."

"I have called her Lola," I said, "but you may, of course, call her what you wish."

"You are Lola," he said to the slave.

"Thank you, Master," she said, named. She put down her head and, gently, kissed his feet.

"Lola," he said.

"Yes, Master," she said.

"From the first instant, long ago, when I saw you in Port Cos, I wanted to own you."

"And from the first instant in Port Cos, so long ago," she said, "I wanted to be your slave."

"You now are," he said.

"Yes, Master," she said.

"Here," I said. I threw Calliodorus an eighteen-inch black binding strap. It was identical to the one I had earlier given to Aemilianus.

"Thank you," grinned Calliodorus.

"Bind her well," I said.

"Have no fear," laughed Callidorus, "she will know herself bound."

There was then laughter, and Gorean applause, congratulating Calliodorus on his good fortune, and me on the loveliness and generosity of my gift. Then again we sat down. The gift, nude and collared, curled lovingly on its side near him, its hand touching his knee.

"It is time now," laughed Tasdron, "for me to add something to the evening." Peggy looked at him, puzzled. "On your feet, Slave," said he to her, "and go to the tiles at the foot of the table."

Startled, Peggy did as she was told. She then stood there, frightened, in the brief white tunic. She had no idea as to what was to be required of her. She had thought that she had been brought to the supper merely to attend Tasdron, her master.

"Strip," said Tasdron.

Swiftly, unquestioningly, knowing herself a Gorean slave girl, Peggy unbelted the tunic, parted it, and slipped it from her shoulders. She then blushed crimson. She had been forced to make herself nude, in the presence of others, before the man she loved.

"Slave," said Tasdron.

"Yes, Master," said Peggy.

"In the tavern," he said, "you have seen various dances, have you not?"

"Yes, my Master," she said.

"You have seen among them, have you not," he asked, "the Sa-eela?"

"Yes, Master," she whispered, turning white.

"Dance it," he said.

"I am not a dancer!" she cried.

"Must a command be repeated?" he asked.

"No, my Master!" she cried, and gracefully flexed her legs, and lifted her hands, their backs to one another, above her head.

"Splendid!" said Glyco.

How beautiful Peggy was, and how frightened!

Tasdron lifted his hand.

The Sa-eela is one of the most moving, deeply rhythmic and erotic of the slave dances of Gor. It belongs, generally, to a genre of dances commonly known as the Lure Dances of the Love-Starved Slave Girl. The common theme of the genre, of course, is the attempt on the part of a neglected slave to call herself to the attention of the Master.

Tasdron then signaled to the musicians.

And then Peggy began to dance.

I remembered her then from long ago, from Earth, also from the restaurant, where she had worked as a hat-check girl. She had worn a black ribbon in her blond hair, a long-sleeved, white-silk blouse, panty hose of black netting, and a brief, black miniskirt. Her long, shapely legs had been well revealed. She had been very lovely. I did not find it hard to understand that she might have come to the casual attention of a Gorean slaver.

"I thought she was not a dancer," said Glyco.

"I have never thought of her as a dancer," said Tasdron, puzzled. "I have never used her as a dancer."

The former Peggy Baxter, of Earth, nude and in the steel collar of Tasdron of Victoria, her master, now danced before us, a Gorean slave girl.

I sipped a Turian liqueur.

I sensed the lovely little dark-haired slave kneel down quite close to me, behind me and to my left. She put her hands about my left arm.

I savored the liqueur, and observed the dance of the slave.

I also smiled, detecting the swift, astonished breathing of the little slave near me.

"Such movements, of course," Glyco was saying, "are instinctual in a woman."

"Yes," said Tasdron.

"Oh," breathed the little slave near me, "oh!" I smiled. I gathered that she had seldom seen the dance of a female slave.

The Sa-eela, usually performed in the nude, as though by a low slave, and by a girl freed of all impediments, except her collar, is one of the most powerful of the slave dances of Gor. It is done rather differently in different cities but the variations practiced in the river towns and, generally, in the Vosk basin, are, in my opinion, among the finest. There is no standardization, or little standardization, for better or for worse, in Gorean slave dance. Not only can the dances differ from city to city, and town to town, and even from tavern to tavern, but they are likely to differ, too, even from girl to girl. This is because each girl, in her own way, brings the nature of her own body, her own dispositions, her own sensuality and needs, her own personality, to the dance. For the woman, slave dance is a uniquely personal and creative art form. Too, of course, it provides her with a wondrous modality for deeply intimate self-expression. "They all wear collars," is the first portion of a familiar exchange, of which Goreans are fond. The second, and concluding, portion of the exchange is, "But each in her collar is different." This exchange, I think, makes clear the attitude of the Gorean toward the slave girl. In one sense she is nothing, and is to be treated as such, but, in another sense, she is precious, and is everything.

A familiar bit of advice given by bold Gorean physicians to free women who consult them about their frigidity is, to their scandal, "Learn slave dance." Another bit of advice, usually given to a free woman being ushered out of his office by a physician impatient with her imaginary ailments is, "Become a slave." Frigidity, of course, is not accepted in slaves. If nothing else, it will be beaten out of their beautiful hides by whips.

I felt the small hands of the lovely little dark-haired slave tight on my arm.

"She is not bad," said Tasdron, observing the dancer.

"She is superb!" breathed Glyco.

I looked across the table, to my right. Lola, half kneeling, half lying, in the arms of Calliodorus, his hand in her hair, could not take her eyes from the dancer. She was breathing deeply. I glanced to my direct right. Florence, in the brief yellow tunic, knelt behind Miles of Vonda, clutching him, her fingers caught in his tunic, her chin on his right shoulder. She, too, was breathing deeply. "Master," she whispered to him. "Master."

I took another sip of the liqueur. It was quite good.

Peggy now danced upon her knees, at the end of the table, using the table in the dance, thrusting her belly against it, and touching it with her hands, and her body and lips.

"Ohhh," said the little slave, holding my arm.

I smiled. The Sa-eela, of course, is not the sort of dance which could be performed by a free woman.

Peggy, then, was back from the table, on the tiles, on her back, and sides, and knees, and then prone, and then again supine, and then writhing, as though in frustration and loneliness.

I observed the dancer, closely, the striking of her small, clenched fists on the tiles, the scratching of her fingernails at their smooth surfaces, the turning of a hip, the flattening of a thigh, the lifting of a knee, the turning of her head, the piteous scattering of her hair from side to side. She lay on her back, and, whimpering, struck down, in misery, stinging the palms of her hands, bruising her small heels. She might have been in a cell, locked away from men.

She then rolled to her stomach, and rose to her hands and knees, and, head down, remained for a moment in that posture. It is at this moment that the music enters a different melodic phase, one less physical and frenzied, one almost lyrical in its poignancy. She crawls some feet to her left and lifts her head. She puts out her small hand. It seems that it there encounters some barrier, some enclosing, confining wall. She then rises to her feet. Swiftly she hurries about, in the graceful, frightened haste of the dancer, her hands seeming to trace the location of the obdurate barriers, those invisible walls which seemed to contain her. She then stood and faced us, and put her head in her hands, bent over, and then straightened her body, her head and hair thrown back. "I?" she seemed to ask, looking out, as though some rude jailer might have come to the gate of her pen. But there is, of course, no one there, and, in the performance of the dance, that is clearly understood. Then, in poignant fantasy, within the pen, she prepares herself for the master, seeming to thoughtfully select silks and jewelry, seeming to apply perfume and cosmetics, seeming to be bedecked in shimmering, diaphanous slave splendor. She then crosses her wrists, and moves them, as though they have been bound. She then extends them before her as though the strap on them had been drawn taut. It then seems that she, head high, a bound slave, is being led on her tether from the pen. But, at the gate, of course, her wrists separate, and her small palms and fingers indicate for us, clearly, that she is still confined. She retreats to the center of the pen, falls to her knees, covers her head with her hands, and weeps.

The next phase of the music begins at this point.

She looks up. There is a sound in the corridor, beyond the gate. She leaps up, and backs against the wall of her pen. This time, it seems, truly, there are men there, that they have come for her. She puts her head up; she turns away; she feigns disdain. Then, it seems, as she, startled, looks about, they are turning away. She then throws herself to her belly on the floor of the pen, calling to them, lifting her head, holding out her hand piteously to them. She pleads to be considered.

It then seems, as she shrinks back, lifting herself to the palms of her hands, frightened, that the gate to her pen has been opened. She kneels swiftly in the position of the pleasure slave. Obviously she fears her rude jailers. Twice, it seems she is struck with a whip. Then she, again, assumes the position of the pleasure slave. She nods her head. She understands well what is expected of her. She is to perform well on the tiles of the feasting hall. "Yes, Masters!" it seems she says. But how little do her jailers, perhaps only common and boorish fellows, understand that this is precisely what she, too, deeply and desperately desires to do. How long she has waited, in cruel frustration, unfulfilled and lonely, in her cell for just such a moment, that precious opportunity in which she, a mere slave, may be permitted to display and present herself for the consideration of her master. How can they understand the poignance, and significance, of this moment for her? She is to have an opportunity to present herself before the master! Who knows if she, in such a large house, one with such cells and jailers, may ever again be given such an opportunity?

It then seems that she is hauled to her feet and that her wrists, tightly and cruelly, are bound behind her back. Her body and head are then bent far over. Her head twists. It seems a man's hand is in her hair. Not as a high slave, clothed in jewelries and shimmering silks, tastefully bound, is she to be conducted to the site of her performance, some aristocratic banquet; rather, cruelly bound and nude, she is to be thrown before masters at a drunken feast. She then, with small, hurried steps, bent over, described a wide circle on the tiles. Then, it seemed, she was thrown to her knees, and then her side, before us. Her hands were still held as though tightly bound behind her. She looked at us. We were, of course, the "masters," before whom she was to perform. She rose to her feet. She twisted, as though her hands were being untied. She then flexed her legs and lifted her hands over her head, as she had in the beginning, back to back.

The final phases of the Sa-eela then begin.

In these phases the girl, in all her unshielded beauty, and naked except for the collar of slavery, attempts to arouse the interest of her master.

In the former Peggy Baxter, of Earth, I now saw little left which was reminiscent of her planet of origin. Before us there danced a Gorean slave girl.

I glanced about, to the small, dark-haired slave clutching my arm, to Lola, in the arms of Calliodorus, to Florence, kneeling behind Miles of Vonda, to she who had been Shirley, in her yellow gauze, kneeling to one side, now the slave of Aemilianus. They were breathing deeply. Their eyes shone. In fascination, and in arousal, and fear, they watched the beautiful slave. They knew that they, too, wore collars.

Peggy's body gleamed with sweat. She had small feet, and lovely, high arches. Her body was superb. She had retained, by means of diet and exercise, her block measurements, those measurements which were hers when she, after having been prepared for sale, was marketed from a slave block. The master commonly has a record of such measurements and many masters, using a tarsk scale, used for small livestock, and slave tapes, periodically check their lovely properties, making certain that they are maintaining the measurements. And woe to the girl, in such a case, whose measurements are found to depart to any significant extent from the block measurements! Such a departure can be an occasion for corrective discipline, and of a quite severe sort. Sometimes, when one sees a fearful girl refusing the smallest of sweets and exercising, almost in desperation, one may suspect, in amusement, that the day on which her master plans to check her measurements is not far distant. The lovely figures of slave girls are not accidents. Only free women are permitted to become unkempt and gross.

Peggy was dancing well.

She had lovely arms, and lovely, slender wrists. They would look well roped, or clasped in slave steel.

She had now entered into the display phase of the Sa-eela. In this portion of the dance the girl calls attention to the various aspects of her beauty, from the swirling sheen of her cascading hair to her ankles, from her small feet to her tiny, fine fingers.

Women are so incredibly beautiful. It is a wonder that men do not scream with pleasure, seeing them.

It is little wonder that Goreans put them in collars, and own them.

"Oh!" gasped the naked, collared little beauty kneeling near me. I smiled. I recalled that she had seen little on Gor of the dancing of female slaves.

I looked at her.

"She is so sensuous, and female!" she whispered.

I shrugged. "She is a slave," I said. Free women, incidentally, are seldom permitted to witness dances of the erotic power of the Sa-eela. The major reason for this, interestingly, is not that they might be offended or outraged, but for their own protection. Many times lovely, young free women, sometimes thinking that they have cleverly disguised themselves, donning male garments, pretending to be boys, thus seeking admission to the dances, find themselves set upon and stripped. Soon, in chains and well ravished, they find themselves as much slaves as the dancer. Perhaps, in their turn, too, they will be taught to dance. On their way to the market they may, if they wish, reflect upon what they, at that time, are likely to regard as their folly. Later, at the feet of a strong man, they may become clearer on the nature of the motivations that took them to such a performance in the first place. They were courting slavery, begging, in their way, for the steel of the collar, pleading to be subject, if they were not pleasing, to the cut of the whip. They had not truly been free women; they had only been, unbeknownst to themselves, slaves in search of their masters.

"I am hot, Master," said the little slave kneeling beside me.

"A bold admission," I said, "for a former Earth girl."

"And I am frightened," she whispered, suddenly.

"Of course," I said. "You now realize, even more clearly than before, what it might mean to be a slave on Gor."

She then clutched my arm, even more tightly, and then, she kneeling beside me, small and naked, helpless and vulnerable, her throat locked in the steel of my collar, on the tiles, we watched the dance of the female slave.

The music now, pounding and throbbing, mounted headily toward the climax of the Sa-eela.

In these, the final portions of the Sa-eela, the slave, in effect, puts herself at the mercy of the Master. She has already presented before him, almost in a delectable enumeration, many of the more external and rhythmic aspects of her beauty. She has displayed herself hitherto before him rather as an object in which, hopefully, he might take an interest. A woman may do this, of course, from many motives, such as fear or her desire to be purchased by an affluent master, only one of which might be her authentic, poignant desire to be found pleasing by him, for her own sake. In such displays there can be, though there often is not, a subtle psychological distinction, detectable in the behavior, between the merchandise, so to speak, and the girl who is displaying herself as merchandise. In the first case, where no true distinction exists, which is the authentic case, the girl, in effect, says, "I am for sale. Buy me, and love me!"

In the second case, the girl, in effect, says, "Here is a fine slave. Are you not interested in her?" In the second case, of course, the Gorean is interested, though the girl may not understand this clearly, in not only the merchandise but the girl who is displaying the merchandise. She might truly be terrified if she understood that it was she herself he intended to own, and, in fact, was going to own, she the exhibitor of the merchandise as well as she, the merchandise exhibited. Goreans, as I have mentioned, are interested in owning the whole woman, in all her sweetness, depth, complexity and individuality. They, and their whips and chains, settle for nothing less. To think of the imbonded woman as a slave object is in one sense quite correct, but, in another sense, it is a perversion of, and a failure to understand, the intimate and beautiful relations which can exist between masters and slaves.

The girl now, in all her helplessness, in all her desperation, in all her sensual splendor, was dancing not aspects or attributes of her beauty before her master, but was dancing her own passions, her own needs and desires, her own piteous, needful, beautiful, intimate and personal self before him. There were no restraints, no reservations, no compromises, no divisions or distinctions. Her needs were as exposed as her collared body. She danced herself before her master.

The music swirled to its climax and Peggy, turning, flung herself to her back on the tiles before Callimachus of Port Cos. As the music struck its last, rousing note, she arched her back, and flexed her legs, and looked back at him, her right arm extended piteously back towards him.

Callimachus, sweating, overcome, trembling, fists clenched, rose to his feet. He looked down at the supine slave, sweating, her breasts heaving, at his feet.

"She is, of course, yours," said Tasdron. "Jason and I thought you might find her of interest."

"Bring me binding fiber!" cried Callimachus, throatily, joyfully. "I must tie her!"

Lola fled from the table to search out binding fiber and, in a moment, returned to the table and knelt before Callimachus, head down, handing him a generous length of soft, silken, scarlet binding fiber. In another moment, Peggy, wincing, had been helplessly trussed, hand and foot, on the tiles.

"Escape!" ordered Callimachus.

"I cannot, Master!" cried the girl, struggling futilely. "You have tied me too well. I am helpless!"

"Escape!" commanded Callimachus.

"I cannot," wept the girl, "nor do I wish to, Master!"

I turned her over and examined the knots on her wrists and ankles, and then put her again on her back. "The knots are excellent," I said. "She has been securely bound. She is a well-tied slave. She cannot free herself."

Callimachus then cried out with joy and went to Tasdron, whom he embraced. He then came to me and seized my hand, and then embraced me, too, weeping. "My thanks," said Callimachus. "My thanks to you both!"

In his joy he had immediately tied the slave. He had waited not a moment longer than necessary to put her in his bonds. The practical and symbolic significance of binding the woman is, I gather, clear to all. It is a joyful, meaningful way of demonstrating power over the slave, and showing that she, in effect, belongs to you. It is a thrilling, exciting act for the master who binds, and for the helpless, dominated slave, who finds herself bound. "He who ties a woman owns her," is a Gorean saying. To be sure, strictly, a woman might find herself tied by a man who does not own her legally, but even in such a case, she will experience herself as being owned in a rather practical and significant sense, that sense, namely, in which she is completely at his mercy and under his control, that sense in which he may do with her as he pleases. Consider then the joy of binding when the master knows that he literally, and legally, owns the woman he binds; and she knows that she is the full and legal property, with no hope of escape or rescue, of the one who binds her.

Callimachus looked down at the bound slave. "From the first instant I saw you," he said, "I wanted you as my slave."

"And from the first instant I saw you, my Master!" cried the girl, looking up at him, "I was your slave!"

And then he reached down and seized her and, holding her by the upper arms, before him, she unable to stand, as she was bound, he began to cover her face and mouth, and throat, and breasts, with kisses.

"Oh, Master," begged Florence, "please take me home, and use me! Please, my Master, take me home, and use me!"

"It has been a pleasant evening," grinned Miles of Vonda, rising to his feet.

We all rose.

"I shall call you 'Peggy'," said Callimachus to his new slave. "It is a superb name for an Earth-girl slave."

"Yes, Master!" she said. "I am Peggy. I am Peggy!"

Tasdron signaled to the musicians, that they might now leave, and, quietly, not calling attention to themselves, they began to gather together their various instruments and other paraphernalia.

"Come, Slave. Step quickly. Off with the garment," said

Aemilianus to the voluptuous slave, who had been Shirley, whipping out the binding strap I had given him earlier.

Quickly she ran to him, stripped off the yellow gauze she had worn, turned her back to him and crossed her wrists. He then tied her wrists behind her back.

"May you get much service and joy from her," I said.

"I shall," he said, "if she wishes to live."

The girl trembled, and there was much laughter about the table.

"What will you call her?" I asked.

" 'Shirley'," said he. "That is an excellent name."

"An Earth-girl name!" laughed Glyco, meaningfully.

"You are Shirley," said Aemilianus to the slave.

"Yes, Master," she said. "I am Shirley." She trembled, her wrists helplessly confined in the loops of the binding strap. She had been given an Earth-girl name. She then realized just how perfect and complete would be the slavery to which she would be subjected in the house of Aemilianus. It would be a slavery at least analogous to that in which an Earth girl is held in a Gorean house. It was little wonder, then, that, hearing her new name, she had trembled in terror.

"Oh!" cried Lola, wincing, standing with her back to Calliodorus. He had tied her wrists behind her back.

He then turned her to face him. "Do you object, Lady Lola, of Port Cos?" he asked.

"I am not the Lady Lola, of Port Cos," she said. "I am only your lowly slave."

"Do not forget it," he said, lifting her head up with his fingers and, bending down, kissing her gently on the lips.

"No, Master," she whispered.

The last of the musicians had now filed from the house. I thought they had been superb. I would later, in a few days, send a tip for them to the tavern of Tasdron.

I glanced at the small, dark-haired slave. I expected that I would be spending the next few days muchly in the house. She, watching Calliodorus and Lola, did not realize that I had glanced upon her. That, I suspected, was just as well. Such heat and desire as might have been revealed in even so casual a glance might have frightened her. She would learn soon enough, lovely little collared beast, what it was, fully, on Gor, to be a master's slave.

I saw that Callimachus had now removed the binding fiber

from Peggy, with which he had so joyfully asserted his power over her, that he might bind her and make her helpless, and his ownership over her, that she was his to so bind and to so make helpless. She was on her knees before him, kissing at his feet and weeping. "Do you have another binding strap," asked Callimachus, sheepishly, "something to take her home in?"

"By some odd chance, I do," I said, grinning, and threw him such a strap. I had brought three such straps to the table, one for each of the girls who was to be awarded as a gift. In a moment Peggy was on her feet and her head was back. She winced and then laughed with joy. Her wrists had been tightly tied. She knew then that her life with Callimachus would not be easy, nor did she wish it to be. She did not want a weak man; she wanted a man strong enough to elicit, dominate and control the woman in her; Callimachus, a Gorean master, she now realized, would do so; she now realized that he would not compromise with her; she would be kept in total slavery, under the strictest of disciplines, fully owned and uncompromisingly mastered; she would serve him perfectly; she was joyful.

"Please, Master," begged Florence, "bind me in some way."

"Very well," said Miles of Vonda, kindly.

Peggy, her hands tied behind her back, went to kneel before Tasdron. He had given her to Callimachus. She kissed his feet in gratitude. "Thank you, Master," she wept, "thank you!"

"Thank you, Master," breathed Florence to Miles of Vonda. He had locked her hands behind her back, in slave bracelets. She, too, now had been bound by her master. His desire for her, and his mastery over her, had now been, to her joy, by the steel of the confining bracelets, attested. She extended her head to him, her lips pursed, her eyes closed, to kiss him, but he seized the sides of the opening of her slave tunic, the left side in his right fist, the right side in his left fist. "Master?" she asked, opening her eyes. The sides of her tunic were held tightly. "Master?" she asked. "Are you not a slave?" asked Miles of Vonda. "Yes, Master," she said. Then, suddenly, laughing, Miles of Vonda jerked open the tunic and tore it down about her lovely, flaring hips. He then thrust it open and back on her hips. Its upper portions hung back, depending from the belt, still in place, about her braceleted wrists. "Yes, Master!" she said. "March me naked through the streets as your slave. I love you!" Miles of Vonda then picked up the lyre, which she had used earlier in entertaining us. With its strap he slung the small, lovely, curved, stringed instrument about her body, the strap over her right shoulder, the instrument behind her left hip. The delicacy of the instrument, with its suggestion of refinement, gentility and civilization, contrasted nicely with the barbarity of her luscious, enslaved nudity, the shreds of her tunic and her helpless, steel-clasped wrists.

"I love you, Master!" she cried. She pressed her body to him and he, clasping her to him, with force and possessiveness, kissed her as his desired and owned slave. I had little doubt that when he arrived home he would play well upon her body, making it the instrument of his attentions. He would draw forth from her by his skills rhapsodies of movements, cries, moans, utterances and admissions, a music to the ears of both the conquering master and the delicious, yielding slave, she who finds, and can find, her most glorious victory only in her most complete and devastating defeat. "I love you, Master!" she was weeping. "I love you!"

Tasdron, with a snapping of his fingers calling Peggy to her feet, removed his collar from about her neck, and she ran to stand, head down, deferential and bound, near Callimachus. I threw Aemilianus the key to the collar of Shirley, and he removed it from her. I myself took the steel of my collar from Lola's throat.

"Thank you for giving me to Calliodorus," she said.

"Serve him well," I said.

"I shall. I shall!" she said.

Slave girls, of course, may speak the name of their masters to others, for example, as in locutions such as, "I am the girl of Calliodorus of Port Cos," or "I come from the house of Calliodorus." It is only that they are seldom, in addressing the master himself, permitted to use his name. He is usually addressed simply as "Master," or as "my Master."

"I have an announcement to make," said Tasdron, "for which I have waited until now." We regarded him. The slaves knelt. A free man was speaking. "The forces of the Vosk League are soon to be organized," said Tasdron. "It is my honor and pleasure to inform you that one among us has agreed to act as the commander of these forces. He is, of course, Callimachus, of Port Cos!"

"Congratulations!" I cried to Callimachus, shaking his hand. There was Gorean applause.

"The appointment was made earlier this afternoon, in a secret session of the High Council of the Vosk League," said Tasdron, "that body sovereign in the league, composed of representatives drawn from all the member towns." Tasdron smiled at me. "This time and place," he said, "seemed appropriate for making the first public announcement of the appointment."

"Thank you, Tasdron," I said. He had honored my house. Peggy was looking up at Callimachus, from her knees, her hands bound behind her back. Her eyes were shining. How proud she was of her master.

"But what of Port Cos?" asked Calliodorus. "Are you not to return to Port Cos, to replace Callisthenes, to become High Captain?"

"That post is yours, my friend, Calliodorus," said Glyco.

"My thanks!" said Calliodorus.

We applauded him, congratulating him and expressing our approval of the wisdom of the appointment. On her knees beside him, her hands tightly bound behind her back in the black binding strap, Lola pressed her lips fervently against his leg, and looked up at him. Her eyes shone, too. How proud, too, she was of her master!"

Tasdron reached into his pouch. "I am sure that you recognize this," he said. He held, in his hands, two pieces of rock.

"The topaz!" said Aemilianus.

"The topaz!" said Calliodorus.

"What you do not know," said Tasdron, "is that long ago, over a century ago, this stone, unbroken, was the Home Stone of Victoria."

We were startled. There was silence in the room.

"Over a hundred years ago," said Tasdron, "it was carried away by pirates, and broken. Since that time Victoria has not had a Home Stone. What had once been our Home Stone served then as nothing more than a pledge symbol among the buccaneers of the river. In a few days we of the council of Victoria will go down to the river. There, from the shore of the Vosk, we shall select a common stone, not much unlike others. That, then, shall be the new Home Stone of Victoria."

There were tears in my eyes.

"What of the topaz?" asked Aemilianus.

"It has been broken," said Tasdron. "No longer may it serve as a Home Stone."

"Why have you brought it here?" asked Calliodorus.

"Ar's Station and Port Cos," said Tasdron, "are mighty powers on the river. I brought it here that I might give one half to you, Aemilianus, and one half to you, Calliodorus. In all that may later ensue, whatever it may be, do not forget that you once fought together, and once were comrades."

Tasdron then gave half of the topaz to Aemilianus and the other half to Calliodorus.

"My thanks," said Aemilianus.

"My thanks," said Calliodorus.

Then Aemilianus looked at Calliodorus. "Let us never forget the topaz," he said.

"We will not," said Calliodorus.

We then went to the door, and, as pleasantries were exchanged, our guests, one by one, began to take their leave. Miles of Vonda left first, heeled by his curvacious, auburn-haired beauty, Florence, once, too, of Vonda. On the street, below, at the foot of the stairs, he ordered her to precede him. She then did so, well exposed in the shreds of the tunic, the delicate lyre slung behind her left hip, her wrists fastened behind her, with Gorean efficiency, in her master's steel. She walked before him, her shoulders back, her head high; she walked before him, happily, beautifully, a loved, paraded slave. Aemilianus next left, heeled by Shirley. Following him, Glyco and Calliodorus, both of Port Cos, left, the pair being heeled by Lola.

Tasdron and Callimachus paused at the door.

"Tasdron," said I, "when the council arrives at the shore of the Vosk, it is my hope that I may be there."

"It is our hope, too, that you will be there," said Tasdron, "with the others of Victoria."

We clasped hands. Tasdron then left. He carried with him the brief white tunic which Peggy had worn, and the collar which he had taken from her throat. They would fit other girls.

"Congratulations, again!" I said to Callimachus.

"Thank you," he said. "I shall, of course, need strong men, men from the various towns, men tried and true."

"Doubtless you will find them," I said. "The finest swords on the river will be eager to place themselves in your service."

He then casually thrust Peggy ahead of him through the door, and she hurried, bound, down to the first landing of the stairs, some yards above the street. Callimachus followed her a step or two, and then he turned, and faced me.

"The temporary headquarters of the forces of the Vosk League," he said to me, "will be in the private serving room of the tavern of Tasdron. You know the place."

"Of course," I said. We had met there, many times.

"In five days," said Callimachus, "you will report to me there."

"Report?" I asked.

"I have selected you as my second in command," he said.

"Callimachus!" I cried.

"Or do you, now that you are rich, fear the travail of the service, the offices of such a guardsman?"

"No!" I cried.

"Then you have your orders," he said.

"Yes, Captain!" I said.

He then went down one or two stairs, and then turned, and again faced me. "We might discuss this at greater length, but, as you might understand," he said, jerking a thumb at the nude, bound Peggy, waiting for him on the landing, "I am in a hurry to get this slave home, and use her."

"Yes, Captain," I grinned.

He then joined Peggy on the landing. He regarded the lovely, bound slave. She drew back. "Am I not to heel you, my Master?" she asked.

"Precede me," he said.

"Yes, Master," she said.

"Thus," said he, "should any of Victoria be abroad at this hour they may observe the value and the quality of the animal, this lovely gift, which I have been given."

"Yes, Master," she said.

"And, too," he smiled, "I wish to anticipate the pleasures which I am shortly to derive from you."

"Yes, Master," she laughed, and hurried down the stairs ahead of him.

I then closed the door, and threw the bolts and bars in place. I then turned and looked at the small slave standing near me. "Go to a place near the table," I said, "and kneel there on the tiles, with your head bowed, deferentially." "Yes, Master," she said, and hurried to obey. I then went about the house, locking and securing it. The dancers, and their master, of course, had gone long ago. I had made many improvements in the house. I set the bars and bolts in place at the back door, leading from the kitchen. I attended, too, to the windows. When I returned to the vicinity of the table the house, in effect, had been transformed into a small fortress.

I looked at the small slave, kneeling, head down, on the scarlet tiles, in the light of the lamps.

"We are alone," I said.

"Yes, Master," she said.

"You may lift your head," I said.

"Yes, Master," she said.

I walked about her, examining her. She was very beautiful.

"May I speak, Master?" she asked.

"Yes," I said.

"You brought three binding straps to the table," she said.

"Yes," I said.

"But you brought none for me?"

"No," I said.

"Ah," she said.

"Your gift to me, your performance, during the course of the black wine," I said, "was very beautiful."

"Thank you, Master," she said. "But it was not a mere entertainment. I had long fantasized stripping myself before you, and offering myself to you as your slave."

"Really?" I said.

"Yes," she said. "And in many fashions, and ways."

"You shall enact these for me in the future," I said.

"I shall be pleased to do so, Master," she said.

"How long have you entertained these fantasies?" I asked.

"Even on Earth," she said. "I can even recall attempting to decide what might be the most sensuous way I could remove a bikini before you."

I took her by the upper arms and put her forward, on her belly, on the tiles, and then I crossed her wrists behind her body, and her ankles. It is a standard binding position. She then retained this position, not having been given permission to break it, while I went to the tiles at the foot of the table and gathered up the two golden straps with which, earlier, she had simulated the footwear she had worn at the restaurant. I then returned to her side and crouched down. I then began to tie her, her wrists with one of the straps, and her ankles with the other.

"Had you fantasized thusly," I asked, tying her, "the removal of your clothing, the white-sheath gown, and such, and the offering of yourself to me as a slave, on the night of our meeting at the restaurant?"

She winced. I checked the knots.

I then turned her to her back.

"Yes, Master," she said, looking up at me, "but then, of course, I did not know that slaves were not permitted purses nor, without their master's explicit permission, a nether closure to their garments."

I stood up, and looked down at her.

"You have tied me," she said. "I am helpless! You own me!"

"But you were testy, ill-tempered, belligerent in the restaurant," I said.

She squirmed on the tiles, bound. "I was a confused Earth woman," she said. "I did not know what to do!"

She tried to pull her ankles apart. "Please untie my ankles, Master," she begged. "Let me throw them apart for you!"

"It seems you now know what to do," I said.

"I did not know then what I was," she sobbed. "I know now what I am! Please untie me now, Master! Please let me serve you!"

"You will be untied if, and when, I please," I told her. "Yes, Master!" she sobbed. I then sat down, cross-legged, a few feet from her. I wished to think. She was an interesting, complex slave.

The former graduate student in English literature, bound, nude and collared, struggled to her knees. She looked at me.

"It is rather different from Earth, isn't it?" I asked.

"Yes, Master," she said.

"Do you know your place, and condition?" I asked.

"Yes, Master," she said. "My place is at your feet. My condition is that of a slave."

I then gave myself to thought.

"Master," she asked, "may I speak?"

"No," I told her.

"Yes, Master," she said.

I then considered many things, Earth and its miseries, the nature of life, genetic endowments, biology, civilizations, chains and collars, and the small, excruciatingly desirable, curvacious beasts that are human females.

I heard her whimper. I looked up. "Yes?" I said.

"May I speak, Master?" she asked.

"Yes," I said.

"Thank you for tying me," she whispered.

I nodded. In tying her I had, of course, demonstrated her desirability for me. She was worth tying. Too, I had demonstrated for her, in a way that is incontrovertible for a female, my mastery over her. I had tied her. Too, of course, I had enjoyed tying her, making her helpless and mine. It is a great pleasure for a man to tie a woman. It is interesting to consider, when one thinks of it, that there are probably many men who, in all their lives, have never tied a woman. These, of course, are not Gorean men.

I stood up, and looked down at her. She shrank back. This amused me.

"Alas," she said, lightly, "now I must clear the table, and finish the dishes, and put the house in order."

"Such things can wait," I told her.

"Oh," she said.

I continued to regard her.

"Doubtless I am now to be locked in my kennel for the night," she said.

"No," I said.

"Oh," she said.

I continued to regard her, amused. She squirmed on her knees.

"Master gave away two girls tonight," she said, lightly. "But he kept me. He kept me in his collar."

"Yes," I said.

"Is that meaningful?" she asked.

"Perhaps," I said.

"I am now the only girl in the house," she said.

"Yes," I said.

"Am I to be kept for full service?" she asked.

"Doubtless you have much to learn of cooking and sewing," I said, "but I have no doubt that you are already a superb little maid and laundress."

"Does Master intend to buy other girls?" she asked.

"That will be decided later," I said.

"I shall endeavor to be such that master will find the purchase of others girls unnecessary," she said.

"But then," I said, "you would have to render a full service."

She put her head down, shyly. "It is my desire," she said, "to render my master a full service."

"A full Gorean service?" I asked.

"Despise me, if you must, my Master," she said, "but the answer is a most emphatic 'Yes!'"

"It had better be," I said.

"It is," she laughed. "It is, my Master!"

I walked over to her, and looked down into her eyes.

"But will you not, sometimes, remember that you knew me from Earth?"

"Yes," I said.

"But you made me serve your guests naked," she said, reproachfully.

"Of course," I said. "There were two reasons for that. Neither of them, of course, need be made known to you."

"Please, Master," she said.

"The first reason," I said, "was for your own instruction. In performing such servile tasks for the guests, and while naked, were you not fully conscious that you were a slave?"

"Quite, Master," she said. "I am certain that I have profited well from the lesson."

"Secondly," I said, "you are very pretty. Thus your nudity contributed to the pleasure of the guests and myself, thereby improving the course of the liqueurs."

"Then you might have me serve nude anytime?" she asked.

"Of course," I said.

"Even though you knew me from Earth?"

"Of course," I said. "Do not expect, simply because we are both of Earth origin, that this will soften your slavery. It will only make it more delectable."

"Yes, Master," she said. "Master," she said.

"Yes," I said.

"I do not want my slavery to be softened," she said, "for any reason."

"It will not be," I told her.

"I beg to be kept in a full, and hard, slavery," she said, looking up at me.

"You will be," I told her.

"Without compromise," she begged.

"Without compromise," I said.

"Thank you, Master," she said. "It is how I have always wanted to serve you, even from the first moment I saw you, on the campus of the university."

"And, too," I said, "from the first moment I saw you, it was the form of service I wished from you."

"It is now yours, my Master," she said.

I then crouched down and gently lowered her, to her back, on the tiles. I then stood up, and looked down at her, naked and bound, at my feet.

"Please rape me, Master," she said. "Please subject me to slave rape."

"Why?" I asked.

She looked up at me, startled. She squirmed in the bonds. There were tears in her eyes.

"I beg to be raped," she said. "Please, Master, rape me! Rape me!"

"Why?" I asked.

"Is it not obvious?" she asked, weeping, twisting in the golden straps.

I smiled.

"I—I," she stammered.

"Say it," I said.

"I—I am hot in my collar!" she wept. She then blushed crimson.

"What a vulgar little slave, you are," I said.

"What a beast Master is," she said, "to make a girl so explicitly confess her needs."

I then crouched down and untied her ankles, but I held them together in my hands. I felt them trying, straining, to move apart, but they could not do so. She had little leverage and, in any event, her strength was as nothing compared to mine. They would not be thrown apart until I wished.

"This will be the first time that you have truly had me, as my own Master," she said. "You took me in the Street of the Writhing Slave as a Coin Girl, a mere rent girl, a street girl, a gutter wench, and you have taken me, I a helpless slave, I not knowing you, in the guise of my unknown Gorean master, but this will be the first time that you have had me, so to speak, in your own name and right."

"Yes," I said.

"Please, Master," she said, "may I beg one thing! Let it be swift, efficient and uncaring. Put me under your lust, as a mere object!"

I regarded her. Obviously at my least touch she would go into orgasm. I had never seen a slave more ready for exploitative penetration. She wanted her first having by me, in my own name and right, to be one which would make it clear to her that she, in my arms, was only a mere slave.

"Oh!" she cried, as I flung apart her ankles. She looked at me, in sudden fear. Then I took her.

"Oh, yes! Yes!" she cried.

Then I withdrew from her.

She lay at my feet, on her side, her hands bound behind her. "Oh, yes, yes," she whimpered.

I had had her casually, swiftly, ruthlessly, without sensitivity or tenderness. I had had her as a meaningless piece of slave meat.

"Yes," she moaned, softly, "yes, yes."

I looked down at her. Sexuality in the human female is a marvelous, deep, complex and total thing. Consider the female at my feet. I had scorned to show her the least respect. I had treated her as trash, and a worthless slave. Yet she moaned, bound, on the tiles, in joy. She had been treated as she had wished, as one who was merely mine, and must submit, in the order of nature. I looked down at her. Her entire body, in all its curves and beauty, cried out her vulnerable sexuality. What scoundrel, I wondered, would refuse to satisfy the needs of the female of his species?

I kicked the girl with the side of my foot. "You are now in your place, Slave," I said.

"Yes, Master," she said. "You had me well."

With my foot I rolled her to her back on the tiles before me.

"Will Master keep me?" she asked. "Did I please Master?"

"You were not entirely displeasing," I said. "At least for the time, you will be kept."

"I will try to work out," she said.

I looked down at her, on her back, her hands tied, on the tiles at my feet.

"I will try desperately to work out," she said.

"On your belly," I said. Then I went to her and untied her

hands. Quickly she rose to her knees before me. She held my legs and, softly, kissed my left thigh.

"Now that I have had you, and I have decided to keep you about, at least for the time," I said, "we must try to think of some name for you."

"Yes, Master," she said.

"But there is no great hurry in the matter," I said.

"No, Master," she said. For now she would continue nameless. Many times, incidentally, a new girl is not immediately given a name. If one doesn't know if she will work out, or be kept, it is sometimes not thought worth the while to waste a name on her. Similarly, sometimes a master waits a few days to name the slave, to see if an appropriate name, one seemingly right for the girl, suggests itself. Most of the time, of course, it must be admitted, the girl, like a pet sleen, is promptly named. It makes it much more convenient to refer to her, and summon her. The name she is given, of course, is a function of the will of the Master, and names may be changed, as he pleases. Sometimes, for example, a girl may be rewarded with a lovely name, or punished with an ugly one.

"Thank you for my slave rape," she said. "It is how I wished first to be had by you."

"It seemed appropriate for a low slave," I said.

"Yes, Master," she said. "Thank you, Master." I felt her nibbling at the tunic at my thigh, and kissing, softly, through it. I felt the dampness, the wet, from her small, warm mouth, and, too, through the cloth, the movement of her tongue. "Master did not even remove his tunic," she said.

"Do you object, in the least?" I asked.

"No, Master," she said. "I am only a slave."

"To your work," I said, jerking my thumb toward the table.

Startled, she rose swiftly to her feet and went to the table, where she, kneeling down, began to gather together the dishes and stack them.

It pleased me to see her, naked and in my collar, engaged in this necessary and menial labor, fitting for a slave. This also gave me the opportunity I desired, unseen by her, to fetch forth from the chest an object which, long ago, I had purchased for her on the great concourse near the wharves.

I moved quietly behind her, as she knelt, working, at the

table, the object, in several loops, held between my hands. I then, with one motion, slung the loops over her head and body, and jerked back, straightening her body, and pinning her arms to her sides. "Chain!" she cried. "Master!" She tensed her body and struggled, but only for an instant. I tightened the chains. She ceased struggling. The chains were tight in her flesh. "Master?" she asked. I then lifted the chains from her, and held them out, before her. "It is beautiful," she said.

She saw now that the chains had been the loops of a single, graceful body chain, sinuous and glossy, closely meshed and dark, ornamented with colorful beads of wood, semiprecious stones and bits of leather. Its full loop is some five feet in length, and it can be wound and looped, and twisted and strung about a woman's body in a variety of intricate fashions. It is light and the closeness of its meshing allows it to follow closely the contours of a woman's body. It is unbreakable. It may be worn with or without clothing. By means of small clips, snap clips or lock clips, it may be used to secure as well as adorn a woman. It is to be worn, of course, only by a slave. "It is beautiful, my Master!" she said. "Is it mine?"

"It is mine," I said, "as you are. You own nothing. It is you, rather, who are owned."

"Yes, Master," she laughed, "but did you not buy it for me?"

"For you, or for any other slave," I said, lightly.

"I think I am the slave you had in mind," she said.

"Perhaps," I said.

"The first time you ever looked at me, on the campus of the university," she said, "you looked upon me as though I might be a slave."

"I did?" I asked.

"Yes," she said. "Do you think a woman does not know when she is being looked upon as though she might be a slave? We are not stupid, my dear Master. Furthermore, you looked upon me as though I might be your slave."

"I was not, at that time, clearly aware of such things," I said.

"And, in my heart, beneath those ridiculous garments of Earth I then wore, I knew that you were right."

"You would scarcely greet me," I said. "It seemed you would scarcely deign to recognize my existence."

"I was afraid," she said. "Everything was suddenly so different. Can you imagine what it would be for an Earth girl, with all her conditioning, and her education and training, to suddenly recognize that she is a female, and has met her master?"

"Doubtless it would be a troubling insight," I admitted.

"Put the chain on me, Master," she laughed. "I am eager to see how I look in it!"

"Vain slave," I said. Then she stood and I, from behind, looped the chain about her. She hurried to one wall, where there was a full-length mirror, and, turning and posing, and adjusting the chain on herself, she examined herself.

"It is beautiful," she said, turning. "How I pity poor free women who cannot wear such things." Then she looked at herself, frontally, and, skeptically, tilting her head one way and another, experimented with the chain, varying its lines, loopings and tensions. She adjusted it with her small hands with meticulous care and fastidious taste. "I think I would bring a high price," she said, not taking her eyes from the mirror.

"In a market," I said, "you would not be sold in the chain."

"Even so," she said, "if I were a man, I think I might buy me."

I did not respond.

"Of Shirley, Peggy, Lola and myself," she asked, "who is the most beautiful?"

"Most men," I said, "would probably pay most for Shirley, as most men would regard her as the most desirable, if not the most beautiful. Then I would think that Peggy would bring the next highest price, and then Lola, and then you."

"I would be last?" she asked, still looking in the mirror.

"I think so," I said, "clearly."

"But surely some men would find me attractive," she said.

"Of course," I said.

"I think I would bring a good price," she said.

"You might," I said.

"You do not find me unattractive, do you, Master?" she asked, lifting her hands to her head and throwing back her hair, regarding herself.

"You are being kept," I pointed out, "at least for the time."

"You do find me attractive, don't you, Master?" she asked, turning to face me.

"You are not found to be entirely displeasing to my senses," I said.

She swiftly came to where I stood and knelt down before me, and kissed my feet, and then lifted her head, looking at me. "That pleases me, my Master," she said.

I then lifted her to her feet, but did not permit her to press her lips to mine.

"Do you like the chain?" I asked.

"Yes, Master," she said, "it is beautiful."

"It is not expensive," I said. "It is a common piece of slave jewelry."

"Fit for a low slave," she smiled.

"It also has certain features of which you might not be immediately aware," I said.

"Oh!" she said. Then she tried to pull her wrists apart, from behind the back of her body. "I am chained!" she said.

"Yes," I said. With the small clips, using convenient portions of the chain, I had fastened her hands behind her. With the clips, of course, she may be chained by the hands and feet, and waist and neck, in almost any conceivable position.

"I now see why free women do not wear these things," she smiled.

The chain was now secured with snap clips, which are usually perfectly adequate, as the girl, as she is chained, cannot reach or undo the snaps. I had also, however, purchased a set of lock slips, which are useful in some chaining situations or out-of-doors, where, say, one would not wish a stranger to be able to gag the slave, undo the clips and carry her off from where, perhaps, she has been chained to a post. The body chain I had purchased, though efficient, and attractive and sturdy, was not an expensive one. Some such chains, of course, such as those sometimes worn by high slaves, are quite expensive, being of gold and set with such stones as rubies, sapphires and diamonds.

She moved away from me, and turned before me. "Am I pretty in your chain?" she asked.

I wanted to scream with pleasure, the little she-sleen! How

well the little beast knew what she was doing! What a slave she was.

"I see that you think I would bring a good price," she said.

I clenched my fists.

"You do find me quite attractive, you know," she said.

I said nothing.

"Masters find it so difficult to conceal their desire," she laughed.

I said nothing.

"I am helpless, you know," she said, trying to pull her wrists apart.

"I know," I said.

"May I approach Master?" she asked.

"Yes," I said.

She came and stood quite close to me, within the cricle of my space, close, as a slave may stand to her master. Her nearness was almost overwhelming. I thrust her back. She regarded me, amused, observing me scrutinizing her bared beauty. She knew I owned it.

"Doubtless I am now to be unchained," she said, "that I may attend to my domestic labors, clearing the table, and such, but then, perhaps, it was not for that reason that Master chained me so helplessly. Perhaps he has other plans in mind for me. I know that he need not reveal to me his intentions with respect to me, but, naturally, I am curious."

"Curiosity is not becoming in a Kajira," I said.

"Granted, Master," she said, "but, as you must understand, in certain situations, as when a woman finds herself naked and chained before a man, a certain amount of curiosity on her part regarding her fate is almost unavoidable."

"I think it is time to throw you in your kennel," I said. "There you may ponder your cleverness." I seized her angrily by the arm and pulled her, stumbling, toward her kennel. "No, Master!" she cried. "Please, no!"

In moments I had thrust her into the low, cement, steel-barred kennel. She scrambled about, on her knees, on the blanket on the cement floor, her hands chained behind her, to face outward, just as the steel-barred gate clanged down, locking, in front of her. I saw the shadows of the bars on her face and body. She thrust her face, and beauty, against the bars. "Please, Master," she begged, "don't kennel me!"

"Why not?" I asked.

She regarded me, through the bars, her face pressed close against them. She was on her knees. A girl cannot stand in the kennel. Its low ceiling, about four feet in height, does not permit it. She drew back, slightly, from the bars. "The kennel is cold, and hard," she said.

I turned away.

"Master," she cried, "please don't go!"

I turned again, to face her.

"I will try to be a good slave," she said, "humble, docile, loving and obedient."

Again I turned from her.

"Master," she cried, "let me beg for what I want!"

I turned to face her.

"Let me beg on my belly for what I want!" she said, her face pressed against the bars, tears in her eyes.

I went to the gate of the kennel and unlocked it, and flung it upwards, and stepped back.

The slave then, on her belly, squirmed forth from the kennel. I stepped back five paces, that she must follow me. Then she lay before me, submitting and prone, on the tiles.

"Did you wish to speak?" I asked her.

She lifted her head. "I beg your touch, Master," she said.

I looked down upon her. The depth, extent and distribution of sexually active areas on the female body is, of course, considerable. Indeed, in sexual arousal, her entire body can become sensitized, and, so to speak, sexually vulnerable and flammable. Her sexual response can become one of the entire squirming, yielding, overwhelmed organism. When a woman yields it is all of her that yields. Her response, of course, is far more than crudely physical. It constitutes a psychophysiological ecstasy, a rhapsody of being owned and had. Her sexual response, thus, is far more than a simplistic response to physical stimuli. It is a function of an entire situation and condition. It is, thus, perhaps, that the female slave, knowing herself slave and owned, attains sexual heights and depths, orgasms and totalities of response, forever denied, in the nature of things, to her ignorant sisters, cool and inhibited, smug in their prides and freedoms. The slave girl, in effect, is the woman in her place in nature. It is there, in her own place and world, and there only, that she can attain her biological destiny, that she can find her total female fulfillment. Free, she is enslaved, the prisoner of inhibitions, artifices and conventions; enslaved, she is free, liberated to the self-fulfillment of her deepest nature. Free, she is enslaved; enslaved, she is free. That is the paradox of the collar.

"I am the only woman in the house, Master," said the slave.

I did not speak.

"Do not lock my softness away from you tonight, in the kennel," she begged. "Let it be near to you."

"Do you have sexual needs?" I asked.

"Yes, Master," she said.

"Do you want them satisfied?" I asked.

"Yes, Master," she said.

"Do you confess yourself to be a lowly and passionate slave?" I asked.

"Yes, Master," she said. "I am a lowly and passionate slave."

"One who is eager to please her Master?" I asked.

"Yes, Master," she said.

I looked down at her, on her belly, her small hands chained behind her. The passions of the female slave are a mystery to many free women who, unaroused and sexually inert, never collared and owned, cannot even understand them; to most free women, of course, the passions of the female slave are not so much a mystery as a source of envy and fury; she senses that they, deep and precious, making the slave so helpless and vulnerable, are far beyond anything which she herself possesses. Sometimes, perhaps, twisting on her couch at night in frustration, the free woman may dimly sense what it is to be an aroused slave, a woman so much at the mercy of men, and so precious and beautiful to them; the free woman clenches her fists and moans; the slave may throw herself to the feet of men and beg to please them, as she cannot.

"Master, Master," whimpered the small slave, lying before me.

I looked down at her. Her passions had been well ignited. This had been done, doubtless, by her condition, and by masters. She was a slave.

"Do not kennel me, Master," she begged. "Sleep me at your slave ring."

I smiled. The girl whom I had known on Earth, now my

nameless slave on Gor, had begged to be slept at my slave ring.

"Chain me by the neck at the foot of your couch, my Master," she begged, "as you might a slut or a she-sleen. You need not even touch me. It will be enough for me, if I am merely allowed to lie near you."

"On your feet," I told her.

Swiftly she scrambled to her feet and stood before me. I looked at her, and she, swiftly, deferentially, put down her head. "Now you are beginning to be pleasing," I told her.

"Thank you, Master," she said.

I touched the side of her face, gently. She lifted her head. "Perhaps I will deign to touch you," I said.

"Thank you, Master," she whispered.

"Strip me," I said.

"But I am chained!" she cried, trying, futilely, to pull her wrists apart.

I smiled.

"Forgive me, Master," she laughed. "I am such a stupid slave!"

Then she fell to her knees before me and, with her teeth, untied the sandals and removed them from my feet. She then stood, and, bending over, her hands helplessly chained behind her, bit and pulled at the knot in the cord that belted my tunic. When she had freed this knot she went behind me, first to my left shoulder, and then to my right shoulder, and, with her small, fine teeth, drew the tunic from my body.

"Ohh," she said, softly, "Master is beautiful."

"I cannot be beautiful," I said, rather irritatedly. "I am a man. I might be good-looking, or handsome, perhaps, but I cannot be beautiful. And even such things, I suspect, would be rather controversial."

"To me," she said, "you are lean, and strong and beautiful."

I looked at her, angrily.

"And you own me," she smiled.

"That, at least, is uncontroversial," I said.

"Shall I heel my Master to his bedroom," she asked, "or does he desire that I precede him?"

"I shall carry you," I said.

"As Master wishes," she said, breathlessly.

I put my hands on her.

"Oh!" she said.

I then rubbed my fingers and smelled my hand. "Slaves, too, it seems," I said, "sometimes find it difficult to conceal their desire."

"Yes, Master," she laughed.

"Oh!" she said. "You are going to carry me like this," she asked, "upside down and in front of you?"

"Yes," I said, "and as I ascend the stairs slowly, you will please me."

"Yes, Master," she laughed.

At the top of the stairs I stopped, and shuddered, and cried out.

"Perhaps I should have gagged Master," she said.

I then carried her, over my shoulder, into the bedroom, to throw her to the foot of my couch, beneath the slave ring.

XXI

THE SLAVE RING;
THE WHIP IS KISSED;
BLACK WINE;
A SLAVE IS NAMED;
ECSTASY

How small and soft she was, and how beautiful, lying in my arms, on the furs of love, at the foot of my couch, in the soft light of the ravishment lamp.

About her throat, over the slender, identificatory collar, a heavy, thick iron collar had been locked, with a heavy chain, leading to the stout loop of the slave ring, some eight inches in width, fixed in the foot of the couch.

"I am so happy, my Master," she said. "I am so happy."

Her first taking had been on the floor of the bedroom, she still locked in the body chain. I had then relieved her of its restraint, that the evening might properly begin.

With her own hands I had forced her to spread the furs of love and light the ravishment lamp. I had then had her kneel at the foot of the couch, and had chained her by the neck to the slave ring. I had then had her kiss the whip. I had then again taken her.

Before this last having of her she had lain on her back on the furs crying out with joy, feeling the heavy collar on her throat, and the weight of the chain that fastened her by the collar to the slave ring. "I cannot slip it," she had said, trying to force the collar from her. "No," I had said. "The chain is so heavy!" she had purred. "It will hold you well," I had told her. Then she had risen to her hands and knees. She had reached out and touched the slave ring with her right hand, and then she had crawled to it, and kissed it. She had then turned to face me, on all fours, the chain dangling down from her collar. "I love being chained to your slave ring," she had said. I had then drawn her towards me and thrown her on her back. "Yes, Master," she had whimpered, eagerly throwing her legs apart.

"I am so happy," she whispered, lying in my arms. "I had never dreamed I could be so happy."

I thrust the whip again to her mouth and, tenderly, softly, holding it to her lips, she covered it with kisses.

"You enjoy kissing the whip, don't you?" I asked.

"Yes, Master," she said.

"You know well what its lash can do to your softness, do you not?" I asked.

"Yes, Master," she smiled.

"And yet you kiss it lovingly," I said.

"Yes, my Master," she said.

"Why?" I asked.

"I do not know," she said. "Perhaps it is a symbol, plain to my vulnerable womanhood, of your manhood, which makes me such a yielding slave. Perhaps it is a symbol of your dominance over me."

"Does it seem to you that you are kissing a symbol?" I said.

"Perhaps on some level it seems so," she said, "but I experience it rather differently. It is, you see, a real whip, and one that can be used on me. Thus it seems to me that what I am really doing is kissing a whip, your whip. The whip, in itself, is not a symbol. It is a real whip. It may, of course, have symbolic significance."

"Kissing the whip is for you," I said, "apparently a rich sexual, and emotional, experience."

"Yes, Master," she said. "And even if you were a hated master, it would still, for us slaves, be such an experience."

"Even if the master were a hated one?" I asked.

"Yes," she said. "On one level we might hate to kneel before him and kiss his whip, but on another level we would be thrilled that he had made us do so. He would be showing us that we are women. Master, perhaps, being a man, cannot fully understand, or understand in its total fullness, what it is for a woman to kneel naked before a man and be forced to kiss his whip. It is, I assure you, a very meaningful experience, and one which she understands in every bit of her body. Indeed, after having kissed a man's whip it is very difficult to continue to hate him, even if he wishes us to do so, enjoying perhaps the humiliation and taming of a woman who hates him. Rather, as slaves, now taught by our master, we find ourselves, almost against our wills, considering how we might perhaps better serve and please him."

"I see," I said.

"All women want to be owned by a man strong enough to make her kiss his whip," she said. "What woman would want to be owned by a man of any other sort?"

I said nothing.

"You will be strong with me, will you not?" she asked. "You will make me do, and be, uncompromisingly, and as a slave, what you want, will you not?"

"Yes," I said.

"Then I kiss your whip," she said, "and love it."

"You enjoy being a slave?" I asked.

"I am a slave," she said, "and I love it."

"You know that you cannot change your mind on this matter," I said, "and that there is no escape for you on Gor."

"I know it well, Master," she said. "On this world, the law even, as I am a slave, in all its force, puts me in your total power."

"In the total power of any Master," I said, "to whom you might legally belong."

"Yes, Master," she shuddered. "But it is my hope that you will be kind to me."

"I shall see if you serve well," I said.

"I shall serve well," she said. "I think that you will find that the girl you knew on Earth, now collared on Gor, will supply you with wonders of service."

"Serve me now," I said.

"Immediately, and in any way Master wishes," she said.

She lay on her stomach, on her elbows beside me. I lay on my back, looking up at the ceiling.

"Several collars were removed tonight," she said, "those of Shirley, of Lola and Peggy."

"To be replaced with other collars shortly," I said.

"My collar was not removed," she said. "You kept me."

"Yes," I said.

"I think you like me," she said. "You could have taken me to the market and sold me. You could do that easily. You are a Gorean master. But you did not do so. I think that perhaps you like me."

"Perhaps," I said.

"That will not endanger our relationship, do you think?" she asked.

"I do not think so," I smiled.

"You are rich, aren't you?" she asked.

"As Goreans go," I said. "I think, yes."

"You could buy many girls?" she asked.

"Yes," I said.

"But I am the only girl in the house," she said, pointedly.

"At the moment," I said.

"Oh," she said.

I regarded her, smiling.

"I will try to be such that you will feel neither the need nor the desire for others," she said.

"Do you think that you can do the work, and supply the love and service of several, Nameless Slave?" I asked.

"Yes, Master," she said, fervently, "yes, a thousand times yes!"

"I shall give you an opportunity to prove yourself," I said.

"I ask nothing more," she said.

"You need training," I said.

"Train me!" she cried. "Train me, piteously, mercilessly, to your standards and pleasure!"

"I shall do so," I said, quietly.

"Yes, Master," she said, trembling.

I held her in my arms, looking down into her eyes. She looked up at me, lovingly.

"I do not need to report for five days," I told her. "I think that will give us time to become better acquainted."

"I thought we were already rather well acquainted, Master," she smiled, "and intimately."

"I do not even know your name," I said.

"You have not yet given me one!" she laughed.

"I want to know millions of things about you," I said.

"I am your chained slave," she said. "What else do you need to know?"

"Everything," I said.

"The talents of my tongue and fingers?" she asked.

"Everything," I said, "even your smallest movements and most trivial thoughts."

"You want to own all of me, don't you?" she asked.

"I do own all of you," I said. "It is only, now, that I am growing curious about what I own."

"You wish to make inquiries into the nature of your property?" she said.

"Yes," I said.

"I am a girl, and a slave, and I love you," she said.

I kissed her.

"I can tell you my measurements," she said, "and my collar size, and the sizes of the wrist and ankle rings that will fit me. I was forced to memorize these things before my first sale."

"I am tempted to grow fond of you," I said.

"Of a slave?" she asked.

"To be sure," I said, "the thought is surely foolish."

She suddenly lifted her lips to mine and kissed me, deeply and softly, rather helplessly, almost in desperation. "I am almost melting with love for you, my Master," she said. "I know my will means nothing, but I beg to be had."

I then again, this time gently and at length, with tenderness, took her.

I looked down at her, curled on the love furs, so small and curvacious, in the heavy collar, chained by the neck to the slave ring, asleep.

The light of morning was in the room, filtering through the shutters. It was warm and bright outside. We had slept late. I had been downstairs to get some food. I could hear birds in the garden.

I kicked her in the side. "Awaken," I said.

"Oh!" she said, moving with the chain on her neck.

"Position," I said.

Swiftly she assumed the position of the pleasure slave, on the love furs, head up, back straight, kneeling back on her heels, her hands on her thighs.

"You kicked me," she said.

I cuffed her, backhanded, striking her from her position to her side on the love furs. She looked up at me from the furs, her eyes wide, blood at her mouth. Then she resumed the position of the pleasure slave.

"Last night," she said. "Did it mean nothing? Surely you love me!"

"Be silent, Slave," I said.

"Yes, Master," she said.

I picked up the whip.

"Am I to be whipped?" she asked.

"If it pleases me," I said.

"Yes, Master," she said.

I held the whip to her mouth, its blades folded back.

She kissed it, and shuddered, and I placed it on the couch.

I slid the bronze pot toward her, across the tiles, to where, going to the end of her chain, she might reach it. "Relieve yourself," I told her, "facing me."

"Yes, Master," she said and, backing toward the pot, and squatting over it, she did so.

I enjoyed making her perform this simple, homely act in my presence.

"I am a slave, aren't I?" she asked.

"Yes," I said.

I then slid the pot to the side of the room, and gave her a pan of water and a rag, with which she might freshen herself. When she had done this I put the pan and the rag to one side. She then knelt again in the position of the pleasure slave, on the furs, the heavy chain dangling between her breasts, and then lying over her left thigh, thence descending to the furs and lifting to the slave ring.

"Good morning," I said to her.

"Good morning, Master," she said.

I fed her some dates, by hand, by putting them in her mouth, from a tray of food I had brought up from the kitchen.

"You struck me," she said.

"Do you object, in the slightest?" I asked.

"No, Master," she said. "You may do with me as you wish."

I held a date before her, and she leaned forward, stretching her chained neck to reach it, and I drew it back. She then knelt back again, on her heels. Whether she were to receive the date or not was my decision. I then gave it to her, putting it in her mouth.

"My Master feeds me," she whispered. "The slave is grateful."

I then put a shallow porcelain bowl of water on the floor, and pointed to it.

She drank from it on her hands and knees, lapping from it, as a she-sleen. "My Master waters me," she said, looking at me, from her hands and knees, the chain hanging from the collar on her neck. "A slave is grateful."

In so simple a fashion, by hand feeding, and floor watering, not permitting the slave to use her hands, I had demonstrated to her, in the Gorean fashion, that her food and water, even such simple things as whether she was to eat or drink, or not, were in my control.

"You may now sit back against the foot of the couch," I said.

"Yes, Master," she said.

I joined her there.

We then, from the tray, feeding ourselves, taking dates, and slices of larma and pastries, breakfasted and chatted.

It is pleasant to have breakfast in bed, so to speak, with a naked young lady, especially when she is chained by the neck to your slave ring.

We chatted of many things, including our former lives, on Earth, and our experiences in the university. She was loquacious and animate.

"I have a surprise," I told her.

I brought up from the kitchen, where I had been keeping it hot, a vessel of black wine, with sugars, and cups and spoons. Too, I had brought up a small bowl of powdered bosk milk. We had finished the creams last night and, in any event, it was unlikely they would have lasted the night. If I had wanted creams I would have had to have gone to the market. My house, incidentally, like most Gorean houses, had no ice chest. There is little cold storage on Gor. Generally food is preserved by being dried or salted. Some cold storage, of course, does exist. Ice is cut from ponds in the winter, and then stored in ice houses, under sawdust. One may go to the ice houses for it, or have it delivered in ice wagons. Most Goreans, of course, cannot afford the luxury of ice in the summer.

Immediately the girl, kneeling, prepared to serve me. "I believe Master prefers his black wine 'second slave,' " she said.

"Yes," I said.

I watched her pouring the beverage. She did so carefully, deferentially, being careful not to spill a drop. I noticed how her breasts depended from her body. How marvelous it is to be served by a beautiful woman.

"There are two cups," she whispered.

"One is for you," I said.

"Black wine is expensive," she said.

"Pour one for yourself," I said.

"Even though I am a slave?" she asked.

"Yes," I said.

"Am I a high slave?" she asked.

"Do you wish me to hold your head back, my hand in your hair, your back almost breaking, and force the spout of the vessel between your teeth, pouring the wine as it is, black and scalding, down your throat?" I asked.

"No, Master!" she said.

"Your brand is pretty," I said.

"Thank you, Master," she said.

"You are not a high slave," I said. "You are a low slave. You are the lowest of low slaves."

"Yes, Master," she said.

"And do not forget it," I said.

"No, Master," she said.

"Now pour yourself a cup of wine," I said.

"Yes, Master," she said. "May I mollify my beverage?"

"Yes," I said.

I watched her as she mixed in a plentiful helping of powdered bosk milk, and two of the assorted sugars. She then left the small, rounded metal cup on the tray.

"Why do you not drink?" I asked her.

"A girl does not drink before her master," she said.

"I see that you are not totally stupid," I said.

"Thank you, Master," she said.

I then sipped the black wine. She, too, then, after it was clear that I had drunk, lifted her own cup to her lips.

"Yes," I said, "you may drink, Slave."

She then, head down, holding the small cup by its two tiny handles, sipped the beverage.

We drank the black wine in silence, sipping it, looking at one another.

How beautiful she was, and I owned her!

"I love belonging to you, Master," she whispered.

"Finish the wine," I told her.

"Yes, Master," she said. I put my own cup on the tray.

I looked at her, from her small feet, to her ankles and calves, her sweet thighs, the sweet belly of her, her waist, and marvelous breasts, her shoulders, and arms and hands, her fair throat, chained, her lovely lips, her sensitive, delicate features, her deep, vulnerable eyes, and the marvelous wealth of her dark, cascading hair, perhaps never cut, except for shaping, since she had been brought to Gor.

Timidly she put her own small cup on the tray. "Master desires me," she said.

I moved the tray to the side, well away from the furs.

She was half kneeling, half crouching, near the far corner of the large couch. I saw that she was frightened.

"Do you sometimes fear the desire of your Master?" I asked.

"Sometimes," she said. "Your eyes."

"What is it that you see in my eyes?" I asked.

"A Gorean lust," she said, "and I, a chained slave, know myself the helpless vessel upon which it will be vented."

I snapped my fingers. She, even though frightened, must come to my arms.

I threw the chain back over her shoulder, and held her. She half tried to pull away, frightened.

"How can you feel such desire for one who is only a slave?" she asked.

"How could one feel such desire," I laughed, "for one who was not a slave?"

She shuddered. It was pleasant to feel her enslaved beauty trembling in my arms.

"To be sure," I said, "you are only a nameless slave."

"Has Master considered a name for me?" she asked.

"Down!" I said. "On your hands and knees on the furs, head touching the furs!"

Swiftly, fearfully, she complied.

I slapped her. "Oh!" she cired.

"I can think of a name for you," I told her.

"Please, no, Master!" she cried.

I then put my hand on her. She squirmed. "You seem well informed as to the desires of Masters," I said. "I trust you are similarly well informed as to the desires of slaves."

She whimpered.

"I can think of another name for you," I said.

"Please, no, Master," she said.

"But then why should I publicize so blatantly the heat of my little slave?" I asked.

She sobbed.

"I can name you anything, you know," I said.

"Yes, Master," she said.

"Now on all fours, arms straight, head up!" I said.

Immediately she assumed this position.

"Please do not put me in the slavery of the she-quadruped, Master," she begged.

"I will put you there, and keep you there, if it pleases me," I told her.

"Yes, Master," she said.

"Perhaps I should call you 'Princess' or 'Trixie'," I said. I used the English expressions for these names, as there are no precisely equivalent Gorean expressions for them.

"Master may do as he wishes," she said.

"But such names are perhaps better reserved for our occasional private sport," I mused. "Too, they would make little sense to our Gorean friends."

I walked about her. "You would make a pretty poodle," I told her. I used the English expression 'poodle,' of course, as the animal is unknown on Gor.

"Thank you, Master," she said.

"You might be interesting as a poodle," I told her.

"Doubtless I shall perform for Master in many ways," she said.

"You will," I told her.

"Yes, Master," she said.

I then took her by the hair, and twisted her about, so that she lay on her side, I crouching beside her. "But, generally," I said, "I think I shall keep you as an enslaved human female, for that is what you are."

"Yes, Master," she said, wincing.

"I could give you the name of a Gorean girl," I said, "but since you are of Earth origin, and are a low slave, it seems more appropriate that you be given the name of an Earth girl."

I then flung her to her back, threw apart her legs and entered her.

"Ohhh," she sobbed, softly.

"You are a hot slave," I observed.

"You are going to name me, in the having of me, aren't you?" she asked.

"Perhaps," I said.

"And you will give me the name of an Earth girl, won't you?" she asked.

"Perhaps," I said.

"Even knowing what such a name will do to my slavery," she asked, "making it the slavery of an Earth girl on Gor?"

"Of course," I said.

"Cruel Master," she said.

"I am rather fond of Earth-girl names for slaves," I said.

"And so, too, are Goreans, the brutes," she said.

"Earth girls are commonly regarded as being among the most desirable of slaves on Gor," I said.

"At least among the lowest and most helpless," she said.

"True," I said.

"I shall tell you a secret, Master," she said. "So much a slave am I that I desire to wear no other sort of name."

"I know," I said.

Then she clutched me. I saw that she was on the brink of orgasm.

"Do not move, in the slightest, Slave," I told her.

"Please, Master," she said.

"No," I said.

"Yes, Master," she said.

"There are many fine Earth-girl names," I said.

"Please, Master," she said.

" 'Phyllis' is a lovely name," I said.

"Name me," she begged. "Name me!"

" 'Tracy' and 'Stephanie', too," I said, "are lovely names."

"Anything," she said, hoarsely. "Anything! Name me, I beg you. I cannot stand it! I must move! I beg to be named!" I felt her fingernails digging into my flesh. Her eyes were wild. "Name me, my Master," she whispered, begging, "name me, name me, please, name me!"

"Very well," I said, and began to move within her. Immediately she was clutching me and shuddering. She looked at me, wildly. Then she threw back her head, helplessly. "I name you 'Beverly'," I said.

"I am Beverly!" she cried. "I am Beverly!"

Then, in a few moments, she was sobbing, and clutching me. "I am Beverly," she sobbed. "I am Beverly!" Then, after a time, still holding to me, she lay trembling in my arms. "I am Beverly," she whispered. Then, in a few minutes, she lay softly on her side on the furs, facing away from me, her knees drawn up. "My Master has named me," she said. "I am Beverly."

I stood up and looked down at her. She rolled to her back, and looked up at me.

"What is your name?" I asked.

"Beverly," she said.

"I do not think you will forget your name," I said.

"No, Master," she smiled.

"Do not forget, either," I said, "that you wear it now as a mere slave name."

"No, Master," she said. "I shall not forget." She knew that, as a slave, she had no more right to a name than a tarsk or sleen, or any other form of domestic animal. She then rolled to her stomach, and began to kiss my feet. Then, tenderly, she rose to her knees, still kissing my feet, and then began to kiss my ankles, and calves. "I love you, Master," she whispered. When she lifted her head, tears in her eyes, she seemed suddenly startled, troubled. She put up her hand to my left arm. "Master," she said, "forgive me! I have hurt Master!" There was blood on my arms, from the gouging of her nails, and blood at my left shoulder, from the cut of her teeth.

"It is nothing," I told her.

She rose to her feet, and kissed the wounds. "Am I to be punished, Master?" she asked.

"No," I said. Masters are commonly indulgent of the uncontrollable spasms of their female slaves.

"Thank you, Master," she said.

I then held her by the upper arms. She was so beautiful!

"Doubtless I must soon be released from the slave ring," she said, "that I may attend to my work."

"Oh!" she cried, thrown brutally to the furs at the foot of

the couch. She looked up at me, frightened, the chain on her neck.

"That decision is mine," I said, "not yours."

"Yes, Master," she said.

"Do you hear?" I asked.

"Yes, Master!" she said.

"Who hears?" I asked.

"Beverly!" she said.

"Who does Beverly hear?" I asked.

"Beverly hears her Master!" she said.

I then crouched down, and took her in my arms.

"Yes, Master," she said.

It was pleasant to hold her, as a yielding slave.

"It is evening, Master," she said, lying beside me.

"Yes," I said.

I had refilled the ravishment lamp and then had had her relight it. She was beautiful in its soft light, lying on the furs, the heavy stone of the couch and the iron of the slave ring, to which she was still attached, behind her.

"All last night, and all today," she said, "you have kept me at your ring."

"I have waited long to own you," I told her.

"Yes, Master," she said. She rolled onto her back, looking up at the beams in the ceiling. "Callimachus has selected you to be his second in command, in the forces of the Vosk League," she said.

"Yes," I said.

"I am the slave, then, of an important man, am I not?" she asked.

"Perhaps," I said, "but remember that you are only his slave."

"Yes, Master," she said, "that is well understood by this enslaved female."

"You may serve me wine," I said.

She reached to the wine, a sweet Ka-la-na of Ar, and filled the goblet to the third ring. Then, as I sat back against the couch, she knelt before me. She, head down, pressed the heavy metal goblet deep into her lower abdomen, and then she lifted it to her lips and, holding it with both hands, kissed it lingeringly and lovingly. Then, kneeling back on her heels she put down her head and, humbly, her arms extended, her head down between them, proffered me the goblet. "Wine, Master?" she asked.

"Yes," I said. I then took the goblet from her, and drank. She lifted her head, and watched me.

"I think you know how to serve wine well," I said.

"Master should know," she laughed.

I indicated that she should approach me. "Keep your hands on your thighs," I told her.

"Yes, Master," she said.

I then, crouching beside her, my hand in her hair, controlling her, gave her to drink from the goblet, letting her finish the last ring. I then gave her the goblet, and she put it to the side, with the wine vessel.

I then sat back again, against the foot of the couch.

She, kneeling to the side, in the lovely position of the pleasure slave, watched me.

"Lie down here," I said, "beside me."

"Yes, Master," she said.

She lay beside me, in her chained softness, and beauty. She kissed me on the hip and then, with a rustle of chain, put her head down to the furs. "Do I please Master?" she asked.

"You are not entirely displeasing," I told her.

"That pleases me," she said. She laughed.

"What is wrong?" I asked.

"Nothing," she said. "It is only that I thought it amusing. On Earth many boys, I think, would have liked to get me to their bed. But here, on Gor, you have not yet even permitted me to ascend to the surface of your couch."

I smiled. She had served only at its foot, at the slave ring.

"Will Master permit me sometime to ascend his couch?" she asked.

"We shall see what progress you make in your slavery," I said.

"I shall endeavor to make progress," she said. A Gorean slave girl, incidentally, does not simply take a position on a couch as might a free person. Commonly she will kneel at its lower left side, or bottom, and then kiss its furs, or covers, after which she will crawl into it on her belly. Unless otherwise instructed she will remain near its foot, rather in the manner of a pet sleen. She may also, of course, be whipped or beaten to the couch, or forced to it, her arm twisted high, and painfully, behind her back, or carried to it, or thrown upon it, perhaps chained or bound.

"Master," she said.

"Yes," I said.

"Do you recall, long ago, in the restaurant, when I spoke to you, daringly, I think, for a then-unenslaved slave, of the dreams, strange then to my mind, which I had been having?"

"I recall," I said.

"I had often then dreamed, as I recounted to you, and as you will perhaps remember, that I was a female slave, that I was kept in rags or naked, that a steel collar had been put on my neck, that I had been branded, and that I was subject to discipline—and that I must serve a man."

"I remember," I said.

"There was one thing about those dreams, dear Master," she said, "which I did not dare to tell you."

"What was that?" I asked. I recalled that I had suspected, from certain subtle cues, and silences, that she had not fully expressed herself to me on that occasion.

She looked down.

"What was it?" I asked.

She looked up. "That the man I must serve was always the same," she said.

"Yes?" I said.

"And that he was you, my Master," she said.

I took her gently in my arms.

"You see, my Master," she said, "you are, for me, a dream come true."

"And you, for me, Sweet Slave," I said, "are, too, a dream come true."

"Master?" she asked.

"Many times," I said, "did I fantasize you thusly, in my arms, an owned slave, mine to do with as I pleased."

"I am here now, my Master," she said.

"I know," I said.

"And it is where I want to be," she said.

I looked at her, in the light of the ravishment lamp.

"Gone now," she whispered, "are the pains and shames of Earth."

I kissed her, gently.

"How strange I once would have thought it, on Earth, so long ago," she said, "had I been told that I would find my fulfillment only on a distant world—and chained by the neck to the slave ring of a master."

"You are a woman," I told her.

"Yes, Master," she said.

I then caressed her gently into ecstasy.